MEET ME
AT
MIDNIGHT

To the Red Herrings, whose imaginations run wild and who conquer fear to create new worlds with their words. We believe in you!

- C.J. Redwine & Mary Weber, editors for The Writer's Sanctuary.

CONTENTS

Introduction

Dear Reader,

In 2013, The Writer's Sanctuary held its first event—a retreat for writers at every stage of their career. Some had multiple books published already. Some were still working to finish their first manuscript. We brought them together for a week of rejuvenation, teaching, connection, and community.

In 2018, we expanded to multiple events a year. In 2020, when Covid made holding live events impossible, we pivoted to offering online webinars, publishing conferences, and virtual retreats. Our community began growing rapidly as our mission to create a welcoming, safe place for all writers to receive teaching, mentorship, and connection at an affordable price drew more and more storytellers to us.

In 2023, we launched the Red Herrings Society, a "secret" society for writers that offers a monthly masterclass, a bonus webinar, a newsletter full of strategies and insider information, a giveaway, community writing sessions, an active Facebook group, and more. We dove headfirst into mentoring this special community, and out of that mentorship, the *Meet Me at Midnight* anthology was born.

Some of these writers have published books you can add to your shelves! Some are currently seeking publication. And some are just finishing their first manuscripts. All of them are fabulous storytellers.

Be prepared to laugh, cry, swoon, and turn the pages as fast as you can because you're going to need to see what happens next. Meet us at midnight, dear reader. It's going to be an unforgettable experience.

UNDER
THE
CYPRESS

KATIE PHILLIPS

Chapter 1

BEKAH

The fireflies are already dancing under the pine trees, the heady scent of evergreen and damp earth hanging in the warm, humid night. It's only May in North Carolina, but the woods are rushing into summer just like everyone else.

I take a deep breath to steady my nerves, but my heart pounds against my chest just the same. *Tonight, I'm gonna tell him.*

I'm not gonna chicken out, like always.

I'm probably lying to myself.

A twig breaks under my heel on the hard-packed dirt path leading to the swimming hole. The crack is louder than the comforting chorus of cicadas and courting frogs.

Wish me luck, froggie friends. I hope you find your true love.

A shadow moves under the old cypress tree that stands guard beside the pond, and my heart leaps into my throat. Tucker's already here.

Meet me at midnight, his note had said, tucked into my hand earlier today during the jubilant crush of flapping gowns and pointy flat hats and parents taking pictures of our small town's few seniors.

We've been meeting under the cypress tree since we were knee-high to a grasshopper. Building stick houses. Playing hide and seek. Swimming in the pond with the moon overhead and pretending not to be scared.

We haven't met every day the last few years. Not like we used to. Him, distracted by swim team and football and whichever popular girl he happened to be dating. Me, by my art and helping my parents with their business.

But most Sundays, we meet at midnight under the tree and talk about life and our dreams and go for a swim under the stars.

Tonight—will be different.

The shadow at the knobby-kneed base of the cypress unfolds into Tucker's tall frame, and he grins. I return it, brushing my sweaty palms on my cut-off jean shorts.

"Hey, Ribbit."

I roll my eyes. The nickname will never die.

"Hey, idiot."

Tucker laughs, rich and deep, and my nervous stomach turns over.

"Your mom make lemon cake?" He pulls a towel out of his backpack.

"Of course." My mom celebrates every special occasion with her signature lemon glaze cake, topped with blackberries from our own vines.

Tucker grabs the back of his shirt and pulls it over his head. The moonlight through the branches touches the smooth muscles of his shoulders and flat stomach.

Don't make it awkward.

I swallow hard and look away, dropping my own towel to the grass and easing my shirt off. I already put on my simple one-piece swimsuit underneath my clothes.

"And you didn't bring me cake?" His voice draws closer.

I shimmy out of my cutoffs and toss them beside my wallet on the ragged-edged bath towel.

"Get your own cake. Mom can't tell you no."

"Is it my fault women can't resist me?"

I snort-laugh, turning back to him. Tucker's standing behind me, grinning his stupid grin, arms crossed over his chest like he doesn't know how good he looks.

He knows. Unfortunately.

"Last one to the rock is a snapping turtle!" I run for the pond with mud squishing between my toes, and jump.

Cool, murky water closes over my head. I surface, gasping in mouthfuls of warm night air. A second splash nearby.

Tucker. He'll beat me!

I strike out, the water flowing smoothly over my skin, washing away my worries. Falling into my rhythm, I listen for Tucker.

Nothing. He swims like a ghost.

I reach the massive boulder on the opposite edge of the pond, but Tucker's already there. He always wins. But that's not really the point.

I try to gulp in more air only to get a mouthful of muddy water and lapse into coughing and sputtering.

Tucker just laughs, plants his hands on the edge of the flat boulder, and heaves himself out of the pond. I'd enjoy the sight if I wasn't choking on fish-water. I wipe bedraggled hair out of my eyes and clasp the hand he extends down to me.

Tucker hauls me up onto the rock beside him. With a final cough, I settle onto the smooth surface still radiating warmth from the day.

He smiles at me, I smile back, and we both look out over the pond, listening to the frog song in companionable silence.

Tell him, the braver voice in my head prods.

He'll reject you and it'll ruin everything, the cowardly voice argues back.

The words stick in my throat. Back in the trees, an owl hoots a soft reproach. Tucker shifts, sighs.

"I have something I need to tell you," he says out of the dark, his low

4

voice rough.

My heart starts hammering again. *Maybe . . . he feels the same way?*

"Me too," I croak.

"You first."

I shake my head. It's probably better if he admits the truth about us, what's been simmering the last couple years. *This is it. This is really happening.*

"You go," I mumble.

Tucker shrugs, looking at me closely and then back out over the water. A firefly lands on the rock between us, a faint glowing light.

"I've decided to join the navy," he says. "And become a SEAL."

My heart freezes, imprisoned in my rib cage, pain lancing through my chest. His words rattle around in my brain, real and yet somehow not.

But what about me? I gulp down the selfish words. *He—he doesn't feel the same as me.*

I blink back tears and clench my shaking hands around my knees, searching desperately for a "normal" response. *He can't know. He can never know.*

"Isn't that—dangerous?" My voice comes out a squeak.

He shrugs. "In the SEALS you're on a team. I'm a strong swimmer and a good shot. My parents can't afford to send me to college, and my grades aren't good enough for scholarships."

Tucker twists to look at me, and I try desperately to pretend I'm not dying inside with every matter-of-fact, *true* word coming out of his mouth.

It does make sense. Too much sense. I understand, and I wish I didn't. There's nothing holding him here. No reason to stay, except . . .

Me. I thought he'd stay for me.

I'm such an idiot.

"I have to get out of here," he's saying softly, urgently. "There's nothing for me here, Bekah. No future for me."

Nothing.

My heart throbs, the word repeating in my ears like the steady refrain of the frogs calling for their mates. *No-thing, no-thing, no-thing.*

"When?"

He shifts uncomfortably. "I leave tomorrow morning."

Tomorrow! In a matter of hours, he'll be out of my life, and he didn't tell me. *I thought we were friends. How could he not say something?*

"I'm sorry to break it to you like this. I just got final confirmation today."

Tucker clears his throat, running a hand through his damp hair and making it stand on end. He draws in a deep breath, his shoulders rising and falling.

I look away. Swallow hard.

"Look, Bekah. When I get to boot camp, I can get mail. Will you write to me?"

I glance back. His eyes shine with earnest affection, and a touch of uncertainty. It's the latter that gets me. What kind of friend would say no, just because I love him and I'm disappointed he doesn't feel that way about me.

"Of course." I force a smile. "I might even send cake."

"You're the best, Ribbit."

Our eyes meet, his slow smile the most gorgeous thing I've ever seen, and it feels like the whole night is holding its breath. The frogs pausing their song, the fireflies slowly winking, the breeze whispering through the wispy, swaying branches of the cypress.

And him and me, caught in this moment of midnight magic. His breath coming fast, my own stopping altogether. Just him and me, with the weight of all the years and unspoken dreams between us.

He leans closer, his gaze drifting, my heart trying to beat its way out of my chest to join his . . .

And Tucker clears his throat and leans back, letting out a heavy breath and looking away. He crosses his arms over his pulled-up knees.

He wasn't going to kiss you. I focus on the cypress across the pond, its familiar shape blurry with tears. *He was never going to kiss you.*

Tucker sighs. "I'd better go. Gotta be up early."

"Yeah." What else is there to say?

He stands and looks down at me, his outline against the night sky all smudged around the edges.

"I'm gonna stay a bit longer. You go ahead." It's shocking how normal I sound when my world feels shattered.

"Okay." Tucker waits a moment, staring down at me. *Please. Just go.*

"Promise you'll write?"

I bite my lip. It's better than nothing.

"I'll write."

I tell myself I won't watch him swim back across the pond, cutting through the water like a sleek fish. Won't stare at the shadow of the path until every flicker of movement disappears.

But I'm far, far too good at lying to myself.

Chapter 2

TUCKER

Five years later . . .

I turn over the plain white envelope, my name written on the front in a familiar sprawling script. Sinking down onto my cot and brushing off the ever-present desert dust, I take a deep breath at the nerves tightening my chest. I feel Bekah's presence, like a missing part of myself. Always have, probably always will.

I was just too much of a young idiot to recognize it when I had the chance. I'd been so wrapped up in proving myself, in getting out of that small town and becoming *someone*, that I hadn't truly realized what I'd left behind.

Good coffee and her weekly letters had gotten me through the hardest days of my life. Kept me from giving up and ringing the bell during Hell Week. Nothing but her curved lips that May night had ever felt so tempting.

I shoulda kissed her. I'd wondered, ever since. But I couldn't stay. Couldn't promise her anything. *Shouldn't be thinking about it now, either.* I love my job. Have a great team I trust with my life. But still, some days . . .

I carefully tear open the envelope and pull out the sheet of paper covered in Bekah's untidy handwriting. I scan her opening greeting and smile.

"Hey idiot," it says.

I talk to my parents as often as I can, but Bekah is my real source of news from home.

Our neighbor's goat escaped and ate my mom's rhubarb out of the garden. Bekah's mom made lemon cake for our classmate's baby shower. The mayor of twenty years lost to a young newcomer—beauty shop opinions are still divided.

I grin, tucking her letter in the pocket of my fatigues. I'm due for a briefing at 14:00, but maybe afterward I can write back. *Not that I have much to say.* Most of what I do is classified, and not what I'd want her knowing anyway. *Maybe after this deployment I should get a dog, just so I have something to write about.*

I'm not brave enough to say what I really want to say, to ask what I really want to know.

If I didn't re-up, when I come home—would you give me another chance?

Most men wouldn't call me a coward, but I guess I am when it comes to her.

Chapter 3

BEKAH

I *finally did it.*
I sit frozen in the front seat of my beat-up Crown Vic, parked in the gravel driveway of my parents' farmhouse, and stare at my phone. *I can't believe it.*

After years of living with my parents, working for them and trying to build my client base and barely scraping by, my dream design studio saw my work, called me up, and offered me an interview. If I get it, I could move to Raleigh, start my dream job in a matter of weeks.

This can't be real. Nothing this good ever happens to me. I blow out my breath slowly.

The hard part will be telling my parents. They'll be excited for me, of course. But I'm their only child, and they've gotten used to having me around.

I've gotten used to being here. But I have to move on with my life. Move on from him. I climb out of the car, slamming the door shut, and notice the tan sedan parked in the driveway. It belongs to Tucker's mom.

His last letter sits unanswered on my desk upstairs. I want to reply, but I also dread it. Because I know what I have to say. *This will be my final letter, Tucker. This isn't good for me. I hope you can understand.*

And he will. I know he will. He's just that kind of friend, who knows you better than you know yourself. I don't think he'll even be surprised.

But the idea of not getting his letters anymore, not even his comically brief notes that I almost memorize every word of . . .

It hurts too much. I haven't been able to make myself do it yet. *But I will. I'll get the job. I'll move on with my life.* I spot our moms talking on our front porch. Tucker's mom twists to look at me.

My heart stops in my chest and my knees give out. *No.*

Her face is ashen, her always impeccable make-up smeared under her eyes. She clutches her purse in a white-knuckled grip.

It's Tucker. The moment that's haunted my dreams since the last night I saw him has finally come.

Today's the day.

I let myself sink onto the sidewalk, reaching for a breath and not finding it. My mom hurries toward me, speaking, but the words are muffled. Distant. She tucks her hand under my arm to lift me up. I get my legs working and make it to the front porch steps, digging deep for words.

"Is he—?"

"He's alive," she says gently. "He'll recover."

A breath rushes back into my chest, and I force myself to take another. And another. The pressure on my sternum pushes back.

My mom, and his mom—they've been best friends for as long as I can remember—exchange wordless glances. I swallow hard, my shaking hands twisted together in my lap. Tucker, hurt. Tucker, in a hospital somewhere. Fighting for his life.

The comforting circles of my mom's warm hand on my back don't falter, and I've never been more grateful. Tucker's mom clears her throat and pulls an envelope out of her purse.

My stomach drops.

"He asked me to give you this."

I take it and lower my gaze, staring at a pebble resting in the dirt by the paint-peeling step. Tucker's mom walks slowly to her car, thin shoulders hunched. A plume of dust hangs in the air behind her as she drives away down the long dirt road.

"I'll give you a minute," my mom says, squeezing my shoulder and turning to go back in the house. The screen door bangs shut.

I stare at the envelope in my hand, my thoughts drifting to Tucker's unanswered letter on the desk upstairs. I tear open the envelope and unfold the single sheet of paper. It's not his blocky handwriting—someone must have helped him.

There are only four words on the paper. Four words and a date several months away.

Meet me at midnight?

I crumple the edges of the sheet of paper and let myself cry like I haven't since that May night long ago with only the frogs to hear.

I want to. I want to so desperately. My head says *no*, but my heart says, *try again.* I swipe away the tears running down my cheeks.

Move on. Meet him. I hear the frog chorus again. *Move on. Meet him. Move on. Meet him.*

Maybe this is what I need. Closure. For him. For me. A chance to actually leave that long-ago night behind me.

I'm not the girl I used to be. It's time.

Chapter 4

TUCKER

I lean against the rough bark of the old cypress tree. My still-healing muscles are screaming. But I told Bekah I'd meet her here, and I'd have to be dead to not keep that promise.

That is, if she comes.

I shift my weight off my bad shoulder, letting my head fall back. She probably won't come. I know that. Understand it.

I've held on to her and given nothing back. She has every reason to not give me the time of day. Weekly letters, the occasional call for birthdays and Christmas. Just friends. *I can't do it anymore.* I want more. And she deserves better.

Adjusting my ball cap, I take a deep breath to release the tension flowing through my body and making my shoulder cramp painfully.

A twig cracks, and my heart leaps, but it's just a bird fluttering away in the undergrowth.

If she's gonna come, she'll come. No use stressing. But my nerves aren't interested in my logical pep talk. They're circling and stamping in my chest like teenagers at a barn dance.

I'm sweating, running through my speech in my head, when I spot a small figure moving down the path, curvier now than she used to be, but no less beautiful.

Finally, my nerves settle in my stomach and harden into resolve. *Today's the day. I'm gonna tell her. Don't screw it up.*

She pauses, the moonlight falling on her face. I use the tree to shove myself to my feet, gritting my teeth against the quick flare of pain. We stand there a moment, taking each other in, with only the frogs and the fireflies as witnesses.

"Hey, Ribbit," I say softly, carefully. Uncertainty and something a little bit like longing flickers across her face.

The corner of Bekah's mouth turns up. "Hey, idiot."

Tension melts away, and we're grinning at each other like kids.

"Swim?" Bekah tilts her head at the pond.

I'll pay for it tomorrow, but I'm not about to tell her no. I've already changed into my swim shorts. I pull my shirt over my head, sucking in my breath against the stabbing pain in my shoulder.

Here goes. I don't let myself turn away as Bekah's gaze moves over my body, slowing on the angry, red scars marring my shoulder and chest. She lifts her eyes to meet mine, her expression holding concern, but not horror or pity.

"Should you really be swimming?" She raises an eyebrow.

I relax and smirk back. "I won't tell, if you don't."

Rolling her eyes, Bekah slips out of her shorts and tank top—and takes the air right out of my lungs. Those curves definitely weren't there last time. She's gorgeous.

She sends me a sideways glance, catching me staring, and freezes when I don't drop my eyes or look away. *That's right. I'm interested.*

But will she give me another chance?

The question is left unanswered. She turns and sprints for the water. I let her, since my top speed now is *slow.*

The water's just as cold as I remember—but I've swam miles in much colder. I take a practiced stroke, ignoring the fire shooting through my shoulder.

Bekah beats me to the rock. No surprise.

She climbs up, squeezing her long hair out like some mythical siren in the moonlight. I forget to breathe, let alone swim, and end up sinking and swallowing water. A kick brings me back to the surface. *Smooth.* I grasp the edge of the boulder, cursing under my breath at my arm that's shaking from the effort. Nothing like being stuck in a hospital bed to undo years of intensive training.

I plant my hands on the boulder, set my jaw, and heave myself out of the water. Bekah grabs my arm, saving me from a humiliating fall back into the pond.

I hate it. But it's my life now. She doesn't let go until I've settled on the rock, gasping heaving breaths as the waves of pain recede.

"You shouldn't be swimming," she says dryly.

"Probably." I grin, stealing a glance.

She leans back on her hands. Water runs down her smooth skin, inviting my gaze. I look away, so I won't get distracted from what I need to say.

"Thanks for coming." I clear my throat.

The owl hoots in the tree overhead. My speech is gone. *Blunt honesty, it is.*

"I don't know how you feel about me. If you want to just be friends." I draw in a deep breath and take the plunge. "But I love you, and I want a future with you."

Silence.

A very long silence.

My heart is trying to pound out of my chest, my palms sweating. I listen to the frog choir cheering me on for a moment, then turn to look at her.

She's crying. Tears running down her cheeks. My stomach drops.

"I'm sorry, Bekah. I didn't mean to hurt you." I put my arm around her, pressing my cheek to her hair.

"You're an idiot," she whispers, her voice shaking.

"I know." I force my words to come out steady. Reassuring. "You were always right about that."

She slowly pulls away, wiping her face, and I reluctantly let her go. "I got my dream job. I live in Raleigh now."

"Okay." I let out my breath slowly, folding my arms over my knees so I'm not tempted to reach for her. "Congratulations. Good for you."

Bekah sighs and looks over at me.

"I was going to write you back, tell you that there wouldn't be any more letters. That I had to let you go. Move on."

That one hurt. More than getting shot.

"I almost didn't come," she says softly, her voice thick with tears.

Guess I was right to be afraid. But what she didn't say echoes.

"So, why did you?" I meet her gaze and hold it.

Bekah takes a deep, shuddering breath.

"Five years ago, I met my best friend right here at midnight, hoping he loved me the way I loved him. Dreaming that we could have a life together."

I clasp my shaking hands. I've never been so scared in my life. But, somehow, I find the courage to force the words out, my voice low and rough.

"And now?"

Bekah reaches out and slides her hand around my arm. I close my eyes, afraid for a moment I might cry with relief, and shift to draw her into my arms. This time she lets me, curling against my chest, resting her head on my shoulder, her skin like silk against my own.

"I'll go where you go," I speak softly in her ear. "Stay where you stay. I just want to be with you." *Years and scars and all.*

Bekah lets out a long sigh, her breath warm against my chest. She draws away enough to see my face and a smile curves her lips.

"You promise?"

I've never been more sure of anything in my life.

"I promise."

"Then I do, too."

She looks at me quietly, and I stare back, my heart pounding in my ears. Somehow this moment feels both miraculous and inevitable.

"Kiss me, idiot," Bekah whispers.

I break into a grin. "Sorry. I'll get right on that."

And so I kiss my best friend under the shadow of the cypress tree, while the fireflies dance around us in the light of the midnight moon.

About the Author

Katie Phillips is a developmental editor and author coach, as well as head fiction instructor for the Author Conservatory. She loves treating her readers to atmospheric prose and authentic characters that feel like friends. When she's not writing contemporary romance or fantasy novels, she enjoys evening walks with her husband and chasing after her toddler daughter. Connect with her for author services at www.katiephillipscreative.com, or follow her writing mom adventures on Instagram @authorkatiephillips.

MAGNOLIA GOES TO JAIL

AMY FORTENBERRY

I never set out to attract trouble, just like I didn't go outside hoping to attract all the mosquitoes in Souligner Parish.

And yet, I couldn't avoid either. Grandmama always said: "Magnolia, you find more problems than a gravedigger finds dirt."

Ironic, as she'd often been the instigator. At her funeral, I'd had the passing thought that now maybe Grandmama would be an angelic influence on me. Instead, she'd decided her "mansion above," as the gospel songs say, would be my house here on earth.

Decidedly not angelic.

No one had been more surprised than me when, a few days after her funeral, Grandmama popped into my sitting room wearing her favorite pink linen pantsuit. I screamed. She told me to hush my caterwauling.

And that was that.

My house *is* fabulous, so as haunt choices go, hers wasn't the worst. I'd inherited a former sugarcane plantation from my husband, Gus, who'd dreamed of making Belle Soeurs a world-class travel destination.

Gus had been my college sweetheart and the love of my life. We eloped the day after our graduation from LSU with our whole life mapped out, but a boat explosion a month later wiped those plans away much like Hurricane Katrina did to the Gulf Coast. At twenty-three-years-old, he'd left me a widow.

While I worked to make his one-time dream a reality, I also attempted to rebuild my shattered heart. Belle Soeurs turned out spectacular; my heart resembled a kindergarten craft project.

And that brings me to my current predicament.

Grandmama claimed I'd spent enough of my fruitful years pining after Gus and the life we'd planned.

Nonsense. It's not like I hadn't dipped my toes into the dating world. I'd been on a few dates.

First dates, anyway. I believed in being cautious.

Grandmama said I purposely picked losers so I couldn't lose my heart again.

Mostly, I ignored her. I'm a thirty-year-old woman with a successful business and a satisfying life; no man needed.

However . . .

I inherited more than my ample curves and love of the color pink from Grandmama (although I favored sequins and ruffles, whereas Grandmama had a more subdued Southern Lady aesthetic). I also got a dangerous double dose of her stubborn streak and competitive spirit.

Which is why, on Christmas Eve, when Grandmama bet me I wouldn't actually ask a decent guy (defined as one who didn't sponge off his mama or draw unemployment) on a date, I tumbled headfirst into her trap.

I'd like to swear I did so because of what she offered as a prize if I won, as it would save the sanity of more folks than just me. But I'm not that altruistic. I was in it to beat Grandmama.

In a huff, I picked out my target: Sheriff Everett Toulouse, a non-spongy, fully employed man I'd known for years, seeing as he'd been buddies with Gus. I knew I was playing right into Grandmama's hands, but the thing is, Grandmama wasn't totally wrong. Gus had been gone for eight years, and no matter how much I touted my enjoyment of the single independent female life, perhaps she knew my heart better than I'd like to admit.

So, here we were, with Grandmama's deadline of Epiphany tomorrow—meaning she'd barely given me twelve days to do the deed—and I was already a couple of hours into our community's annual Twelfth Night Gala at Belle Soeurs. I'd been consumed with getting every detail right for this year's theme of Midnight Fairy Tales, and I'd lost track of the days. I had very little time to corner Everett and do my asking, because Epiphany—and Grandmama's gloating—began at midnight.

***

I heard the scream on my fifth trip to the kitchen for more king cake.

I should have been cornering Everett instead of being a gofer, but I wanted my staff to enjoy themselves, too. And my head chef, Uncle Sally—Grandmama's baby brother—had consumed more spiked punch than any seventy-year-old man cosplaying as Little Bo Peep (don't ask) should and was absolutely no help.

My beautiful costume, inspired by Anderson's *The Wild Swans* and covered in vines and fresh blossoms in shades from deep purple to barely-there pink, dropped petals all over the tile floor as I jumped in shock. The king cake followed them down, but I barely noticed.

The scream had come from the basement. Great.

Belle Soeurs' basement, a rabbit warren of rooms and hallways, was used for storage now, but during the plantation days, it contained the kitchen, the corn crib, a chicken coop, and even a jail. The kitchen was long gone, as were the chickens, but the jail's iron bars remained as a reminder of former days.

The large clock hanging above the commercial-grade refrigerator read 11:15pm. Forty-five minutes until I lost my bet with Grandmama.

I didn't want to investigate the scream, but someone had to.

Maybe I could kill two gators with one stone! Who better to investigate with me than the sheriff? I'd report the scream to Everett and slip in a dinner invitation while we investigated. Not the most tasteful timing, but desperation knows no bounds, apparently.

Slip-sliding through the king cake mess, I made it to the ballroom in record time before my luck fizzled. I spotted Everett immediately, but unfortunately, the majority of Souligner Parish's citizens danced a Cajun two-step between us. It would take me forever to fight my way to him, and I wasn't totally self-absorbed: the haunting scream still echoed in my ears.

I needed a new plan.

Everett was out of reach, but his deputy Whalen Finnick wasn't.

Finn, another of Gus's childhood friends, had returned from military duty last year and joined Everett's staff. And now he was only a few feet away, leaning his long body against the wall and observing the dancers. I grabbed his arm and pulled him towards the kitchen.

"Hey, slow down. Where's the fire?" Finn's voice, low and amused, tickled my insides, and I squirmed. Why couldn't he have been Everett? Discombobulated, my answer came out in a jumble.

"I heard a scream from the basement, and I'm not going down there by myself, and I couldn't get to Everett, so you'll have to do."

"A scream? Magnolia, have you been drinking the punch?"

The bloodcurdling sound came again, saving me from answering.

"Stairs?" Finn barked the question, his trained gaze already sweeping the room for possibilities.

I pointed towards the door just past the refrigerator, and he took off. When I tried to follow, one of the surprisingly strong vines stitched to my gown caught on the island and jerked me backwards. Cursing, I ripped myself free and raced down the stone steps, trying to catch up to Finn without tripping over the trailing decoration.

Finn stood at the bottom of the stairs, no doubt trying to decide the best place to start in the maze of rooms. Another scream rang out from our right, and we simultaneously turned in that direction.

I had a sudden thought: if Grandmama was behind this somehow to make me lose, I was calling a Catholic priest for an exorcism. I didn't care that Grandmama had been Baptist all her life.

Finn motioned for me to stay back as he crept forward.

I ignored him, of course, and followed less stealthily, as satin ball gowns make a lot of noise, no matter how much one tries.

The end of the hall was empty, and Finn frowned. "Is this some kind of trick?"

Before I could tell him exactly what to do with his suspicion, something tugged sharply on the blasted vine I'd snagged upstairs, spinning me like a top right into Finn.

Being as how I'm a substantial woman, even without the additional weight from the ruffles, Finn staggered backwards through the open door of the jail's single cell with me in his arms.

Gravity took us both down, and as we fell, Finn's foot kicked the small metal box holding the cell's iron door open, sending it skidding into the hallway. Without it, the door slammed shut with a definitive click.

19

And on the other side of the now locked door, the real culprit finally showed himself, the tail-end of my gown's embellishment hanging from his mouth: a goat, complete with horns, creepy horizontal pupils, and a smell that could chase fish out of the bayou. As if to remove any doubt, the goat opened its mouth and let out a bellow worthy of the darkest demon from hell, spraying out masticated pieces of my dress as it did so.

Finn laughed.

I did not.

I'd been tricked by a stinky farm animal, and now I was locked up in the basement with Everett's best friend instead of Everett. Nothing against Finn, but he wasn't going to win me the bet.

I should have taken my chances in the ballroom.

"This isn't funny!" I tried to scramble to my feet, but, you know— ruffles and petticoats and extra pounds. Finn, who'd leapt to his feet as easily as a frog jumping a log, pulled me up.

"It's kind of funny." He nodded at the goat, who had found another piece of my dress.

I grabbed Finn's wrist to check his watch. Thirty-five minutes until midnight. Okay. I wouldn't panic.

"We're locked in, no one knows we're down here, and it's almost midnight! NOT funny."

A tiny bit of panic, then.

"Relax. We're not." Finn tried the cell's door. It didn't budge. "Hmm."

He added a foot against the bars for extra leverage. Still nothing.

He turned to me. "Why are we locked in?"

Of all the dumb questions . . . "Uhm, hello, goat? Headbutt? Have *you* been drinking the punch?"

To his credit—or maybe to placate the crazy lady—he remained calm. "Okay, but who keeps a functional jail in their basement? Are you into some kinky stuff?"

"No!" Well . . . I hadn't thought about that . . . "No. Absolutely not. And anyway, that's why we kept the door propped open. So that no one gets trapped in here again."

He raised an eyebrow. "Again?"

"Uncle Sally got locked in once for a few days. But we stored extra kitchen supplies in here back then. Cooking sherry and breadcrumbs saw him through just fine."

"So, you're saying your uncle was stuck in here for days, and that didn't encourage you to disable the lock?"

He had a somewhat valid point. "I would have gotten around to it eventually, and besides, that's why we keep a key in here."

I grabbed his wrist again. Thirty-two minutes. That whole inane conversation had taken three minutes of my time.

Now I was panicked *and* angry. "Why are you here instead of Everett?"

"Because you—wait. Did you say there was a key in here somewhere?"

Jumping crawfish, I had. "YES."

I shoved Finn over to get to the nearest stack of boxes. "It's in here, somewhere . . . just have to find it."

I tore through the top box, throwing Christmas paper over my shoulder in a red and green frenzy.

"Do you normally keep a key with your Christmas decorations?"

"Duh, no."

"Magnolia?"

"What?" I found ribbon and some tape, but no key. I kept digging.

"Why are you looking in the Christmas boxes then? Also, why do you keep checking my watch?"

"I—" I looked around at the layers of wrapping paper covering the concrete floor. My shoulders slumped. "You wouldn't understand."

"You could try me." Finn took my hands out of the Christmas box and closed the lid. He turned me in the direction of a raggedy wooden desk and pointed at the small box resting on its surface which was a more likely key-hiding spot.

I searched through it while Finn rummaged through the desk's drawers. "Do you believe in ghosts?"

"Is that a trick question?"

I cut a glare at him, and he wiped away his grin. "Okay, sure. I've seen some things."

"Belle Soeurs has plenty, but only one makes me want to scream." I slammed the box shut and tossed it aside. "My grandmama."

That caught Finn off guard, sending the collection of dried-out pens he held clattering back into the drawer. "Your own grandmother? That's—"

"Crazy, yes. On many levels, the worst being she made me a bet I was fool enough to take. I have until midnight, but if we don't get out of here, I'll lose because I need Everett, and you clearly aren't him." I poked his chest for good measure.

"What does Everett have to do with this?"

I moved to another box before answering. "Everything. Grandmama doesn't think I've moved on from Gus, so she bet me I wouldn't ask out a guy with serious potential before Epiphany, which starts in—"

"Twenty-nine minutes. Yeah, I'm aware. Why Everett, though?" Finn's voice sounded peculiar, but I couldn't say why. Maybe my mention of Gus had brought up painful memories.

"Keep looking!" I pointed at his idle hands. "And why Everett? Uhm, hello? Have you looked at him?"

"Clearly not in the same way you have."

That made me laugh. I didn't remember Finn being so funny. Or tall.

It was my nature to be flippant and I tried, I swear, but brutal honesty is what came out.

21

"Because maybe Grandmama is right. And I hate it when she's right. I don't want to be the woman that's still pining eight years later, who goes through life afraid and just sleeping with— er, dating losers because it's safer. Everett—I know he won't hurt me. And maybe it's time to try something real."

Finn studied my face, and I could see true understanding in the depths of his midnight-blue eyes.

That bothered me almost as much as losing the dang bet to Grandmama. Almost.

I concentrated on the blasted key. I'd insisted it be kept inside the cell so that if someone got locked in again, they'd have it.

My eyes landed on the box Finn's foot had caught as we went down earlier. The one way across the hall.

"Noooooo." All I could do was point, but Finn caught on right away.

He grabbed a ratty old broom and tried to reach the box. "What do you get when you win?"

"Grandmama stops calling taxis to carry her back and forth from New Orleans. Do you know how many cabbies she's sent to therapy?"

Not that I did either, but I'm guessing it was more than one.

And guess who got stuck paying the cab fares? Even though Grandmama had brought a change of clothes to her afterworld, she'd conveniently forgotten her pocketbook.

Finn snorted. "And if you lose?"

I crossed myself. I'm not Catholic, but I needed all the protection I could get. "I have to rent a limousine to take Grandmama and her friends to New Orleans for some ghost party at City Park's Singing Oak. Seriously, the whole thing is ridiculous."

"Well, we have twenty minutes to keep that from happening." Finn kept his tone light, but it was clear he wasn't having much luck with the broom.

If only that dang goat wasn't still standing there, gloating at our predicament.

How had that beast even gotten into the basement to begin with?

Uncle Sally dressed as Little Bo Peep popped into my head.

I pushed Finn behind me and grabbed the cell bars with both hands, pushing my face as far through them as I could. "You stinking pile of fuzz. You're going to make a delicious goat stew, and I'll make Uncle Sally cook it. That'll teach . . ."

I trailed off as the goat stepped closer and sniffed one of the few vines still attached to my gown. I had an idea.

Not a great one, but at this point, what did I have to lose?

I ripped the remaining greenery off my skirt. Snatching the broom from a startled Finn's hands, I tied the vines to its handle.

"Watch out, Finn. I'm going goat fishing."

The cell walls didn't go all the way to the ceiling, so by standing on my toes, I could just clear the top with the broom. Thankful I'd been a tomboy before I discovered sequins and glitter, I cast my line—er, vine—so it landed on the box that literally held the key to our escape.

The greenery danced across its scratched surface, catching the goat's attention. He moved closer, curious, and I jerked the vine back out of his reach, teasing him.

"You do know that's not a cat?"

"Nobody asked you. Time?"

Finn checked his watch. "11:45."

I held my breath and tossed the vine again. This time, when the goat approached, I waited until he bared his teeth before jerking the broom back over my head, wincing as it connected with something solid.

Success! The goat, frustrated at losing his snack, charged after the vine. His hoof caught the box and sent it skittering across the cement floor right to me.

Dropping to my knees, I pushed the goat away as it tried to nibble my hair and pulled the box to me. Inside, precious as rubies, was the key.

I struggled back to my feet and fumbled for the old-fashioned lock. I couldn't see what I was doing, but miraculously the tumbler clicked into place and the iron door swung free.

Careful to block the door from closing again, I put the key in the safest place I knew - my cleavage - and turned to high-five Finn.

"We did i— uh, Finn?"

Finn lay on the ground, knocked out cold.

Sweet crawfish; I remembered the thunk of the broom handle hitting something hard.

That something? Finn's head.

Everett would never go out with me if I'd just murdered his best friend.

The goat, sensing this was all well above his pay grade, gave the abandoned greenery a good tug and scampered away with his prize floating behind him.

I lifted Finn's wrist to check the time again, flinching as it dropped back to the floor with a thud. I had a few minutes left before midnight—enough to run upstairs, find Everett, and ask him out, and then get back to the basement to see to Finn.

But without the goat smell burning my nostrils, I caught a faint coppery scent in the air. Blood flowed from Finn's temple, disappearing beneath the curls teasing his ear.

I'm proud that I debated longer than I should have. It wasn't so much Everett as Grandmama.

But Finn . . .

My heart jerked in a way I hadn't felt in a long, long time. One that reminded me I was a woman, and here was a man who needed me.

A man who still hadn't moved.

Grandmama, the bet, and even Everett left my mind, replaced only by Finn. I leaned over him to listen for proof he was alive, but gravity is not a big girl's friend.

After almost tumbling headfirst on top of him, I decided to try a different way. I hiked my ballgown up to my thighs and straddled Finn's midsection, which let me safely place my ear on his chest.

His heartbeat thumped loud and strong.

I practically melted against him. Now that I knew I wasn't a murderer, I found it rather relaxing to be pressed against a warm man. There was no more *eau du goat*, and through the basement's open windows faint music from the ballroom floated above the nightly chorus of crickets. I could get used to this.

Finn's watch chirped just as a clock from somewhere in the vast basement began its own announcement of the hour. As it chimed for the twelfth time, Whalen Finnick opened his eyes to find a woman he barely knew straddling him. On the filthy floor of a jail, somewhere under a former sugarcane plantation.

I really hoped Grandmama wasn't seeing this.

"Good God Almighty." Finn jerked to full consciousness, and faster than I could say peanut-butter pie, had me flat on my back with my hands pinned above my head.

Alright then.

"Hello to you too," I drawled, impressed at his quick reaction and maybe, just maybe, a little turned on.

Finn pulled me to my feet, wincing as his head wound made itself known.

I made him perch on the corner of the splintery desk and used my sleeve to gently dab at the gash. "So, I may have accidentally whacked you with the broom."

Finn's eyes searched my face. "Accidentally?"

"100%. But I got us out of jail!"

His eyes flashed to the door before returning to me. "It's after midnight."

"Nice! You aced your cognitive test."

Finn grabbed my hand, pulling it away from his head. "Magnolia."

"It's fine. I've lost bets with Grandmama before."

Finn didn't let go of my hand. "You could have asked me."

"What?" I tried to step back but Finn kept me close.

"You may not have noticed, but I, too, am a good man. Same as Everett."

For the second time tonight, my sarcastic mouth failed me. "It's after midnight."

Finn's lips lifted in a crooked smile, and his hand tightened on mine. "So? Ask anyway."

I didn't let myself stop to think. "Would you—"

A cacophony of voices interrupted me as my party guests spilled into the basement, led by Everett. Uncle Sally brought up the rear with the blasted

24

goat on a leash, who, not to be left out, bellowed a scream that made his earlier ones sound like a lullaby.

Everett pulled me from Finn's hold into his own. "When that goat burst into the ballroom eating your costume, I thought maybe you'd fallen down the stairs or worse."

He paused to catch his breath. "And all I could think was I'd missed my opportunity to ask you out."

Grasping my chin, he peered into my face. "Are you hurt? You're so pale."

I pulled his hand away. "I'm fine. It's probably the dang goat smell, which, speaking of . . ."

I stared around Everett until my uncle met my eyes. "Now Magnolia, I know what you're thinking."

"Really?"

"I wanted to win the costume contest! So, I needed Sam here for authenticity's sake."

"Little Bo Peep had sheep. Not goats."

I took a step towards him, but he wisely melted back into the crowd, who, now that I'd been found whole and alive, began heading back upstairs for more king cake and spiked punch.

Everyone but Everett.

"So? What do you say?"

I turned my attention back to him. "Sorry?"

"Go out with me." Everett pushed a frizzy blonde curl off my forehead, watching me with soulful brown eyes.

Which reminded me of the inky blue ones I'd been gazing into just moments before. "I, er—"

I turned to look at Finn, but Everett and I were the only ones there.

Embarrassment rolled through me. I'd probably imagined Finn's interest, and here was Everett, clearly letting me know how he felt. He had asked me out.

I took the arm he offered. "I'd like that. But no goats."

"No goats," he promised, and I grinned, although my heart wasn't in it. I couldn't shake the feeling that I'd lost something more than Grandmama's bet tonight.

✳✳✳

Two months later . . .

The limousine cut powerfully through the dark as we journeyed towards New Orleans. As far as the driver knew, I was his only passenger.

I'd held up my end of the deal, getting Grandmama and her friends a limousine, and we were on the way to the Ghouls Gathering at the Singing

Oak.

Everett had offered to go to New Orleans with me, not knowing about Grandmama, but I'd gently declined. It was Mardi Gras night and he and Finn would have their hands full with the inebriated miscreants in our own parish.

At the thought of Finn, I flushed. I'd seen him once or twice since the Twelfth Night Gala, but we acted like strangers.

Well, not exactly: strangers wouldn't be eaten up with embarrassment.

One day I'd remember to appreciate what was actually in front of me instead of hankering after what wasn't.

Grandmama poked me, turning my skin to ice. "Are you listening? I have a new bet for you."

"Nope."

At least I'd learned one lesson.

About the Author

Amy Fortenberry is a lifelong Southerner recently transported to the Salt Lake Valley of Utah where she lives with her sweet (and terribly spoiled) rescue dog Nola and more nieces and nephews than she can shake a stick at (also terribly spoiled—can you find the common denominator?). Her favorite city is New Orleans and its special brand of living lends flavor to all of her writing. Follow her on Instagram @amyluluwrites or visit her at www.amyluluwrites.com.

SHATTERED SILENCE

DAKOTA FOSTER

Breathe in.

Deeper.

Slower.

Pause.

Stuck. Trapped. Breath that can't be released. Burning lungs and knotted throat. The exhale won't come. My skin screams. Every touch of clothing and brush of air stings as raw and tender as a fresh sunburn.

It's only a panic attack.

Blood races through my veins, thunders in my chest, trembles my unsteady hands. But it will pass. I'll live.

Probably.

I hope.

Or maybe I don't.

It could all end now.

Stop.

Spiraling thoughts only fuel the panic. Remember my plan. Focus on something in the here and now.

Three things I can see.

- The pale, flickering bulb of the bathroom light overhead. Cold and unsteady like the oily tendrils of lies that slither through my head . . .

- The dying cricket in the corner, twitching on the stained, cracked tile beside a bloody pile of discarded tissue.

- The smeared, chipped mirror above the sink showing a girl who looks too young to be here: twenty-two, but the world thinks she's a teenager still, innocent. Small. With slick brown hair, stringy and oily, charcoal smears of bleeding mascara beneath soft hazel eyes hidden in sunken sockets above deep shadows on pale skin, like purple bruises betraying the sleepless nights that haunt my exhausted soul and whisper that it would all be so much easier if I swallowed all the pills . . .

Stop.

My vision blurs at the edges, and my skin tingles now, the needle-prick pain of my face and fingers falling asleep. I'm not getting enough oxygen. My knees give out. I crumple to the foul, filthy floor, hot tears rushing down my cheeks. My hands are tainted now from the vile residue coating this unwashed tile, and I can't even brush away the saltwater anguish on my face.

Focus.

Two things I feel.

1) The stab of my thumbnail on the pads of my fingers, rubbing back and forth. I didn't realize I was moving my hands. Why can't I be normal?
2) The pinching of my toes in my too-tight heels.

Why did I come here? I hate bars. Hate the way alcohol burns and the terror that takes over the second I fear I might lose even an ounce of control over myself. I want to not feel. I want to not be alone. But coming here is so much worse. Alone while alone hurts so much less than alone surrounded by people.

My heart dances. A frantic, too fast jazz number. Unsteady. Uneven. This feels like dying. Is this a heart attack? Am I . . .

Stop.

Panic attacks are like this. Push through.
One thing I smell.

- Piss, dried on the floor. No. This isn't helping. I'm supposed to have a mantra. Crud. What is it?

All is well. All is well. All is well.
It's not, though. All is in shards now. It broke at midnight like an effed up Cinderella's pumpkin.

***

Midnight.
Two hours ago.

Sitting at the coffee shop while warm espresso fills the air with rich, earthy hues.

Open mic night.

I scratch doodles in my notebook, psyching myself up to speak. To walk up to the platform when my name is called and read my poetry.

> *One dark knight I was crumbling.*
> *His sword too sharp, too cruel.*
> *His lust for power overcame me . . .*

The words scrape out. My voice raw. Chest tight. My eyes hot with tears I choke back.

He leers at me. Why is he here? This isn't his scene. He's not a creative. Not an artful soul. He doesn't belong here. He takes everything he wants. He ruins it.

I squeeze the mic too hard, sweating hands shaking now. My voice too small. My body too stained with shame.

He wraps his arm around a girl who looks just like me except for the smile on her innocent face. He whispers in her ear, and she laughs.

My black sweater is too tight, too scratchy. It scrapes my skin. Slices me open. My words have stopped, but my feet haven't moved. The light is on me. On the darkness in me as I bleed.

No.

My hands fly to my throat, the cool of my palms soothing against my burning skin. He's laughing now, too. Shouting words I can't hear over the storm inside my head. I wanted to be brave. But I wasn't enough. I was too much. I race out into the suffocating night, stale, humid air choking me. The hands of the courthouse clock show twelve o'four. Just past midnight.

The bar across the old downtown square of shops promises cheap drinks and forgotten problems.

But now I'm here, on the filthy bathroom floor, gasping for breath.

The door opens. Did I not lock it? Why am I such a mess? A girl walks in, black ripped jeans and combat boots. She sits beside me. Chipped nails. Bandaged palm.

Her voice is like rain on a summer day, "I heard your poem. I know what he did to you. He did it to me, too. I'm willing to tell the police now, if you are."

Her hand rests on my knee. I lean my head against her shoulder. My voice is like thick fog on an autumn morning. "I am."

About the Author

Dakota Foster is a writer and professional photographer living in small town Texas with her sweet, wild, big family and an abundance of cats and dogs. She has Sensory Processing Disorder and anxiety disorders, and she's passionate about breaking the stigma on mental health disorders and neurodivergence. For more raw, relatable conversations about navigating the ups and downs of life, follow her on Instagram @read.write.coffee and visit www.dakotafoster.com.

FEAR NOT

DEENA GRAVES

FEAR NOT

I f kissing Liam were a drug, I'd be an addict. He'd finished his Hot Tamales before I pulled him in for one last goodnight. The spicy cinnamon of his tongue burned against my own.

I backed away, savoring the lingering, fiery kick. Liam sighed, twirling a dark curl out from behind my ear, reminding me I was about a week overdue for a haircut.

"Want me to come in?" The purr in his voice about undid me.

With equal parts frustration and want, my throat vibrated with a groan. "Nah, Dad'll be home soon." A glance at the dash clock told me it was a lot closer to midnight than my 11PM curfew.

Liam settled back into the driver's seat, concern tightening his brown eyes. I gazed out at the dark neighborhood with sparse suburbanite streetlights, not really seeing anything.

Dad's rules were as archaic as they were unnegotiable. We didn't agree on much, especially regarding unsupervised visits from my boyfriend. Mom was the only one who hadn't treated me like a pariah since coming out freshman year. Her warm hugs and bright smile made up for my father's cold disappointment that I felt in my bones. Or the surety that if he could somehow force the gayness from me without fracturing his pristine, cookie-cutter image, he would. Every one of his words or flat stares stoked an ember of fear in my gut, like an unspoken promise.

"Any news on the investigation?" Liam tucked a skinny, golden-tipped loc back with the others tied low at the base of his neck and slid on his dark-framed glasses. He hated them, but, for me, they completed the whole package that was Liam.

Most of the football team dated cheerleaders, but I fell hard for the editor of the school paper—a Triple B threat: a bookish boy with banter.

I shook my head, frowning at the dash. "Nothing. It's been a week and not a peep."

"I'm so sorry, Trey. I can't believe your mom took off like that."

She needed the space; I'd heard the arguing. Mostly about me—how it was Mom's fault I turned out gay. She was too soft on me, too protective. The note she'd left for Dad said she'd gone to visit her sister in a nearby town, but she never got there, per my aunt. Some clothes, a small suitcase, and her bathroom stuff were missing, along with her Camry.

"Yeah." I took Liam's warm hand, threading his deep-brown fingers with my fair-skinned ones. His brows knit as though he struggled to say something else. I smiled, but it fell flat. "Thanks for picking me up from practice."

"Of course. I know Coach is hell-bent on running you into the ground before the game against Lincoln." The left corner of his lips curled upward.

"But seeing you all sweaty in football pads is absolutely worth it."

I laughed. "Is that all it takes? I've been playing this all wrong."

"Ass." His sudden smile dazed me. "Thanks for showering, though. There's only so much I can do to ward off post-practice boyfriend smell." Liam flicked the candle-shaped thing hanging from the rear-view.

"Anything for you, babe."

Liam smacked my shoulder and I about doubled over. It felt good to laugh, and Liam excelled at dragging it out of me ever since he wrote a piece on me, Varsity Captain, for the school paper. The playful look in his eyes didn't quite match the worried set of his delicious mouth. I slid my hand around the back of Liam's neck and pulled him in for another kiss. *Yum, cinnamon.* "See you tomorrow."

I grabbed my practice gear from the floorboard, climbed out of his beat-up compact, and tossed my Varsity jacket on the seat. A pre-snow breeze burned inside my nose. Its clean iciness mixed with wood-smoke and filled the November Midwest air.

"Trey?" Liam leaned over the gearshift to look up at me. "They'll find her. You don't have to worry, okay?"

My gut clenched and I forced my gaze to the back of my Varsity jacket in the passenger seat. The stitching for my name, Rizzo, had frayed around the edges and came loose. Mom would've been able to fix it.

I frowned, fighting the catch in my throat. "I know."

I wanted to believe that. I wanted them to find Mom, and then we'd go have ice cream and resume all the normal crap, and this would all be over. Hell, I'd take more of the arguing over another day in a silent house. Each passing day brought less news from the local authorities. I couldn't stomach the weighted resignation in their words or the defeat on their faces.

"Elephant shoes."

"Elephant shoes," I said with a grin.

Last year, we'd watched a comedian's bit about mouthing the words 'elephant shoes' to a chick he didn't like because it looked as if he'd said 'I love you.' We both cracked up. It stuck after that. I'd say the actual words since I meant them, but this seemed more us.

I grabbed my stuff and walked up the sloped driveway to the empty, dark house. Each step begged me to turn around, to get back into Liam's car and drive away. Anything to not have to face my father alone in this tomb.

I flipped on the porch light when I stepped inside. Dad worked a lot these days, avoiding me as usual. Too bad I looked just like him, with all his Italian glory, complete with identical black hair that curled when it grew too long, or he might convince others I was a bastard. That's how he treated me, anyway, despite possessing the highest QB passing rating in the state, having an enviable GPA, and college scholarships padding my email inbox.

Screw him.

I tossed my gear at the foot of the stairs and walked past the shrine-like table full of pictures of me over the last seventeen years and into the designer-bland white and soft gray kitchen. After emptying my pockets onto the massive granite island in a clatter of phone and house keys, I grabbed a protein bar from the pantry organized by category and then alphabetically. If I lost myself in my studies, I could ignore Dad when he got home just as he would ignore me.

I turned back toward the hall, and my body locked in place.

My heartbeat stuttered into a sprint and goose flesh rippled over my skin as though ice water trickled down my spine. The door to the storage room under the stairs, which stayed locked—always—was open, and the shrine-table sat at an angle like someone had shoved it out of the way.

Most kids would've loved a mysterious closet under the stairs that promised letters of admittance to faraway magic schools. Not me. For as long as I could remember, I'd had nightmares about being trapped in there, being sucked into frozen darkness with a silent scream on my lips. They were so bad, doctors had medicated me since grade school. The little magic pills made sure I didn't remember any dreams, and Mom set up the picture table so I didn't have to see the closet.

I took a step backward, gaze fixed on the closet door while snapshots of medically blurred dreams flashed through my head.

A blanket of cold latched onto my skin, biting at my lips and nose like our harsh Midwestern winters and freezing me in place. My shaky breath puffed out in frantic billows as tendrils of silvery light swirled around me like an illuminated cloud. Eyes dark as pitch appeared, as if I were nose-to-nose with another person. A scream crouched in my throat, ready to spring free. The room tilted as my knees gave out. Then, everything went black.

***

When I came around, impenetrable darkness surrounded me.

I jerked upright and cracked my head against something. My forehead throbbed as I inspected the area above me. A low ceiling, not much taller than where I crouched, sloped upward. I scrambled forward, disoriented by the dark, and banged my shoulder into a wall. Lunging backward, I hit another wall. The tightness of space closed in on me. Cold panic clawed its way up my chest. My pulse beat a frantic throb in my head. Breath made raspy from stale, moth-ball air scraped along my dry throat. My hands began to shake.

Too tight. Too dark.

I curled my fingers into my hair, tugging at the scalp. *Get a grip, Rizzo!* I forced out a breath between clenched teeth and tried to focus on one thing at a time. I stretched out my arms, gauging my space. My elbow brushed something other than a wall. Square. Cardboard. Boxes?

Settling on my knees, I pushed the box away from me. Wouldn't budge.

I pulled it toward me and reached an arm beyond it. My fingers met a rough and chalky surface. Plaster. Another wall.

I shoved away from the boxes, my back slamming against the opposite side. My head brushed the ceiling where I knelt. *Don't think about how close the walls are. Don't think about the dark, the cold. Think about Liam and his smile.*

Liam!

I jammed my hand into my pocket for my phone before remembering I'd left it on the counter. *Shit!* Not like I could tell him where to find me. Or what happened. Or how I got here. Wherever *here* was. Raking my fingers through my hair with a breath, I tried retracing my steps. Came home, dumped my pockets, grabbed a snack and—

The closet door! And the weird, misty cold, but after that was a massive blank.

My hands started shaking harder, and I hunched over my knees, rocking back and forth. *Okay, don't freak out, man.* My chest burned with each ragged breath. My stomach twisted up worse than pre-game jitters.

I needed to figure this out. Now. The sooner I figured out where I was, the faster I could get the hell out! Clenching and unclenching my fists, I reached for the wall to my right. My fingers traced a slender, vertical frame and wooden surface. A door? I lunged forward, feverishly running my hands over the wood, searching for the knob. My knuckles cracked against a metal object—an oval no larger than an egg. And it refused to turn no matter how hard I twisted.

Wait. I stopped, frozen, as I stared into the darkness.

Locked door?

Angled roof?

Boxes?

"Dad!" Panic broke my voice as realization hit. "Dad! Let me out! This isn't funny!" *How the hell did I get into the closet under the stairs?*

I slammed my palms and fists against the door until my knuckles bled. Warm liquid slid between my fingers, making them sticky. Tears burned behind my eyes. Was the room getting smaller? Sweat slicked my face and neck. My sweatshirt clung to my clammy skin as tingles electrified every nerve ending.

"Dad . . ." I slumped in defeat, my forehead thumping against the door. Is this how he punished The Disappointment? By trying to scare me straight?

My throat thickened. "Mom . . ."

Something cold grazed my cheek like a finger.

"Jesus!"

I threw myself against a wall, away from it. A faint, misty light gathered near my feet like some Halloween fog machine. I couldn't move. The stagnant air of the closet frosted over. My hot breath formed puffs in the dim light. Goosebumps rose in a wave along my arms and down my legs.

"Dad!" My hoarse voice failed to penetrate the dead air. I pounded raw knuckles against the door. My clammy hands slipped from the grip on the tiny knob. "Get me out of here!"

I looked over my shoulder. The misty light swelled and billowed into a silvery cloud a few feet tall. Its pulsating shape grazed my shoe, sending an icy jolt up my leg. I pulled my knees toward my chest, but the closet wasn't big enough for both of us. My stomach churned until I almost puked. I focused on my bladder so I wouldn't piss myself.

"Dad!"

"Trey."

I stopped pounding and spun around, pressing my back against the door. The word whispered through my head like a near-forgotten secret.

The cloud cast a faint glow, bathing the tiny space in a silvery-blue light. It was semi-transparent; the outlines of boxes and contours of Dad's golf clubs were just visible through it. The floor beneath the cloud twinkled as if frost crystals had formed. My chest heaved as I tried to breathe.

"Boog."

I stopped breathing. The whisper in my head again, but this time, I heard the nickname only Mom used.

The cloud shifted and slithered into a vague human form with shoulders and a head. It had a fluid quality—the center was almost solid, with outer edges softening into a fine mist. And it moved like swirling storm clouds in time-lapse.

I then saw eyes. And a smile. Both were familiar.

"Mom?" I gasped.

The smile in the mist broadened with warmth.

"Are you—" I swallowed. Tears warmed my cold cheeks. "Are you . . . dead?" The last word caught in my throat. She couldn't be, not my mom.

Anguish. Sorrow. Pain. They weren't words, but sensations passing through me as if I'd experienced them—like my soul felt them.

"Mom?"

Frustration. Irritation. The swirling mist roiled and darkened to pewter like storm clouds in the spring.

"I don't understand. What's going on?"

The mist's dark eyes hardened, and *anger* plowed through my skull, so potent, sulfur burned in the air. My heart skipped and I backed into the door again.

Regret washed over me in a cool current. The Mom-mist eyes softened, and the torrent of swirled mist settled into silvery wisps of light. A sensation similar to *comfort* spread through me like warm hugs after a rough day.

"What happened, Mom? Where are you? The cops have been looking for you." I had so many questions, but the Mom-mist only watched me.

I took a deep breath and rubbed my face. Mom-mist couldn't answer questions the way I asked them. I had to work around this.

"Okay." I choked back tears and nodded to myself. "So, you're—" I couldn't say it. "You're . . . gone." Her encouraging smile urged me to keep going. "Do you know where your . . . body is?"

Sadness, but *determination*. I took that as a yes. How to find her, though? I tried to formulate a question she could answer when the sulfuric *anger* rushed back. I coughed at the potency.

"Did you wreck?"

The *anger* winked out. Not a wreck.

"Are you still in the car somewhere?"

Nothing.

Dread sank into my gut.

"Were you—" I licked my lips. "Was it *not* an accident?" My heart pounded in my temples as *compassion* flashed through my brain.

This couldn't be happening. I scrubbed a sleeve across my face. "Do you know who did it?"

Something close to *pride* glowed in her with the brilliance of a blazing star. Her misty form almost appeared solid.

"Holy shit, Mom! Who?" The sulfur *anger* came back with a vengeance. I sneezed.

"Alright, Mom. Calm down. We can figure this out." I took a breath. The Mom-mist closed her eyes as if taking one as well and her swirls steadied. "I need to find you. To find your . . . body."

Pride blazed and her megawatt smile brought tears to my eyes again. "*Boog.*" My bottom lip trembled, and I closed my eyes. "*Trey.*" How could I hear my name and nothing else? A familiar weight settled across my shoulders, complete with the hint of a light patting against my back that Mom would do.

I opened my eyes, and the Mom-mist swirled all around me, bathing me in light as a soothing blanket of *love* settled over me. The intensity of it rocked me, and the confidence in Mom-mist's eyes gave me the courage to hold it together. Shadowy tendrils from medicinally forgotten nightmares teased at the corners of my mind.

I shifted my position to work out a cramp building in my calves. The shorter ceiling here made moving around awkward. As I maneuvered to my hands and knees, a floorboard wiggled under my right hand. Confused, I felt around the loose board and reshuffled pliant cardboard boxes that smelled like the antique shop downtown Mom used to drag me to.

Eventually, I discovered there were several loose, rough-cut boards, and cursed as a splinter dug its way under my fingernail. Gripping the lip of one with my fingertips, I lifted.

"Oh, God—" A sickeningly sweet odor, like rancid meat, flooded the small, dark space. It reeked worse than week-old garbage or a deer carcass on the side of the road. I fought the urge to vomit and pulled the collar of my sweatshirt over my nose and mouth. My watery eyes met Mom-mist's. *Sadness. Regret.*

Her dark eyes lowered to the space between us and back at me. "You've got to be kidding me."

Mom-mist's subtle glow did nothing to penetrate the pitch-black beneath me. I knew what I would find if I reached into the crawlspace. I needed to do it. Mom needed me to do it. I fought to push past the knot of fear and grief that froze me in place.

A cool, tingly sensation blanketed me. My head and heart filled with so much *love,* I thought I'd burst at the seams. Mom-mist surrounded me again. The tears wouldn't stop as Mom-mist hugged me. I rocked back and forth on my knees, wanting nothing more than to have Mom's arms around me, holding me tight, so I knew everything would be okay no matter what. She was a tiny thing, my mom, not quite reaching my shoulder, but I was the small and breakable one in the dark.

"Trey."

Something clicked into place. When she whispered in my head, it wasn't so much my name but a mother's limitless love I heard. Not even death could sever that kind of love.

I sat back, and Mom-mist settled in front of me. The determination in her eyes mirrored what hummed in my heart. I scrubbed my face with my sweatshirt and reached into the darkness below the floorboards.

The uneven, roughly-cut edges of the support beams under the subfloor scraped my hands. Fabric. Canvas? A leather-wrapped handle. I pulled out the small suitcase.

Feeling along the edges, I found the zipper. Once unzipped, I bit down on the inside of my cheek as Mom's perfume circled around me. I'd know that jasmine scent anywhere. The bottle must have busted. Carefully reaching into the case, I discovered clothes bunched up by the handful.

I closed the suitcase and shoved it onto the boxes I'd restacked behind me. Taking a steadying breath, I watched Mom-mist. Her dark eyes were full of purpose and *confidence* settled over my shoulders, squaring them up.

Shifting onto my stomach, I reached into the hole that might be about three-foot square. My hand met the sturdy yet soft material of denim. A leg. A thigh. Gentle fingers skimmed over her hip. Her body bent at the waist, knees toward her chest. The silky fabric of her blouse had stiffened in places from the below-freezing nights. I flinched at the coldness of her arm. The frozen skin felt mealy under my fingers like super over-ripe fruit.

Something wiggled under my touch. I snatched my hand back with a curse but banged my elbow on rough-cut support beams. A string of profanity curdled on my lips as I reached back into the dark hole and did my best to ignore whatever bugs had found her. My brows pinched and my lips trembled. Her shoulder. Hair.

I rested my palm on the back of her head and held my breath against the sobs threatening to break free. Tears still burned down my face. How could this be happening?

My breath quivered and I tried to push away the grief. I'd come this far, so I could keep going. *Patience. Admiration. Love.* They all swirled around me, mixing with the lingering scent of Mom's perfume and the gag-inducing sweetness of decay.

She lay wedged under the floorboards in a shallow section of crawlspace. How did she die, though? I searched for her neck. The flesh was bloated and sort of spongy, but found nothing. Her skull didn't seem fractured.

I shifted for a better angle when my pinkie grazed something. I tucked my hand in my sleeve, covering the skin, and reached out again. *Damn it!* The handle of a knife stuck out from her chest, wedged between her knees.

I sat back, measuring Mom-mist. Her steady eyes held mine.

"He knew, didn't he?" I asked even though she couldn't answer. "The bastard knew you were leaving him."

Respect. I nodded at her confirmation.

"They won't believe me, Mom, not without concrete evidence. Doesn't matter how this looks. I've watched enough FBI dramas to learn that. We can't let him walk."

Bitter *rage*. Mom-mist's eyes lowered to my lap. I followed her gaze and caught the faint silvery outline of my hands on my thighs. I stared at Mom-mist, not understanding what she meant. She met my eyes, and then pointedly looked into the pit where her body lay. I frowned and she repeated the stares. My hands. My eyes. Her body.

Her hands!

I lunged forward and reached into the hole again, fumbling around until I found Mom's hands. Her fists were in tight balls, but the familiar curls—the same curls I inherited from my father—trapped between her fingers should be enough.

Pulling myself out of the crawlspace, I watched Mom. Firm *determination* and her familiar *pride* welled in my heart. I nodded to her as she smiled her megawatt smile. *Love* so pure and vibrant brought tears to my eyes as Mom-mist faded away in smoky tendrils. Before the storage closet once again fell into complete darkness, Mom's perfume scent blanketed me and the feather-soft sensation of *peace* filled my heart.

"I love you too, Mom."

With a deep breath, I rubbed my face. "Now, I just have to figure out how to get out of this damned closet."

A soft click, and my head snapped around, heart in my throat. The storage room door swung open with a sigh, revealing the dim light from the kitchen flooding the hall outside.

As I gazed out the angled doorway, a small smile tugged at my lips. The icy fear that clawed under my ribs when I thought of this room was gone. Instead, as I sat on the floor, I discovered I wasn't scared at all. I knew what needed to be done.

I crawled out and staggered into the kitchen as the grandfather clock in

42

the living room clanged away the hour. Aside from the light above the stove, the dark house showed no sign of Dad. I grabbed my cell phone from the counter and dialed without hesitation.

"Yeah." I cleared my throat. He won't get away with this. "I'd like to report a murder."

The front door opened.

"Trey?" Dad's brown eyes, mirrors of mine, took in the open storage room door and settled on me in the hall. A flicker of wariness I'd never seen on him, flittered across his features. "How did you open—Who are you calling at this hour?"

I squared my shoulders on the twelfth gong of the old clock, knowing I had nothing to fear from him ever again.

"Yes," I told the emergency dispatcher. "The killer is here. He just came home."

About the Author

Deena Graves grew up in Northern California, nestled between the Bay Area and the majestic Sierra Nevada Mountains. It wasn't until she moved to Tennessee as an adult that she developed a deep love of lightning bugs, a neat bourbon, and the magic of fictional worlds. When not writing, Deena can be found submerged in Marvel movies (again), trying to befriend her local crows, or teaching herself DIY woodwork. For more [mis]adventures, follow her on Instagram @panicwritten.

FEAR NOT

44

HAUNTED

MARY E. DIPPLE

S he didn't know what caused him to appear.

It may have been the smell of decay that came when the green of summer gave way to the russet and golden colors of autumn.

Or it could be the sound of dry leaves skittering over her stone floor, blown in by the wind as her last customer left the shop clutching a shawl against the chill.

Maybe it was because she hadn't slept in over six days.

Whatever it was, it had weakened the magical barriers in her mind and now he stood in her shop, a dried-up husk of the man he'd once been. His gray skin appeared as if someone had dried and stretched it before draping it over a skeleton. She forced herself not to look at him. She couldn't react to his presence, even if it was only in her mind, because to do so would only weaken the barrier further.

She flipped the sign in her window to "Closed" before locking the door. When she returned to the counter, the smell of cinnamon and cloves surrounded her, and she felt the barest brush of a kiss across her cheek. Warmth filled her hands, and she raised a mug of hot cider to her lips. Fire crackled in a hearth behind her as her mother stood and turned to her father. She smiled as her parents embraced.

But it was wrong.

Her mother was dead.

He'd killed her and so many more.

With that thought, the memory faded, and the man in her mother's arms became the apparition that stood before her once again. She stiffened and unfocused her gaze so as not to look directly at him. She buried the feelings of warmth and safety the memory he had triggered brought with it. He was not the man that one-time child had believed him to be. He was, and always would be, a monster.

She placed her hands on the counter to steady herself before pulling out and counting the till for the day. She recorded the amount in her ledger and mumbled an enchantment over the lockbox to secure it for the night.

He never spoke.

Never moved.

He just stood watching her, his silence creeping up her neck and demanding she look at him.

She blew out the lamps, plunging the shop into darkness. A darkness she knew could not hide him.

Taking the last candle with her, she readied herself for bed then sat on the hand-stitched quilt with her legs crossed under her, hands folded in her lap, eyes closed. The barrier in her mind needed to be rebuilt. She would never rid herself of him, but she could close him out of her waking thoughts. She could force him back into his solitary prison. Back into the hole where she'd locked him so long ago.

She touched the flame of life that blazed in her core and drew a thin strand from it, like drawing wool from a wheel. She threaded the golden life force through her fingers and wove a new barrier. A barrier that would lock out all thoughts, all memories, of him.

"Your barrier gets weaker every time," his voice rasped. "One day, you won't be able to lock me away. One day, you will face what you've done. And then it will be my turn."

When she opened her eyes, she was alone. The house sat still, except for the clock in the shop striking the middle hour of the night. The day he spoke of would come. She knew it, and she feared it. For when it did, when he was free once again, the world would burn.

About the Author

A lover of all things magical, Mary E. Dipple uses her talent of spinning stories to shine a light into the darkness that so easily entangles our lives. She is currently writing her epic-fantasy series, The Lotus Chronicles, publication date to be determined. When Mary isn't slaying the darkness with story, she enjoys spending her days tending her ever growing rose garden, playing with her lovable furry assistants, and writing flash fiction. You can find more about Mary and her stories by visiting her Instagram @mary.e.dipple_author or website at www.marydipple.com.

THE
MIDNIGHT
REQUIREMENT

JENNIFER DYER

O f all the evenings to leave my wand at work, this is the worst. I zip through the dim and silent halls of Fairy Godmother Headquarters, the frantic beating of my wings reflecting my rushing thoughts. I need to get my wand then zoom home to my second (okay, third) bowl of berrydew ice cream. Anything to forget tonight's betrayal. The pressure tightens in my throat again, but I refuse to give in to more tears.

Purple and pink fireworks flash outside a nearby window, the sky-lighting portion of the Queen's High Summer Ball. Aside from the food, it's one of the parts of the ball I love the most. I turn away so I don't have to see them.

A magic mirror flashes to life as I skulk past, displaying a fairy godmother in a sparkly pink gown fluttering over a flowery meadow, shooting fairy dust from her wand. In a cheerful voice, she trills, "And they lived happily ever after." She winks at the viewer while writing in sparkly gold appears next to her. *Use your wish today. Your HEA awaits.*

I resist punching the mirror because I'm allergic to pain. Plus, as the Fairy Godmother Assistant Intern, I already clean up enough messes around here. But seriously, the adverts make it sound like wishes grow on blackberry bushes, yet each fairy only gets one in their lifetime. Flapping my wings, I glare at the shimmering surface showing a kissing couple. "Lies. Happily ever after doesn't exist."

A shadow blocks the path to my desk, and I nearly run into a tall, muscular fairy. Before he utters a word, I already know who it is. And I don't want to hear what he has to say.

Still, he can't help himself. "Don't let Lulu hear you say that." His deep voice grates up my spine and to the tips of my wings. Perfect. Just what I needed. Hunter Driftwood.

As always, Hunter wears black from his raven hair to his boots. When we're on the ground, he's three centimeters taller than my fifteen centimeters, so I flap to gain equal height. His narrowed eyelids almost obscure his bright emerald irises, and his full lips curl into a sneer. "Why're you here dressed like that?"

I step back and follow his gaze. My soft blue ballgown sparkles in the low light, well . . . except for the purple berrydew ice cream stains marring the bodice and the flower petal skirt. And instead of the satin heels I'd bought for the ball, I'm wearing caterpillar slippers with purple flower noses. But perhaps the crowning achievement is my name tag. Since I'd forgotten my wand, with its unlock spells for Headquarters, I'd had to use the visitor entrance. The desk fairy had started her High Ball celebrating early and had gotten my name wrong, spelling it, *Silly Bum* instead of Silybum Marianum. I go by Mari at any rate, but no one around here remembers.

I flap my wings to edge around him. "I'm just here to pick up something."

"Your wand?" He folds his toned arms over his chest, not that I care about his muscles.

I gave him a heated look and slide past, catching a hint of orange mixed with sandalwood. "Go count your pencils, Driftwood."

He follows. "Weren't you supposed to be at the ball?"

"Changed my mind." Yep. That's totally what happened. The pressure behind my eyes intensifies to a burn. I blink, refusing to give in.

Hunter huffs what could be a laugh if it came from someone capable of such frivolity. "Where's Mr. Perfect? What's his name again? Shiplap? Shifty?"

"Shut up." I scoot to my tiny cubical, shoving aside piles of paper, plants, and my collection of kitten miniatures before I locate the wand under the thick Fairy Godmother Assistant Manual emblazoned with the acronym FGAM. I resist the urge to slam it on Hunter's toes.

Hunter is still scowling when the mirror behind us activates and flashes bright pink. He groans. "Not another FGE."

It takes me a moment to shuffle through the hundreds of acronyms FGH (Fairy Godmother Headquarters) uses. Right, FGE is a Fairy Godmother Emergency. My eyes meet Hunter's, and it's like the two of us are on the same page for the first time ever. We both bolt for the door. If they don't find us here, they can't make us—

Our manager Lulu pops into the hallway, blocking our escape. Her embroidered purple dress stretches tight across her apple-shaped middle, and she's carrying a delicate saucer piled with lemon-lavender tarts and dainty burnt sugar chocolate swirls.

My mouth waters at the food that obviously came from the ball. More of my favorites. I fight the urge to knock the plate out of her hands.

She pops an entire tart into her mouth, making a smacking noise. "Driftwood, Silly Bum. Glad you're here."

"It's Mari, and I was on my—"

Lulu waves me off. "It's a Code Five, and since you don't have anything else to do tonight—"

"I have plans." Eating berrydew ice cream at home constitutes a plan.

She finishes her last pastry and waves the saucer away with her wand. "Giselda's granted an unauthorized wish. And you know how she is. Doesn't do a lick of paperwork, so she's gone and left the magic on again. It's got to be turned off by midnight, or . . ." She grimaces. "We can't have a repeat of the '08 disaster." She glances my way, as if noticing my outfit for the first time and tsks. "Show some pride in yourself."

I shoot back a frown of my own. "I requested the night off, so I can wear whatever—"

"Everyone knows your plans changed."

My mouth opens but all that comes out is a tiny "ock."

Hunter scowls. "This is a punishment, and you know it." His deep voice rumbles through the room.

Lulu waves a pudgy hand like she's showcasing something precious. "It's an opportunity."

Hunter's arms and shoulders go taut. "It's a waste of my skill set."

My wings snap shut. "What skills would that be? Acting like a total—"

Lulu shushes me. "There's no way around the midnight requirement."

Hunter's normally pale face flushes. "First I'm relegated to a bureaucracy, now I'm demoted to grunt work with incompetent low flyers."

"Excuse me?" How dare he imply the fairies in my department weren't skilled enough to fly at higher altitudes? Like we were too stupid? "You arrogant wasp. I'll have you know, us Fairy Godmother Assistants—"

"Don't work in MIT." His green eyes glow like evil magical amulets.

"Oh, pardon me, Mr. Magic Information Technology. Didn't realize I had to curtsy in your presence."

Lulu snaps her fingers between us. "Figure it out, or you're both fired."

My jaw drops, but Hunter's wings flap so hard he raises several centimeters off the floor. Suddenly he's less a technology "grunt" and more like a dragon. "You can't—"

"Figure it out." Lulu flies off, wings flapping at hummingbird speed.

I fist my wand.

Hunter's suddenly in my face. "This is your fault."

I stand my ground. "What in your deluded brain—"

"Facts." He counts off on his fingers. "If you hadn't skipped out early to coat your face in six layers of sludge, Giselda wouldn't have forgotten to file her paperwork. And if you hadn't forgotten your wand and come back looking so miserable, I wouldn't have been in this room getting trapped into doing your job. Therefore, we wouldn't be in this situation."

That's the most he's ever said to me, but the "doing your job" bit stings like flying into thorny bougainvillea vines. And what does me looking miserable have to do with anything? "Your paychecks are signed by Headquarters, same as me, Magic Tech."

He glowers and spins, almost knocking me back with his wings, and stalks down the hallway.

Good. I sink onto my stool, rubbing my temples, my hands coming away tinted with the pink glitter Juniper insisted would be perfect for the ball. I wipe my hands on a report for Lulu, not at all sorry when glitter smears across the numbers.

A shadow looms and Hunter is back, broodier than ever. "Are you coming, or do they pay you to stand still and dribble pixie dust?"

My eyes snap to meet his. "Apparently, they pay me to interface with artificial intelligence." I flap my wings and zoom past him, ready to find the rogue FG and get home to some chocolate. Still, maybe it's better having to work. This way I have a legitimate reason to avoid the ball.

Hunter clears his throat and points down the hall to his left. "I've prepared a briefing."

"When? It's been like ten seconds."

"While you were pouting."

"I wasn't—" Ugh, this guy. "Wouldn't it be *briefer* to find Giselda and get the paperwork filed? We've only got—" I wave my wand for a show-me-the-time spell, but only a few pitiful sparks spit out.

Hunter looks heavenward like I'm the biggest annoyance in Hidden Wood. "Didn't charge your wand again?"

"What business is it of yours?" And how did he know this was the second occurrence this week? I've been so swamped with ball preparations, details have slipped my mind. I flit past him. "I'll charge it then meet you for your stupid briefing."

Headquarters is fortunate enough to have a wand tree and a watering well on premises, so charging can be quick. I exit our floor into the central courtyard where a golden-trunked tree grows in the center, stretching far into the sky. Leaves that range from glossy forest green to light gold are tinged with silver in the moonlight.

Next to the tree, the well is a small, white bricked circle. It's old fashioned, with a crank handle to bring up water one bucket at a time. The Elders insist magic works best when we do things the traditional way.

I flutter to the base of the tree and stick my wand into the soil. Wands are recharged with magic by resting in the soil of a wand tree then being watered, preferably from a sacred well.

A glance at the well reveals no bucket, and it's not in the courtyard either. All I find is someone's half-full coffee cup with a purple lipstick stain that looks like Juniper's color. I resist an irritated hiss. How long had Juniper and Shade been planning—nope. No time for that now.

I grab Juniper's day-old latte and chunk it on the soil around my wand. Coffee's almost the same as water, right? It'd be fine. Time is short, so instead of waiting the recommended five minutes, I give my wand a quick swish, wipe the soil off, and flutter back to Hunter's office.

I know where his cubicle is, but I'd have found it anyway because of the screams and shouts coming from his magic mirror. What is he watching?

He's so intent on the image that he doesn't acknowledge me. On the surface, what might have been a lovely garden party has turned to horror. Fairies scream and flutter away as a table turns into a pumpkin, then the chairs, then another table. The pumpkin spell spreads. I gasp as a hanging lantern turns into a spaghetti squash and crashes onto two screaming fairies.

Hunter clears his throat. "Guess the spell's not confined to pumpkins, but gourds in general."

"That's what concerns you?"

"What concerns me is that we have less than an hour to find Giselda if we want to prevent that."

My eyes are wide. "This is the disaster of '08 Lulu mentioned?"

Hunter pauses the mirror with a wand flick. "This should be included in all FGH trainings. Fairies died in the '08 crisis."

We're silent for a moment, taking in the reality. If we fail, the results could be deadly. I speak first. "Okay, we find Giselda and problem solved."

With a flick of his fully charged wand, he waves black-lettered charts into the air. "She's gone offline." He points to one of his charts, a map of Headquarters. "Her last known location was here."

"Uh, that's my office."

"Right, so obviously, she came to see you, found you had left early, and failed to turn in her paperwork."

"This isn't my fault." Still, the berrydew in my stomach churns. "Juniper was covering my calls while I picked up my dress."

"Then we need to get in touch with her."

I snort. "She's at the ball." Not going near there, and I had no plans to speak to Juniper again after what she did. "Plus, there's no mention of Giselda in our daily log. I don't think Juniper saw her."

Instead of arguing that we should head there stat, he nods and runs a hand through his thick hair. "What would you suggest?"

I wait for him to say something sarcastic, but he leans a hip on his desk and folds muscular (again, not that I care) arms across his chest. Hmm. When he didn't have a twig up his rear, he was cute, in an objective way, of course. I shake off that thought and get down to business. "We could use a wish-tracer spell."

He gasps like I'd suggested harming puppies. "Do you have a warrant?"

I wave that off, which is the wrong thing to do.

"Under section six-three-two of the manual—"

I flick my wand to show the time, but instead of my usual purple writing, the numbers come out green. And runny. Ummm. Still, I pointed. "We only have forty-five minutes."

"The wish subject could be anywhere. Even in the human realm."

That makes my stomach twist worse than before, but braving the humans and their machines would be better than the ball.

He pauses at his desk, staring into a drawer then back at me with a conflicted look.

I motion to the door. "You going to organize office supplies or come with me?"

That earned me the narrowed eyes again, but his gaze lands on the mirror, frozen on the image of a cute garden house complete with moss and flowers. Except the house is half orange, morphing into a pumpkin. My legs grow heavy. Were fairies trapped inside?

Hunter slides a bottle out of the drawer and motions for me to follow him.

"What's in the bottle?"

"Shh."

"Don't shush me. What, is it sunscreen? Afraid the moon will shine too bright?"

He grunts and leads me out a side window, shooting through the trees. Whoa, that fairy could fly. I pant to keep up with his larger wingspan, regretting skipping air aerobics for the last . . . um lifetime. But tomorrow, I'm committed. Maybe.

Finally, he pauses on the far side of a crepe myrtle, ducking into its branches. "Can I trust you, Mari?"

I pause. He's used my preferred name, the one Lulu's never bothered to learn. "Uh, yeah."

He shakes his head, running a hand through his hair. "I can't risk—"

The tense shift in his muscles shakes me. "Hey, you can trust me. I swear on every future bite of chocolate."

He must realize how serious that promise is because he nods. "It's not like I have that much more to lose."

Whoa. What is he talking about? Before I can ask, he uncorks the bottle and waves his wand. Blue smoke swirls out like a tiny tornado.

"What's that?"

"A wish tracer I've been working on."

"Isn't wish tracing illegal without a warrant?"

"This is different from a wand spell." He gives me a side eye. "But still probably illegal." His lip crooks up, which makes him look less perfect, more . . . bad boy.

I force my eyes back to the smoke, which is forming a trail to the center of Hidden Wood, toward the castle. The two of us scoot shoulder-to-shoulder and . . .

"No." We say the word at the same time because the wish subject is apparently at the ball.

***

The wind is against us, so it takes too long to fly to the queen's courtyard where the ball is being held. The whole time my thoughts swirl faster than the wish trail. I don't want to go into the ball, especially with smeared mascara and caterpillar slippers, but visions of pumpkin-pocalypse haunt me. So many fairies might get hurt, even Juniper and stupid Shade.

High hedges block off the courtyard, but we peek in through a gap. Hundreds of fairies hum around the lush courtyard, eating and dancing, and a full orchestra plays in the corner. The clock tower in the center of the courtyard reveals we have less than five minutes until midnight.

Hunter leans closer to be heard over the music, and my neck tingles at his low words. "I'd offer to do this solo, but I can't go in. The queen—"

I gasp, cutting him off. The trail swirls forward, leading to a couple leaning in for a kiss. Juniper and Shade. The truth hits me harder than a wing cramp. "This is why Juniper offered to cover my desk. She knew I had Giselda's contact info. That little moth wished for my date to fall for her." The betrayal washes over me, stealing my breath.

Hunter scoffs. "What do you see in him anyway? He's a total dandelion."

"You wouldn't understand."

"No, I don't. He doesn't deserve you. You're so far out of his league, he's not even inside the stadium." Hunter's emerald eyes come into focus, staring at me as if I was something . . . beautiful.

He grimaces. "I'm sorry I've been such a thorn to you. The one thing I look forward to every day is seeing you smile, but you waste all your energy on him. Tonight, when you came in crying, and I knew it was Shade's fault . . ." He shakes his head. "We don't have time for this."

I swallow. Did he mean to say he cared for me? He was right, we didn't have time for this, but I was going to stop the end of the world so we could discuss it more. I brandish my wand. "Let's go." We zoom into the garden. Our best chance is to get Juniper to unwish the spell, thereby turning off the magic. Surely, she'll listen to reason.

I start talking before we land. "Juniper, you've got to undo the wish."

She gives me a double take. "What wish? Come on, Silly Bum, this really is sad."

Liar. By the way Shade's eyes are glazed over, it's obvious he's so far under her spell he can't think straight.

Hunter moves toward us, but three guards converge on him, dragging him away. One says, "You're not welcome here, Driftwood."

Struggling, Hunter yells to me, "One minute."

Juniper grips Shade's arm. "Face it, I won."

Had she always been this shallow? "This isn't about winning. Giselda didn't set the magic to turn off at midnight, and if we don't stop it, the spell will go rogue. Fairies could die—"

Juniper glares. "Liar. Ugh. For the last year, you've talked about Shade as if the two of you were the only fairies in Hidden Wood, but I've known him longer." She taps her chest, shaking green fairy dust off the icy petals of her dress. "You never once considered that I was in love with him. You don't care about anyone except yourself. I had to make this wish, and I'm never undoing it."

The clock tower strikes the first bell of midnight. If we get to twelve . . . "Please, Juniper." I stare around, wondering if we'll be at the epicenter of the pumpkin-quake.

She digs her nails into Shade. "Let's go."

The second gong sounds.

I chase after them. Maybe if I can get them away from the crowd, no one will get hurt, but Juniper ducks behind a couple guards and yells that I'm harassing her.

Third gong.

Strong guards fly me toward the exit. I wave my wand to stop Juniper, but only a stream of latte comes out.

Gong.

The guards toss me outside, and one waves his wand at me.

Gong.

Several feet down the garden, Hunter's in the middle of a fistfight with two guards. I try to run back in, but my guard must've hit me with a blocking spell. Crab apples. I'm stuck outside.

Gong.

What was I going to do? Lulu firing me paled in comparison to the carnage that could ensue.

Gong.

I fly to the top of the hedge, but the blocking spell holds.

Gong.

A gust of wind blows me into a tree, and my dress tangles in the branches. *Gong.* Was that the ninth chime?

By the time I pull free of the tree, two more gongs have sounded.

I race forward, but the last gong sounds and a blast of magic passes through me, raising the hairs on my neck.

Below, where Juniper and Shade had been dancing, a ring of orange forms, growing more solid. I press my hands to my mouth. If that pumpkin erupts, the two could be crushed. In a desperate move, I utter the words I can only use once in a lifetime. "I wish to stop this, Giselda."

My heart twists from using my one and only wish, but a glowing light shines around me, and Giselda pops into view. Her pink dress and wings sparkle. "Took you long enough, dearie."

Below, someone screams. And someone else. It's happening. I point downward, my wings so tired I lose altitude. "Please, make it stop."

A leaf turns into a squash and plummets to the ground, smashing a cello. More fairies scream.

Giselda waves her wand. Below, one of the tables is turning orange, but it doesn't go full gourd.

I sag with relief, sinking to the ground. Hunter flattens the last of his guard trouble and runs to meet me. "You okay?" His cheek is bleeding, and his tunic is torn. He looks . . . amazing.

"I think it's over." I rip off a petal from my skirt to press onto Hunter's bleeding cheek.

Giselda gives her wand a little tap and giggles. "Whoops. I *have* made a mess of things, haven't I?" She flicks her wand at Hunter, mending his torn tunic and getting rid of the swelling in the side of his face. "There." She steps back, clapping her hands. "More than two wishes have been granted tonight." With a wink, she's gone, leaving behind a trail of pink sparkles.

I dab at Hunter's face. "What was with all her winking and clapping?"

He catches my hand and leans closer, eyes dropping to my lips. "Like she said, more than two wishes were granted."

Does he mean he wants me to fall for him? My heart melts like warm chocolate chips in a cookie. For the last year, I'd worked with Hunter, arguing, competing, and pretending I hated him, but maybe what I felt was quite the opposite. And by "forgetting" to turn off the magic, Giselda had given me and Hunter a reason to unite.

I stare into those intense green eyes and lean in for a kiss. As I always imagined, sparks fly. And what do you know? Turns out it was the perfect day to leave my wand at work.

About the Author

Growing up, Jennifer Dyer aspired to be a ninja-Jedi princess and has been imagining adventures ever since. No matter the genre, she's a sucker for a good romance and loves when baking and books collide (well, perhaps not in the same bowl . . .). She's received several writing awards, including first place in the Toronto Romance Writers' Catherine Contest and the Windy City Romance Writers' Four Seasons Writing Contest. For more magical worlds and adventures filled with second chances, swoony romances, and chocolate, follow her on Instagram @JennDyerBooks and visit her website https://jenniferdyerbooks.com.

THE CREATIONIST'S CURSE

COLLEEN BROWN

T he brass bell in the clock tower struck midnight, and the world hidden beneath the veil came alive with ancient magic.

Tonight, the world sat on the cusp of the autumn equinox. Rain that had pelted the city of Margoza ceased, and the sky lit up with stars. The glow of the moon cast deep shadows in the wake of stone buildings.

From the hill at the center of the city, the Royal Centre of the Arcane loomed like the gargoyles that decorated its façade. From the second floor, where the rarest enchanted books and deadliest occult artifacts sat under magical securities, one could see the pattern Margoza was built in— a spiral. It started at the large manor on the outskirts and worked its way toward the Royal Centre.

Evelyn Awbrey, the Curator of Arcane Books and the Occult, stared out at the city below. Her gaze lingered on the manor, and she wondered after her daughter who lay sleeping there.

Was the music box on the nightstand still playing? Were the fairy lights Evelyn had conjured to ward off nightmares dancing above her head?

Sleep well, darling. I'm watching over you.

Evelyn turned, and her long, wavy hair colored as though licked by flames swayed against her black ruffled blouse. The heels of her dark brown leather boots echoed against the hardwood floors as she returned to her office.

She could smell the orange tea wafting over the Annex before she pushed the door open. She scanned the small room, the pale grey walls broken up by chestnut paneling, papers strewn about, and books left open.

Evelyn pinched the bridge of her nose and chose to ignore the clutter. She sat down at her desk, welcomed by the picture of her family, and reached for the bottom drawer. Twisting the key abandoned in the lock, she reached until her hand hit the false back.

"There you are." Her eyes trailed over the black silk scarf as she set it before herself.

Silver stitching wove constellations on the outside while the reverse revealed zodiacs in gold. Inside, a tarot deck lay tucked away.

Evelyn ran a finger reverently over the delicate rose-gold designs of the inky black card on top of the deck. Tiny sparks traveled through her fingers, electrical currents racing through her veins.

The ancient magic the cards were infused with was distinct— powers of a Creationist, a caster who could create seemingly anything from nothing. Evelyn could see its tendrils fluctuating in the rose-gold hues as though it were alive, ebbing and flowing like water.

Evelyn handled them with care as she shuffled, but though hundreds of years old, they felt new. *And as beautiful as the day they were crafted no doubt.* She drew three cards, lining them in a row, as she asked a silent question.

The High Priestess. The King of Pentacles. The Moon. All upright.

Evelyn licked her dry lips, hand hesitating over the deck. She drew a final fourth card and laid it beneath the others. The ending to the story the cards told wasn't what she'd wanted, but it was what she'd expected.

The fourth card was The Tower, also upright. This meant chaos, destruction, and unavoidable upheaval. It was a card far more terrifying than Death.

"Oh, Mina." Evelyn breathed her daughter's name as her slender fingers traced The Moon's feminine face. It made her chest tighten.

The card signified her daughter. The Tower, her future.

I tried to keep her safe, my love. Evelyn's eyes flitted to the photograph.

It was one of few sunny days in Margoza, which was normally plagued by grey clouds and pelting rain. Evelyn held little Mina, who was only a baby then, in her lap amongst fields of lavender. She could still smell the wands of delicate purple blossoms as Mina's father tickled their daughter's nose with them.

It breaks my heart that she's grown up without you.

Mina's father had disappeared on an expedition into the ruined city of Valenbeuge. A group of twelve had gone into the castle that had once belonged to a powerful sorceress, and only one had returned— Nathaniel Browning.

Nathaniel had been a close friend of her late husband and a fellow colleague at the Royal Centre, Curator of the Codex—a hall of records for tracking magical genealogies and history. While he had believed the tarot was a replica, Evelyn had uncovered it was genuine.

Created by the sorceress of Valenbeuge Castle, the family sigil decorating the back of the cards was indisputable.

Three lines, three dots within three concentric rings—the Awen.

The sigil was an ever-present reminder throughout Evelyn's home of her ancestor, Elvira Awbrey. She had been a Creationist who had done marvels, but using her abilities took a toll. Elvira had lost her mind before the end when the Council of Margoza hunted her down and barricaded her within her own castle.

A heavy thud echoed from the Annex. Evelyn shuffled the cards back into her desk, locking it and pocketing the keys.

"Is someone there?" Evelyn called and moved to the door to peek out. "Martha?"

The light from her office sprawled across the floor in a warm glow. Bookshelves rose like giants, floor-to-ceiling structures only broken up by the upper-level landing. Moonlight spilled from the large windows on either side of the Annex, its milky white sheen casting an eerie radiance.

Evelyn crept out into the darkness. The hum of magic crackled in the air. It pulsated within her blood.

Chains rattled from the restricted rows, the books there monitored closely by enchanted knights in their polished silver armor. With a wave of Evelyn's hand, the knights lifted their swords for her to pass. She ducked, despite their blades were held well above her head, always worried the charms giving them life may be faulty.

Never can be too careful where magic is concerned.

Evelyn's eyes caught a book on the floor thrashing against its bindings. She recognized it as a rather savage piece. The stitching was messy, and the pages were stained with age. It was covered in vellum that she was certain had been pulled and stretched from human flesh.

Barbaric. Evelyn pitied the poor soul who had been used in this way.

A gentle stroke and a few careful words settled the book. She picked it up, alabaster skin a stark contrast to the tanned hues of the cover.

As she turned to walk it back to its stand, Evelyn's eyes caught the floor twinkling. *What is that? Glass?* She reached down and hissed as her finger swelled with a bead of blood.

Evelyn looked for the source, hearing the soft whistling of the witching hour wind. She followed the glass like breadcrumbs, discovering a broken window at the back of the Annex.

Someone broke in. The hairs on her neck stood up. Her palms tingled. *How did they get past the guards?*

Dropping the tome, she ran, hair flicking like sparks of fire as she skidded to a halt at her office door. Out of breath, panic prickled in her veins.

Bookcases toppled, some complethoely mangled. The walls were torn open with plaster and paneling shattered. She hadn't heard it, hadn't felt the violation of her office, but she smelled the powdered-sugar scent of a concealment spell clinging to the air.

She rounded the desk. Drawers were dismantled, but the false back, which was hidden from the naked eye by a charm, was intact.

It's him. He's finally come for these.

Evelyn scrambled to pull out the deck, holding the cards close as she exited her office. Racing to the entrance of the Annex, she tugged on the mahogany doors, but they wouldn't budge. She sensed a hex on them—the dark magic that created it was familiar, poisoned.

Turning, she scanned the dark bookshelves and tables as shadows crept closer. She wasn't alone.

Sprinting for an iron staircase, she flew up its winding steps to the upper-level landing where she knew a secret passage sat behind one of the bookcases.

The shadows chased. They stretched, reaching for Evelyn's shadow, and caught it easily. With a tug, they brought her crashing to the floor, pulling her through the rungs of the railing.

Evelyn plummeted, clutching the cards to her chest as she instinctively outstretched a hand. The familiar fiery sensation of magic in use curled around her arm, thrusting through the palm of her hand as she came to a screeching halt. She hovered above the floor for a moment before lowering completely.

Applause echoed as the shadows slithered across the ceiling, descending over windows and walls. They converged on a set of leather shoes.

"Bravo Evelyn." The clapping slowed patronizingly. "I must say, I was expecting more of a fight to get in here."

Evelyn snarled, all teeth and claws like a cornered wildcat. With a shakiness that she attempted to hide, she picked herself off the floor and watched him and the shadows he commanded.

"Should I call you Huxley? Or are we still pretending that's not your name, dear?" Evelyn's laugh was bitter. The name tasted strange on her tongue and pain bloomed in her chest as her heart raced too quickly, betrayal running deep.

She had only ever known him as Nathaniel Browning. The man who had healed her broken heart after her husband's disappearance, had married her, had acted as a father to her daughter even.

"Clever," Huxley nodded slowly. "Figuring out my name, I mean."

She had never seen *this* side of him. Huxley Caddell was an intense man, menacing even, like some kind of dark fae from a fairytale Evelyn had read about in a book. His brown wool vest and starched white shirt were replaced with black silk and crimson; a black tie knotted at his throat. His drab, chestnut hair was slicked back from his face, putting his spritely cobalt eyes on display.

Sudden dread turned her heart to stone as her mind drifted to Mina. What would happen to her if Huxley escaped?

"Let me guess." Huxley clicked his tongue, running it over his teeth. His eyes narrowed pointedly. "I'll have to go through you, yes?"

"Would you expect anything less?"

He shoved his hands into his pockets, voice brittle. "I've had enough of the games, *darling*. Give me the deck. Go home to Mina."

"What poison did you fill her mind with?" Evelyn noticed the shadows slinking into the rows of books.

The clock tower chimed twelve-thirty, and the magic in Evelyn's body thrummed. She had a small window before the ancient magic that had slipped through the veil seeped back into the earth again.

Evelyn was strong without it, but Huxley was stronger.

"You should be angry with the Council also." Huxley fiddled with the hound-head cufflinks on his sleeves. "They laughed at us. Called us zealots. They didn't think so much power could be amassed in one caster, yet here I stand unscathed. Meanwhile, they kept dirty little secrets."

The shadows grew, stretching into impossible forms as they reached into Huxley's silhouette and merged. The shape—monstrous.

You tampered with forces no one dared disturb, gave your soul to the darkness. For what? To make those old fools pay?

"Your soul is corrupted by dark magic. Is that a feat?" If she could stall, maybe one of her colleagues—perhaps Martha, whose office sat below the Annex and also worked late tonight—would hear them.

If Martha were here, we could take him.

"Destroying the Council will be. I'll pave the way for those like me." Huxley's lips curled, his smile bloodcurdling. "Those like our little Mina."

"You're insane." Evelyn agonized over what might have happened while he and Mina were alone. *I left Mina alone with this monster so many times. What did he say?* Her heart fell. *What did he do?*

"Insane?" Huxley's face pinched, upper lip quivering as he outstretched a hand. "I need the scroll that crone hid in those cards. Then we'll see how insane I am, Evelyn."

"I'd rather die," Evelyn spat. "Then allow Mina to grow up in a world corrupted by *you*."

Evelyn thrust out a hand and sent a shockwave barreling toward him. Huxley rocketed back, sliding across one of the tables and toppling over the edge. Evelyn pocketed the deck in the cup of her bra, close to her heart, and ran. She turned down a row, the books rattling on the shelves as the Annex grew impossibly dark.

"Good show, Evelyn. Good show!" Huxley bellowed as he sprung back up. He fixed his hair, straightening his vest and tie.

Evelyn could hardly see, feeling her way behind a knight clad in armor holding a shield and mace. She pressed her back against the pedestal the knight stood on. Her heart hammered in her chest like the wings of a hummingbird against a bony cage.

Huxley's shadows slithered across the floors, hunting her.

"I can smell the ancient magic rolling off you." Huxley licked his lips, closing his eyes and inhaling deeply. "It's *delicious*." He maneuvered through the aisle of tables. "The veil is fading. That magic you're borrowing, using to conceal yourself from me, has almost run out."

Evelyn saw shadows curling up the load-bearing pillars—ornately carved into human shapes to honor those who had created the Royal Centre. Their faces darkened, lines deepening as the shadows filled the spaces. Their wooden heads swiveled, hoping to catch a glimpse of her.

I'm trapped. The thought stung. *My only chance is the window he used.*

Evelyn twisted and placed a hand against the cold calve of the knight. "Protect the artifacts. Defend their secrets."

She poured herself into the charm, feeling the strain of using her abilities. The knight sprang to life, clinking as it descended the pedestal. Magic swept from it into other knights around the Annex, each one groaning to life.

A shadow lunged, blocked by the knight with its shield. The mace swung at the creature's billowing mass as Evelyn fled deeper into the Annex.

"Stop her!" Huxley bellowed as a rigid, crooked finger followed Evelyn.

Just a little more. The ancient magic coursing within Evelyn guided her through the Annex. *Please, help me, Elvira.*

Soon the witching hour would pass as time crept closer to one. That power would wilt like a flower in winter when the bell chimed in the clock tower. Evelyn could almost hear the hands of the clock ticking away with each step she took, feeling the mechanisms grinding with every heavy beat of her heart.

All she could think about was escaping the Annex, guarding the deck. *No,* that meant nothing compared to protecting her daughter.

"The window!" Huxley screeched, the sound more fiendish than human. Books rattled, chains clanking against the shelves.

Evelyn stopped at the window, climbing up onto the blue velvet cushion. She hissed as soon as she touched the glass, cradling her hand back as a burning sting raced up her arm.

He's hexed it. The window shimmered red, sparks traveling over the glass as if it were electrically charged. *He's too powerful.*

Despite the thoughts, Evelyn tried again. The dark magic reacted violently and tossed her like a ragdoll off the cushion. The cards fell from her shirt, exploding across the floor.

Evelyn could hear the knights moving about the Annex. Swords clanked and shields thudded as the moonlight spilled in through the window behind her.

A crow, feathers silken and shimmering in the moonlight, perched itself outside the glass. Its dark eyes gleamed like hardened gemstones as it watched Evelyn pick herself up. She met its stare with surprise.

What're you doing here? Where's Alaric? She couldn't believe the crow was real, sitting there, tilting its feathered head at her as though it heard every word she thought. *Find your master. Bring Alaric to the Annex!*

With Alaric at her side, they could end Huxley Caddell. Once and for all.

The crow cawed, flapping its wings urgently as it took flight into the darkness. Rays of moonlight became a spotlight, settling on a card that sat expectantly on the floor.

The High Priestess stared back at Evelyn against the backdrop of a rose-decorated veil. Pillars stood on either side, one silver and the other gold— the dueling nature of magic. Clutched tightly in the High Priestess' right hand was a scroll.

"Release to me what's locked within," Evelyn spoke quietly.

Her hands hovered over the card, palms emitting a golden hue. Magic spooled from the card into the air like sparkling dust in shades of rose, silver, and gold, before disappearing into the moonlight.

If only you or Mina were here to see this, love.

The card lay blank as Evelyn picked it up. She flinched as the cut on her finger reopened, sliced along the card's thin edge. She watched a drop of blood trail down the front and vanish into the inky blackness.

"*Evelyn* . . ." Huxley taunted, footsteps silent as he moved in and out of the shadows.

Evelyn could sense his dark magic. It was a sour, toxic presence that burned the nose and churned the stomach.

She moved to the load-bearing pillar separating two bookcases in her row. It had been carved to resemble a founder; a pointed nose held spectacles from falling off his hollow face. Evelyn's lips moved wordlessly, the base of the pillar glowing a soft gold as she crafted a hidden compartment and sealed the scroll within.

Either you'll be found by someone who can use you for good, or you'll be lost to time.

Evelyn's finger glowed as she carved a rune into the wood— a simple shape representing inheritance. It reminded her of a fish swimming toward the heavens.

Evelyn felt a pull deep inside her, shoulders rounding forward as though a tether tied to her heart was being jerked. She gazed at her hands. They became ethereal, coiling as though smoke swirling in the air.

The Creationist's Curse! Elvira must have created a fail-safe for anyone who tried to steal the scroll. My blood must have set it off.

The empty card that had absorbed her blood was now finishing her, inking in the blank space with a new image.

The magic of a Creationist came at a steep price. While their power was believed to be produced from nothing, no energy could be created or destroyed. Only borrowed. Transformed.

"Don't take me from Mina." Evelyn knew in her heart it was pointless.

She closed her eyes and pictured her home on the outskirts of Margoza. She envisioned her daughter asleep in her green nightgown decorated with lavender flowers. Evelyn hoped good dreams fluttered around her mind like fireflies.

Mina likes fireflies.

"I'm sorry sweetheart." Evelyn was fading. "Remember, rabbit," the nickname made her smile as she blinked back tears, "magic always comes at a price."

She looked over her shoulder at the moon. Autumn's breath, crisp and sweetly scented of fallen leaves, went unnoticed against her skin. She felt the final tug and was gone with nothing more than a soft exhale.

***

The doors to the Annex erupted.

"Evelyn, several of the guards are dead. We're under attack!" Martha, a stout woman with hazel eyes bulging behind thick-rimmed glasses, stormed in. Her berry-colored dress rounded out her plumpness and made the rosy undertones of her clay-colored skin glow. "I heard shouting, and the doors were hexed. Evelyn?"

Martha raised her hands, a soft green radiating from her palms.

"Martha!" A man in a gray tweed suit and a deep rose-colored pocket square appeared at the Annex doors.

"Here Alaric!" Martha called.

The small black velvet rose pinned to Alaric's lapel jostled as he moved briskly. His silver hair caught the moonlight as he passed each row, dispelling the shadows with a wave of his hand. A crow flew over Alaric's head, perching on the top of a row of bookcases that Martha had turned down.

Without either's notice, shadows slinked back to their owner who lurked in the opposite row. Huxley's eyes glowed in the dark, watching closely.

"There's a broken window, just as that crow of yours told you." Martha scanned the scene, shaking her head of tight brown curls. "An artifact too. No Evelyn though."

"How could the Council let this happen under their noses?" Alaric's breath came in quick, shallow bursts as he skidded to a halt beside Martha. He lifted a clenched fist to push his wire-rimmed glasses up his sandy-colored nose.

"Those old farts wouldn't know a charm from a hex if it bit them in the arse." Martha mocked and the crow rattled its beak. "Whoever did *this*, they're powerful. The hex on the doors—complicated. Nearly didn't crack it."

Martha collected cards from the ground. Wind whistled through the fractures in the window, but with a wave of her hand, the glass was repaired.

"Evelyn was here. I found Elvira's tarot." Martha stood. "She's been studying it since, well . . ." She met Alaric's stare, a silent understanding passing between them. "I've never seen this one before."

She handed him the deck and tapped a mauve-colored nail at the card. Alaric examined it, shaking his head.

A woman in a flowing dress sat at a window, flowers adorning the sill. She stared up at the stars, hand lifted as though to catch the moon.

Alaric's finger brushed over the artwork. Something felt amiss. "Surely, Evie wouldn't abandon these so carelessly."

The crow broke out in a heated caw, voice filling the Annex.

"Evelyn was frightened," Martha's voice became a whisper. "Mentioned someone was after Elvira's artifacts. She insisted that cursed scroll was hidden in this deck."

Alaric looked at the cards again, sensing nothing overly powerful about them. At least, nothing more powerful than any other artifact collected from Valenbeuge Castle. But the woman in the image kept calling to him.

"If it were ever in this deck, it's no longer here." Alaric slipped the tarot into a pocket inside his jacket. "Knowing Evie, she's hidden it elsewhere for safe keeping."

Martha tapped her fingertips against her chin. "Oh dear, something's happened to Evelyn then?"

"I'm growing more certain every moment we don't bump into her,"

Alaric confessed.

"What will happen to Mina?"

"I'll go to Awbrey Manor and talk to Nathaniel."

"But you—"

"I'm her uncle, Martha," Alaric said, body rigid. "Nathaniel's her stepfather."

Martha nodded. "Will you give Mina the deck then? Or Mr. Browning?"

"Not Nathaniel. They belong to an Awbrey." Alaric sighed heavily. "I'll keep the cards safe until Mina's old enough. She must control her abilities first before handling anything Elvira created. A Creationist in these times . . ." he shook his head solemnly. "The Council will label her a Chaotic before her eighteenth birthday and condemn her if they find out."

"Very well. We need to report the break-in and Evelyn's disappearance to the Council. *Immediately*." Martha marched passed him and headed for the doors.

Alaric stopped at the end of the row. He gazed back at the moon spilling in long milky ribbons that danced across the cherrywood floor. The smell of dust, leather, and something sweet like lavender added to the mystery of the Annex.

"I'll take care of Mina, Evie. I promise." Alaric touched the cards that sat against his breast before turning towards the exit.

He stopped again when the crow cawed, flapping its wings in urgency. Alaric looked at the bird on the railing of the upper-level landing, then cast a leery stare back into the Annex.

Shadows clung like tar.

Alaric outstretched his hand, fingers splayed as his muscles strained. Veins bulged in his forearm as he ordered the shadows forth. They soared across the floor into his own shadow, swallowed up by his silhouette.

"From one Shadow Caster to another," Alaric's voice soured, venom dripped from each syllable. His dovetail eyes flitted about the room. "If I find you, I'll tear the magic from your marrow. Keep away from my family."

Alaric's footsteps trailed away, the crow following behind.

Huxley stepped out from the back with a scowl, walking to the nearest window. He watched the crow soaring towards Awbrey Manor as the courtyard of the Royal Centre hummed with excitement at the break-in.

"I've waited this long, *Ric*. What's a few more years? Mina *will* give me what I want, one way or another." Huxley turned, disappearing like a shimmer of black smoke.

The clock tower struck one and the violet eyes of the girl, asleep in her bed beneath twinkling fairy lights, snapped open as a crow tapped lightly on her window.

About the Author

For more dark fantasy and psychological horror, follow Colleen at authorcolleenbrown.com or on Instagram @ColleenBrownAuthor.

A Tooth
for
Trulian

AD UHLAR

S hylah returned the vials and potions to their designated shelves and sat beside the hearth for a drought of honeysuckle tea. The crackling of the wood and the sweet smell wafting from the dainty white flowers floating in her cup always took her back to that day and her mother's smile before she and her sister, Trulian, left to collect the same blooms from a nearby field. It was a day she wished to forget, but she wanted to remember her mother's smile, her face, her love.

In the early years after her village was burned, Shylah could see her mother every time she closed her eyes, but now, six years later, she was forgetting. The only way to bring her mother back to life, now, was the mixing of honeysuckle with the smells and sounds of burning wood. Whenever her sister delivered their potions to Naamah, Shylah desperately needed to remember life before her bonding with Naamah, who, in her great mercy, had *saved* Shylah and her sister from the uncertain fate of orphans. Still, even servants and slaves had more rights than bonded—any unbonded could tell Naamah no, even if they rarely did. Part of Shylah was grateful, while the other part suspected Naamah or her Green Willow Guard had set the fire. She had no proof, of course, and even if she did, there was no one to oppose Naamah and her Guard, who were everywhere and nowhere all at once, so bonded they stayed.

At nine and fourteen, the sisters had been placed in the care of a bedraggled and inflated elixir trainer, Apollyon. They couldn't walk from the front door to the hearth without climbing over mountains of potions, ingredients, and all manner of books in his shop. It had taken them nearly a month to organize each salve, vial, herb, and book into designated spots. Trulian struggled with potions, while Shylah had surpassed Apollyon, so for the last two years, Shylah had become the primary brewer, and Trulian delivered them. Despite no problems, Shylah was never at ease waiting for her sister to return, especially when that delivery was to Naamah herself, and especially when Shylah had made substitutions in an elixir.

She drank the last bit of her tea and washed the cup. She never knew why Naamah wanted the potions; although she had her suspicions, she knew never to question, only to obey. That was the power of the bonding—always claimed, never independent. She placed the cup on the mantel and fingered the small vase of delicate viola blooms, her sister's favorite. Trulian should be back by now. It had been nearly two hours since she left with the potion.

The temperature dropped. Shylah's nails dug into the mantle beside the violas as the cold gripped her body. Naamah's hands combed Shylah's flaxen curls, intensifying her terror with every caress. Shylah's neck tensed; her heart pounded. She searched the small potions room. She needed something, anything to ward against Naamah's specter. The dried herbs and newly mixed potions wouldn't help. Neither would the blade she used to cut the comfrey. No matter how real the caresses felt, she wasn't there–not really–at least Shylah didn't think she was. Shylah searched her memory. Had the door opened or feet crossed the floor? No. Naamah couldn't be here. It had to be a projection. Shylah needed something that would change the air–the fire. It was dying down, but the wood near the edge seemed to have enough flame to free her from Naamah's grasp.

She lunged forward and bounced off an invisible wall. Pain shot through her scalp as she landed on her back. Naamah stood above, her blood red lips turned down. Shylah tried to scramble backward, but Naamah's hand shot out, grabbed her hair, and yanked her up. Her stomach flipped. The potion.

"I didn't have any wyvern fang. Apollyon said—"

"That. Insipid. Beast. Knows. Nothing." Naamah twisted her hand, wrapping Shylah's hair around it with each word. "You *will* get the fang and recreate the potion, my dear."

The way Naamah said "my dear" turned the needle pricks on her scalp into flames that burned to Shylah's toes. The involuntary shudder of her body sent a fresh wave of pain through her, expelling a satisfied grunt from her taskmaster.

Naamah leaned close, hot breath on Shylah's ear. "Let me remind you, chattel." She flung Shylah to the floor like a rag doll and conjured an image of Trulian. The sight of her sister, with her red locks, shackled in the dungeon, arrested any escape plan. "If you don't—" she smirked at the floating image "—I have plans for your sister." The vision disappeared, and Naamah grabbed Shylah under the chin, bringing them face-to-face. "I will return at midnight. The potion will be corrected if you want to save your sister." She pushed Shylah back and disappeared.

Why had she listened to Apollyon? She should've known the wretched man would be wrong, but there was no time to point blame. Only eight hours until midnight, at least two hours to get to the magma pits and two to return. Shylah grabbed her satchel and hastily flung in the blade, several potions, and an empty jar for collecting teeth before sprinting through the door. She only stopped when she reached the cliffs overlooking the magma pits just beyond the capital walls.

The pause in momentum gave her body the seconds it needed to voice its complaint. Elixir designers didn't do much running; her lungs burned, and her muscles ignited in miniature explosions. She instinctively bent in half, resting her hands on her knees before clasping hands above her head and filling her lungs as deeply as she could between coughs.

Once she could breathe without coughing, she opened her satchel and took inventory. Gingerly, she set the empty jar and potions on the ground beside her. Five, only five potions. Two that would momentarily stun the beast, one to paralyze it, one healing, and a memory-wiping potion. She sighed. Why hadn't she thought it through and grabbed more paralyzing potions? Only six hours to find a tooth, return to the city and remake the potion. Her fingers probed the loose herbs and oils from her last excursion. Where did the blade fall to?

"What are you doing?"

The surprise of a voice, let alone a male one, made every muscle jolt, and she nearly dropped the satchel, but she managed to secure it and shove a hand inside. Her fingers continued stealthily hunting for the blade. Sharp metal pressed into her shoulder.

"Hey, I'm talking to you."

She turned and faced her inquisitor, a boy a full head shorter than her. He looked about fifteen, like Trulian, but the six years Shylah had on him didn't settle her nerves. He had a sword, and she didn't; on his chest—the mark of Naamah. His azure hair looked familiar, but she couldn't place it. With his sword still aimed at her, he turned the tip and stepped toward her.

"Naamah sent me to get a wyvern's tooth," she blurted out.

"My mother loves sending servants to do pointless tasks."

"I am a Bonding," she corrected.

"Oh." He nodded, sheathed his sword, and stepped toward the pits. "Sometimes I wonder what it would be like not having parents."

Was that pity in his voice? "What do you mean, pointless tasks?"

"She has a chest full of wyvern teeth at the foot of her bed. You're her entertainment." He bent over to pick up one of the potions she had placed on the ground beside her before his introduction rattled her. "I'm Jorden. You don't have to do everything she says; there are ways to shield yourself, even as a Bonded." He stood.

She reached for the potion, but he yanked it back with a grin.

"It isn't just me I have to protect."

He raised his eyebrows and nodded. "What's your name?"

"Shylah."

She picked up the rest of the potions from the ground before holding out an open palm toward him. "I don't have time to spit the gall with you. I need to get that tooth." She snatched the potion from his hand and started down the narrow path cut into the side of the cliff.

"Wait!" Jorden caught her. "How? Do you even have a sword?"

She stopped. That would have been a good tool. She clenched her fist and faced him. "I have five potions and a dagger. I only need one tooth."

"Well, you better not miss, then." He smirked and motioned to the pit. "There are five wyverns down there. Can you take on all five?" He leaned against the cliffside and crossed his arms.

Why did he keep shooting holes in her plan? No, she couldn't take on five. She thought there would be only one. She squinted at him. Was he playing with her, like his mother? He knew her bonding extended to him, and she couldn't refuse his request. Was he making a request? "How do you

77

know there—"

"I watch them." He looked at the sky. "Once I can mount one, I will ride it away from here."

Shylah scoffed. "You would choose to live as an orphan? When you have everything. You value nothing, it seems."

He locked eyes with her, and she tensed. She was never good at holding her tongue with men, especially young ones . . .

His shoulders dropped. "I am not my mother. I will not abuse your bonding."

"Well then," she crossed her arms, "what's your plan? It will be dusk soon, and unless you're the one who manipulates beasts . . ."

He looked to her right.

"Wait." She furrowed her brow and shifted into his eyeline again. "You are! What are you waiting for then?"

He pushed his shoulders back. "I can only work a single beast at a time, and I'm better the younger it is. These," he motioned to the pit, "are a family, and they never leave the young ones alone."

"Never?" She crossed her arms.

"Not long enough for me to get to one anyway."

"Why don't you use your mother's Green Willow Guard to help you?"

He scowled. "I told you; I'm not my mother. I don't force people to do things or intentionally put them in danger."

"How do you know they won't just help you?"

He sighed." You're only here because she's forcing you. She probably has someone captive you care about.

She dropped her hands.

"See."

Shylah gripped her satchel. "Okay. I'll help. How do I get a tooth, and you get some alone time with a wyvern?"

He stood straighter and grinned. "Might you have enough in there for a few sleeping potions?"

"Yes." A fire ignited in Shylah's mind; she couldn't believe she hadn't thought of it herself.

They used the random potions she had grabbed in haste and the extra herbs from her satchel to make seven sleeping bombs; it was better than none, but not by much. Jordan took a single potion so he could wield his sword if needed. Shylah put the rest in her satchel, took thin fabric scraps, and wrapped her hands. They'd put four wyverns to sleep before they could get airborne. Otherwise, any advantage Shylah and Jorden might have would be gone. If they timed it right, he'd have about twenty minutes alone with a young wyvern, while she'd grab a tooth and save Trulian. Plenty of time. After all, wyverns lost teeth every few years, so all she had to do was find one.

They slunk down the cliff. Her ears twitched, and she held her breath every time their steps dislodged a pebble or snapped a twig. Jorden didn't seem as concerned and walked upright, almost skipping the entire way down the path. Shylah silently slid between the boulders and peered around each curve. No wyverns. Jorden jumped out onto a rocky divide and started yelling.

"Shh!" She reached up to pull him down, but he jumped away. She tried to keep up with him, but he was more agile on the boulder tops than her heavy skirts allowed.

A cross between a low growl and a loud rattle bounced off the rocks, and a burnt crimson wyvern emerged from the shadows. Jorden threw a potion ball. He missed sending a plume of blue powder into the air.

"Shylah, throw one! We have to get it before it flies!"

Adrenaline pulsed through her as she ran toward the wyvern and ducked behind a rock in time to see flames push past on both sides. The heat curled the light hair on her arms into dark dots.

"Shylah! Now!"

She popped above the edge of the rock to find herself two arms away from the fire-dripping face of the wyvern. She froze.

"NOW!"

Jorden's call snapped her back, and she threw the bomb.

A direct hit.

The wyvern reeled and flailed before succumbing to the potion. One down. Relief mingled with excitement making her steps surer.

"Shylah, behind you!"

She turned. Two more wyverns, one the color of burnt wood and the other of tarnished copper, headed her way; they moved like oil over the tops of the rocks, wings pulsing with each step of their front claws. What would they spit at her? She blindly groped for a potion in her satchel, slowly stepping backward. She couldn't take her eyes off them.

Jorden flew through the air and hit one square in the face with the flat of his sword—the verdigris one still locked on Shylah; its slinking became a run. She looked down and searched even faster for another bomb. Her backward collision with the sleeping wyvern sent her fingers into a fist around one; rolling off, she launched the potion. It exploded in a blue cloud. She held her breath. She couldn't fall asleep too. The wyvern reeled and stumbled around like a drunk soldier, tried to step on a rock, but slid to the ground in a heap. Two down.

Jorden sprinted toward her, the charcoal one in close pursuit. He was out of potions. Grabbing a sleeping bomb, she waited till he was a few boulders away and tossed it to him before ducking behind a nearby stone. A loud thud, followed by a cloud of magma dust, engulfed her. Three down.

Shylah peered around the boulder in time to see Jorden sprinting into the cavern's mouth. She followed; there were five. Skidding to a halt, she scanned the pit and the sky before stepping toward the entrance that swallowed

Jorden. He emerged, luring the fourth wyvern from the cavern. It was a smaller indigo one a few shades darker than Jorden's hair. Why wasn't it already asleep? And where was the last one? The image of a burnt crimson wyvern bursting through a blue cloud of smoke momentarily flashed into her mind; he may have had a sword, but he had lousy aim. She approached the cave's entrance, eyes still jumping from one crevice to another.

"*Go!* Hit the young one and get your tooth!" His eyes locked with his wyvern.

"But—"

"Go!"

She ran in and hit the final cowering amethyst wyvern. The potion hit its shoulder; she dodged frosty breath. After three more close calls, it started stumbling and finally came to rest near the side of the cave.

She grabbed the jar from her satchel, and it hit the ground at her feet. Her heart sank. Even one crack meant she couldn't use it to collect the tooth. She wiped her sweaty hands on her skirt, the fabric scraps almost saturated. Picking up the jar, she inspected every curve and edge. Confident it would hold the acid the tooth expelled, she twisted the jar upright in the soot at her feet and began searching.

She ran to the farthest wall, never wholly turning her back on her sleeping foe. She didn't want to be surprised if it hadn't breathed enough potion. The dim light made it hard to see, so she stirred the soot with her foot feeling for a hard tooth in the powder.

Nothing. Not even a tiny pebble to give her false hope.

Caution dissipated, and she sifted through the powder with her hands, working toward the entrance. Her desperation deepened, and her breathing shallowed. She crawled on all fours, sweeping her hands in wide arcs.

She reached the purple mound and stopped. No teeth. Her chest tightened, and she stood, scanning the small cave. Turning back to the wyvern, she clawed at the powder cradling the purple scales. Only soot. Its tale shifted, and Shylah jumped back. Her gaze fell on its head, laying sideways, mouth opened. She stepped toward its mouth and slipped her hand into her satchel. She had to get a tooth.

Again, she wished she had brought a sword but produced the three-inch dagger instead. Pulling back the upper lip, she took a deep breath and reached in. She began cutting and digging the flesh around the nearest tooth. Her mind willed her hands to move faster, but everything felt like walking through mud while the blood and saliva made fast work of her cloth wraps. The burning acid made her bones feel like strings inside her arms, weakening her muscles.

"Keep going, Shylah!" She said, as if saying it out loud gave it power. She kept sawing the black tooth bed until the tooth moved, and she pulled it out. The wet pop of saliva and flesh filling the void snapped everything back to normal speed. How long had that taken? She sealed the tooth inside the jar and wiped her hands and dagger in the soot before tucking everything in her satchel.

There was no time to waste; the fading light meant she would be running home by moonlight. Shylah ran back to the center of the magma pit and skidded to a stop. Jorden and his wyvern flew toward her like a bird flying into a storm. It banked so severely that she thought Jorden would crash to the ground just before it shot up the side of the cliff and disappeared in the darkening sky. She sprinted after him, wondering what it'd be like to fly away with Trulian—away from Naamah, but rocks and ash were a hazardous combination to dreaming and running. She face-planted, getting a mouthful of magma dust. The burnt crimson wyvern shifted and shook its scales. She pushed back up and hurled the last bomb at the beast. Her lungs burned. Near the top, she slipped, and her knee hit the ground. Pain shot to her hip, but the bone-shaking screech and crack of electricity splitting the air behind her pumped adrenaline into her system. She welcomed its numbing effects and how it chased any thought of resting from her mind.

The trip back was painfully slow. She could have used a ride on Jorden's wyvern. Then again, manipulating a wyvern—even a young one—was almost more than Jorden could manage. Someday, they'd escape Naamah's reach. Fear pinched her throat. Her mouth went dry. She'd helped Naamah's youngest son run away. Had she sealed Trualian's fate while trying to free her? What if they never escaped? No. Focus. She shook the image of Jorden flying away from her mind and sped up her pace, leaning into the mind-numbing pain in her knee. It was dark when she finally pushed through the workshop door and collapsed on the table, her breath escaped in shallow gasps.

Save your sister.

She stood. Light flashed behind her eyes. Squeezing them shut, she touched her knee. She could tell it was swollen through skirts. She bent it. Nausea rippled through her chest. Grabbing a nearby mug of water, she splashed her face—not water. Vinegar. She gasped, spit, and wiped her face.

She hobbled along the table edge to the cabinet and grabbed the healing salve. Sitting, she saw the bright red skin pulled taught from the swelling. She massaged in the salve and wrapped it before collecting the potion ingredients: spikehog quills, finger-root, thelyphonid venom, fennec blood, branchia, fire onion, swilk, water, and the tooth.

Save your sister.

Her knee gave way, and she collapsed into a chair. Squeezing her eyes shut, she rubbed her upper thigh. Each time she neared her knee, a flash of red lit the dark, followed by pricks of light. She rested her forehead on the table. The salve should have been working by now. It wasn't. She pulled her skirts up, removed the fabric, and applied more salve. Her knee had nearly doubled in size, her skin the color of a Nammah's lips. The salve seemed to be doing more for the acid burns on her hands than her knee.

Save your sister.

The pressure had to be released, but the thought of cutting her own knee sent a new wave of nausea. Sitting back up, she closed her eyes and breathed deeply.

She gripped the dagger with one hand and grabbed the table edge with the other. Taking a deep breath, she cut into the red flesh. A jolt of fire shot through her muscles. Her nails dug into the table as blood poured from her knee. She exhaled the pain, and by the time her lungs were empty, her knee only ached. Her grip loosened, and breathing deeply, she wrapped the wound.

Now, she could put weight on her knee. She moved slowly, but she moved. She crushed the spikehog quills, swilk, and wyvern tooth into a paste, set it aside, and started the water boiling over the fire. She hastily cut the fire onion and finger root, nearly cutting her finger. Once the water boiled, she tossed in the chopped ingredients and the branchia to steep. Over the candle, she warmed the thelyphonid venom and fennec blood until it formed a viscous amalgamate. She removed the water from the fire and stirred in the thick liquid before adding the paste, making a lumpy, deep red mixture that smelled of decay with a hint of rose blossoms. She retrieved a clean flask, a funnel, and a piece of clean muslin to separate lumps from the liquid. There was no time to let the potion cool, so she gritted her teeth and squeezed the muslin ball of goo. A scalding blood-red liquid oozed out, dripping down her hands and into the funnel until the flask was over half full. The pain rivaled her knee, but she had to save her sister. She could treat blisters later. She tried to wipe the red stain off her skin without popping the blisters that peppered her palms and grew across the backs of both hands.

"Once stained, they never come clean." The fire flickered, and all the warmth was sucked out of the room.

Midnight. Shylah turned to meet the black eyes of Naamah, who grabbed Shylah's hands. "Not burned badly." She frowned. "The scars will be minimal, but that red will stain the bone." Shylah looked away. Naamah gripped her chin and turned her head back, forcing their eyes to lock. "*You* are stained."

Something like a smile flashed across Naamah's face before she turned to the table and picked up the flask of foamy red liquid. She smelled it and swirled it like mulled wine.

"You saved your sister," Naamah said and stepped toward Shylah, who moved the chair between them. Naamah chuckled and added, "For now."

She turned, a flurry of red and black fabric, and was gone.

Shylah leaned on the chair, and her muscles shook. She sat before her strength could leave altogether. But then her eyes rested on the empty tooth jar.

Trulian.

She sprang to her feet, rushed into the night, and tumbled over a mass of skirts outside.

Shylah rolled over. "Trulian!" she yelled, squeezing her arms around her sister.

"Shy . . . can't . . . breathe . . ." Shylah loosened her arms, and Trulian gripped tighter. "Thank you."

About the Author

AD Uhlar is constantly searching for hidden treasure in the real and imagined world which lead her to complete her MFA in writing from the University of Nebraska. In research for one of her novels, she forged a sword and learned general blacksmithing, thanks to the GRACA grant awarded by UNO. When she isn't writing or teaching, she farms, plays board games, reads, raises rambunctious two legged and four legged creatures while making fairy houses, although she has yet to find any fae to occupy them. Unearth treasure with her on her website www.aduhlar.com or by following @aduhlar on Instagram, Facebook, or TikTok.

A
CRUMBLE
OF MAGIC

DANA BLACK

S age Buecking was buried under a mountain of profiteroles, and he'd had enough, thank you very much. Alas, there was no "having enough" pastry when your family made them for a living. And for the joy of it. And for the magic in it.

No, being a baker was in the Buecking blood and had been since the formation of the world. Or at least since Layrn had become one of the Seven Western Realms. It was an honor to be a member of the Bakers Guild, and it was an even bigger honor to provide the sweets for the Earl of Asterwoode's Summertide Gala.

Which is why thirteen-year-old Sage was buried under a mountain of profiteroles, with only eighteen hours left before they were expected at the manor house for delivery, and three more desserts to bake and assemble before then. The whole Buecking family would be up all night.

The bell tinkled over the door of the bake shop, merrily oblivious to the panic bubbling in the back room like the caramel sauce on the stove. "Hello?" a girl's voice called out from the front.

"Be with you in a moment," Sage called, stacking the loose creme puffs on a tray so they wouldn't tumble to the floor. Where were his mother and uncle? They were due back from the market ages ago. Satisfied with the state of the pastries, Sage dusted his tan hands on his apron and strode into the front of the shop.

"Welcome to Buecking's Bake Shop, purveyors of the finest sweets and breads in all the Seven Western Realms. How can I . . ." he trailed off as he looked up at the customer. His stomach soured. "Oh, it's you."

"What a way to treat a paying customer," the pale girl said with her nose in the air. She had a fine hat perched atop her golden curls and what looked like new ribbons trailing from the brim. Cressida Alder was the poshest— and meanest—girl in their class at school. Her only redeeming quality was she wasn't training to be in Sage's magic Guild. She was working toward the Clothiers Guild, and Sage certainly didn't need any fancy clothes.

"Sorry, we're closed. Private event." Sage turned toward the kitchen.

"There's no sign saying you're closed, and the door was open," Cressida argued in her prim voice. She always tried to act older than thirteen. It was annoying.

"Ugh, fine. I can get you anything that's already in the case, but I can't make anything special today. We really do have a big order to fill, and I need to get back." Sage leaned against the counter and pointed to the display case, which was filled with an impressive selection of beautiful cakes, breads, pastries, and truffles.

"That's hardly ideal." Cressida studied the case. "Mamá will be so

87

disappointed. Are these fresh?"

Sage narrowed his eyes. "Of course."

Cressida held up her hands. "All right. No need to snap, Sage. I'll take a dozen of the miniature lavender ice cakes, six cherry-lemon dandies, and six ginger-cinnamon scones."

Sage nodded tersely and started pulling trays out of the display case. He put the lavender ice cakes in their own box to protect the tiny sparkly purple confections. They were a bestseller this time of year, partly because they looked nice on a fancy dining table, partly because they were infused with a secret family recipe of sun drops, a concoction that both warmed you and created the feeling of a lazy day at the lakeshore.

"Do the dandies have anything special in them today?" Cressida asked as Sage moved to the second tray of treats. He was about to retort that all of their treats had something special in them, when she interrupted. "I mean, do they have any magic?"

Sage's shoulders dropped down from where they had crunched by his ears. "Oh. Uh, no, but I could add something if you want." He looked around behind the counter for the toppings. "I've got memory sprinkles, sympathy syrup, and . . . joy dots. Those are lemon flavored, so they'd go with the cherry and lemon that's already in there."

"Yes, that will do."

He pressed a sunny yellow joy dot into the center of each cookie, in the middle of the bright cherry compote. The dots shimmered as they settled in, making themselves at home. It was the perfect addition to the cookies. He always loved that part, when the magic just fit.

He quickly finished packing up the baked goods, told Cressida the total, and counted her change back. "Do you need me to call the delivery boy to take these home for you?"

"No, Pierre is outside. I assume you'll be at the gala tomorrow?" She had an unreadable look on her face. Sage couldn't tell if she wanted him there or hoped he wouldn't show up.

"Kind of a requirement when you're providing the desserts . . ." Sage gestured toward the back room.

"Sage?" A new voice called from the back. Not his mum's. A second of silence passed, followed by a resounding *crash*, a squeak, and a quiet, "Oh no!" from the voice.

"Gotta go." Sage left Cressida to wrestle with her boxes and ran into the back room.

There, in a heap on the floor, were his cousin Tashandra and all two hundred profiteroles.

***

"I'm sorry. I'm so sorry," Tash kept saying over and over, tears running down her warm brown freckled cheeks. She picked up a handful of ruined creme puffs and stared at them like they were a scrying orb. "I don't know what happened. I walked in and was looking for you, and the next thing I knew, something bright orange streaked in front of me, I lost my balance, and landed on the tray." She dropped the pastries in her lap and buried her face in her hands. "I've ruined everything! Those will take ages to remake," she mumbled, then started crying again.

Sage sighed. It was an accident. What they needed to do now was fix it. "It's all right, Tash. You didn't do it on purpose. Let's clean these up and get back to work." He grabbed the trash bin and started scooping up the ruined puffs. "It's too bad we don't have a cleaning charm." He cracked a smile at his cousin, hoping she would feel better.

Tash sniffed and tried to return the smile but failed. Her face crumpled again. "But we're hours behind now. How can we get everything done by tomorrow afternoon?"

"We'll come up with something," Sage said. "We're terribly clever, remember?"

Tash managed a real smile, and she picked up an armload of profiteroles. They stayed silent for a few minutes as they cleaned, Sage's mind whirring as he thought through the options.

They still needed to make four batches of sugared lemon butter tarts with peace elixir to make sure no one talked about politics, plus Calliope Savoy's famous cardamom cake drenched in dragon's breath cordial for the centerpiece. Tash was right. They were hours behind now, *and* he had to come up with something to replace the creme puffs. They were too fussy and time-consuming to remake.

And where were his mum and Tash's dad?

"Oh, they won't be back for a while," Tash said, tossing the last of the puffs into the bin and cleaning her hands.

"What?"

"You asked about Da and Auntie Amrita while you were muttering to yourself."

Sage's cheeks heated. His brain moved so fast sometimes, he didn't always realize when words made their way out of his mouth. "Oh."

"I saw them at the market on my way here. The whole place was buzzing with news—the Earl of Asterwoode's son is visiting from Draven, and he's on some sort of mission for the Fanos. Da and Auntie got a summons to an urgent meeting with *them*"—she gave Sage a knowing look—"and Da said to keep working, and they'll come relieve us when they're done." Tash shrugged like it was nothing and wandered over to the wall filled with recipe books.

But it wasn't nothing. Tash might have been almost two years older, but she didn't pay as much attention as Sage. He'd heard all the rumors. He'd spent every afternoon and weekend working in the bake shop the last year to practice his magic, and if there was one thing people liked to do in shops, it was talk.

Some people thought the Earl's son, Theophilus Savoy, was a traitor for marrying the young queen of Draven, their neighbor to the southwest. But Sage thought he was a genius. Sure, he'd heard all the stories about how they'd fallen in love at that boring, non-magical school in Draven, but he knew there had to be more to it. Giving up life in a magical realm to live somewhere freezing cold and close-minded sounded like the worst possible thing a man could do.

Theophilus must have been searching for a way to restore magic to Draven, and the only thing guaranteed to work was Queen Radhika's legendary Sun Gem. It was rumored to have been destroyed by Gerard the Fearful when he launched his coup in Draven ages ago. But in Layrn, they knew better. It wasn't gone, it was just missing. The Fanos had been on the hunt for it for generations, and they must be getting close if Theophilus left Draven to join the search. That had to be the reason he was back in Layrn: he needed help—most likely of the magical variety.

"A dream cake!" Sage shouted, making Tash jump and drop the stack of recipe books she'd been carrying to the worktable.

"Stars, Sage, are you trying to kill me?" She half glared at him while she piled the books on the table.

"Sorry. I figured out what we need to make," he said, dashing over to the table and sorting through the books. The one he needed wasn't there. He moved to the bookshelves. "We need to change the centerpiece cake. Turn the cardamom cake into petit fours to replace the profiteroles." He pulled a heavy leather tome from the shelf. "And do this for the centerpiece instead."

Sage flipped to the page marked by a rust-colored ribbon and pointed triumphantly at the recipe. Tash leaned in and gasped.

"Oh, Sagey, no. We can't make a dream cake. The magic is too complicated."

Sage waved away her concerns. "I've helped Mum make a hundred of them. Every Layrnian gets one on their coming-of-age day. I know the mechanics. How hard can it be?"

He tried to ignore the pricking sensation in his gut telling him *exactly* how hard it would be. "We can do this, Tash," he said, more trying to convince himself than her.

"You know I've never gotten a baking charm right on my own. I keep trying to convince Da to let me switch to the Horticulturists Guild, like my mum, but he's so stubborn about me being a Buecking." Tash looked like she was going to start crying again, so Sage employed his second-best skill: deflection.

"What if I promised you wouldn't have to use any magic?" He elbowed her. "You know how to make a regular cake. So maybe you could work on the cardamom cakes while I get started on this?"

Tash frowned. She looked back at the dream cake recipe. "'*Baker, be warned, for dreams are fragile precious things, formed in the depth of night to light our way,*" she read. "This is a bad idea. Who's it going to be for, anyway? Dream cakes need to be incredibly specific, tailored to the recipient."

"Theophilus Savoy," Sage said, drawing the two words out almost like a hushed prayer. Tash's eyebrows shot up. "It has to mean something big that he's back and gathering people for secret meetings," Sage continued. "If we're going to be members of the Fanos soon, we might as well start helping how we can."

"We're technically children, Sage. What can we do aside from mess things up?"

"I'll be fourteen next week. That's old enough to do something, even if we're not of age yet. We have magic, which is more than the sad children in Draven can say. Maybe Theophilus is trying to restore it. What if he's searching for the Sun Gem? Wouldn't that be worth it?"

Tash threw her hands up. "Ugh, fine. I'll bake the cardamom cakes."

"Yes!" Sage punched the air with his fist.

"But," Tash interrupted him, "you're going to help me with those too. Because rule number one of dream cakes is they have to be made at midnight. I thought you said you knew what you were doing." She rolled her eyes, then went to tie on her apron.

"Right. Of course. I knew that," Sage sputtered, hoping he sounded confident and not foolish. But Tash could see right through him. She always had.

***

Even with magic involved, it was harder to accomplish their goals than Sage had assumed. His kind of magic couldn't keep last-minute evening customers away, and they couldn't just close early when the next day was a holiday and people expected to be able to buy treats for their celebrations.

Between the customer flood and the lack of adults to help them, Sage and Tash had barely gotten the cardamom cakes out of the ovens by the time the clock struck eleven. In the quiet of the empty shop, Sage closed his eyes and leaned against the counter, listening. It took a minute to find it, but eventually he did: the faint golden hum of magic. It whispered around him and settled on his skin and hair, lighting him up inside and reminding him of the reason for his sleepless night ahead.

Everyone deserved the chance to experience this, and if he could do something to help Draven get their magic back, he had to try.

Tash banged back into the kitchen, breaking the hush of the moment. "Okay, shop is cleaned and closed, and I've packed up the remaining items for tomorrow. Are you ready for this foolishness?"

Sage grinned. "I was born ready."

"Good." Tash nodded and held out a tiny tray with sweets on it. Four perfect truffles—two rolled in cocoa and two dipped in pink icing—sparkled up at him. She handed him a chocolate one. "We're going to need these."

"Smart thinking." Sage took the truffle and popped it in his mouth. Tash ate hers more slowly, but now wasn't the time to savor the treats. The flavors of chocolate, orange, and coffee burst on his tongue, shocking all his senses. Tash chose well. The awake elixir worked immediately, making his fingers tingle slightly.

Tash pointed at the pink truffle. "Save that one for just before midnight, when we need the most focus."

Sage nodded. "If you want to keep working on the cardamom cakes, I'll let you know when I need help."

Comfortable silence settled in the kitchen as they worked. Sage consulted the ancient recipe book as he buzzed from shelf to shelf. He'd watched Mum make hundreds of dream cakes, but Tash was right. This was very advanced magic he hadn't practiced. And if he got it wrong . . . well, the consequences could be disastrous.

One key element of the dream cake was the addition of hidden trinkets, chosen specifically for the recipient, which required a complex bit of magic. He needed several ingredients that reminded him of Theophilus.

"What do you know about Theophilus Savoy?" Sage asked.

"Um, he's got bright blue eyes. All the Savoys do." Tash started mixing buttercream. The scents of cardamom and vanilla filled the air.

"Blue eyes." Sage grabbed a bottle of cabbage broth and the jar of bicarbonate of soda and mixed them in a bowl. "His daughter is the crown princess, so something to represent her . . ."

"What about a splash of princess rose water?" Tash went and found it on the shelf. Into the bowl it went. Pink sparkles lifted into the air from the mix.

"Perfect. What else is important to him? Maybe something from Asterwoode?" Sage ran to the shelf with the herbs, scanning the labels until he found it: garland bezel syrup, from a tree that only grows in the region of Layrn between where they were in Hielt and Asterwoode down the road.

He tipped the jar so two drops dripped into the pinkish-blue paste. It hissed and sizzled, and the whole mixture turned a weird gray-green color.

"Is it supposed to do that?" Tash asked, peering into the bowl with a grimace, then backing away. "Ugh, it smells rotten!"

"That's probably the cabbage broth. I'm sure it's fine," Sage said. He consulted the recipe. "Okay, three elements to represent Theophilus, mixed well." He poured the goop into a round cake pan. His eyes watered from the scent. It really was rancid. Nothing he could do about it though. "The recipe says to let it cure in the oven for ten minutes, and when it's done, we'll have the objects to bake into the layers of the cakes."

Sage shoved the pan in the oven, closed the door, and prayed it would work. "Cake time." He clapped once. "We need three flavors, so I was thinking lemon-lavender for one, strawberries and clotted cream for the second, and . . . one more."

"Raspberry and vanilla," Tash offered. She went back to work cutting the cardamom cakes into tiny cubes. "No, wait. Blueberry thyme."

"Perfect." Sage mixed the base batter for the cakes. They'd all start the same, then he'd add the different flavors in separate bowls. "Here's the tricky bit," he said, reading from the book again.

"We haven't already done the tricky bit?" Tash wiped flour off her forehead and re-tied her poof of nutmeg curls up on top of her head.

"Not even close. Once we have the batter ready and the trinkets are done, we have to place the objects in the batter *and* get them into the oven at midnight. Not before or after. We'll have one minute or the whole thing could be wrecked."

"No pressure," Tash muttered. "You know," she said, waving a spatula of buttercream at him, "plant magic doesn't have these time constraints. It's much more flexible."

"The horticulturists at school are always complaining about fiddly harvests. What about the moonbeam flower? That one is tied to midnight too. And if you don't collect it on the right day, doesn't it burst into flames?"

"It turns to ash, but that's not the point. The point is—" But whatever the point was got lost in a terrible rattling sound, a swirl of acrid gray-green smoke, and Tash yelling, "Sage, get down!"

Sage dove away just as the oven door burst open, spraying putrid gunk all over the work station he'd abandoned.

Shaking, he sat up and looked at the horror before him. The clock chimed. Only fifteen minutes to midnight. "No, no, no." Sage stood up. "What happened? We'll never finish in time now." He knocked his fists against his forehead, and a chill seeped into his toes. Two disasters in one night were too many to deal with. Not on such an important day.

"If we hurry, we can try again," Tash said. "We'll have to figure out what went wrong. And use a different oven." She screwed up her face at the mess and the smell, then inspected the damage. "It looks like the cake batter is okay. We just need new trinkets."

"Good. But how do I fix the mixture?"

"Sage Idris Buecking," Mum said from the back doorway, "what in the stars happened?"

"Mum, I'm so sorry. We'll clean it up," Sage said, scrambling toward her.

Mum waved him away. "Messes happen in the kitchen. What happened to your bake?" She scooped up a fingerful of the dream goop and sniffed it. She wrinkled her nose. "Wrong combination?"

"Apparently. You make dream cakes look so easy. How do I fix this?"

Mum laughed. "It looks easy because I've practiced a long time. I've made several like this too. This is for tomorrow? Who's it meant for?"

"Theophilus Savoy. I thought he might need it since he's back in Layrn."

"Wise thinking." Mum glanced at the clock. "You need to work quickly. Choose something related to his Guild, something that reminds you of him, and something connected to whatever compelled you to make the cake. Can you think of things?"

"Oh!" Tash ran over and thrust something into Sage's hand. "Eat this!"

It was the focus truffle. Perfect. Sage shoved it in his mouth and chewed. Ideas flooded his brain. Theophilus was in the Cartographers Guild, so northern brambleberry juice would work. The Savoy blue eyes were well-known, but cabbage was a bad idea. "We need something blue—not cabbage."

Tash's eyes lit up. "I know just the thing." She grabbed a jar of tea and poured out some blue flower bits. "But we need the full flower." She pressed her fingers into the petals and a perfect butterfly pea flower formed in their place. She handed it to him with a grin. "Told you I need to switch Guilds."

Sage grinned back. "Well, I'm glad you're in ours right now. Thanks."

Only one more item . . . what had compelled him to make the cake? The Sun Gem. Candied orange and lemon peel could represent that.

He mixed them all quickly and put them in the oven that had been waiting for the cakes. Eleven minutes to midnight. They'd have one minute to get it ready. His pulse stuttered.

Uncle Amal returned then, and they cleaned and finished the cake batters while they waited. At eleven fifty-nine, Sage opened the non-exploded oven, holding his breath. The mixture had transformed into a tiny lantern, a compass that pointed southeast, and an oddly shaped mirror with a sunburst of orange and yellow gems on the back. Sage exhaled. It worked.

"Ten seconds," Mum said. "Concentrate on your intention for the cake."

On the first clock strike, Sage placed the items into the cake pans. He picked up the first batter to pour. *I want to help Theophilus find the Sun Gem and restore magic to Draven.*

They pushed the three cakes into the oven on the last clock strike. Midnight. A blanket of magic floated over them, bringing calm. He looked at his family, and they all laughed. Never a dull moment at Bueckings' Bake Shop.

***

The next night, with most of the Layrnian nobility gathered, Sage and his mother presented the dream cake to the Earl of Asterwoode and his family. They exclaimed over the swirling blue, pink, orange, and yellow icing, depicting a perfect Summertide sky. Even Cressida Alder said it looked nice.

When Theophilus cut into the cake and found the mirror, his eyes widened. "How did you know?" Theophilus asked.

"I didn't," Sage said, the true magic of the dream cake dawning. "I just knew I wanted to help you. The recipe did the rest."

Sage hoped it would be enough. The warmth in his gut told him maybe it was.

About the Author

Dana Black writes middle grade and young adult fantasy tales mixed with magic, humor, and heart, and an extra sprinkling of glitter whenever she can get away with it. You can find her on Instagram @missdanablack and on her website, missdanablack.com.

MIDNIGHT KEY

HEATHER TABATA

The little bell over the shop door tinkled as Mrs. Witt stepped out of the swirling, sea salt air. She shifted her basket of blueberry crumble bread from her right to left arm, and the smell drifted across the wooden shelves of candles, hand creams, and perfume.

Elise smiled up at the woman. "Good morning. I'll be finished here in just a moment." She carefully smoothed a label over the little ceramic jar, a thin layer of paste holding it fast. A hand-drawn sprig of lavender rested under the words, "Lavender Honeysuckle, Barrett's Chandlery, Kingdom of Marilon."

Blinking back tears, Elise placed the candle on the front window display and finished humming a verse of Mama's song. She brushed a finger over the label and turned to Mrs. Witt. "How can I help you?"

"Ah, just what I was looking for." Mrs. Witt's silver-streaked chestnut hair swung over her shoulder as she picked up the candle. "I adore this scent and was afraid it was out of stock." Her smile crinkled just a bit next to her eyes.

"It's my favorite too, but that may be the last of it for a while." Elise rubbed a smear of paste on her work apron. "I still haven't been able to get the scent extraction and the blend right. It was Mama's guild secret."

Mrs. Witt pressed a hand to Elise's shoulder. "We all miss her too."

The door jingled again, and Sheriff Stolzfus swaggered over the welcome mat. His cane tapped a hollow cadence on the stone floor as the door smacked closed. "Well, it's that time again." His voice grated like gravel crunching under a wagon wheel. "Queen's levy is due. That'll be 125 pence."

Elise's hand hovered over the jar. "Last month it was 120." And he was here four days early.

The sheriff swiped a finger over a shelf, mouth pursed before he even lifted it. He brought it closer to his face, squinted, and put his hand back at his side with a huff. "Her Majesty's expenses are increasing, what with the banquet for the ambassadors and the Princess Royal's wedding."

Elise might like to have a new dress or pair of shoes every month, but that didn't mean she could raise prices whenever she wanted. She took another coin from a second jar and added it to the rest. It still wasn't the full total. "May her Majesty rule long and well."

The Sheriff counted the coins and slid his gaze back up. "The levy isn't optional."

"I wasn't prepared for it today. It isn't the last day of the month."

He dropped the coins in a bag. "I'll be back in four days for the rest of the payment. Surely a shop that is prosperous enough to continue will be able to pay the levy by that time."

A gust of sea air rushed in as the door banged shut.

Mrs. Witt held out the candle. "I'd like to buy this, and I'll pay in advance for the next one of this scent you make."

Elise worked her thumb in her other hand. "I'll be glad for you to have that one, but I don't know when there will be more."

The sun streamed in on shelves that, despite careful arranging, couldn't hide being nearly bare.

Mama had kept the shelves stocked two high and three deep. But without the recipes and instructions that Mama'd refined passed down to her, Elise's candles were novices next to a master's. This would have been the year Elise could have joined the guild as a junior member, and then she'd know more than just the basics. Until then, she'd have to muddle on the best she could and pray that she made enough to pay the monthly levy.

Mrs. Witt wrapped her hand around her basket handle. "You need your mama's box, don't you? If you could see her recipes from the guild vault, you could keep going, couldn't you?"

Elise's throat burned. Mama's polished maple wood box with the little lock on the front held all her notes on making the goods for the shop. Handwritten cards from Mama, Grandma, and two more generations back were tucked in there for safekeeping. She'd seen the box once, but only guild members were allowed to read what was inside.

She swallowed, trying to make sure words would come out. "I think I could. I don't want Jane and Andrew to grow up in the city working in warehouses." Even though her brother and sister were nine, they would be put to work too, and there'd be no more school for them.

Elise glanced outside at the herb garden below the window. The sun glinted off Jane's wheat-blonde hair as she carried her rag doll. She chased Andrew's stick figure knight with its bits of silver painted paper standing in for armor around the narrow, pebble bordered paths. Apparently, Jane's princess wasn't the one who needed to be rescued.

Mrs. Witt stood a little straighter and set her jaw. "As a member of the guild, I declare this an emergency. Go to the vault at midnight. Don't be late. You can open the door for only a single minute."

With a deep breath, Elise nodded. "Mama told me that the door will open then without a key. Does it just unlock and then lock back?"

"No, there's more to it than that. I can't tell you the rest, but if you're able to figure it out, then the vault finds you worthy of being a full member. You'll be given a key and the complete support of the guild." Mrs. Witt tapped a finger on her basket. "Just remember, you can't take anything out of the vault, so know exactly what you are looking for before you get there."

Elise pressed a hand over Mrs. Witt's. "Thank you so much. This gives me a chance to keep the shop. I can't stand the thought of Jane and Andrew not growing up here."

Mrs. Witt smiled. "You're very welcome, dear. Just don't be late." The bell tinkled as she walked back out into the street.

***

Light from the streetlamps scattered across the cobblestones, wet from evening rain. Elise's slippers splatted through puddles in the shadow of houses and shops as she darted around pools of light. Two streets down from home, she passed the clock tower, waiting to mark the change of one day to the next.

There was one more dull tap on the pavement after her last footstep and then stillness. The back of her neck prickled with the eerie feeling of someone being nearby. She leaned against the wall of the cobbler's shop and held her breath, mouth open.

If she got caught breaking curfew, she'd be fined. Without the money to pay, she'd be sentenced to labor at the docks for several days, and she'd have to close the shop until that was finished. The queen's levy would be impossible to pay if that happened.

The clock tower chimed a half hour to twelve. If she wasn't at the vault at midnight, it would lock again until tomorrow, and there'd be no time to make anything to sell before the sheriff returned.

Money, and who got how much, accounted for most of her problems.

She lifted her foot to take a step around the corner and into the light.

Another tap echoed from down the street, crisp and hollow.

She held her foot mid-air and wobbled. With her fingers spread, she touched the cool plaster of the shop wall. Then she eased her foot down without a sound.

The tap came again in a steady rhythm, growing louder and closer. Softer pats surrounded it.

A cane and footsteps.

The sheriff.

Elise darted to the cobbler's shop. She lifted the wooden cellar door and slid inside. The hinge creaked a bit as she lowered the door above her head. Taps, muffled now through the thick wood, came faster. The door wasn't quite closed, but if she moved it, it could squeak again, and the sheriff was close. She scooted her feet more squarely onto the rock step.

"Who goes there? 'Tis after curfew," he called. "Show yourself, and the crown may show mercy." The cane rapped closer and closer until it sounded directly outside the cellar. Then the dim bar of light that came through the opening vanished into heavy air smelling of dirt and roots.

The crown had never shown mercy and never would. Elise's arms ached with supporting the heavy door overhead.

"Last chance. Two days at the docks instead of three." The sheriff tapped his cane twice and made a raspy sound in his throat. "Have it your way. When I find you, you'll wish you lived in another kingdom."

101

The clock tower chimed a quarter to midnight.

A strand of hair stuck to Elise's forehead. If she wasn't at the vault wall at midnight sharp, she'd miss her chance.

The sheriff stomped down the street. When the last tap of his metal-tipped cane faded, Elise counted to thirty. No more sound.

Her muscles quivered as she eased the cellar door open and crawled out.

A chilly, wispy mist materialized over the lanes as she hurried to the edge of town. Cobblestones turned into a dirt path that wound through the forest toward the capital. Just before the dense cover of trees, an old stone wall formed a square, too tall to see over, that held the guild vault. Everyone knew it was here, but only members of the guild were allowed inside.

A faint echo of the midnight bells knelled from the tower as Elise pressed a hand to the wall. Her ragged breathing muffled a faint melody coming from the stones. She ran her hands along the wall, searching for the door. Her fingertips brushed damp moss and crusty lichen in the crevices of the stone, but she couldn't find the door.

The same tune began playing again. It sounded familiar, but there was no time to think about that now.

She frantically brushed her hands along the wall toward the forest, but there was no door. She only had one minute. Where was it?

The music grew louder then abruptly stopped again. The tune wasn't finished, and that's where it stopped last time.

She darted farther down the wall, and when the music started again, she stepped directly in front of the sound. The wall was only stone, but there was a tiny gap between blocks running taller than her head, across, and down. This must be the door.

She knew those notes. They were from the song Mama hummed when she worked in the backroom of the shop.

Elise caught the place in the song and hummed like she would have with Mama as she checked the edges of the door for a latch. There was nothing, not even a keyhole.

The tune stopped again at the same spot, but Elise kept humming, imagining Mama standing there with her. Now was not the time to panic. She finished the song and started it again, but no more music came from the wall. What was she supposed to do?

Then there was a scraping as the section of blocks swung in.

Elise gasped and covered her mouth.

This was the vault.

A soft glow filled the area. Brick pathways meandered around flower beds and pruned shrubs. Scattered through the small garden were little boxes with roofs, almost like birdhouses.

As she stepped onto the pathway, the door rumbled shut behind her.

The first box had a picture of a spinning wheel painted on the side. This must be for the weavers. She walked past boxes for the potters, carpenters, smiths, and leatherworkers. In the back corner, in front of a stand of lavender and with honeysuckle climbing the wall behind, stood a box painted light blue with a sunflower yellow roof. It had a candle painted on the front.

She lifted the lid, and inside were bound books, linen sachets, a couple small jars, a mortar and pestle, and a polished wooden box. She opened the box to a stack of recipe cards on thick parchment with careful handwriting in four different styles of penmanship. The top cards were Mama's.

There was the recipe for her trademark lavender honeysuckle scent. Elise read through the instructions three times, committing amounts and the process to memory. If only she could take the card home.

The notebooks were a sort of diary for each of the last four chandlers to keep track of what worked and what experiments didn't go well. Elise picked up one of the sachets and worked at the drawstring.

"Who's skulking about in there?" The sheriff's muffled, breathless voice came from outside the door. "It's after curfew. Open this door!" Several hard raps sounded on the stones. He must be trying to break in.

Elise grinned. The vault was protecting her.

"Is that you, Mary Robbins?" He paused and there was another smack against the wall. "Nora Witt?" He made that noise that was not quite a growl but not exactly clearing his throat. "I know I saw a woman go in there."

Elise ran the drawstring through her fingers. So he didn't know it was her.

"Come out now and tell me who you are, and the crown may be merciful and lower your fine."

Why did he keep suggesting punishment would be lessened? It never had been for anyone.

"If I have to root out which household is missing a person right now, I'll do it. But I'll demand the maximum reparations possible." Another solid smack to the wall. "Have it your way." His footsteps hurried down the path as quickly as a middle-aged man with rheumatism in both knees could go.

She'd have to get home before he got to her house, and that meant taking the long way around without the path. The door stayed closed. How was she supposed to get out? She ran to it and checked all along the inside of the edges. No knob. No latch.

Maybe the song. She hummed a few lines, but nothing happened. She tried again. The sheriff would get to her house first if she didn't get out of here fast.

She began another song Mama sang sometimes. With the first notes, there was a low scuff from the center of the garden. A section of the pathway slid away from a set of stairs leading down into a tunnel. Inside, a series of torches lit in succession down the walkway.

Elise shivered but hurried down the steps. As she walked farther in, the first torches winked out. She jumped and looked back. A mechanism with gears spun a metal torch snuffer over the next one and extinguished it. She'd love to study how it worked, but there was no time. Maybe, one day, she'd be back.

The torches that had easily kept up with her slowed. She hurried on, but no more lit. Then a heavy wooden door slammed shut in front of her. A metal door knocker made in the shape of ivy bounced twice against the door from the jolt.

What just happened? She knocked on the door and tried to turn the knob. Nothing.

Bouncing on her toes, she looked all around the door. There was no way past it.

Then the torches farthest into the tunnel winked out, and a pair lit in the direction of the vault. The next two closest to her went dark, and another set blazed closer toward the way she'd come.

She followed the light, but it was the wrong direction. The sheriff would just barge in her house if she wasn't there. If she was missing, he'd charge a fine for sure. Jane and Andrew would be terrified.

Back on the path at the vault, Elise rubbed a hand over her face. She had to get out. Trying to slow her breathing, she leaned forward with her palms on her apron. Something crinkled in her pocket.

She snatched it out and saw Mama's neat handwriting. She must have accidentally put it in her pocket when the sheriff scared her.

Elise scurried to the chandler's box, tucked the card back in, and skidded back to the opening in the pathway.

She ran down the tunnel, and the torches lit in front of her faster as she sped up. This time, the wooden door in the tunnel stayed open. Her legs burned like hot wax had been poured inside them when a set of stairs appeared ahead. She ran up, and a trap door slid open ahead of her.

Slowing, she gazed into the shadows. Where did the tunnel take her? She stepped out onto square black and white tiles. A wooden staircase spiraled above her. It was the clock tower. Her house was only two streets over.

She opened the door, and from just outside of town, the sheriff's cane tapped furiously. Elise closed the door behind her and ducked into the alley. She ran through shadows to their back door just as the sheriff reached the front.

As noiselessly as she could, she tiptoed up the stairs to her room as he pounded on the door.

"Show yourselves, everyone who is inside!"

Elise threw on a shawl and lit a candle. "Just a moment," she called as she walked past an open bedroom door.

Andrew sprawled across the bed, one arm hanging off the edge. Jane's wide eyes stared back at her. Elise held up a finger to her mouth and winked.

Then she hurried back down the stairs, taking pins out of her hair so it tumbled free.

She opened the door and squinted. "Can I help you, Sheriff? My brother and sister are trying to sleep upstairs."

His face turned bright red in the dim light. "Did you manage to get into the guild vault tonight?"

"What do you mean?" Elise rested a hand on the front candle display.

"Someone was at the vault. I saw a woman, and none of the guild members seem to know anything."

Her knees wobbled. "How could I get in? Only members can open the door."

He peered from her loose hair to the long shawl hiding her dress. "Ned Atkins said someone went inside his cellar just before midnight, and the description he gave fits you." He circled his cane on the floor and twitched his mustache to one side.

Elise crossed her arms over her stomach and tilted her head a bit. If he couldn't explain it, she certainly wouldn't help. "I'm not in the habit of sneaking into other people's cellars. As you can see, I'm here, in my own house, and would appreciate getting the rest of the night's sleep. I have a shop to open early in the morning."

The sheriff rapped his cane twice. "I believe, since I'm here, I'll just go ahead and collect the levy."

Elise's shoulders rolled in. "One moment." She ducked her head and turned to the counter. After she closed the shop earlier that evening, she'd checked, and there wasn't enough.

"Unless you'd prefer to surrender the shop now, rather than in three days." The sheriff tapped his cane triumphantly.

Elise paused next to the empty shelf that waited for Lavender Honeysuckle candles. The same shelf Mama put them on. With the same recipe she now had memorized.

Jane and Andrew were snug upstairs, believing she'd take care of them.

She raised her head.

Straightened her shoulders.

Turned to the sheriff. "I have three more days before the levy is due. I'm sure the artisans and the queen's ambassador wouldn't like to hear that the amount was being required early, especially from a single young woman raising her siblings. At midnight, no less."

He took a step toward the counter, but she stood in the walkway. "Are you refusing to pay the levy?"

"No." She nested a hand in her pocket. "I'm agreeing to pay it when it's due."

The sheriff made a grating noise in his throat. "See that you have it." He spun and stalked out into the night.

Elise hurried to the door and closed it. Her hand shook as she turned the latch and rested her forehead against the smooth wood of the door. A giggle escaped her throat, and she pressed a hand over her mouth. She turned and leaned her back against the door.

Shadows stretched through the shop, but faint bars of light slid through the windows.

Her shop. To keep running. To keep her family.

Tomorrow, she'd make a batch of candles. The next day, she'd advertise a sale and set up a temporary stall in the town square next to the ocean wall to draw more attention. And on the third day, the sheriff would have his levy.

She walked up the staircase, hand trailing the railing, to tuck in her two little people.

About the Author

Heather Tabata is from Kentucky but slips into a British accent at random times thanks to Jane Austen. When she isn't taking pictures of clouds, you can find her on the front porch reading or crafting journeys that always end well. For more adventures and capturing beautiful everyday moments, follow her on Instagram @heathertabata and visit www.heathertabata.com.

THE ALL
HALLOWS
CLUB

HAYLIE HANSON

108

My shoulders press against the tombstone at my back until the chilly granite becomes indistinguishable from the icy foreboding knotted inside my chest. Swirling mist whispers threats as dark as the moonless night. An obsidian raven perched atop an obelisk of the long-since deceased stares down its beak as tendrils of fog curl over the heavy stone.

"Turn back now," the harbinger bird breathes one final offer of safety. *"Get out while you still can."*

I clamp my palm over my mouth, siffling a cry of horror. There's no logical way the raven whispered words into my head and heart. It's stone, inanimate. My fear manifested them. That's the only explanation . . .

. . . isn't it?

Screaming wind tears the sky, rattling dead tree limbs like bones. I duck further behind the tombstone, squeezing my eyes tight before forcing them open. Panic sticks in my throat. I force myself not to imagine the dark fate waiting amongst these graves if I fail my initiation.

Get out. Get out. Get. Out.

Why did I agree to this ridiculous challenge? I don't know anyone in the All Hallows Club. But if everybody else in this town is intent on ignoring my presence, pretending like I don't exist, completing the Club's initiation challenge on Halloween night is my last chance to make new friends, and no longer be alone.

Or, it could be my last night in existence.

"It's just a dare," I remind myself. "One silly dare." Come to the graveyard on Halloween night, make it all the way across and solve the mystery of the golden lights before the last stroke of midnight, then report to the Club leaders waiting at the farthest gate.

Oh, and if I fail even one of the tasks, I'm banished from the Club. Forever.

I glance at the clock on the nearby church steeple, rising into the sky like the blade of a dagger. Fifteen minutes to midnight. What if I don't make it across the graveyard to the gate? What if the lights never appear?

What if I . . .

"First midnight Halloween challenge?"

"AH!"

I leap high, grazing the raven's beak before sinking back to the ground. A boy my age slips behind the tombstone beside me, someone I've seen lurking around alleys and dark corners with a mischievous grin I want to trust, but don't know if I should.

"Don't do that!" I hiss.

"Sorry, new girl, I didn't mean to scare you." His bright smile pierces the black veil of night. "Then again, scaring's the whole point of Halloween, isn't it?"

"I guess so." A pause floats between us. "My name isn't 'new girl,' it's Ruby."

"Ruby. Sorry." I don't think he's sorry, but the nonchalance in his voice has a strangely calming effect on my nerves. "I'm Eddie. You're the latest initiate into the All Hallows Club, aren't you?"

"If they decide to let me in." My admission into this exclusive society is by no means certain, despite how much I desperately want it.

"It's a great Halloween. Midnight with a new moon is always extremely creepy." Eddie turns his pale face toward the watchful raven, brushing a dark swath of hair away from even darker eyes. "There's an old poem about a raven and ghosts. 'Once upon a midnight dreary . . .' Do you know it?"

Poetry seems like an odd topic of conversation, given the circumstances. "I'm a little busy for recitation. I'm crossing the graveyard so I can watch for the golden lights."

"Are you?" Eddie arches an eyebrow. "You haven't made it very far."

As if I needed another reminder I'm too terrified to move. A gale howls through the tombstones, and I grasp my arms tight, shuddering at the unearthly sound. Above me, the raven's blood-red eyes lock onto my petrified gaze.

"I told you so." Words slither through my mind as if flesh and bone are little more than crepe, the raven's words defying reality to reach me. *"Get out while you still can . . ."*

It's my imagination, nothing more. Just my mind playing tricks. Vivid, awful, terrifying tricks.

I duck lower, becoming one with the earth, but Eddie lounges against the obelisk like he's the king of the graveyard, this pillar of granite his own personal throne. How is he *not* afraid on a night like this? He must be a seasoned Halloween competitor. But he seems nice enough—and the only Club member who's bothered to show his face all night.

"How long have you been initiated?" I ask.

"Oh, you know. A while." Well, that's frustratingly vague. "Enough about me, new girl—"

"Ruby."

"Yes. Ruby." He swishes fog away from his face until it settles in his misbehaving hair. "What's your story? Fresh initiates *always* have a story."

"It's just like you said, I'm new here." I shrug my shoulders. "Is it wrong that I want to make friends?"

"Nothing's wrong with friends," Eddie says. "But we're the All Hallows Club."

"What does that mean?" I frown. "Are you a gang?"

"Not exactly."

"A coven?"

Eddie grins. "Last I checked, there was only one witch in our ranks." He tips his chin. "For somebody so eager to join up, you don't know very much about us."

"I know you're the most secretive group of oddballs in existence." I hold his gaze so he can see how little I appreciate the enigma. "I had to go on a wild goose chase, hunting clues hidden in alcoves and between cracks in walls, just to figure out the initiation challenge was taking place in the graveyard. 'Meet me at midnight where the dead doth dwell, in All Hallows moonlight the clock shall knell.' Isn't that a little cliche for Halloween?"

"The cliche mystery is part of our charm." He winks obnoxiously. "Our *secretive* charm."

"Charm. Sure."

"Now you're catching on." Eddie's smile vanishes like a puff of smoke, revealing sudden seriousness. "Secrets and oddballs aside, you still want to join, even though you're scared out of your mind."

"I'm not scared."

Eddie sees through my lie in an instant. "Of course you are. You're scared of the graveyard, the darkness—but you're even more scared of something else." He leans in until we're face to face, his eyes as inky as the heavens. "You're terrified you'll never have another chance to figure out why you feel so alone: that you're lost forever, because your story isn't worth telling. It's an aimless shadow—just like you."

I bite back the urge to give voice to the fear and loneliness Eddie's assumptions unearth. Instead, I square my shoulders and ask, "How do you know anything about me?"

"Because all new initiates have a story, and we were *all* new initiates." Eddie's smile returns. "Remember now: cross the graveyard. Learn the secret of the lights. Meet the Club members at the far gate. Easy!" His gaze lands on the church clock. "It's almost time."

I look up, finding the clock face. Ten minutes to midnight. Dread drops into my gut, heavy as the mossy stones under my fingertips. "Any final strategies or tips before I—"

When I glance over my shoulder, Eddie is gone, swallowed entirely by the graveyard and the woods beyond.

"Come on, Ruby. Don't be afraid. This graveyard won't cross itself." Yes, pep talks are good. Especially since my only sympathetic companion abandoned me. Thanks, Eddie, you lousy good-for-nothing.

"Never too late to turn back," the raven muses. Erm, not the raven. Because stone doesn't talk.

"Shut up, bird-who-can't-speak-in-the-first-place." I have half a mind to throw one of these rocks at its face. "If my imagination is going to communicate through you, I could do without the negativity."

"Negativity? Really?" The raven's tone shifts in my mind, rendering it incredulous. I prefer malevolent, personally.

111

"I told you to shut up." Slowly, I slink away from my tombstone hideout, crawling on hands and knees across wet grass and slimy tree roots. The gate where I'm supposed to meet the Club lies across miles of endless gravestones.

Alright, not *miles*, but it looks that way from my perspective.

"Flying would be a nice bit of magic right about now." I glance over my shoulder at the raven before fog obscures its glossy wings. "I'll bet you wish you could fly. And talk. And do any of the things I've imagined you doing tonight."

"So imagine it, then. I'd love to fly."

Why has the bird developed a sense of humor when I'm about to face horrors unknown? Five minutes ago, it was intent on terrorizing me.

"Since you're a figment of my imagination, I don't have to do anything you say," I tell the raven. "Goodbye."

I slip across the graveyard, darting behind one tombstone to the lee of another. The further I venture into the cemetery, the older the markers become. Lettering that once was clear transforms into little more than scratches. I glance at the tombstone at my back, searching for a name, a date—but I'm frightened out of my wits by what I see.

Are those . . . *claw marks?*

"No. No, no, no." I dash under another decrepit piece of stone in the shape of a cross, claw marks not included. Leaning back, I gather myself, until—

CRACK

"Eek!" I roll away just in time. The top of the cross crashes where I rested my head mere moments ago. "That was a close one."

Quickly, I seek out a new tombstone in the midst of broken rubble. Ah, here we are! This one is sturdy, shaped like a rectangle, but I examine the edges and center just in case. No claw marks or hidden cracks. "What a relief."

The moonless sky thickens with clouds, and the wind shrieks through skeletal birches and elms in the forest beyond these graves. There's no safety out here. All any lurking monsters or ghouls have to do is sneak up to my hiding spot and snatch me. The only sanctuary is the locked, empty church that's as far from me as sunrise is from the next sunset.

"Why did I agree to do this?" I pose the question to myself. "The whole thing is a fool's errand."

"Yes, it is."

A voice.

A hollow, spectral voice.

I go numb with terror, turning my head slowly, slowly, until . . .

"*You?!*" I leap to my feet, staring slack jawed as my bone-chilling fear turns into disbelief, then shock. That belligerent raven! It's materialized on top of the broken cross that just tried to smash my head. "How did you get

112

down here? How are you *actually* talking?"

"You said flying would be a nice bit of magic," the raven replies through its disturbingly stationary beak. "I thought I'd try it."

"Obsidian ravens can't magically fly, or talk. Physically *or* telepathically. You're nothing but an apparition conjured by an agitated mind to menace me into giving up."

"Menace? That's not very nice."

"Please, stop talking."

"Perhaps you're only imagining me talking. But everything I'm saying is what you ought to be telling yourself." Glowing red eyes stare at me critically, like this bird statue believes I'm as silly and desperate as I feel. "All of this is nonsense, isn't it? You should go back to where you came from."

"Yes, I should. I've lost all sense, conversing with a stone bird. I need to get out of here."

"That's a good idea," the raven agrees. "The way you came in is just over there."

The bird turns stiffly on creaky joints, pointing its beak. The archway bearing the cemetery's name appears through a glimmer of silver fog.

"All Hallows Cemetery." I never noticed it before. "How very original."

"The Club is cliche, as you pointed out," the raven reminds me. "Not the kind of friends you want."

"Except I don't have any friends at all . . ."

Pain aches through every inch, reaching my fingertips and toes, until I give in to the misery of how alone I've been, how lost. A drifting soul with nowhere to turn, just existing, day-in and day-out, hoping I can find a sense of belonging and purpose. It's what led me to the All Hallows Club and this graveyard on Halloween night: to prove I have a story that's more than forlorn, aimless wandering. A story that's worth telling.

But is the Club the answer to all those things in the first place? Or is the truth buried somewhere else?

"These All Hallows delinquents make you do dangerous things to prove you're worthy of friendship." Can the raven read my thoughts, too? Everything else it does defies logic, why not mind reading? "Friends should accept you just as you are."

"I agree," I say.

"You do? That's a first." The raven's wings gleam a reflection of the starless sky. "Tell me, why are you still hanging around?"

"Is the answer another riddle I've got to solve?" I scoff. "I think I'll take Eddie and his poetry over you."

"Nevermore," the bird squawks. "Is that better?"

"No, it's not." I close my eyes, searching for the meaning behind a decision I have to make before it's too late. To stay and complete the challenge, and be initiated into the Club no matter the cost . . . or leave right now, always wondering why I wasn't worthy.

And yet—

Who decides my worth and purpose in coming here tonight? Eddie? This raven? The oddball Halloween club? Who decides how the night ends, and whether or not I'm truly alone?

Does the All Hallows Club tell my story, or me?

"This isn't just about the Club," I tell the raven. "If I cross the graveyard and solve the mystery of the golden lights, I *might* have friends. I *might* not be lonely anymore. *Might* isn't a good enough reason for everything I've gone through—but I have another reason to see it through. A better one."

The raven tilts its obsidian head. "Go on . . ."

"The initiation isn't about proving something to the Club. It's about proving something to myself." My voice grows stronger, steadier. I'm as assured of my own words as I've been of anything. "Even if I fail the challenges, even if I'm alone, I still faced what made me most afraid. Maybe that's the story I'm supposed to tell."

The raven hops up and down. "What will you do now, Ruby?"

"If I can do one thing that terrifies me, I can do a million things." Yes, *this*, at last, is my challenge. "The choice to stay or go is mine. But first, I'm learning the truth about those golden lights."

After all, who *wouldn't* be curious to know why the lights are so important to the Club?

"Nevermore, indeed."

Nevermore, really? "Can you stop saying—" But the raven's gone, vanished into thin air just like Eddie. "Of course the bird shows up with advice, then disappears. Is it named Eddie, too?"

I rise, standing tall, and look across the graveyard. The far gate remains scarcely visible through the fog. Yes, it's far—across a harrowing stretch of tombstones surrounded by funereal mist, a sight that sends shivers of horror down my spine—but I can do this. I *have* to face my fears. Forget the Club, this is for me. For Ruby. To prove I can write my own story: even something as terrifying as finishing my Halloween graveyard tale.

Swift as an eagle, I soar through row after row of tombstones, eyes on the far gate. No sign of the golden lights, just the church steeple and clock cutting a hole through the night. Where are the lights? I almost crash into a tall pillar with a weeping angel atop its zenith, but avert my eyes, and keep going.

"I'm going to make it." The far gate looms before me. "I did it. I faced my fear."

A smile parts my lips, and I almost wish Eddie and the raven were here so I could gloat my triumph, until—

"Hey, Kelsey, over here!"

Voices. Ones I don't know. They don't belong to Eddie and the raven, at any rate. But who are they?

I stop dead in my tracks, but can't see anything, not even outlines of forms or shapes in the blanket of fog.

"This is so stupid." A girl's voice trembles nearby. "Why did I let you convince me to do this? Do you scare the pants off every new kid at school, or am I special?"

A group of people laugh at her. "You chickening out, Kels?"

"Carter, Alex, Emma! Where are you?" The scared girl, Kelsey, calls into the night. Not only is she terrified, she's panicking. "Seriously, did you guys ditch me?"

I scan the graveyard, but I don't see anything that looks like golden lights. Are they real? Or did I get lured out here the way this girl Kelsey did, only to be abandoned by her so-called friends in the graveyard on Halloween?

"It's alright!" I attempt to cry out and reassure her, but the words come out strange. Instead of my normal voice, it's creaky, and cracks like the birch branches in the forest.

Just my bad luck! Spending all this time in the cold and fog is going to make me sick.

Sick . . .

I was sick not too long ago, wasn't I?

"What was that?!" Kelsey screams.

"Kels, did you hear one?" A second voice pierces the gloomy fog.

Hear one of what?

"I don't know, I d-don't know!" She chokes, stuttering and talking too fast all at once.

"What's going on?" Another voice joins in.

"Kelsey heard one!"

"I heard it, too!" One last voice joins the group.

I look around, frowning. What could she have heard? The graveyard has gone eerily silent.

"Can we just go home?" Kelsey sounds on the verge of tears. "I should have taken my little brother trick-or-treating instead of coming to this freaky old bone yard to look for ghosts."

Ghosts? I've seen a lot of things tonight, but not a ghost. Eddie and the talking raven certainly aren't ghosts.

Aren't they?

"Seriously, who makes their friends do a weird scavenger hunt for clues before leading them to a graveyard on Halloween?" Kelsey's trying her best to talk herself out of sticking around. Sounds familiar. "'Meet me at midnight where the dead doth dwell.' So dumb."

A strange sensation comes over me, something like the disembodied spirits she's hunting. *Meet me at midnight*—I thought those notes and clues were for me, left by the All Hallows Club. Were they left by Kelsey's friends for *her*?

Or were they somehow meant for both of us . . .

"Please, I'm begging you guys, let's *go!*" Kelsey sobs.

Poor girl, I know how she feels. Haven't I spent most of the night horrified by this place, too? At last, I spy her through the fog, huddled over with her arms around her middle. She needs a friend the way I've needed a friend—a real one, not somebody trying to scare her for a laugh or trick her into proving herself.

If her awful peers aren't going to comfort her, I will. I might not make it to the far gate by the last stroke of twelve, but I'm not worried about the Club's initiation. Helping her is more important.

I come to Kelsey's side, grinning when I reach for her shoulder. "Don't be afraid, I'll be your friend."

But my hand passes through her, as though my fingers are nothing more than air.

"SOMETHING JUST TOUCHED ME!" Kelsey pulls a cylindrical, red object from her back pocket.

Click—

Golden light floods my vision. First, Kelsey's. Then three more, one for each of her friends. Their eyes land on me, and widen, horrified. Every one of their faces turns the color of ash, and their mouths gape like caverns, steaming with shallow breaths on the verge of ceasing.

"What's going on?" I look between them, confused by their fear, and hold my hands up to my eyes. They shimmer in the golden light. Translucent.

The golden lights . . .

"A GHOST!" All four voices scream, brimming with the worst kind of horror.

A ghost.

I am a ghost.

The golden lights are flashlights. They belong to ghost hunters who come to this graveyard on Halloween.

I *was* sick recently, and I didn't get better. I only got worse.

The All Hallows Club isn't a club at all. It's a society of—

"Ghosts! Run! Before they attack! Run!"

Kelsey's so-called friends flee, their golden lights fading with them, but she stands, rooted and firm. A strange look crosses her face as she stares at me. It morphs from horror into defiance, then bravery . . . it's everything I felt tonight, too. We face each other in our truth, no longer afraid of what we might find waiting in the dark.

"You're not as scary as I thought you'd be," she says.

I shake my head and smile. None of this is as scary as we thought. Understanding flows between us until Kelsey smiles, too. "Those scaredy-cats think they're so cool, but *I'm* the one face-to-face with a ghost. Maybe I was meant to find you, so I wouldn't be afraid anymore."

Maybe I was meant to find you, too. I reach for her. Kelsey reaches back until the tip of my finger grazes hers.

"Kels!" A teenage voice cries. "Where are you?!"

"I gotta go." Kelsey spares me one last glance. "Thanks, ghost. I've got an unbelievable story to tell everyone."

I watch her go, alone but unafraid, until the golden lights are gone. Maybe, I helped her finish her Halloween story the way she helped me finish mine.

DONG

The church bell strikes the first toll of midnight, and it dawns on me I completed all the Club's challenges in time.

"Well done, Ruby."

Eddie materializes near the cemetery gate, the riddling raven perched on his shoulder. It's no longer carved obsidian, but a mystic, ethereal bird as haunted as the rest of the graveyard. It flaps its wings, a sound like dead leaves rustling across the tombstones.

"See, Ruby?" the raven says. "I could fly all along."

Yes. I see everything now.

"I know the truth about the lights, Eddie, and why I had to come here— I had to face my fears so I could tell my own story."

Eddie smiles, his dark eyes shining. "Like I said, all new initiates have a story, and we were *all* new initiates."

From the damp earth, more ghosts rise to join Eddie and I near the gate. Dozens of Club members welcome me into their ranks, spirits who once made the choice to stay in the graveyard on Halloween night: ones who, like me, needed to write their tales this side of midnight.

DONG . . . DONG . . . The bell tolls, counting down the seconds before Halloween ends. I meet Eddie's gaze with a measured look.

"What happens now?"

"Now you've got another choice." Eddie extends his hand. "You can stay with us and help new initiates every Halloween, or you can go your own separate way. Where that leads you, none of us can tell."

Stay, or go . . .

I did their challenge. I faced what made me afraid. The choice to stay or go is mine.

I chose to open up to Eddie and his raven, even though I was scared of rejection and being alone. I chose to cross the graveyard, even though I didn't know what I'd find on the other side. And I chose to help Kelsey stand up in front of her peers and face her fear, too.

How many people and ghosts are lost and fearful, in need of a friend as they traverse their darkest nights? How many stories do I have in me to tell?

After all, if I can do one thing that terrifies me, I can do a million things.

I reach out, take Eddie's hand, and nod.

The ghosts around me cheer, and Eddie grins, grasping my fingers as his raven hops up and down with excitement.

"Welcome, Ruby, to the All Hallows Club."

About the Author

When Haylie Hanson isn't writing stories about ghosts, she can be found drinking iced coffee and trying not to kill house plants. For more geeky fun that may or may not be Halloween related, follow Haylie on Instagram @therealhayliehanson, and visit www.hayliemhanson.com to sign up for her newsletter!

SINGLE EXTRA-LARGE GARBAGE BAG

HEATHER LINDAHL

I t was the rainstorm. Nothing else would have driven Dana inside the bustling café rife with assorted misfits perched in equally unkempt chairs. Avoiding the large counter, where all the germs were sure to live, she found a small table near the window. A harried waiter eyed her cleavage as she ordered a cup of coffee, black. Ignoring his lingering gaze, she dug into her bag.

Thick paper napkin—*spread across the surface to avoid contact.* Package of wet wipes—*left corner.* Disposable cup with lid—*front and center so no one touches.* Nitrile gloves—*only need one to pour the coffee, no need wasting the spare.*

Stale piss and tobacco assaulted her sinuses, warning her to lean towards the wall as one of the café's rancid customers stumbled past. He grabbed the back of her chair to stable himself. Dana went completely still even though every nerve screamed. He might have mumbled an apology, but she was too focused on the bag clutched in his right hand. 110th St. Mission. The rumored haunted orphanage that had been turned into a homeless shelter. A small shudder passed through her before she jerked her spine straight again.

She knew it wasn't just rumors. A dark magic, perhaps called forth by all the blood soaked into its foundation, permeated that place. She'd only allowed herself to set foot on those grounds twice since the orphanage closed when she was fourteen, just long enough to know the ghosts of the past were indeed still there.

Breathing through her mouth, she memorized the man. White male. 5'10". 163 lbs. Red and black flannel with a torn left sleeve at the elbow. Half-eaten package of chocolate covered mini donuts in his left hand. Stone washed jeans caked in over a year's worth of grime. White tennis shoes with a faded blue racing stripe—right sole flopping off at the toe. And an ill-fitting, grimy blonde toupee that had slid over one ear.

This time she calculated the supplies needed without even blinking.

Nitrile gloves - *at least six pairs needed, double glove to avoid filth.* Package of wet wipes—*if done right, only ten would be used.* Disposable poncho—*tuck sleeves into gloves to avoid using more wipes.* Shoe covers—*in this weather, two pairs would be necessary.* Extra-large black garbage bag—*one would be plenty if the joints were done carefully.*

The waiter made his way back as the truth slammed into her. She'd used her last garbage bag the night before. Dumping the coffee into her disposable cup, she sniffed the bitter liquid and sighed. Restocking supplies and hunting on the same day led to rushing, and rushing led to getting caught. Taking several sips of the black liquid, Dana let the bold heat wash away anything but discipline.

Suddenly, hands black with frostbite and putrescence slammed down on her table. The toupee slid off and hit her package of wet wipes as the man pushed his face within a foot of hers. His lips peeled back in a toothless grimace, ragged pieces of his gums and strings of spit wiggled like worms trying to escape a bird's clutches. His clouded blue eyes snapped into singular focus as he tilted his head.

"We're waiting in the boiler room."

Dana bolted to her feet, her disposable cup crushed in her fist. Ignoring the burn of the liquid dripping down her gloved hand, she stared at the man trying to see what his actual features were before decades of life on the streets wore him down to a discarded penny. It couldn't be him. That was impossible. But she'd know that voice anywhere. Her first.

Before she could force air through her increasingly dry throat, the man's eyes slid out of focus. He scooped up the toupee and attempted to affix it back on while mumbling about keeping the rainstorm out of his head. Shuffling away without even a second glance in her direction, he shouldered the coffee house door open and disappeared into the sheets of water.

Snatching up her bag, she bolted for the bathroom, desperate to scrub the encounter off her skin. Tap—*all the way hot, three pumps of soap. Wash— rinse—repeat twice more.* Strip glove off—*turn completely inside out to avoid contamination—toss in garbage.* Three pumps of soap—*wash—rinse—repeat twice more.*

As she held her hands under the scalding water for three counts of sixty seconds, she caught her own gaze in the mirror and let the heat burn the uncertainty away. He was dead. Nearly a decade ago, she had spent fourteen hours–an hour for every year of her life–separating his limbs and carving up his torso until only 3x3 inch pieces remained. Her first in so many things, he'd taught her all about fear, pain, violation and the sweet numb of reducing a man to a single extra-large garbage bag.

And every single lesson had been taught in the boiler room.

Shutting the water off with her wrist and grabbing paper towels in two sets of three, Dana slipped back into the café dining room to find the storm had spent itself into a light drizzle. Tossing the hood of her raincoat over her head, she flung herself into the dreary afternoon. It was time to go shopping.

***

Three nights later, Dana melted into the shadow of the giant maple tree in the crumbling courtyard of the 110th Street Mission, letting the calm of the night wash through her. She'd watched as the man from the coffee shop meandered in through the front door not long after she'd arrived. Lights out had been nearly two hours ago, and yet she waited, hands on the straps of her backpack. Mentally tallying the supplies inside, a wicked smile ghosted across her face as her fingertips brushed the hunting knife sheathed at the small of her back.

Finally relinquishing her post, Dana weaved through the overgrowth to the side door near where the storerooms once were. Making quick work of the old lock, she slipped inside and locked it behind her. A loud clang tore through the night, and she leapt behind a nearby stack of boxes. Again, the chime struck, and with it, the grimy wall she'd tucked herself against transformed into the cheery, bright yellow paint of her childhood.

Dana held still and waited as the old clock, long since defunct, finished ringing out the midnight hour and, she realized with a spark of glee, transformed her into her twelve-year-old self. It had been this way since that night; that night she'd ended it for all of them. If any of his remaining Lucky Thirteen set foot on the blighted 9x9 tiles again, the past claimed the present.

Brynn had been the one to find and warn her, only a few years after they'd all been scattered to the foster care system. The twins had snuck in, back when it still lay empty, too high to care about anything other than a place to hook up their next fix and found themselves right back where it all started.

She'd tested the abhorrent magic several times—never getting much further than where she stood now—finding herself caught in a Cinderella type spell where everything was real but only until the clock struck six am. Then time would unspool and return to the present. Each time, it had pulled her back into that night when she was fourteen—the one where changing her actions wouldn't make a difference—and so she'd quickly returned to avoiding this entire section of the city altogether.

But how could she refuse the invitation so flawlessly delivered by the vagrant at the coffee shop? Especially since the magic had finally brought her back to a time before that fateful night when she was fourteen.

She made it halfway down the hallway before the sharp slap of a trio of patent leather shoes approached from the nearby recreation room. Dana hid a groan and marched forward only to find her path blocked by Melanie and her toadies.

"What are you wearing, freak?" Melanie tossed her curly brown hair over her shoulder and smirked at Toady 1, who eagerly nodded.

Toady 2, not wanting to be left out, shoved her face into Dana's, motioning to the rain poncho she wore. "Is that a trash bag? The freak knows she's nothing but trash."

Melanie's face split into a triumphant grin as she shrieked a giggle. Dana's fingers curled, itching to reach for one of her blades and give Melanie a permanent smile. Instead, she did what twelve-year-old Dana had always done. Nothing.

The teenage tyrant circled her, flicking the poncho's hood off her head. "Maybe if you weren't so ugly, your mom wouldn't have dumped you here."

Georgia and Ryan stuck their heads out of the library door nearly twenty feet away and quickly disappeared again. No one was going to volunteer to come between Melanie and her favorite target. They were just grateful Dana took their place.

Melanie sunk her fingernails into Dana's arm and yanked her forward. "It's your lucky night, freak. *He* wants to see you."

A shiver crawled down Dana's back, spilling across her skin in goosebumps. That it would bring her back tonight of all nights. The night she'd learned the lesson of how easily a small body breaks beneath his hands. Her heart began to pound, but tonight it wasn't from fear.

She allowed herself to be pulled along down the windowless stretch of corridor. The twins slinked past, two sets of eyes refusing to meet hers. As Melanie and the Toadies herded her into the concrete stairwell lit only by a flickering overhead bulb, Dana was greeted by the cloying tendrils of mildew in the air and the five boys lining the tiny landing. They had their arms raised over their heads, fingers touching creating a skin lined tunnel of pre-teen B.O. the girls were forced to scramble through.

Dana twisted and contorted to avoid any true contact as the Five Musketeers—the boys' not so clever self-moniker—began to chant, "Boiler Room. Boiler Room. Boiler Room." She tucked her lips in between her front teeth to bite back a smirk. Within less than a year, they truly would be the Three Musketeers as two would never make it out of said boiler room.

It didn't take long to leave both the mildew crusted stairwell and the Five Musketeers behind. By the time they reached the heavy steel door, Dana was sure to have lasting half crescent divots in her arms from Melanie's nails. Toady 1 and Toady 2 wrestled the door open and Melanie dragged Dana inside where he stood, waiting. He stroked Melanie's face and praised her for being his best girl. Toady 1 and Today 2 lined up hoping for his scraps as Melanie basked in his approval.

Dana took the opportunity to tuck her hair back into the rain slicker, slide her pack to the floor and kick it into the nearest corner. At any moment, he would dismiss all but her and instruct Melanie to fetch little Tammy Jo in exactly 2 hours. Her fingers inched to the base of her spine and closed around the perfectly balanced handle of her hunting knife. If she did this just right, she could save more than one life tonight.

Closing her eyes, she counted her heartbeats–*1, 2, 3, 4, 5, 6, 7, 8, 9, 10*– until the slamming of the door announced she was finally alone with him. The choking scent of his aftershave coated her throat as he stepped into her space and leaned forward. Still, she counted–*30, 31, 32, 33, 34, 35, 36, 37, 38, 39, 40*. His fingers plucked at her poncho in an unspoken question, and she smiled–*50, 51, 52, 53, 54, 55, 56*.

Her eyes snapped open and honed in on his pulse beating wildly on the side of his throat. "60."

He never saw it coming. Just like the first time. But this time, she was practiced, efficient, each movement effortless despite being in an untrained body. This time, she dragged him over to the unfinished floor and allowed him to watch his life drain out while she worked. And this time, despite pausing two hours in to send five-year-old Tammy Jo back to bed unscathed, it only took her five hours to pack him into one extra-large garbage bag.

Standing and stretching, free from all her protective wear, Dana felt an odd warmth spread through her chest. Unbidden laughter poured from her lips until she could barely stand. The blood-soaked, hardened earth beneath her feet remained undisturbed. No small mounds calling the sudden adoptions of other children a lie.

The magic had brought her back in time to save them all.

Dana retrieved her pack, quickly slipped through the now quiet orphanage and stole outside, breaking the spell. Checking her watch by the light of the moon, she confirmed that only one hour had passed. She could feel over a decade of new memories flood in and bared her teeth triumphantly. But he hadn't acted alone.

One down. Twelve to go.

About the Author

Heather is a writer of all things paranormal and magical realism, a foodie chef, and an obsessive seashell collector. When she isn't writing stories or taking care of her family of rescued cats, she can be found playing Dragon Age, watching Forensic Files, or walking on the beach. Share a cup of coffee and spill the murder tea on Instagram @heatherclindahl.

A WITCH WITH A CURFEW

FALLON WILLOUGHBY

The house loomed out of the dark, a black stain against the night sky. An old Victorian, its tall tower blocked the stars and seemed to absorb their light. Leaning onto the pillow I'd put in the back seat, I rubbed my eyes, tired from the strain of watching this blasted haunted mansion for yet another night. My phone buzzed in my pocket, and I scrambled to sit up and pull it out. Almost midnight. I was going to miss curfew again. My parents were already messaging to check on me. Judging by all the exclamation points, Mom wasn't going to be happy.

The only thing that kept me from growling out cuss words was the fact that I was trying to be quiet. I got out of the backseat, heading to the driver's seat to go home. It was just then that I heard the sound—something like footsteps on concrete. Tensing, I stopped moving, trying not to make any noise. It had to have been someone walking near the house. I slowly turned on my heel, looking back towards the mansion—a two story monstrosity that had been abandoned a decade before when the old couple who'd lived in it died mysteriously one night.

Rumors said their ghosts still made mischief there, and kids liked to dare each other to explore it in the dark. A couple of weeks ago on Halloween night, a nineteen-year-old was murdered in the empty mansion. Probably went in there on a dare. The cops had no leads and no witnesses. Whoever had murdered him disappeared.

The ghost stories were true, though. I knew that Emma and Edward haunted the place. Edward liked to throw his toupee at intruders (not that it did anything), as he was a grouchy old man who had probably yelled "Get off my lawn" while he was alive. Their mysterious deaths? Not so mysterious—they were just old, and tall tales had gotten the times wrong– the wife died two months after the husband.

That's what comes from my "gift" of being a witch. An odd witch at that, given that my powers run towards death. Not that I killed people. No, I can just see it. Sense it. I know when someone has died within a few miles of me, and as I've gotten older, that sense has grown. I feel them, and if I get close enough to a body, I can see their last moments. Ghosts, who know I can see them, love to talk to me. Some of them love to annoy me in public, as I try desperately to ignore their existence. No one likes looking crazy.

My parents didn't know what I was doing, but I did have to follow curfew–21-year-old college student or not–while I lived at home. This case though . . . the guy had been a few years below me in school, and I didn't remember much about him. But I really wanted to know what had happened. Unfortunately, I hadn't managed to get close enough to touch the body and see his last moment. Now, I was waiting and hoping his ghost would come to the mansion, to haunt it as Edward and Emma had.

I hadn't moved, and I hadn't heard any more footsteps. Had I been so lost in my own thoughts that I missed it? Crap. I leaned against my car and studied the house. No one had come down this road, and it dead-ended past the mansion. The town wasn't far off, so some light trickled down the street but that was it. No one had come this way via the sidewalks. So, what had made that noise?

I pondered walking up to the house. There was still a murderer on the loose, and whether I knew ghosts on the inside or not . . . it seemed foolish to risk it.

Snap.

Creaaak.

Almost dropping my phone, I peered into the dark. There had been crime scene tape around the doors. The police searched the area for days, hoping to find clues.

Could it be someone who knew something? Crime scene tape was fluttering in the wind, no longer attached to the door. Had someone entered? Should I really trespass a crime scene and risk getting arrested for answers?

Would the killer really come back here, even after the cops had marked it off?

Then again, that was how some of them got caught. They liked to . . .

Then again, maybe I'd been reading too many crime novels . . .

I looked back at my car, then down at my phone that had buzzed more times than I could count as my parents texted me. Clenching and unclenching my hands, I tapped out a quick message that I would be home soon and started towards the house, cursing my stupidity the entire way. If I was going to help solve the murder, I had to find that kid's ghost.

Besides, it could just be an animal. Or something falling. Or the wind.

I repeated that over and over in my head as I trudged up the hill towards the house, avoiding the easy steps in plain view of the front door. Odds were if someone was here, they knew I was too. But no reason to make it easy for them. I mean, you zig and zag, right?

It was even darker up here close to the house, and a deeper dark section indicated where the front door should be closed. Crime scene tape flapped in the wind and draped across the porch. I tried peering in to see if I saw any movement, and the lights flickered. Freaking flickered in the kitchen—Emma and Edward's favorite room. With a deep breath, I threw myself into the house, and ran into the kitchen.

Where Emma and Edward were dancing about, laughing.

"Seriously, guys? Don't you have anything better to do?" I asked, glaring.

"Callie! Our favorite person," they said as they continued dancing.

With a heavy sigh, I leaned against the wall. Since I was here . . .

"Have you guys seen the young man who was murdered here?"

"Terrible business, that. Glad we weren't around for it," Emma said. They twirled about the room some more.

Ghosts can wink across planes, or so they tell me. I don't know what any other plane looks like, but apparently, they aren't bound here. Some of them just enjoy the chaos of making mischief (playing with lights that shouldn't turn on, having objects fly, making you think you hear someone talk) like Emma and Edward, or they have unsolved issues, or they can't let go of their life, or are afraid of what is next. At least those were all the reasons I knew for why ghosts refuse to move on.

Edward and Emma stopped across the island and leaned against it, smiling at me. "What is new in this mortal realm, my darling?" Emma asked, as Edward followed with, "We've been having a blast since Halloween."

"Nothing new, now have you seen the young man?"

"Nathaniel? He's in the bedroom he was killed in."

"WHAT?" I yelled. Then, remembering someone else might be around, I whispered, "Why didn't you say that in the first place?"

"Simmer down," Edward said, tossing his toupee at me. It flew through my side, a feeling much like that of a cold chill up and down your spine coming over me. Most people wouldn't have noticed it at all.

I glared, and he came over to pick it up. "You'll spoil the mood. And I told you, didn't I?"

Giving up, I shook my head at them, and then turned towards the staircase. The lights were out, so I clicked on the flashlight on my phone. I thought about asking Edward to make the lights come on, some ghostly magic I didn't understand that allowed them to manipulate the world around them as they gained strength, but decided I didn't want anyone else to see and start poking around. At the top of the stairs was a wide landing and several rooms. I knew, though, that Nathaniel had been in the bedroom closest to the stairs, so I went in that direction.

"Nathaniel?" I called out hesitantly.

I heard a muffled squeak that almost sounded like a mouse and then nothing, then another squeak like someone trying not to make noises and failing.

I pushed open the door and found Nathaniel on the covers, looking like he had tried to pull them over him and hide. His hands were up by his head, like he was holding onto covers over his face.

I decided to announce myself with facts, "Sorry, it takes a long time for ghosts to manipulate the world—and even then, most aren't good enough for that."

He looked up, realizing the covers hadn't moved.

"My name is Callie."

"You went to my school," he said as recognition dawned on his face.

"Yep."

"You can see me?"

This was a common question with new ghosts I ran across. Another conversation I was tired of having.

"Yes. And I've been hoping you would come. I wanted to find out if there was anything I could tip to the cops."

Nathaniel sat up at this. "Tip?"

"About your murder. About who killed you."

"Killed me? I wasn't . . ." His eyes turned kind of glassy, and he zoned out.

My phone vibrated again, and I switched it to silent. I hoped I had enough battery to last through this.

"Nathaniel?"

His body shivered, and his eyes refocused on me. He shook his head. "It doesn't matter. You can go. Don't worry about it."

"What?"

"Don't worry about it," he repeated. "Cops wouldn't believe a girl who sees ghosts anyways."

"Hey, I've successfully tipped them off a few times now without saying anything about talking to ghosts."

"Look, just leave, okay?" He stood up, agitated, pacing in the small room.

"I don't understand . . ."

Then . . . I heard a sound. Someone was coming up the stairs. A few seconds later, the back of Edward appeared in the hall outside the bedroom door, a silvery outline lighting him in the darkness.

"I said get! Go! Get out of my house," Edward shouted towards the stairs before turning back to me. "A boy, Callie. Hide!"

There wasn't more than a second, and I didn't have a chance. The guy came shuffling into the room, looking freaked out. Then, he noticed me standing beside the bed.

Damn. I should have turned off the flashlight.

"What are you doing here?" he asked, his voice vibrating with false bravery. He was skinny, wearing all black, but with blonde hair so pale it was almost shocking in the dark. I couldn't see his face well, with my little amount of light.

I paused, unable to say, "Talking to a ghost." I looked at Nathaniel, and realized he was looking at the guy in front of me like he knew him.

I finally settled on, "I was curious. Why are you here?"

"Uh. I was dared."

"Well, dare achieved. You can leave."

But the guy's eyes kept darting around the room. He looked worried, but I couldn't make out much in the dim lighting my flashlight gave me.

"Everyone okay in here?" Emma's ghostly voice nearly sent me jumping off the bed. I hadn't expected it. The sound was followed by her shadowy form appearing beside her husband in the doorway.

The guy gave me an odd look, which I understood since I seemed to be jumping out of my skin for no reason. I just nodded vaguely at the door, unable to say anything. "You okay, dude?"

"Dude" nodded his head, not looking at me. He answered with, "Yeah. I uh, might stay for a while. You can go."

Nathaniel hadn't stopped looking at the guy in front of us. I had an idea.

"You know a guy was killed in here, right?"

I heard a shuffle of feet from him.

"What's your name?" I asked again.

"Why do you want my name?"

His voice had gotten hard on that sentence, and I thought he looked surer now.

"No reason. Just hard to talk to you without it."

He shook his head. "No dice. Leave."

"No. I have unfinished business."

"Well, so do I."

There was a tense silence. I was also trying very hard to ignore Emma and Edward, who were now dancing on the landing. It was sweet they had checked on me, even tried to warn, but really? Dancing?

"Corey . . ."

I looked at Nathaniel, and realized he was trying to get Corey's attention. It wouldn't work, and I didn't want to reveal what I could do. There were other options though.

"If you were just coming up here on a dare, then what do you need to do?"

"Look, it doesn't matter. Just leave me alone in here, okay?"

"No, I won't, Corey."

I heard his gasp, and then saw him come closer into the light.

"How did you know my name?"

"Because you knew Nathaniel."

"How the hell did you know that or Nathaniel?"

I paused. Okay, so clearly that wasn't my best idea, but I don't like being told what to do. And besides, if "Corey" was a murderer, he was a pretty scrawny one.

"Look," he said, stammering, "you need to leave."

Something glinted in his hand. A gun. He wasn't pointing it at me, but he had it at his side. Which wasn't good considering he wavered between being brave and scared shitless. My phone screen lit up again.

"What was that?"

"My parents are furious I'm not home."

He smirked. "Go home, then."

"I . . ."

But as I started to speak, Edward came in, flitting about the room. My eyes followed him, curious, and distracted.

"You what?" Corey asked, moving the gun closer to his side.

I held my hands up, and replied, "I just wanted to find out who killed Nathaniel, is all. I can go."

And just like that, the gun came up. *Yep. Should have kept my mouth shut.*

"How did you plan to do that?" Corey asked, his voice angry.

Nathaniel moved closer to us, standing by Corey. He was shaking his head.

"I told you to leave it alone." Nathaniel whispered to me.

This was the first time I'd had a gun pointed at me. I had to say, I wasn't fond of it. Maybe I should quit the ghost helping business unless specifically asked? Though that had got me in trouble too . . .

Oh hell. Screw it.

"I can see him. Nathaniel. His ghost is here. It's how I knew your name. And he seems to be worried about you."

Corey's eyes flicked back and forth, looking around the room.

"You can see him? Is he okay?" his voice sounded small this time.

Nathaniel nodded. "I'm fine."

"He says he is, yes. But Corey . . ."

An odd suspicion was coming to me. Corey had been coming here alone with a gun. That didn't bode well. "Corey, what are you wanting to do with that gun?"

"What?" Corey asked, his voice a whisper. He looked at the gun in his hand. "I . . ."

Nathaniel's eyes went wide, and he looked at me, really looked at me for the first time. "Don't let him. Tell him not to worry."

"Nathaniel says not to worry. Corey, what happened?"

Corey raised the gun again, pointing it at me. Then himself. Then he started looking around the room. "Nathaniel, are you really here?"

I wasn't afraid for my life anymore, and I really hadn't thought Corey would do it before. But now I was afraid for him. Nathaniel was trying to show Corey he was there by waving his hands in his face. I shook my head.

"He's too weak to do anything to prove he's here. New ghosts can't interact with our world very well."

"Then how do I know you're telling the truth, huh?"

Corey aimed the gun back at me, but it wasn't straight. I thought for a minute, then looked at Edward who was still on the other side of the room. I raised an eyebrow.

"HOO DOGGY!" Edward shouted, and suddenly the lights flickered in the room.

Nathaniel jumped, and so did Corey, who looked at me startled and terrified. "He's really here?"

I nodded.

"Nathaniel, I'm so sorry. I'm so sorry." He crumpled to the floor, and held the gun, looking down the barrel.

"Nathaniel, you better tell me quickly what happened." I looked at him desperately, unsure how I was going to stop this.

He had leaned over Corey, and I saw him try to hold him.

"Were you two here together?"

Corey and Nathaniel both answered yes. Nathaniel kept talking.

"We met here, once a week. We . . . we were together. But Corey's parents didn't know. And . . . we . . ."

Corey's cries got louder, and I saw the gun move.

"COREY!" I shouted. Edward decided to help and made the table move a bit. Corey shook all over, but the gun stopped moving.

"You were in love with him, weren't you?"

Corey nodded.

"What happened?"

"He fell. We were getting ready to leave when he tripped and fell and hit the table. Hard. It all happened so fast. I tried to check his pulse, but there was so much blood. I couldn't feel anything, and if I'd been caught here . . . Man, my parents would kick me out of the house. I'd have nothing. So, I ran. I ran and then when I was far enough, I called the ambulance from a store phone."

Nathaniel was now crying, silver tears running down his face. I walked over to Corey and bent down even with him on the floor.

"It's not your fault. It was a terrible accident."

"I don't blame him, I was gone pretty quickly, anyways." Nathaniel had that faraway look in his eyes again.

"Nathaniel doesn't blame you. Says he'd probably still be dead. He doesn't want you to die too."

"But I don't have him. I don't have anyone who . . ."

I gently reached out and took the gun from his hands. He let me take it. I slid it across the floor. I'd need to wipe it clean and get it out of here.

"Corey, it wasn't your fault. And there are people out there who will be there for you. Maybe not your parents, but there are plenty of us who will help you."

I sat beside him and held him while he cried. Nathaniel sat opposite me, watching. As the grandfather clock in the basement chimed midnight, Nathaniel began to fade. He faded more with each tone, and I realized that he no longer needed to stay here. His unsolved business had been solved.

"Tell him I love him. And there is someone else in this world he is meant to find."

"I will," I whispered. As the twelfth tone rang, Nathaniel faded out completely, gone from this world. I didn't know if ghosts went to another plane when they left, or heaven or hell, or where exactly their souls wound up. But I hoped for him, it was somewhere wonderful.

My parents buzzed my phone again, so I messaged back I was safe. They'd really lose it after this. But I'd saved a life today, and sort of solved a murder.

Now to face my parents . . .

About the Author

College Professor by day, Fallon Willoughby is a mom/wife/writer and more by night! For more fantasy and chaos, follow her at @fallonwilloughby on TikTok.

THE
NEXT
CHAPTER

CAIT MARIE

Chapter 1
LILA

The soft clinking of something hitting Lila's window woke her from a dead sleep. She blinked, trying to let her eyes adjust enough to figure out what was going on. Her bedroom was still dark, save for the small light she always left on in the corner. She rolled over and grabbed her phone from the other side of the bed. Squinting at the bright screen, she groaned. It wasn't even midnight yet.

After an exhausting day working at the Summer Scoop, she'd come back to her parents' house and promptly passed out. Tomorrow was the first day of summer, which was their excuse to have all sorts of deals, along with a bunch of fun games and activities down on the beach below the ice cream shop the whole weekend. One would have thought it was the Fourth of July or something with how many families and groups of friends had gathered around the lake. Lila hadn't stopped moving the entire day. Her feet and legs ached so much. She'd wanted to soak in a warm bath when she got here, but she'd been too tired and opted to collapse in bed instead.

Something tapped her window again, and she sat upright. Her heart hammered in her chest as she stared at the glass.

Until it happened again, reminding her of the first time she heard that sound five years ago. Then, her pulse started racing for a whole new reason. With a grin, Lila flipped her sheet off and all but jumped out of bed.

She ran to the window on bare feet. Looking down, she spotted a lone figure standing in the grass. Her stomach fluttered at the sight. Even after all these years, Gavin Miller, the boy next door, still had this effect on her.

Lila unlocked the window and pushed it up. "Aren't you supposed to be in Texas?"

He'd said he would be gone a couple more days. There was just enough moon and starlight to see his beautifully crooked smile as he shrugged. "I missed my girl, so I decided to come home early. Think you can sneak out?"

She chuckled, nodding. "I think I can manage."

"Need me to get the ladder?"

"You know, I think I'm good. I'll be right there," she said. The first time he'd shown up in the middle of the night, he'd climbed up here to convince her to go swimming at midnight with some of his friends so she could check it off her summer bucket list. That felt like an entire lifetime ago.

Grabbing her cardigan off the back of the desk chair, she crept down the stairs of her childhood home. She slid into her flipflops before slipping out the front door. The cool, night air greeted her, and she took a deep, refreshing breath.

"It's not as fun when you use the door," a deep voice said just as she saw his phone's flashlight dancing over the grass that would soon be covered in dew. It might have been summer officially tomorrow, but Indiana had not received the memo. Throughout the day, it had been warm. Once that sun went down though, she swore the temperature dropped twenty degrees.

Lila ran toward Gavin. As she wrapped her arms around the back of his neck, he hauled her up against his chest, their lips meeting without hesitation. She felt the kiss all the way to her toes. He turned in a small circle, holding her as close as possible for one moment, then another. When he finally lowered her to the ground, he still didn't release her.

"Hi," she whispered.

"Hi." Gavin pressed another kiss to the corner of her mouth. "I missed you so much."

"It's only been a couple weeks." Normally, she would have laughed at his dramatics, but she couldn't right now. Not when she'd felt such a deep void in his absence herself. It was as if a part of her had been taken away, and it was so strange to function without him beside her.

He brought a palm up to her cheek. "I don't care. It was way too long."

Letting out a breath, she asked, "When did we become this obnoxious, codependent couple?"

"I think that was about four and a half years ago." He backed up just enough to hand her his phone and help her into her sweater. "After that first semester apart, when I returned for winter break."

Once her cardigan was on, he draped an arm around her shoulders and led her toward the side of the house. He was in his own sweatshirt, which she planned to steal before the night was over, and a pair of jeans, making her feel better about being in her pajama pants and, incidentally, one of his old baseball shirts from high school.

"Where are we going?" she asked as they walked between their families' houses and to the open backyards that butted up to the woods.

"You'll see."

She already had an idea of where he was taking her, but she let him have this one. They passed their old treehouse, confirming her suspicions. She still held his phone with its light leading the way. These little gestures—him giving her the flashlight because of her phobia of the dark without needing to say anything—always made her heart swell. Even after twenty-three years of friendship.

One would think she would get used to it, but that didn't happen.

They reached the break in the trees. The clearing beyond that ended in their small version of a cliff stretched out before them.

It was their spot.

As children, they had often taunted one another about being too scared to get close to the edge, resulting in them proving that they could do it and then getting in trouble by their parents. A lot. To the point where her father built them the treehouse as an alternative.

As teenagers, they came out here to sit and watch the sunrise the morning before her big surgery.

Memories flooded her from that summer, clogging her throat. Her eyes burned from fighting back tears.

When they neared the flat area they liked to visit, her breath shuddered out in a half-sob, half-laugh. A thick blanket was spread out, and there were a few lanterns, a cooler, and a handful of pillows set up for them. Gavin moved to turn on one of the small battery-powered lanterns, and she turned off the light on his phone as she took a seat. He must have prepared all of this before going to get her.

"I can't believe you did this." She curled into his side when he lowered next to her.

He kissed her temple, and she shut her eyes. "It's been five years."

"I know."

Granted, the five-year anniversary of that day was last week, but he'd been out of town. And she knew just how much that ate away at him. He hadn't been able to get out of his work trip though. Well, he probably could have, but she'd insisted he go. Becoming the team physician for the Bennu Firebirds baseball team had been a dream come true for him. She wasn't going to let him jeopardize that or miss out on games and tournaments. Not when they could see each other shortly after that special date.

Gavin turned to the cooler to pull out a bottle of champagne and a couple of plastic flutes. As he opened it and poured them each a glass, Lila stared at twinkling stars high above them, reveling in this moment she never imagined she would be able to experience. At least, not with the man beside her.

Handing her the bubbly drink, he turned to face her. He held his own up. "To being cancer free."

Her eyes swam with happy tears as she whispered, "Cancer free."

Chapter 2

GAVIN

After a celebratory sip of his champagne, Gavin set his flute on top of the cooler. He took a deep breath and faced Lila. The tears in her eyes made his chest ache, even though he knew they were from happiness. When a couple spilled over, rolling down her cheeks, he scooted closer and brushed them away with his thumbs.

They'd waited so long for this moment. The doctors didn't like to use the phrase *cancer free* because there was always a chance it could return, but they'd been told that at five years, the odds of that happening went way down. For now, Lila was in the clear.

She held out her cup for him to put aside too and then snuggled up against him. He wrapped his arm back around her as they sat in blissful silence. Only the familiar sounds of a summer night surrounded them—the buzzing cicadas and croaking frogs, an owl hooting occasionally in the distance. There were few things he enjoyed more in this life than sitting out here under the stars with the woman he loved.

"You know, I was almost to the apartment before I remembered you were staying here tonight," he said in a soft tone.

Her shoulders shook with quiet laughter. "Really?"

"Yep. Totally forgot." He'd been too distracted, mentally running through the list of everything he needed for tonight. His heart raced in his chest, and he wondered if she could feel it.

Lila leaned away enough that they could see each other in the dim light. Her smile eased some of his anxiety. Lifting a hand to her cheek, he pushed a strand of her newly dyed red hair behind her ear. It reminded him of when he had helped her make it pink just after high school. It had been just one of the things on her summer bucket list.

The list she wanted to complete before having her brain tumor removed.

The list that brought them back together after years of arguing and pushing each other away.

"I love you," he whispered.

"I love you too." She closed the distance between them, pressing her lips to his. Gavin pulled her to him. He'd missed her so much the past couple weeks.

He broke the kiss way too soon for his liking, but he needed to tell her more. Wiping his sweaty palm on his hoodie, he reached into the pocket and withdrew the folded piece of paper.

"I made a new list," he said.

"Oh?" She raised a brow, grabbing her champagne once more to sip on it.

He nodded. "In honor of it being five years, I thought it might be fun to create another bucket list."

"Sounds fun. What's on it?" She tried to grab it, but he held it away. Rolling her eyes, she waved her hand, indicating he go on.

Gavin cleared his throat and opened the paper. Could she tell his hands were shaking? "In no particular order—"

"Are they all for this summer?"

"No, most will take some time to work up to." He dramatically cleared his throat again. "Take a trip to another country."

"Ooh, it's the fancy adultier list," she said, waggling her eyebrows. "Where are we going?"

"Wherever you want. Now, hush. Let me read," he said. When she agreed, he leaned in to peck her on the cheek once before continuing. "Go skydiving. Hike up a mountain. Go to Times Square. Go camping with all our friends. Take a cooking class together. Get matching tattoos. Kiss in the rain."

Lila grinned. "We've already done that one."

He remembered very clearly. It was the same day they kissed for the first time, and the day he confessed he'd been in love with her for years.

Gavin and Lila were born exactly three days apart, and their parents were best friends, which meant the two grew up side by side. But some horrible miscommunication and the idiotic brain of a pre-teen boy led to them falling out in middle school. Just after high school, they'd been forced to work in his mom's ice cream shop, where he came across her summer bucket list and knew it might be his last chance at reconciliation.

On a trip to Chicago, things had sort of blown up, and mid-fight, he had kissed her for the first time. He then told her everything, clearing up the past, and they continued on their mission to check items off her list. That included going to a paintball park that afternoon, where it had started to rain as they finished up. He distinctly remembered grabbing her in the parking lot and kissing her against the car. That had been the moment he knew without a doubt that things were finally going to work out for them.

It was the day before she ended up in the hospital and he found out she was sick. She'd been hiding it from everyone for six months. Seeing her in that bed, hooked up to an IV and various monitors, had nearly broken him. It was an image he could never fully scrub from his mind.

He pushed those scary memories aside to focus on the present. "Well, it was fun, and I want to do it again."

Nodding, she smiled. "What else?"

Gavin looked down at the paper, but he knew what the last few items were without needing to read them. His chest constricted, making it difficult to keep his breathing steady, and he clenched the list tighter.

"Get a bigger place to live," he started.

"Definitely." She chuckled and set her flute down again.

After their first year at Maslair University, they'd rented an apartment just off campus. They'd moved a couple times as they finished school and then returned to Summersville to find a new place when they graduated. There hadn't been many options in their small town though, so they were stuck with the tiniest one bedroom he'd ever seen. Most of their belongings had gone to their parents' houses until they could find something bigger.

They had debated whether to search for one closer to Bennu; it was a pain driving an hour and a half to work. But with Lila wanting to take over the Scoop one day, they decided to stay in their small town. Besides, neither were eager to leave their friends and family.

Regardless, he didn't mean they should get just a bigger apartment.

"Buy a house with more than one bedroom," he added in a hushed tone.

Lila met his gaze, and he wondered, not for the first time, what he ever did to deserve her. His beautiful, sweet, smart girlfriend.

The thought nearly made him choke up.

Hopefully, that was the last time he'd ever call her his girlfriend. Even if it had only been in his head.

The love and understanding swirling in her brilliant blue eyes gave him the confidence to go on.

"Have children," he whispered, folding the paper and returning it to his pocket. Instead, he grabbed the small box in there. "Get married."

"Gavin . . ."

"I love you, Lila." He pulled the box out, and she sucked in a breath. "You're my best friend and my other half. I want to keep having adventures with you for the rest of our lives. Because when we're together, I know we can do anything. We can beat the odds and take on the world. We can be our best selves. We can cross off everything on all the lists we ever make."

Popping open the lid, he showed her the ring inside. The princess-cut diamond was set in a silver band with swirling lines of smaller gems spreading out from either side. It was simple but beautiful. And more than anything, it held meaning. The decision to use his grandmother's ring was one of the easiest he'd ever made.

"Lila Weston, will you marry me?"

LILA

Literal crickets filled the silence as Lila stared at Gavin in shock. Sure, she'd hoped they would reach this point, but she hadn't expected it to happen so soon.

Gavin—always optimistic and cheerful Gavin—waited, and then waited some more. When she didn't respond, his smile slipped, breaking her heart.

Moving quickly, she lunged at him, crawling into his lap to wrap her arms around him. She buried her face against the side of his neck and nodded as the tears returned in full.

"Yes," she whispered.

He held her to him, hugging her tightly. His chest rumbled beneath her with quiet laughter. "That was so mean. I thought . . ."

"Sorry." She sniffled and sat back to see him. Wiping her damp cheeks with the ends of her sleeves, she said, "I just—I wasn't expecting this. Not tonight."

Her words cut off, and she covered her face with both hands. He pressed a kiss to her forehead. "So, yes?"

"Yeah," she said with another chuckle before lowering her hands to his chest. She kissed him once, twice. "Yes, I will absolutely marry you, Gavin."

He reached for her left hand. Butterflies cascaded through her stomach as she watched him slide the ring onto her finger. It took her breath away. Turning, she sat sideways in his lap, resting her head on his shoulder and raising her hand. The familiar diamond twinkled in the light of the lantern.

"Grandma Joan's?"

Gavin nodded, winding his arms around her. "She gave it to my mom, who gave it to me."

Lila remembered the older woman well. She'd come to stay with the Millers a lot when they were younger. First because her own husband had passed and she didn't like being alone. Then, when Gavin's father started going on more and more extended work trips, leaving him and his mother by themselves all the time.

Despite being his mother, Grandma Joan hadn't approved or tolerated the man's neglectful behavior. She'd made that more than clear, sparking many arguments over the years. At least, until she passed. Lila and Gavin had been fourteen, and it was one of the very rare times they'd set aside their differences. She'd stood next to him at the funeral, never leaving, never speaking. She just held his hand as they both cried. It was the first and only funeral Lila had ever attended in her twenty-three years.

"She would have been thrilled to know it's now yours," Gavin said, making her smile. "She loved you like her own grandchild."

"I miss her crazy laugh." Lila could still hear it.

Gavin let out an obnoxious, high-pitched imitation of the noise, and Lila snorted. He did it again. "Do you remember when she taught us to play poker?"

"Your mom was so mad."

"Because she thought your parents were going to be upset." He trailed a hand down her arm to entwine their fingers. Lila's dad and Gavin's mom grew up together and had always been thick as thieves. When the former got married though, the latter then became best friends with his wife—Lila's mom. The three were nearly as inseparable as their children.

"My dad was so excited though," Lila said, remembering how he'd shocked them all by starting to play with them.

Gavin's lips brushed the side of her head. "We need to follow that tradition with our kids someday."

"We'll invite him over, make him bring the pennies to bet with," she said with a grin. It was strange to think about having children, but at the same time . . . she wanted that with Gavin more than just about anything in the world. She could picture their little family at the ice cream shop and going to ball games at Bennu.

"And the snacks."

She laughed again but nodded in agreement.

Five years ago, talking about this would have sent her into a spiral. She'd been so afraid of not having a future that she refused to think about it. Now, she didn't want to stop imagining their life together.

But she also knew how important it was to live in the present too.

There were infinite possibilities ahead of them, and she wanted to experience as many as she could with the man holding her in his arms. She wanted to cross off everything on their new list and then continue adding to it for as long as they lived.

When she yawned, Gavin pulled out his phone, showing the time. Midnight.

"It's officially summer," she whispered.

"A new day." He kissed her brow. "A new season." Another kiss brushed her cheek. "A new fiancée." His lips found hers, and her heart felt as if it might burst from joy. Pulling away, he handed her the champagne once more to make another toast. "To another five years?"

"And so many more after that." She clinked her cup against his, ready to marry her best friend and start their next chapter together.

About the Author

Young adult/new adult author Cait Marie has enjoyed reading and creating stories her entire life. Her debut novel, *The Lost Legends*, released in 2020, and since then, she's been publishing and writing in a variety of genres. From adventurous fairy tales to fluffy romance to dystopian sci-fi, and everything in between, she enjoys it all. For more, please visit caitmarieh.com/links and be sure to follow her on social media!

MIDNIGHT MAGIC

GLORIA HERDT

My mother says nothing good happens after midnight. Yet, on the eve of my twenty-first birthday, I'm out to prove her wrong. I sit on the front steps of her cozy Cape Cod, fanning myself so my hair doesn't frizz. My favorite yellow sundress hugs my rib cage then relaxes at my waist. I inhale deeply. The dress may only create the *illusion* of long legs and full breasts, but I'll take it.

Through the glass door, I catch my mother—her long-haired chihuahua at her heels—sneaking into the dimly lit kitchen to fill her water glass. *Again.* I'm only home for the summer, and even though she says I'm an adult—free to make my own decisions—her tone tells me otherwise.

The sun has gone to bed. And she wishes that I would, too.

I sigh heavily. Usually, I'm in bed by nine. The perfect student, gracious daughter, model citizen and devout rule follower.

But tonight, Torin called.

My skin prickles with heat at the memory.

Cooped up in my role of well-disciplined student and daughter, I rarely know what it's like to jump off a cliff and fly.

But when I'm with him, I hear the whispered secrets of my unfurled wings.

I check my linen bag again, my jittery fingers brushing past my Nokia phone, wallet, brush, and—at the farthest depths—my glasses in a case. Only for dire emergencies.

Yawning, I imagine my plush bed. The balmy air—typical of August on Long Island—would lull me to sleep if the cool brick steps weren't kissing my bare legs. I check my watch—9pm—smooth my sundress, and search for headlights on the tree-lined street.

He's an hour late, but I'm not surprised.

He never sticks to anyone's schedule.

Including his own.

My breath catches in my throat when I spot his low-riding, silver coupe.

Beep beep! Blazing headlights. I shut my eyes, then blink rapidly. As I speed-walk to the passenger side—flipping my hair over my shoulder, hoping to appear devil-may-care—I glance up at my mother's bedroom window. I know she's watching with disappointment drawn on her lips.

But as soon as I yank open the door, I swallow my guilt to make room for whatever Torin has in store.

I'm engulfed by blaring punk-rock music. A touch of cool air and woodsy-cologne-aroma draw me into his car. My pulse quickens. Torin's lit up by the glow of the interior light, resting his tanned forearms on the steering wheel. He wears a fitted t-shirt and his signature side grin—setting

151

a thousand butterflies free in my stomach.

I toss him a flirty smile and slide onto the leather seat.

Ahh! I'm stuck.

My butt is *literally* suction-cupped to the seat.

Adrenaline surges, my eyes widen. So much for a sexy entrance.

"Were you waiting for someone else?" He asks playfully, his deep voice making me melt further into the leather.

"Oh, right." I reach for the door, stealthily wiggling my butt to unstick myself. When he peels out of the driveway, I tuck my dress underneath me and exhale smoothly.

"So, before we go to the show, let's get a drink together," he says.

"At a bar?"

"Yeah." He laughs, and it rearranges every molecule in my body.

"But, I'm not twenty-one 'til midnight." I cringe. Because he's twenty-five, he doesn't have to think about the rules like I do, but still, did I have to sound like such a killjoy?

"I mean, we've drank together before. You've seen me."

Oh, dear goodness, this was getting worse by the second.

"I just—I don't know if a bar would let me in, that's all. But yeah, I'm down for whatever."

Real smooth, Summer.

I pretend to gaze out of the window, but really, I'm silently scolding myself.

"I've got an idea," he says, taking a sharp turn onto the highway. His hand moves artfully on the stick shift, sending us into a gear that makes my stomach somersault. We catapult past dozens of cars. My skin tingles. I have no clue where we're going, but the truth is, I don't care.

I can't keep the smile off my face. Even as the car rockets to 90. 95. 100 mph. I grip the edge of my seat. My heart bounces around like a pinball in my chest.

This is what it feels like to be with Torin. Rules be damned, we're flying.

"Don't worry, I won't let anything happen to the birthday girl," he shouts over the engine's roar. When he winks at me under the strobe-like effect of highway lights, I smile so hard my cheeks ache. I can be one of those girls he likes—the ones who are gorgeously daring.

The car stutters down the curved ramp, trees flash in front of my eyes so fast, I'm dizzy. Suddenly, we're in a half-filled parking lot. I squint up at the retro neon sign. *Sunrise Diner.*

I try not to get my hopes up.

Torin doesn't do dates. He's made that very clear.

Not the commitment type, he says, which is probably why there's always a new girl chasing him. Five years ago, I was *that girl*. But I never gave up on the idea of us, even when plenty of others took over the stage. Some may think I'm foolish—waiting for the rare night when I'm in his spotlight—but then again, they can't feel the electricity pulsing inside my body right now.

The smell of butter and bacon wafts through the air as we slide into a diner booth in the back.

"Are you excited about the show tonight?" I ask, peering over my thickly laminated menu.

"Just another night," he replies, his voice lukewarm.

"You're playing a big show, how is that *just another night?*"

"I don't hype up stuff like that. It's fun hanging out with my friends and playing music. That's it." He puts his menu down. Studies me as if he's about to grab his sketchbook and start drawing. "You're right though. It's NOT just another night." His lips crest up like a wave. "*You're* here."

His chiseled jawline and slate-blue eyes make him celebrity-level handsome. When he says things like that, I feel like I'm walking the red carpet on his arm.

I clutch the menu in my sweaty palms. My head buzzes as I search for a witty reply.

I'm saved by the silver-haired waitress who puts two plastic glasses of water on the table. Torin orders a burger, and as soon as he says it, I want one too. But eating a big messy burger is probably *not* my smartest move.

"Um, the chef's salad," I say, my voice unsteady.

"Is that really what you want?" he asks, somehow reading my mind.

I bite my lip, glance at the menu—a glossy burger photo stares back. When I look up, Torin tosses his head back—his version of thumbs-up.

This is one of the reasons I love him.

A tingle of pleasure ripples through me. "The bacon burger," I say, nearly drooling.

"Any fun summer plans?" Torin asks.

"Summer's almost over." My words fall flat on the table. I wish I could pick them up and resuscitate them back to life.

"It's only August," he says, grabbing a napkin from the steel holder.

"Yeah, the *last* month of summer."

"There's plenty of time left." He sketches on the napkin, momentarily consumed. A 70's song plays from another booth's personalized jukebox, punctuating the air with disco flair.

"I wish I saw time the way you do," I say, curling my hands under my chin.

"How so?"

"You don't get hung up on its constraints."

"Time doesn't really exist, it's all a matter of perception," he says, alternating between looking up, then down at the napkin.

"Well, maybe, but we still have to be on time for things. Doesn't it stress you out if you're on your own schedule and no one else's?"

"Not really."

He continues sketching. I shake my head in disbelief.

How could one person be so cool, ALL THE TIME?

When our burgers arrive, Torin tucks the napkin drawing into his pocket before I sneak a peek. We thank our waitress, then dive in. Euphoric hums vibrate over the table. Our love of food is mutual. The bacon-wrapped steam tickles my nose as I sink my teeth into the poppy-seed-covered bun.

Beef juice spills down my chin.

Ahh! Does he see the mess on my face?

In my frantic search for a napkin, I knock over Torin's glass.

Soda splashes onto the table, then my lap.

My temperature rises, making my ears burn. "I'm so sorry," I say, layering the table with napkins.

"I've got you," Torin reaches his muscular arm across the table to help.

"Oh no, my dress!" I soften my voice. "I mean, it's not that bad. I'll get it out."

I rush every breath as I blot the blooming stains with water. I can't show up in a soda-stained dress! My mother's famous quote plasters the walls of my mind and I consider going home.

How much worse could this get?

Soda has devoured my burger, but my stomach is in knots anyway.

"How's it goin' over there?" Torin asks.

"Oh, ya know. *Wet.*" I hold up dripping napkins that I toss into a neat pile.

He laughs.

Did I just make a joke in the midst of my misery? Without trying?

Tension drains from my body, dissolving knots in its wake. Torin cuts his burger in half, stacks fries beside it, then pushes his plate toward me.

"What's mine is yours."

"Thanks," I say, picking up a fry and tapping it to his in mock toast.

"So, you never answered my question." He swallows his fry. "About your summer plans."

"My grandma is coming to town next weekend, so that'll be nice." I sip refreshing ice water. "I've been thinking—" I clear my throat. My heart beats faster. "I haven't told anyone . . ."

I bite my lip.

He leans in closer.

The sandalwood scent of his cologne sends goosebumps racing up my arms.

If anyone believes in my dreams—it's him.

Besides, once a dream is spoken aloud, it's more likely to come true. Isn't it?

I nibble a fry as I plan out my next line, hoping my voice is steadier than my shaking foot beneath the table. "I hear that *Brand New* is looking for a back-up singer."

He nods as he polishes off his half of the burger. The Long Island band scene is pretty much like one big extended family, so it's tough to keep anything an actual secret. "We're supposed to tour with them next year," Torin says after his last bite.

I rush my next words out before they can hide. "I'm thinking of auditioning."

"That's awesome! Do it!"

"But they're looking for someone with songwriting experience."

He raises an eyebrow. "So? You've written dozens of songs."

"Not real songs . . . they're more like poetry musings. And it's *Brand New!* They're a real band and I've only ever played around with music." I trace the beads of condensation on the glass, coaxing out the truth. "What if I don't have what it takes to be a real artist?"

Torin wraps his calloused palms around my hands. My skin sizzles. "YOU ARE an artist, Summer—like me. Artists can spot each other." He leans back, releasing my hands to clasp his behind his head. "You're a brilliant singer *and* songwriter. The next Hayley Williams."

I nibble my burger-half, then dab my face with a napkin, all while secretly beaming. Years ago, I told Torin how much I wanted to be like the lead singer of Paramore—the coolest girl to take the stage.

"It's only a back-up vocalist spot, Torin." I say, dragging myself back down to reality. "Anyway, I'm not cool enough to be a lead singer. I'll always be the backup girl." As soon as the words touch my lips, I realize I'm revealing two secrets.

"What does cool have to do with it? You have a killer voice, Summer." He pushes the plate closer to me. "I know it's only a matter of time before you take the spotlight."

Heat spreads across my body like a wildfire.

The spark was mine, but he fed the flame.

I smile brightly before crunching on a French-fry. Warm salt hits my tongue. I'm aware that a guy shouldn't have so much influence on me. I was taught to be strong—climb mountains on my own without needing someone to boost me up.

But my creativity is only treasured by him—lying dormant 'til he sets it free.

Before we leave the diner, I wash my sticky hands in the bathroom, and scrub my dress with soap, which yields little results. Now, I'm just wet and wearing what looks like a giraffe-print gone wrong.

Luckily, the air is thick and warm when we walk to his car.

"Is your dress still wet?" Torin asks.

"Only damp. No big deal." I'm lying, but the indigo canopy, sprinkled with stars above our heads, is so beautiful that I want to believe there's magic left.

"I have an idea," he says, revealing a black RX Bandits T-shirt from his back seat.

I gasp. "I can't go to your show wearing nothing but a t-shirt."

"No, just while we dry the dress in the bathroom hand-dryer." He raises one eyebrow. My heart pumps harder. When he closes the distance between us, his electric current grazes my skin. "But now that you mention it, I vote you wear just the shirt."

I push him playfully, my hand lingering on his firm chest. I want to trace every muscle on his body. Dive into his mind, swim among his thoughts. A rare spark of confidence ignites inside me. I grab the t-shirt, swing it over my shoulder, and saunter toward the diner with a sultry sway. I peer over my shoulder, fluttering my eyelashes the way sexy people do in mov—

I trip over my flip flop.

Adrenaline goes off like a bomb in my chest.

I throw my hands out to break my fall.

Strong arms wrap around my back, lifting me up before my knee scrapes the ground.

I'm dizzy, but vertical.

"Are you okay? That looked pretty bad."

As I catch my breath, any remaining confidence spills out of me like loose change.

"I'm fine," I say, dusting asphalt pebbles from my hand. "Ya know what, let's go. My dress is almost dry and I'll throw the shirt over, if it looks that bad."

At the backstage door of the underground club, symbols crash and guitars wail. As I nod at familiar drunken faces, I shield myself with Torin's turquoise guitar. We find a couch in the corner perfumed in beer and sweat. Restless energy keeps me standing—pawing at my yellow sundress peeking out from the black t-shirt—while Torin sits against the couch's arm. As he tunes his electric guitar, his lips part as if tasting the notes.

I stop fidgeting, mesmerized by his passion. I want to be held with that kind of devotion. I take a step closer, possessed by a desire to kiss him. But then I look down and remember:

I'm not that cool.

A statuesque woman, with blunt bangs and a raven-black bob, struts past me. She wraps her tattoo-ed arms around Torin's neck—her breasts spilling from her tank-top—and kisses him on the cheek. While they laugh over their inside jokes, my body grows heavy, shrinking towards the floor.

Torin makes the pointless introductions.

"Summer's a singer too," Torin says, grinning at me.

"Really? What band?" Siren asks, tossing her microphone between her hands.

"Oh, I'm not in a band. I'm not even a real singer." I'm sweating, tripping over my words. "I mean, maybe one day, but right now I just write for myself."

Torin adds, "She's really good."

"Cute," Siren smirks.

Instinctively, I smile like a monkey feigning submission.

"You have something—" Siren points at me. "—in your teeth."

I rush to cover my mouth, my pulse competing with the drummer warming up on stage. I excuse myself and disappear into the bathroom—a silent vortex covered in band stickers and old posters. My eyes swell with tears as I stare into the clouded mirror.

A black poppy seed. Sandwiched between my two front teeth.

I squeeze my eyes shut. Give myself a big fat *F* for tonight.

Has anyone ever died from embarrassment? Maybe I'll be the first.

I remove the seed and lock myself in a stall, trying not to breathe the perfume and urine-stained air. I read the scribbled comments on the lopsided door. Fractured memories of hiding in bathrooms as a young teen dig into the soft tissue of my heart.

Haven't I learned that I'm not one of the cool kids?

Plump tears sting my face.

My mother was right. Nothing good happens after midnight.

I wash my hands, wipe my face, then elbow the door open. I will not be reduced to a puddle of tears in *another* bathroom.

When I find Torin, he's lifting an amp off the ground.

"Hey Torin, I'm gonna call a cab, I'm not—"

He turns around. I freeze. The look in his eyes is new, but I know it well. *Panic.*

"What's wrong?"

"My pick. I had it—" He taps his short's pocket. "—and now it's gone."

"Can you borrow someone else's?"

"NO, it has to be *that one*." He rushes toward me and for once, I'm completely calm. "It's my lucky guitar pick. My dad gave it to me before I went on tour."

"We'll find it." My voice carries a surety even as I scan the mess of beer bottles and random clothing.

"Torin! Everyone's on stage, c'mon!" The drummer yells.

"Give me a minute." Torin runs his hands through his hair as if he wants to pull it out.

I squint, checking between used whiskey glasses and under chairs. Everything is blurry. If I'm ever going to find this thing, I'll need my damn glasses. I sigh heavily.

What else do I have to lose tonight?

When I put on my tortoiseshell frames, the world comes into focus, making the room a touch more repulsive. I scour under the couch, craning my neck.

Bottle caps, dust bunnies, old pens, and—

"Wait, it's tiger's-eye-brown right?"

"Yeah, yeah, that's it!"

I extend my arm, my shoulder gets pinched, but I stretch further. I scrape at the floor, latch onto the pick and don't let go until I'm standing.

I smile brightly as I pass it to Torin. He cradles it in his palm.

"You wear glasses," he says inquisitively.

"Yup." I kick dust on the floor.

"Why weren't you wearing them earlier?"

There are so many things I want to say, but instead I shrug.

"They're cute." He grabs his guitar. "Maybe wear them more often."

The compliment has enough fuel to send me to the moon and back.

He disappears on stage. Siren pushes her way to the front. And I keep my glasses on.

It's 11:20pm when the band's horns blare to life, sending the crowd into a moshing frenzy. Fans form an impenetrable circle, so I hang off to the side. While the singer's raspy voice could certainly make someone swoon, it's the overdrive crackle of Torin's electric guitar that makes my stomach flutter.

Since I was sixteen, I've never missed one of his shows.

The sound of his guitar is etched on the walls of my mind.

The precision of his triple-timed pacing matches the beat of my heart.

Bodies dance with abandon to the brassy honks of the trombone and rumble of the drums. The underground ska-punk scene is truly one-of-a-kind, and I can *finally* see it all so clearly. On the second to last song, Max—the lead singer—launches himself off the stage and sweaty fans swarm to catch him.

Boom! There's a crater in the crowd. People shout. Max staggers to the bar at the back. Within seconds, he emerges—a napkin pressed to his face, whiskey glass in his hand. Blood drips into his scruffy beard as he hustles past me. Torin tells everyone they're taking a quick five and meets Max to the right of the stage. They're already deep in conversation when I approach.

"I told you to stop jumping off the stage so late in the show when people are hammered." Torin says.

"Ahh, it's more fun this way," replies Max. He presses melting ice to the bridge of his nose. "Did you see that hot guy with the mustache? Thought for sure he'd catch me." Max growls and we all laugh.

The crowd chants for their last song and Torin throws up his "one-minute" finger to the band.

"So, what do you wanna do?" Torin asks Max.

Max tests his voice, but as soon as he goes for more power, his face scrunches up in pain. He looks at us with watery eyes and brings his whiskey glass to his lips. "The show must go on, right?"

As Max downs his drink, I catch Torin's mischievous grin.

"What?" I'm unable to stop myself from smiling.

Torin eyes the stage then me, then the stage again and I feel like we're back in his car, racing down Southern State parkway at 95mph. He doesn't have to say anything. I'm already shaking my head.

"Think of it as practice for your audition," he says.

"Yeah," I scoff. "Easy for you to say, you're up there all the time. You're used to all those faces staring at you."

"When you lose yourself in the music, you forget about that stuff." Torin gives me a quick hug and I blush. "I'll be right next to you—it'll be you, me, and the music."

Before I can say no, thoughts of late-night adventures with Torin fill my head. Hopping fences to secret places, showing up at concerts without tickets, revealing my singing voice for the first time. My best memories were made when I took a risk.

What if taking the stage tonight—the biggest risk of all—leads to another moment of magic? How could I pass that up?

I face Torin with my hands on my hips. "I'll do it. But you definitely owe me a drink *and* a piece of birthday cake afterward."

Torin shoots me a mega-watt grin. "Deal. Besides, the last song is your favorite," he adds with a wink.

My heart beats double-time as the band meets in an impromptu huddle. From the sidelines, I fiddle with my oversized t-shirt and glasses, remembering how silly I look and it's as if Torin has spotted me doubting myself.

"No one's gonna care what you're wearing. They're here to *feel* something," he whispers in my ear.

Deep down, I know he's right, but it doesn't calm my jittery nerves.

"You're up, Summer." Max holds out his microphone, a knighting of the highest kind.

I take a deep breath, feeling a catch at the top, as my mind reels with the epic fails of the day:

Sticking to the seat, the spilled soda, a wet, ruined dress.

The fall in the parking lot, food in my teeth, the other girl.

Even if the whole thing blew up in flames, could it really get that much worse? And even if it did, wasn't a dream worth failing for?

I open my palm and lock eyes with Max. Tenderly, he passes the microphone, and it feels as if a lightning bolt strikes my chest. It's heavier than I expected, yet natural in my hand. "I won't let you down."

Max hugs me tight. "Give it everything you've got."

As I swear I will, my heart rattles in my chest, shaking the bones of its cage. I inhale rapidly. Ready for the spotlight and one more daring act. As Max disappears into the crowd and the band reunites with their instruments, I grab Torin's hand, pulling him into me. When his face is close enough, I kiss him. *Hard.* His lips return my eagerness, his tongue seeks out mine. Like a star, I burn brightly from the inside out. He runs his hands through my hair and kisses me as if we have all the time in the world—in front of everyone.

When we part, he looks half-drunk. I feel the same, my lips buzzing. We climb the stage steps with smiles plastered on our faces. Torin lassoes his guitar strap over his head, strums, adjusts his distortion settings, then repeats till he gets it just right.

"Happy Birthday, Summer!" he shouts.

It's probably midnight, and I feel like I'm flying. I fill my lungs to capacity, clutching the microphone. Suspicious faces and smiles are intermixed in the crowd. Behind me, drumsticks crack together and an explosion of hurried sound ensues.

My lips move wildly as lyrics dance off my tongue. Sweat clings to my back under the scorching spotlights. I throw my head back-and-forth, letting the energy of the song burn through me; letting the music recover a lost piece of my soul. Pressure in my throat builds as I chase down every word until the dead end of my exhale.

Out in the crowd, people shout along, jumping up and down. I feel the unified hum of their energy.

My whole body vibrates. I've never felt more alive.

I close my eyes, my glasses snug on my face, belting out lyrics of longing to be loved.

I'm not Hayley Williams from Paramore, or Siren, or some sexy girl from the movies.

I'm simply me.

And for the first time, I think that's pretty cool.

When the song ends, the crowd cheers. I'm breathless in a delirious, sweaty haze. Torin grabs my hand and the heated vibrations from his guitar meld with my palm.

"You've always been a star, Summer. You just needed a stage," he shouts above the clamor.

And at that moment, I know my mother was wrong.

About the Author

Gloria Herdt is a Boston-based writer and poet who loves eating tacos, hiking with her rescue dog, and battling her husband in Magic the Gathering tournaments. Gloria loves exploring themes of identity, love, and loss in her writing. For inspiration stories based on her personal transformation journey through trauma, chronic illness, and pet loss, follow her on Instagram @gloria.herdt or Facebook.

Magic Always Exacts a Price

Teri Polen

J ustin knelt beneath the towering weeping willow tree, its trailing leaves dancing in the late-night breeze. He'd inherited the property it stood on after his aunt passed away five years ago, but not because he was a cherished nephew. He was just the only relative left. Even though Aunt Lucy had raised him from the age of eight after his parents died in a car accident, she'd only done it out of obligation and the monthly payout from a trust fund his parents created for him.

He would have sold the property after Aunt Lucy's death and divested himself of those memories if not for one thing—the metal box he'd buried beneath the tree thirteen years ago tonight. Justin had waited all these years to open it at precisely midnight. Maybe thirteen years was too long to hold onto a curse, but time wasn't an issue if it would be powerful enough to give him the vengeance he craved. Dylan had been a friend. A brother, really. But after tonight? Dylan would be nothing but a corpse.

Time hadn't lessened the black hatred Justin tried to lock away. If anything, its roots had grown stronger, deeper, and crept beneath and around the door where it was imprisoned, threatening to destroy the happiness he'd finally found. The happiness he more than deserved. Supposedly time heals all wounds. Wasn't that how the saying went? But it wasn't true, he thought bitterly. At least not for him.

Justin checked the time on his phone then continued digging. Ten minutes to go. He had set an alarm but needed to make sure there were no screw ups. He wasn't even certain the magic would work, but he'd waited too long for this not to see it through. The box had to be opened precisely at midnight. The witching hour.

Aunt Lucy took him to New Orleans after his parents' deaths. His life was full of changes that year—a different home with an aunt he didn't know and who barely tolerated him, a new school, new city. He'd lost everything familiar in his life. He hadn't even been allowed to bring everything from his bedroom at his old home, not even the Lego collection he'd built with his dad. Aunt Lucy said there was no room for his cherished toys or mementos. The truth was, she'd filled nearly every room to capacity with her own collections of knickknacks and junk ordered off a shopping channel. When she died, Justin took great pleasure in trashing most of it.

As that lost kid, he'd consoled himself with the possibility of new friends he'd make at school. At his old school, he'd had a couple of good friends, but they'd been on the other side of the country, and cell phones weren't a thing then. Not that Aunt Lucy would have allowed him one. New friends could have made his situation a little less painful. New Orleans wasn't a small town by any means, but he quickly learned that the old families socialized mainly with each other and cast suspicion on newcomers. The other children in his class had practically been raised together. Cliques had already formed. For them, Justin was an outsider, a charity case. Aunt Lucy made sure everyone knew she hadn't wanted him. She'd only taken him in out of the goodness of her cold, black heart.

A sudden chill swept across his shoulders. Justin dropped his shovel and shivered as he turned up his coat collar. Was this what magic felt like? Did it creep inside you and nestle into the very marrow of your bones? A smile slid across Justin's face at the thought of Dylan feeling the same chill seconds before his death.

Children could be cruel, a fact that never changed. They'd laughed because Justin had no parents. Dylan James, who was surrounded by friends who followed his lead, came up with new insults weekly. Justin tried to make friends in the classroom, at lunch, on the playground, but found himself shunned at every turn. He was the weird kid who didn't fit in. Dylan was the sun and everyone else the planets that revolved around him. So, Justin shut himself off. He sat alone in the cafeteria. He was always chosen last for sports and never invited to parties.

A clang echoed in the night when his shovel hit something solid. Justin threw the shovel to the side, dropped to his knees, and hurriedly dug around the corners of the metal box to free it from its grave. As he dusted off the lid, his thoughts drifted back to senior year of high school. When everything changed.

Justin closed his locker, turned to head down the hall, then skidded to a halt when he saw Dylan James in front of him, his arm draped around his longtime girlfriend, Ashley. Dylan's popularity had only grown after he'd walked into drama club one day and discovered a passion and talent for acting. His future plans included Hollywood after high school, and there was no doubt he had the looks for the big screen. Justin begrudgingly admitted the guy was a talented actor, considering he'd been cast as the lead in half of the school plays since middle school. The other half featured Dylan's biggest rival, Ben Ford, also talented and just as attractive.

Knowing Dylan and Ashley couldn't possibly be there for him, Justin moved to go around them toward chemistry class.

"You coming to the party tonight?" Dylan asked. Justin knew about the party at Dylan's. It was tradition after the opening night of a play whether he was in the lead role or not. Everyone went, not just the drama kids. Not that Justin had ever been invited. He kept walking.

"Justin, dude, didn't you hear me?"

Justin stopped abruptly and tilted his head to the side in confusion. Dylan was talking to him? The same guy who'd tripped him in front of the whole class in fifth grade and laughed loudly as Justin lay sprawled on the floor, his library books crushed beneath him. Who'd taunted him endlessly and made every school year miserable.

Thinking surely he'd misheard, Justin turned slowly toward Dylan, whose stupid, perfect face sported an equally perfect smile that reached his ocean blue eyes. He was unable to detect even a hint of malice in them. "Me?" he asked.

"Sure, bro. It's senior year, and you've never been to one of my parties. You've lived here how many years? And none of us have gotten to know you. Come and hang out with us."

"You should come, Justin, you'll have fun," Ashley chimed in.

Justin stood silent, mouth gaping. All these years he'd never had a civil conversation with either of these people that didn't involve some sort of teasing or harassment from them. Just the bitter memories of some of those pranks helped him find his words. "What kinda joke are you playing this time, Dylan? You've never asked me to do anything other than disappear. Said it wouldn't make a difference to anyone."

Dylan ran the hand that wasn't wrapped around Ashley through his hair, and his gaze cut to the side before meeting Justin's again. "Yeah, sorry about that, bro. I was a major ass to you. Some things have happened in my life lately that made me realize I've been wrong about a lot of stuff. I want to make up for it, and I hope you'll let me."

With his pleading eyes and hopeful expression, his offer seemed legit. But too many years of being the butt of the joke or being ignored prevented Justin from immediately accepting. "Maybe," he mumbled, then hurried down the hall before the tardy bell rang.

After going through the lunch line that day, Justin carried his tray toward his usual table in the corner where he dined alone. Halfway there, a voice called out his name.

"Justin, over here. Saved a seat for you." Justin stopped and nearly dropped his tray in shock. It was Dylan. His table was always full of his friends, but today there was an empty seat right beside him. For Justin. "Come on over," he said again, his expression open and friendly.

Before Justin could process what was happening, his feet turned in the direction of Dylan's table. Eyes still wide from shock, he set down his tray, pulled out the seat, and lowered himself into it. Looks of confusion bloomed on the faces of the others at the table, but they followed Dylan's lead and spoke to Justin like they'd been friends since he moved there in third grade. Justin frowned. What the heck was happening?

Every day that week, Dylan saved a seat for Justin, and soon it just became a habit to join him. He took a chance and attended the party that Friday at Dylan's and surprised himself by having a great time. People spoke to him and included him in conversations. They seemed interested in his opinions and asked him questions. Months of more parties followed, along with sleepovers, hanging out playing video games and watching movies, going to sporting events at school. Justin was at Dylan's so often that his mother started setting a place for him at dinner and invited him for cookouts by their pool. He was even included on holidays. That year was the first time he'd had a turkey dinner on Thanksgiving or received a Christmas gift since his parents were alive. The most Aunt Lucy had ever done was toss a frozen microwavable turkey dinner at him before disappearing in her bedroom to watch television. And that was only one year. She usually spent the holiday with friends, but her plans had fallen through that time. Justin never received an invitation to go with her. Christmas gifts were nonexistent.

Justin was finally included and felt like he belonged somewhere. After being alone and lonely for so long, he had friends. It was like he could breathe again. Life was no longer a black void of emptiness. He woke each morning excited to get to school where no one teased him or bullied him. He was accepted.

Then came New Year's Eve. Dylan hosted a party at his house, and half the school showed up. Dylan's stage competitor, Ben Ford, was there with his girlfriend, Nicole. Rumors had flown when they'd started dating a few months ago. Ben's extroverted, love-the-spotlight personality didn't exactly match Nicole's quiet, blend-in-with-the-paint-to-avoid-being-noticed attitude.

The music was loud, drinks flowed, and laughter filled the air as midnight approached. Without a doubt, this was the best New Year's Eve Justin had ever had, and the last semester of high school looked just as bright.

Right before midnight, everyone congregated around the television to watch the ball drop in Times Square. Justin joined in the countdown with his friends. At the stroke of midnight, couples kissed, friends hugged, and Dylan's girlfriend Ashley even kissed Justin's cheek and wished him a Happy New Year.

Right before Justin's world crashed down around him.

"Everyone gather around!" Dylan said, standing in the middle of the room. "Ben, come stand with me."

Ben kissed Nicole on her forehead, then weaved his way through the crowd to position himself beside Dylan. Justin looked on in confusion, and judging by the other expressions, everyone else was just as clueless.

"Ben and I need your help," Dylan said. "You all know since middle school the two of us have competed against each other for the lead roles in every play. So far, they've been split between us. We both know we're good," he said, flashing a perfectly white, confident smile. "But we wanted to know who the best was on a different kind of stage. So, we came up with an idea."

Something twisted in Justin's gut, a deep-seated instinct developed after years of being kicked to the curb, alone and unloved.

"For the past few months, both of us have been playing roles. We need you to vote on who performed best." Justin's gaze darted over to Nicole, still seated on the couch. Her face paled, and her lips quivered. "I've played the role of best friend to Justin White, while Ben's role has been boyfriend to Nicole Adams." Some people gasped out loud. Others laughed. "Were we convincing?" Heads nodded.

"I knew something was up," someone called out.

Justin glanced back at Nicole. Silent tears flowed down her face as she stood and raced from the room, dodging people in her way as they snickered. She'd been made a fool of just like he had. By someone she'd probably loved. Justin's heart shattered for her.

It was all an act. Justin had trusted Dylan. Believed he'd actually changed and was sorry for all the years of torment. He'd begun to think of Dylan and his parents as his own family. Over four months, they'd softened the near constant ache in his chest. They'd made him feel loved. He'd let his guard down and allowed himself to believe someone cared about him, a thing he'd sworn never to do. And look where it had gotten him.

The wrenching in his gut became a dark rage that erupted from deep inside him. Rage over the way he'd been treated for so many years. That he'd been a pawn in a narcissistic, childish game between two imbeciles who thought nothing of toying with innocent people and manipulating their feelings.

Justin shoved his way through the crowd until he stood in front of Dylan and Ben. "So, it was all a performance? A stupid contest? Four months of pretending to be my friend so you could settle some idiotic score?"

"Uh, yeah," Dylan said. Not a hint of remorse tinted his eyes. "And you fell for it, dude. Believe me, pretending to be your friend and listening to you whine and moan about how much your life sucked was the most challenging part I've played. I deserve an Academy Award."

Blood boiled in Justin's veins. "What's wrong with you? What makes you think it's okay to treat people like that?"

Dylan rolled his eyes. "Get over it, Justin. And while you're at it, you can leave." He turned his attention back to the crowd. "Ready to vote?"

Justin didn't stay for the results.

***

Justin spent his final semester alone. He spoke to no one at school, returned to his regular table at lunch, and ignored every comment or insult hurled his way. He also ignored the laughter that followed him through the hallways and classrooms the first few weeks after the party. And then the next scandal occurred, and he was mostly forgotten. He thought about not going to school, but he needed to graduate so he could get the hell away from these people and never see them again. Make a new life somewhere else. Start over.

Find where he belonged.

One evening toward the end of his senior year, Justin was rummaging around in the attic. Aunt Lucy never came upstairs, so he enjoyed having his privacy. The house had been in the family for several generations, and going through the numerous storage boxes and musty trunks gave him something to do. Over the years, he'd found treasures and learned more about his ancestors.

That night, at the bottom of a trunk full of photo albums and old clothes, he discovered a book. Not a library kind of book, but one that contained handwritten recipes. With its yellowed paper and cracked spine, Justin could tell it had been around for decades and well-used by someone. Drips and smudges from ingredients decorated the pages.

But upon closer examination, Justin realized these weren't food recipes. They were recipes for spells. Potions. Hexes. Rituals. He'd learned his great grandmother had been a little eccentric on the few occasions when Aunt Lucy talked to him after loosening her tongue with multiple glasses of wine. It was rumored she'd even dabbled in witchcraft. After all, it was New Orleans, and that seemed to go with the territory, even if it was kind of cliched.

He'd leaned back against the trunk and paged through the book. Love charms, pet trackers, fertility potions, and so many more. Even a secret ingredient for gumbo. He smirked. That explained all the blue ribbons he'd found for first prize at county fairs in another trunk.

At the top of the last page his great grandmother had written "Magic always exacts a price." Beneath this was a heading titled Ritual for Revenge. He scanned the instructions as a smile slid across his face. An idea began to form.

***

Justin needed a personal item from the target of his revenge. He had a couple classes with Dylan, so he didn't think it would be difficult to take something. It wasn't like his DNA was required. Just an item that was important to him.

But after following Dylan around for two days hoping for an opportunity, Justin was still empty-handed. On the third day, Justin tailed him to the school theater for play practice. Dylan's hand gripped the script for the play the drama club was rehearsing.

The script of a play in which Dylan was cast as lead. Something that was important to him. He wanted to be an actor more than anything. Justin knew he had to steal it for the ritual to work.

The next day Justin slipped into the theater before rehearsal and hid in the shadows, watching for his opportunity to snatch Dylan's script. When the drama teacher said they were rehearsing off book today, Dylan tossed his script onto one of the theater seats, then hurried up the stairs leading to the stage. Once the scene began, Justin crept up to the chair where several scripts sat atop each other. Shuffling through them, he found the one with Dylan's name on the front, then rushed out of the theater, relief washing over him. He'd done it.

According to the ritual, Justin had to wait for the next full moon, which was tomorrow night. He needed to place the book in a box, recite the words, and bury it precisely at midnight. Thirteen years from that night, he'd dig it up, repeat the words, and open the box again precisely at midnight, the witching hour. And Dylan would drop dead. Maybe magic wasn't real. Maybe it was. He remembered his great-grandmother's warning about magic always exacting a price, but what was was losing a few years off his lifespan or waiting a little longer for a promotion at work if it secured him the revenge he craved?

Justin buried the metal chest and then went on with his life for the next thirteen years. He left New Orleans and attended college. He had a roommate who tried to be his friend, but Justin ignored him. Dylan had ruined any chance Justin had of making friends because he trusted no one. Trusting only led to pain and rejection, and nothing good could come of it.

And then he met Marcus Reynolds. Technically, he became reacquainted with Marcus since they'd attended the same high school. Justin barely remembered him, but when Marcus saw him in class at the beginning of senior year, he'd reintroduced himself. Justin nodded once, then stepped to the side and kept walking.

But Marcus was persistent, and that turned out to be one of the things Justin loved most about him. He never gave up on something he truly wanted. They saw each other in that class three days a week. Afterward, Marcus walked with him until their paths went separate ways, talking to Justin the whole time. Even though Justin never joined in the conversation, that didn't deter Marcus. After two months, Justin finally commented about a movie Marcus mentioned. After three, he answered when Marcus asked about his favorite book. By the fourth month, they carried on a conversation over coffee.

By the sixth month, they were in love. Three years after graduation, they married, and Justin had never known love like that. He'd never had anyone to call his own following the deaths of his parents. Marcus became his family. His everything. He'd taught Justin to trust again, had shown him not everyone in the world was out to hurt him, and in return, Justin was happier than he'd ever thought possible.

Eventually, he and Marcus returned to New Orleans where they had a home, careers they enjoyed, and friends they liked spending time with. Justin still shied away from new people but learned to be open enough to give them a chance, and after so many years of pain and loneliness, his life was beautiful.

Marcus remembered the New Year's Eve incident from high school. He'd been in drama club with Dylan, but they weren't friends. Still, everyone knew what he'd done to Justin. In Marcus's opinion, it had been a horribly cruel trick, and Dylan was a classic narcissist of the worst kind. "Karma will catch up to him eventually," Marcus said, and pointed out all the positive things Justin had done with his life despite the hand he'd been dealt. "Dylan only holds as much power as you allow him," he'd add. He also highly doubted anyone's ability to perform magic and had no faith in Justin's ritual. Instead, Marcus urged him to put it behind them and focus on all the years of happiness ahead of them.

In theory, Justin knew Marcus was right. He should have let go of that pain long ago and filled that space with the serenity and contentment he'd found with Marcus. He truly wanted to. But the roots of his humiliation and anger had woven their way into his soul and embedded themselves so deeply they refused to let go.

No matter how hard he tried, Justin couldn't forget about the metal box in Aunt Lucy's backyard. The dirty, rusted box he now held in his hands thirteen years after the day he'd buried it. He checked his phone again. Two minutes until midnight.

Marcus waited for him in their home across town. He knew exactly where Justin was. He'd told him to do what he needed to rid himself of his hurt.

Justin knew Marcus didn't believe in magic. Rather, he believed opening the box would be more symbolic, and he'd finally be free of Dylan.

Dylan had gotten his wish and was now a familiar name in Hollywood. Justin followed his career and seethed silently over his every success. Interviews portrayed him as a courteous, hard-working actor who did what he could to give back to his community. No one knew the real Dylan. But Justin did. And the actor was about to pay for his transgressions.

One minute before midnight, Justin's phone alarm went off. Even after thirteen years he recited the ritual words from memory. At the stroke of midnight, he opened the metal box and retrieved Dylan's dog-eared playbook. A victorious smile slid across his face as he thought of what was happening to Dylan at that very moment. And suddenly, it was as if the weight Justin had borne all through the years lifted at the thought of Dylan's demise. Justin was finally free.

He opened the book and scanned the page with the cast list. Marcus had also been in Dylan's last high school play, but Justin hadn't seen it. He'd even entertained the idea of a career in acting, but lacked the talent needed to compete against Dylan and Ben. He located Marcus's name and slid his finger across the dotted line to the name of his character.

Justin's heart lurched, and he fell to his knees, gasping for breath. This had to be a mistake. Marcus played a character named Dylan. With quivering hands, he frantically flipped to the script cover again. The title of the play was displayed in capital letters across the top of the page and beneath it was the name Dylan. Smaller letters below it read—played by Marcus Reynolds.

Marcus Reynolds read in bed as he waited for his husband to return home. He was dead before his book dropped onto his lap.

Magic always exacts a price.

About the Author

Teri Polen reads and watches horror, sci-fi, and fantasy. The Walking Dead, Harry Potter, and anything Marvel-related are likely to cause fangirl delirium. She lives in Bowling Green, KY with her husband, sons, and black cat. Her first novel, *Sarah*, was a horror finalist in the 2017 Next Generation Indie Book Awards. *Subject A36* was voted one of the 50 Best Indie Books of 2020 at ReadFree.ly. Visit her online at www.teripolen.com.

THE GIRL WHO WISHED

SHANNON MCPHERSON

Marnie Williams's eyes traced the cracks in her bedroom ceiling, the room illuminated by her little sister's bright pink unicorn nightlight. At 13 years old, she often wished she could chuck that unicorn out the window. Marnie doubted any of her friends still slept with a nightlight or shared a room with their seven-year-old sister. She tossed the blanket off her sticky legs and slid them around, trying to find a cool spot. Summers were brutal in their home, even before you counted the way her dad's snores rattled throughout the house. Sleep was almost impossible.

Marnie snuck a peek at her watch, pressing a side button to illuminate the screen. 11:30 PM. She was trying to wait until the last possible moment to get out of bed—only ten more minutes to go. Marnie would get in so much trouble if she got caught doing what she had planned. But, nothing was going to stop her tonight. Sighing, she rolled over on her side, facing her sister. Scout was little more than a lump of blankets in the middle of her bed. Marnie could hear light breathing coming from her side of the room. She thanked her lucky stars that her sister was a heavy sleeper; the last thing she wanted was for Scout to wake up tonight.

Marnie was used to spending her nighttime hours memorizing the lines that zigzagged across her ceiling. Sleep was something that didn't come easy, not for many years. But, tonight, sleep eluded Marnie for an entirely different reason. At midnight, something spectacular was going to happen. It was Wish Fulfillment Day.

She peeked at her watch again. 11:38. Figuring that was close enough, Marnie slowly swept her legs across the bed, gingerly setting her toes on the floor. As she tiptoed across the room, her sister started rustling under her sheets. Marnie froze, her right foot hovering over the ground. Scout turned on her side before settling down again. Letting out a breath, Marnie crept into the hallway.

She'd spent the last few weeks practicing her path from her bedroom to the back door. She knew the location of every last squeak in the old flooring, and now she lightly padded down the hall, past her dad's closed bedroom door, and out the back.

She peered up at the night sky, a blank canvas waiting for stars to arrive. Hurrying across the patio, she reached into a large pot, praying that she didn't accidentally grab a sleeping squirrel instead of the duffel bag she had stowed there earlier that day. She unzipped the bag, making sure her supplies were still secure.

Thermos of hot chocolate—check.

An old quilt—check.

Photo of her mom—check.

In all her planning, Marnie hadn't thought of bringing a flashlight. She was grateful for the half-moon that illuminated her path. With a glance back at her house to make sure no lights had popped on, Marnie began racing across the field behind her house. The tall weeds swayed in the breeze, glistening with little droplets of water. The grass was getting long. Her dad hated mowing the lawn in the summer, but he never said why. Marnie suspected it had something to do with her mom. Mom had spent most of her time in the fields, picking flowers or just going for walks. She always said she liked the feeling of the grass grazing her fingertips as she walked.

Marnie started making her way up the crest of a small hill, her pace slowing as she made it to the top where there were a few large boulders. She spread her quilt on the other side of one. It gave her something to lean on, and it would help shield her from view if her dad happened to look outside.

Pulling out the thermos, she propped the picture of her mom against it. Mom was young in this picture, the photo taken way before Marnie was born. Her long blonde hair was blowing in an invisible wind, shielding part of her face. Her hand was clutching the straw hat atop her head as if she was afraid it would get stolen by the breeze.

Marnie always loved this picture because it perfectly captured her mom's spirit. She kept the picture tucked away in a small box under her bed since her dad couldn't bear to look at it. He could hardly stand to look at any reminders of her mother, especially not near Wish Fulfillment Day. Her dad wouldn't even let them watch TV or listen to the radio the entire month leading up to it.

But despite his best efforts, there was no escaping Wish Fulfillment Day.

Every year, on the last night in June, thousands of shooting stars launched across the sky at midnight. It always happened at midnight, no matter where in the country you lived in. Out of all these stars, only one of them had the ability to grant wishes. The single lucky star could streak across the sky starting on the East Coast before someone on the other side of the country finally saw it and made their wish. It all depended on how hard you looked for it.

Countless people flocked outside each year, staring up at the night sky and making their wishes. Marnie didn't fully understand how it worked. The only thing she had cared about when she was a kid was getting to stay up past her bedtime. Marnie's mom loved Wish Fulfillment Day. She would count down until June, crossing off the days on their calendar. When the clock would hit 11:30 that night, her mom would gather up all their old quilts and grab thermoses of hot chocolate. Marnie, her mom, and her dad would lay on the blankets, burning their lips on hot chocolate as the sky exploded with glittering starlight.

Of course, none of their wishes had ever been granted. But it didn't matter to them. Marnie began looking forward to Wish Fulfillment Day as much as she did Christmas Eve. Well, almost as much.

The night became even more special when Scout arrived, but they didn't last long. Scout only got to participate in one Wish Fulfillment Day, and she was too little to remember it. Their mom got sick soon after that. Days filled with whimsy and joy were replaced by those of darkness and silence.

On the last Wish Fulfillment Day that her mom was alive to see, Marnie was told to stay inside. She crept into the kitchen, peering through the window that overlooked the backyard. She saw her mom standing on the hill behind their house, her skirts whipping in the wind. Her dad stood behind her, begging her mom to come back inside. Mom ignored him, her face turned up to the sky, starlight glittering off the tears streaming down her face.

Marnie never found out what Mom wished for. It didn't matter anyway. Her mother died six weeks later. Wish Fulfillment Day celebrations went with her. Her dad refused to acknowledge the holiday. Marnie never asked if they could go out there to make a wish. She already knew what the answer would be.

But, this year was different. This year, Marnie was going to break the rules. She had something she wanted so bad that she would risk getting in trouble for it. Marnie was going to wish for her mom to come back.

Even if it was just for a day, an hour, a minute—all Marnie wanted was to wrap her arms tightly around her mom and breathe in the floral scent that always clung to her clothes. She wanted just one more afternoon of baking cookies together, giggling as they dumped an entire bag of chocolate chips into the batter. One more movie night where they gorged themselves on popcorn and candy. One more Wish Fulfillment Day where they laid on the same faded quilt that she sat upon now, gazing up at the stars as they clutched each other's fingertips. She didn't even know if it was possible for her mom to come back, but she would never forgive herself if she didn't at least try.

She looked at her watch. 11:50. It was almost time. Marnie leaned back, taking a sip of hot chocolate. There was something magical about the almost midnight hour, even more so when it was Wish Fulfillment Day. It was like the universe collectively held its breath, waiting for the moment when the stars took back the night sky.

"What are you doing?"

Marnie choked, hot chocolate going up her nose. "Scout! What are you doing here?"

Her sister stood on the other side of the boulder, wrapped in a blanket from her bed, a stuffed unicorn clutched in her arm. Her blonde hair was a mess of curls. Marnie didn't look forward to having to comb all the tangles out in the morning.

"I saw you get up, and I followed you." She plopped down on the quilt next to Marnie. "What are you doing?"

"Nothing. Just sitting."

Scout stared at her. "We're not supposed to go outside at night. There could be bears out here."

Marnie was fairly certain no one had ever seen a bear where they lived. "I don't think we need to be worried about bears."

Scout pointed at the thermos. "What's in there?"

"Hot chocolate." Marnie pulled the thermos closer to her out of Scout's reach.

"Can I have some?"

"It's mine."

"But, Marnie!" Scout was getting that pouty look she always got when she wanted something. "I love hot chocolate. It tastes so good when you make it."

Marnie sighed and passed her the thermos. Scout drank greedily. There was nothing Marnie had that Scout didn't take. She didn't always mind it, but tonight Marnie wanted some things for herself. If someone in her family was going to be the one who saw the shooting star, it was going to be her.

"You need to go back to bed," Marnie said, snatching the thermos from Scout. She peered inside. Scout had drunk most of it. Of course.

"I'm wide awake now." Scout glanced up at the sky. "Why is it so black? Is the sky normally this black?"

Marnie blew out a breath, mentally counting to five before she responded. "It's because there aren't any stars."

"Where are the stars? Is it for the wishing thing everyone is talking about?" Despite the fact their dad tried to shield them from Wish Fulfillment Day, there was no way he could completely. Everyone talked about it, including all the kids down at the pool.

"Yeah," Marnie said. "It's almost time."

Scout clapped her hands. "Yay! I want to make a wish. Is that why you're here? To make a wish?"

"Yeah."

"What are you going to wish for?"

"It's none of your business."

"Aw, come on, Marnie. I wanna know."

"No! It's private!" Tendrils of embarrassment started creeping through Marnie's stomach. She knew she shouldn't feel ashamed about wishing to have her mom back, but she wanted to keep one thing just for herself.

Scout laid back on the quilt, spreading her arms and legs out until she took up most of its surface. "Why do you have a picture of Mom out here?" she asked, holding it out.

Marnie grabbed it out of her hand. "No reason."

"You don't have to be so mean about it."

"I'm not being mean."

"Yeah, you are. You always get mean when I talk about Mom. And it's not fair. You have all these memories of her. I barely remember her at all."

Marnie glanced over at her sister. It was true. Scout had been so little when their mom died.

"OK, I'll tell you about my wish. But, you have to promise not to tell anyone."

Scout squealed, clapping her hands. "I pinky promise."

"I'm going to wish for Mom to come back."

"Really?"

"Yes, really."

"Wouldn't she come back as a ghost?"

"No! At least, I hope not." Marnie's stomach started to sink. She hadn't really considered how that would work. "Well, what would you wish for?"

"I don't know. I never really thought about it." She chewed on her lip. "I guess I'd wish for the same thing." She sighed. "Or maybe to have a pet unicorn or something." Scout held up her stuffed animal. "I'd want it to look just like Mr. Sparkles."

Before Marnie could respond, the night exploded with a blinding white light as thousands of stars started shooting across the sky. Both girls gasped. Even though Marnie had seen it before, it always amazed her. They laid back on the quilt and stared at the sky.

Marnie watched the streams of light streak across the sky, wondering which one would be the one to change her fate.

"This is the most amazing thing I've ever seen," Scout said. Marnie turned to look at her, risking a few moments by taking her eyes off the sky. Scout's eyes were glowing with the light of the stars above them. The look of awe on Scout's face reminded Marnie of how she felt as a younger child when she would see the stars racing across the night.

As Marnie turned back toward the sky, she saw it. There was a star that was slightly brighter than the rest of them. It had a fiery tail that seemed to go on for miles. The center of the star pulsed slightly, getting brighter by the second. Marnie knew this moment was special, a one-of-a-kind opportunity that so few people got. She swore to herself she wouldn't waste it on something silly. She focused all of her attention on the star, chanting the wish through her mind like a promise.

The sky went back to normal just as quickly as it started, except this time the usual stars were present.

"Is it over already?" Scout asked, her lower lip starting to stick out.

"We need to get back in bed anyway before Dad figures out we're gone." The girls shoved the quilt and thermos back into the duffel bag, quickly running across the field, trying to stifle their giggles.

Marnie let out a sigh of relief as they got back to their beds, their dad's snores still shaking the windows. She felt exhilarated. There was something magical about this night, but before she could give it too much thought, she was fast asleep.

***

Thud. Thud. Thud.

Marnie groaned, rolling over as she pulled her pillow over her head. She could hear the muffled voice of her dad through the wall. She peeked at her watch. It was 7 AM. Who would be here this early? Scout's bed was empty, Mr. Sparkles left forgotten on the floor.

Someone knocked at her door. "Marnie?" It was her dad. "Someone is here to see you."

Marnie walked out of her room, suddenly aware of the kitty cat pajamas she wore. Her dad simply pointed outside, his face blank. She could see countless vans lined up and down the road in front of her house. People were standing on the other side of their fence.

"Are those news crews?" she asked.

"Yep." Marnie could tell by her dad's clipped tone that he wasn't happy. With a sinking stomach, she headed outside.

A man and a woman waited on the front lawn, both wearing white suits and a golden star pin on their chest which, flashed in the early morning light. Marnie wondered how many times they spilled food onto their suits, but based on their rigid expressions, she doubted that they ever made a mess.

"Marnie Williams?" The woman's hair was gathered into a tight bun, pulling back her skin and giving her a slightly surprised look. "I'm Agatha Montgomery with the Department of Wish Fulfillment. This is my partner Davis Jones. We're pleased to tell you that you are this year's lucky winner."

"Wait, what do you mean?" Marnie's dad asked, stepping forward.

Her partner cleared his throat. "Your daughter made a wish at 12:01 this morning. She correctly identified the lucky shooting star, and her wish was transmitted to our facilities."

Her dad waved his hand like Davis Jones was an annoying fly in his face. "Yes, yes. I know how it works. What I'm struggling to understand is how you even had a wish of hers to grant in the first place."

Marnie dug her toes into the damp grass. It would've been great timing if she had wished to get transported to another dimension where she didn't have to tell Dad what she did.

"Marnie." She looked up, forcing herself to make eye contact with him. "Did you make a wish last night?"

"Uh." Marnie started to feel sweat gathering under her armpits. "Maybe?"

"There's no maybe about it." Agatha pulled a folded-up piece of paper out of her jacket pocket. "We have confirmation of your wish here."

Her dad grabbed it out of Agatha's hand, running his eyes over the text on the paper. "It doesn't say what she wished for," he said, tossing the paper on the ground. He turned to Marnie. "What was your wish?" She thought she saw a flicker of hope dance across his eyes. Marnie knew what he would've wished for. He would've asked to have Mom back.

She swallowed, her mouth suddenly dry. "I wished for . . . I mean, it's kind of silly." Marnie knew what she wished for wasn't a foolish wish. She just hoped that her gamble paid off.

"It's not silly at all, Marnie," Agatha said crisply as she adjusted her jacket. "She wished for her younger sister's wish to be granted."

Marnie's dad whipped his head toward Scout. "Her wish? Marnie, why would you wish for that?"

Marnie shrugged. "I don't know. She hadn't really experienced Wish Fulfillment Day before, and she seemed so excited. I don't know what she wished for though. She said she might wish for our mom to come back." She cleared her throat. "Or have a pet unicorn." Marnie imagined what her dad's face would look like if Mr. Sparkles walked through their front door instead of her mom, and she cringed.

Scout ran down the front steps, stopping directly in front of Agatha and Davis. "You mean I'm going to get what I wished for?"

"Well, that's where things get a bit complicated," Davis said as he adjusted his tie. "Scout did in fact wish for her deceased mother to return."

Marnie's dad stepped forward, putting a hand on Scout's shoulder. "She did?" he whispered.

"She did. Unfortunately, we don't have the capacity to bring people back from the dead." Davis said, his words cutting through Marnie's hopes. He cleared his throat again as if that sound could clear away the discomfort he was causing. "I am so sorry to be the bearer of bad news."

Scout looked up at Marnie and their dad. "I thought for sure they could bring Mommy back. Then you guys would start smiling again."

Their dad kneeled on the grass in front of Scout, the morning dew soaking through his pajama pants. "What do you mean, Scout? We smile all the time."

"No, you don't. All you two do is make sad faces and look at pictures of mom. I thought maybe if she was back, you could start having fun again."

Marnie opened her mouth to protest, to tell Scout that of course they had fun, but no words came out. Scout was right. She and her dad had wrapped themselves up in a cocoon of sadness that nothing could penetrate. They spent their days reminiscing on what life was like, what life would've been like, if Mom hadn't passed away. But, instead of saying that, other words burst out of her mouth.

"Why don't you let us celebrate Wish Fulfillment Day anymore?"

Dad looked up, lifting his hand to shield his eyes from the morning sun that was beginning to burn through the clouds. Words started tumbling from her, as if the dam she had built the past several years was finally cracking and breaking down. "Those days were the happiest memories we had together, and once Mom died, they died with her."

Dad stood up, looking at the crowd of people around them. It was such an intimate moment to be having in front of strangers, but Marnie didn't care.

"I don't know," he said as he scratched his head. "I cherish those memories just as much as you do. I guess I didn't want to replace them with other memories that didn't have her in them."

"But new memories wouldn't be bad, just because mom isn't in them." Silence fell over the group.

"If I may say something that might brighten the mood," Agatha said, stepping forward. "While we may not be able to grant the original wish, we can grant another wish."

Scout squealed. "Really? What can I wish for?"

"Whatever you'd like."

"Daddy, what would you wish for?"

Her dad let out a long breath before saying, "I suppose I would wish for you girls to be happy."

Davis sighed. "While that's a lovely sentiment Mr. Williams, we're the business of granting tangible wishes, not hopes and dreams."

Agatha shot Davis a scathing glance. "Scout, what would your next wish be? If that's okay by you, Marnie, that we still grant a wish of your sister's."

Marnie nodded. "What do you want, Scout? For Mr. Sparkles to come to life?"

"Oh no, I think I want something that's so much better." Scout whispered in Agatha's ear, and a slight smile flitted across the woman's face before her stoic mask popped back on.

"We can make that happen." Agatha stepped away before quietly speaking into a walkie-talkie.

"Copy that," a voice crackled through the line. People started rushing down her street as news reporters started making live reports from their front yard.

Marnie stepped forward, taking Scout's hand. "What did you wish for?" she whispered in Scout's ear.

"Something amazing," Scout whispered back. Marnie shivered, antsy with anticipation at seeing Scout's wish come true.

Out of nowhere, something soft hit her on the head. She peered up at the sky as more pillowy blobs started raining down. Marnie held out her hand, trying to grab one. It was white and squishy.

"What is this?" Marnie's dad asked as he held one of them up to his eye. Marnie looked around in wonder as the tiny lumps started accumulating on the ground, looking like the weirdest snowstorm she'd ever seen.

Scout grabbed a handful of the small globs, tossing them in the air. "They're marshmallows. I wished for it to rain marshmallows." She threw herself on the ground, moving her arms and legs back and forth. "Look! A marshmallow snow angel."

Marnie and her dad made eye contact for a moment before flopping onto the ground next to Scout to make marshmallow snow angels of their own. A cloud that had been blocking most of the sun's rays shifted, and Marnie smiled as she felt an intense warmth wrapping her body in a tight hug.

About the Author

Shannon McPherson looks forward to the day when living in the forest and becoming the resident swamp witch is socially acceptable. Until that time, she amuses herself by crafting quirky tales to entertain herself and others. To stay up to date on her latest musings, visit www.shannonmcpherson.com.

THE
HOLLOW

JANE MCGARRY

Marisol was eight when she met the boy from another world, unexpected and unlooked for, like most of life's pivotal moments. The night air hung like a wet blanket, that oppressive summer heat so common in Arkansas. For the fourth time this year, Marisol ran away from home, her belongings bundled in a small satchel across her back.

In a few hours, she would return home as she had every time before. The illusion of making a choice for herself always faded. Her parents made all the decisions, despite her wishes, the course of their daughter's life long planned out in their minds.

Behind old Mr. Caleb's house, she hurried to her favorite hiding spot amid the unkempt property. Near the creek, boggy ground interspersed the trees, sucking her feet up to the ankles. She went up a rise to drier soil, wiping damp strands of hair from her sticky cheeks.

She slipped through a gap in the hollowed-out remnants of an old tree trunk. Only a few feet taller than her, the hidden burrow opened to the nearly full moon arcing across the sky. Marisol pulled a bedroll from her pack and spread it out, dusty mulch dancing in the air. She laid back with hands tucked behind her head, to watch for falling stars.

A chime echoed across the air. The clock mounted to the front of town hall struck midnight. Marisol counted each resonant peel. When she got to four, a strange shimmer of light appeared on the inside wall of the trunk. At first, she rubbed her eyes, sure she'd imagined it, but no, a sparkling line formed an arch. *Like a door,* she thought. Hopping up, she bent closer to inspect the glimmering outline. Her hand reached out, expecting firm bark, but the surface gave the slightest bit. Intrigued, she pushed, and the bark swung open.

She peered into a rectangular room, oddly ordinary given the circumstance. Four beige walls, a ceiling with a muted light, and directly across from her, another glowing arched opening. Less ordinary was the startled boy who stood in the center.

"Who are you?" he asked, his white teeth bright in his tawny face. A fresh bruise filled his right cheek.

"Marisol," she declared, walking inside. "Who are you?"

"I'm Leonel from Mikana."

He took a step back towards the further doorway, more tentative of this new situation than Marisol. Part of her knew this entire event should scare her, but a bigger part was curious. Besides, Leonel looked about her age and kindness shone in his eyes.

"Where is Mikana?" Marisol asked.

"It's where I live in Esaharia. Where in Esaharia are you from?"

"I'm from Arkansas . . . in the United States . . . on planet Earth." The boy showed no recognition of the locations, so she added, "I got here through a doorway inside a tree. A magic one, I guess. What about you?"

"My door was in the basement of my uncle's shop. It's in a cave hidden behind a tapestry. We sell phachirine." At Marisol's' furrowed brow, he added, "It's a sweet."

"I like sweets," she said, her stomach acutely aware that she had skipped dinner.

"Would you like to come with me to get one?" Leonel offered. "You would have to stay hidden in the cave so my uncle does not get angry."

"Sure," she agreed, excited at the adventure her night had become.

Leonel disappeared through his door, but when Marisol tried, she bounced back as though she'd hit a taut trampoline. He stuck his head back out.

"I can't get through," she explained. "Can you get through mine?"

They tried her door with similar results.

"I guess we can only go through our own door," Leo concluded. "May I ask why you were inside a tree?"

"I was running away from home," she replied.

"Did your parents beat you or something?" His hand flew to his cheek.

"No. Just don't pay me much mind. They have plans for my future, but somehow, they never have time for me. Kids my age make fun of me because I study all the time. Sometimes it's fun to pretend I could leave."

"My parents sent me to live with my uncle and aunt. I had to move from our old town and travel hundreds of leagues after a bomb blew up our home. There's a war, you see. I am safer here, but my uncle drinks a lot and gets angry."

"That sounds bad," Marisol said. "Does he make you wear that dress, too?"

"Dress?" Leonel smoothed out his kaftan. "This is what everyone wears in the desert heat."

"Oh. I'm not near the desert," Marisol said, looking down at her plain t-shirt and sweatpants. "Besides, my parents pick out all my clothes."

"Do you live near the sea?" he blurted, eyes wide.

"No. My parents think time not studying is wasteful. They threaten to lock me in my room if I don't study enough," she sighed. "I've never seen the ocean in person."

"I dream of living by the sea one day." A muted clanging sound emanated from Leonel's door. "I better go. But I come to this place every day. Maybe you can meet me tomorrow? It would be nice to have a friend."

"Sure, that sounds great."

Leonel disappeared through his portal, the wall sealing up behind him. Marisol took a last look around and stepped back out into the trunk. She grabbed her blanket and stuffed it in her bag. No chance was she running away now. A strong grip seized her arm. Her neighbor, Mr. Caleb, looked down, a large silhouette against the moonlight behind him.

"Mr. Caleb," she stammered. "I'm so sorry for trespassing. I was just . . . pretending to be camping."

"Not to worry, young Marisol. You are always welcome on my property," he replied, his voice wrapped in gentleness. His hold on her arm loosened. "I'm just checking you are all right."

"Oh, ok," she managed, her heart still pounding in her ears. "Thanks. I guess I'll be going."

As the clock chimed, she scurried back across the yard and padded down the road to her house. Through the window, her mother and father sat in front of a tv in the living room, a news channel flashing scenes of desolation while commentators argued. Marisol shimmied up the red buckeye tree on the side of the house and dropped back into her bedroom, undetected as always. The clock read 12:02. Somehow, time spent in the mysterious room did not elapse in the real world.

At eleven forty-five the next night, her feet retraced their steps to the trunk. When the clock hit the fourth chime of midnight, the door appeared. Marisol exhaled a breath and realized how much doubt had filled her entire day. She pushed the door open. When her eyes fell on Leonel, a warmth spread in her heart.

"Here I brought you some phachirine." He held out a plate, pride in his smile.

"Thank you. I brought you a book with photos of the sea."

"I can't read it," Leonel declared, pointing at the title.

"Can't read it? But it's written in English, the language we've been speaking this whole time," she exclaimed.

"I've been speaking in Mikanese," he said. "How odd."

With a bewildered shrug, the children exchanged gifts and sat on the floor across from each other. The sweet melted in Marisol's mouth, more perfect than any earthly creation. Meanwhile, Leonel gasped as he turned page after page of the ocean book Marisol had borrowed from the library. They laughed at each other's mutual enjoyment.

"Can I keep this?" Leonel asked.

"For a week, but then I need to return it." Marisol said. At his dejected face, she added, "But I will find some photos and hang them on the wall here. That way, you can look at them whenever you want."

"That would be amazing," he said. "Let's fill the walls with pictures of beautiful things. Even if our worlds have problems, we can make our own better one in here."

Marisol agreed.

Time passed, the friends meeting as often as possible. The room became a haven from the lives they wished to escape. Here she could make choices, and he could avoid the violent hand of his uncle. Colorful photographs adorned the walls. Tan beaches dotted with graceful palms led to crystal blue waters. Meadows filled with an explosion of flowers, like paint bursts on a palette, graced the walls. Paper stars arrayed the ceiling. Marisol found ones that glowed in the dark, and Leonel never tired of looking at them. They named it *The Hollow*, not only for the space where each found it, but for the way it filled the empty spots in their souls.

They discovered *The Hollow* held mystical qualities. Often, items would appear that neither of them brought. A chair, a small bookshelf, paints, and parchment. Items not looked for, but most appreciated. They accepted these oddities as another peculiarity of the room, which seemed to anticipate their needs.

The Hollow allowed their true selves to flourish. Marisol painted seascapes, and Leonel wrote stories with abandon. Their creations covered every inch of the walls, shelves overflowed with trinkets and keepsakes. They reveled in the discovery of clothing, food, and art from each other's worlds. Here, time stopped, releasing them from the grip of abusive uncles and cruel classmates. Here, their authentic selves had the luxury to exist. Here, two sensitive souls found solace and sanctuary.

"Leo, why do you think we both found this room?" Marisol asked one day.

They laid on a mountainous pile of pillows. Years ago, Leonel had built a wooden frame that looked like the prow and stern of a ship. The structure was covered in mismatched bedding, and Marisol draped gauzy fabric down from the ceiling, encasing it like a chrysalis. The stars twinkled against the dull beige overhead. Soft music wafted from Marisol's phone, a device which fascinated Leonel, even after all this time. A strangely shaped shell from his world could also play songs, though she did not understand how. Music, however, was a universal language, creating whatever mood they chose.

"I suppose we both needed someone, someone our own world couldn't provide," he surmised.

Over the last nine years, each had been the other's lodestar. Every emotion, from elation, to despair, gratefulness to rage, occurred in the confines of *The Hollow*. Despite their different worlds, the duo held an intuitive understanding of one another, their bond transcending all else, like the shore pulls the tide in an endless dance. Neither found the same connection from anyone in their own world. In this room, they spent their most cherished moments wrapped in security and love.

One night, Marisol stumbled into *The Hollow*, her eyes red-rimmed.

"What's wrong?" Leonel asked, arms wrapping around her.

"I got into the college my parents want me to go to. It's far away. I told them I wanted to stay at home, but they won't let me." Tears streamed down her cheeks.

"Surely, they will relent when they see how miserable you are. They cannot be so coldhearted."

Even as he spoke the words, he knew such people existed in both their worlds. The kinds who thrived off controlling others, the kind who crushed any trait they deem unworthy. Unfortunately, they were both targets of these all-too-common traits. Him from his uncle, Marisol from her parents and classmates. Leonel wished he could confront those who hurt her, but Marisol's door steadfastly held him back.

"I wish we could leave here. I wish I could go with you to your world, and we could be happy."

"I'm afraid my world would offer nothing different." He rubbed the blooming bruise on his jaw.

"If only we could stay here forever, in our own world," she cried.

"But you've worked so hard at school all these years. You must graduate," Leonel said, knowing the pressure she endured to maintain perfect grades, the ostracism by her peers.

"Promise me when I graduate, we will do it? It's only two more months to wait. I think I can make it that long. Please say we can always be together."

Leonel had never considered parting from Marisol, his missing half. The idea of staying in the room forever swam before his eyes like a dream. Not only would she make her own choices, but he would be safe from his uncle's violence. Leonel looked down into her blue eyes, overcome by the rush of emotion he felt. His head bent toward her, their lips brushing, timid at first, but then more hungrily. Breathless, they parted, and their smiles could have lit up the entire sky.

From that moment on, they planned for a future which rushed to meet them.

"Only one week left until I graduate high school," Marisol said, checking off another day on the calendar. "And I will be free."

"What are you going to tell your parents?" Leo asked.

"Nothing, I suppose. I'll let them think I ran away or something," Marisol replied.

"You don't think they will miss you?' he asked.

"They would force me to go to college to be a lawyer. I have no say in the matter. I think they will miss the idea of who they want me to be." She shrugged.

He nodded. As the date for their plan approached, the flaws became painfully clear. Neither knew how to extricate themselves from their families. But what choice did they have? Even if they could agree on which world to go to, the doors did not let them cross into each other's territory. Not to mention the practical matters of food and other supplies, a topic they noted, yet continued to ignore. Both held fast to the wish that *The Hollow* would provide an answer, as it always did. They parted for the evening after a lingering kiss. Marisol snuck back to her house, up the tree, and into bed.

The next week, Marisol hurried to the tree trunk, her cap and gown in hand. Leo insisted on seeing her in it. She even brought her diploma, oddly proud to show him her accomplishment. At the edge of Mr. Caleb's property, she walked into something cold and hard. With the flashlight on her phone, she saw a chain-link fence around the perimeter. Next to the rental fence sign loomed another placard. "Construction Site." With her heart in her throat, Marisol scaled the metal barrier, heedless of the scratches to her arms and legs.

She ran to the tree trunk, trying to remember the last time she saw Mr. Caleb. It had been a while. At the fourth stroke of midnight, she burst through the door. Leonel took in her frantic eyes.

"What happened?"

She explained the fence and the sign. "They are knocking Mr. Caleb's house down soon. I think he's gone. I don't know what will happen if they knock the tree trunk down. We both need to be in this room when it happens. I'm going to run home and grab a few essentials and come back. You should do the same."

At her door, they kissed. "I'll be right back."

On swift feet, she raced across Mr. Caleb's yard, twigs nipping at her ankles. Scaling the fence, she ran back to her house, all the while making mental notes about what to bring. With only steps left to the buckeye tree, her feet slowed.

Something was wrong.

Her bedroom light glowed brightly when it should have remained dim. Footsteps pounded down the front steps and her father grabbed her arm.

"Where have you been?" His vice-like grip hauled her into the house where her mother hurried down the stairs into the living room.

"Out with a friend," Marisol stammered.

"A likely story. I'm sure you were meeting some boy," he accused.

Leonel's face danced before her eyes, the glimmer enough to incur her father's wrath. He slapped her face and blood tinged the inside of her mouth.

"She was with a boy," her father exclaimed. "That can only mean one thing at this hour."

Marisol's mother shook her head, her mouth a taut line. "And to think, George, we were going to leave this on her desk so she could wake up to a graduation present."

Her mother held a new laptop in her hands. Marisol hung her head. She needed to be smart about this. If she feigned remorsefulness and everyone went to bed, she could sneak out once they fell asleep. Every moment she wasted was one too many.

"I'm sorry to you both. I have no excuse," she muttered.

"And sorry you should be," her father said. "Now, up to your room. And before you think about climbing out that window again, I put a lock on it from the outside, and there is only one key."

He tapped the pocket of his pants. Panic rose in Marisol, the thought of losing Leo blotting out all reason. She bolted for the door, but her father caught her. He carried her upstairs, her arms and legs flailing like an animal in a trap. When they reached her room, he dropped her onto the bed.

"I don't want to be here!" she screamed. "I graduated. I'm an adult now. You can't make me stay."

While her mother looked aghast at this outburst from her normally quiet daughter, the words enraged her father.

"You ingrate. We have sacrificed so that you can go to the best college, and make no mistake, you *will* be going there."

"That is not what I want. It never was. I am not some object for you to brag about, for you to live vicariously through. I am my own person."

"Watch your tone, young lady," George said. "I'm locking you in until you learn your lesson. Come on, Helena."

"Mother, please let me go," Marisol begged.

"How could you do this? How could you shatter all the dreams we had for you? All the hard work to get into an Ivy League college, and now you want to throw it away? I don't know who this boy is, but you need to stay away from him. He does not have your best intentions at heart."

Her mother left the room. When the door shut behind her, Marisol heard the scrape of the deadbolt sliding into place. Though they threatened her with it in the past, she never thought they would use it. Now, she was trapped in her room, with both the window and the door sealed shut against any escape attempt. Marisol pounded with all her might, to no avail. Screams tore at her throat until her voice was gone, but she remained a prisoner.

Leo would think she deserted him. No, he would never think that. He would know she was in trouble, but he could not get through the barrier to save her. The rosy fingers of dawn crept across the steel gray sky before she collapsed with exhaustion.

Late in the afternoon, the lock clicked, and her door opened. Helena brought in a tray of food and set it down. Under her watchful eye, Marisol used the bathroom and showered before returning to her room. Her father waited at the entrance. No sooner had she crossed the threshold when the lock slid back into place. She picked at the food on the tray, its contents clouded by her tears. The promise of a new life with Leo evaporated into hopelessness.

Three days passed in the same fashion. Each day she tried to reason with her parents, who regarded her with pity. She heard them whisper outside the door about the possibility Marisol could not live up to their dreams. *Maybe we should have her evaluated*, her mother had said. *No, she will get over this and do as she is told*, her father concluded. Tears welled in her eyes, and she wiped them on her pillowcase. An idea took shape in her mind. On the fourth day, when Helena entered, Marisol had stripped the bed.

"Could you please change the sheets while I shower?" she asked, her shoulders sagging with defeat.

"Yes, that is a good idea."

Marisol picked up the soiled sheets. She carried the bedding down the hall and dropped it outside the bathroom door. While her mother retrieved clean sheets from the linen closet, Marisol brushed her teeth. Helena's footsteps retreated to the bedroom. Marisol peeked out and grabbed the dirty bundle. After locking the bathroom door, she turned on the faucet in the tub, the water a loud rumble. She looked out the window and saw no one. Opening it wide, she scrutinized the long drop to the ground. Tying the sheets into a makeshift rope, she secured one end to the base of the sink and dropped the other out the opening. Her descent, though clumsy, was remarkably fast.

Once her feet hit the ground, she raced down the street, past a row of dilapidated houses, towards the chain-link fence. Her strides slowed to a crawl while her mind processed what she saw. Mr. Caleb's house was gone, along with all the trees behind it. A flat expanse of dirt filled the entire lot right down to the creek. The world around her blurred. She sank to her knees, one hand locked around a cold metal stave of fence. Sobs rose in her, but her intense grief muffled them, a sorrow beyond sound. Every ounce of resolve drained from her body.

She jumped when a strong hand landed on her shoulder. Expecting her father, she steeled for his wrath. Instead, she looked up into a set of benevolent eyes.

"Mr. Caleb," she whimpered.

"Come, child, I will take you home."

On mechanical legs, she rose and followed him. But instead of turning down the road to her house, Mr. Caleb led her the opposite way. Too numb from her loss, Marisol said nothing. At the creek's edge, he entered a ramshackle shed, the roof barely hanging on to one side of its faded red exterior. Marisol stepped into a room filled with rusted tools and broken fishing lines.

"Usually, I wait for midnight, but given the circumstances."

Mr. Caleb traced his finger against the dusty wood wall and the shape of a glowing arc appeared. He pushed it open and entered, Marisol right behind him. A dejected figure stood in a small, empty room. His head swung up from his drooped shoulders.

"Marisol," Leo cried. "I thought I lost you forever."

The couple embraced, the story flowing out of Marisol between tears and kisses. They pledged their love and agreed to let nothing separate them again.

"Thank you, Mr. Caleb," Marisol said. "I don't know how you did it. But thank you for reuniting us."

Mr. Caleb nodded, his dark eyes crinkling with his smile. "Every once in a while, a singular connection becomes separated between two worlds. It is my job to help those people find one another."

"And we are most grateful," Leonel said. "But we don't seem to belong in either of our worlds."

"No, you do not," the old man agreed.

He walked to a bare wall and traced his finger again. The shimmering glowed brighter than ever before. When a door formed, Mr. Caleb pushed it open. Salt-tinged air floated through, carrying the cry of gulls. Marisol and Leonel peered through at a colorful meadow meandering down to a magnificent sea.

"Where is this?" Marisol asked in wonder.

"It's the world you created together over all the years. Here you will both find happiness and fulfillment. Go now. Start your lives together."

After embracing Mr. Caleb, the couple joined hands and strode through the door, faces radiant with hope. Mr. Caleb smiled, his work done, for these two souls at least. He snapped his fingers, and the rundown shed vanished with him inside, off to continue his work.

About the Author

For more enchanting fantasies and retellings, follow Jane McGarry on Instagram @janemcgarryauthor and visit www.janemcgarrybooks.com

THREE
AT
MIDNIGHT

JM STRADLING

I t'll happen soon.

I huddle on my bed, hugging my legs against my chest, and stare at the large, green numbers on my roommate's clock.

11:58 PM.

Maybe it won't happen this year. Maybe moving away for college somehow threw it off.

Yeah. Right.

It happens every freaking year. For as far back as I can remember. No. Matter. What.

Standing with the door open on my eighth birthday? Yep. Twelfth birthday slumber party where they laughed, called me crazy, and avoided me after? Yep. Sneaking into a bar last year for my seventeenth birthday? Yep.

11:59 PM.

My roommate mumbles something in her sleep and shifts onto her back. Part of me wishes I'd told her the whole thing and begged her to wait up with me. But it wouldn't matter. Others don't hear it, and I'd end up looking crazy again.

I pull my legs tighter against my chest, my breaths coming faster. Any second now. And . . . 12:00 AM.

KNOCK.

KNOCK.

KNOCK.

My roommate doesn't stir.

It's pointless, but I scramble off the bed anyway and adjust my tank top and shorts just in case. After a few deep breaths, I turn the knob and open the door. No one is there. No one ever is. No matter how quickly I open the door. Except . . .

Crouching, I admire the small, black wooden box with my name, Anaya, carved in tiny letters on the lid next to a tiny, carved red rosebud. Gorgeous.

I reach for the box but pull back before taking it. A strange gift after all these years? Weird. And yet . . .

I inch the box closer. The hallway's fluorescent light glints off the golden hinge on the back. Something must be inside. I should leave it there. Shut the door. Forget about it.

But . . .

Picking up the box, I cradle it in my palm. It's warm as though from someone else's hand. This is so wrong. I close the door and carry the box across the room. My mattress springs protest as I sit cross-legged on my bed. I shouldn't open it.

Why not? It's just a box.

The tight hinge resists, but I force it open. A black ring engraved with blood-red roses rests on a bed of red velvet. Pretty . . . but strange. I shouldn't touch it.

Although, a ring never hurt anyone. Besides, it probably doesn't fit anyway.

I try it on each finger. Too small. Too big. Too small. It fits my left ring finger. What the hell? Okay, this is too creepy. Nope. It's going back into the box.

Several minutes of pulling and tugging end in a red and painful finger, but the ring stays.

"Damn it," I yell. A heatwave rolls over me, stealing my breath. It's worse than the triple digit temperature days back home in Phoenix, Arizona.

Wait. What the hell? Giant burning coals have replaced my walls. A gag-inducing stench indicates a pile of rotten eggs and decaying flesh may sit somewhere nearby in the enormous this-is-no-longer-my-dorm room. My bare legs burn—like sitting on sun-heated black leather. I scramble up from the awful reddish-orange rock floor and hop from foot to foot.

I turn and find my roommate's bed replaced by a bright white throne of bone. On it sits a dark-haired, green-eyed god of a man.

"Hello," he says. "Welcome to Hell, Anaya."

"Welcome to . . . what?" I screech. This can't be real.

"You're confused. That's . . . oh, do stop hopping. Here. Allow me."

He snaps his fingers, and silken slippers appear on my feet, ending the burning. Odd. The thin slippers shouldn't be enough protection. I must be dreaming.

"That's better," the man says. "As I was saying, confusion and disorientation are understandable. It happened to the others as well."

I frown. "Others?"

"My potential brides."

"B-brides?" I stammer. He can't be serious.

"If you continue echoing everything I say, I may reconsider your potential." He smiles, revealing perfectly straight, perfectly pointed teeth. Bizarre, even for a dream. "You, Anaya, are one of six possible brides. The last to arrive, I may add. Lucifer won that bet. I expected you first. You were, after all, the only one who opened the door every year. No matter. You put the ring on just the same."

"It won't come off," I mumble, pulling at it again.

"No. It won't. Should you cut off your finger, it'd just grow back with the ring in place. I don't believe you've experienced the joys of dismemberment. And growing the finger back is excruciating. Do try it." He adjusts position as though getting comfortable for a show.

A large knife appears at my feet. "Um. No thanks."

He sighs, and the knife vanishes. "Three of the others tried it. I bet there'd be four. Lost again."

"No offense, whoever you are—"

"Kedar, the Demon King."

Demon King? Fan-freaking-tastic. "Look, Kedar . . . sir . . . Your Highness or whatever. I don't care who you are. I don't want to marry you."

He steeples his fingers under his dimpled chin and leans forward, grinning. "You put on the ring, so your wants no longer matter."

"Seriously? That's so wrong. I wouldn't have done it if I knew I'd end up in Hell and engaged to a demon king."

"We're not engaged, Anaya, not really. You're a *potential* bride. One of six, if you recall. Only one will be my wife. The other four or five will serve my queen however she wishes."

I close my eyes and rub my temples. "Yep, I'm dreaming. That's why the thin slippers protect my feet, and that's why he's not making sense."

He raises an eyebrow. "The slipper fabric comes from my asbestos silkworms. I can take the gift back if you wish." His fingers move into a snap position.

Dream or no, I'll skip the burning feet. "The slippers are nice. Thank you."

He lowers his hand. "And you said I'm not making sense?"

"You said four or five will serve your queen. It can't be four if there are six of us. It can only be five."

He smiles and leans back, caressing the throne's ulna and radius bone armrests. "Four if one contestant returns home."

I nod vigorously. "Home? Yes. I'll choose that."

His deep, booming laugh echoes through the room. "That's adorable," he says. "You can't choose. Oh, I do hope you become my bride. You make me laugh."

I scowl. "Yeah. Hard pass on the whole marriage thing, buddy. I'd rather go home."

He bares his teeth and leans forward again, his gaze burning into mine. "You're new here, so I've controlled myself, but should you continue to disrespect me, you will have consequences."

"Don't piss off the demon king in your dream. Got it."

"It's not a dream."

I roll my eyes. "Yeah, it is."

Kedar leans back, tapping the arm rests. "I've watched you since birth. You're skilled in detecting lies, correct?"

"Yeah. My ears tingle when someone lies, even in my dreams."

He raises a pointy eyebrow. "Have I lied?"

My mind backtracks through our conversation. "Holyshitholyshitholyshit." I gulp shallow breaths, choking on hot air. I'm in actual Hell. Kidnapped by a demon king hunting for a bride. I twine and untwine my fingers until they hurt. I won't marry him. Or serve his queen. I must escape. I clench my fists. Breathe, Anaya, breathe. Don't panic. If I can't think, I can't get out of here.

Breathe in. Out. In. Out. I open my eyes.

"Your panic didn't last nearly long enough," Kedar pouts. "I'm losing all bets today."

Good. I hope he loses me, too. "You said one potential bride could return home. May I know how?"

A table and skull bowl materialize next to his throne. Plucking a human finger from the bowl, he pops it into his mouth, crunching bone as he chews. So disgusting. At least he swallows before answering. "There are souls in hell who know the location of the one and only door back home. Find and torture information out of them."

I gasp. "I can't torture anyone."

A loud rumble shakes the room.

Kedar grins, exposing gory finger flesh stuck between his teeth. "Now, Lucifer, don't be a poor sport. You won the other bets." The rumbling subsides. "No torture, no information. If you change your mind, you'll need your kit." What looks like an old-fashioned doctor's bag appears at my feet. "The kit provides only the specific device needed for each soul. To keep things fun, some souls have information, some don't. You won't know until you torture them. If you find and go through the door home, you lose the contest and forfeit the chance to become my bride."

Lose? Sounds like a win. "Wait. It's a contest?" I ask.

"Of course." He picks another finger from the bowl and uses its long nail to clean between his teeth. "Now, the rules. Entering the wrong door brings instant death and status as servant to my future queen. The contest automatically ends if someone goes through the door home. From among the remaining living, I choose my bride. She decides how the others die and become her servants."

"So, one goes home, and the rest of us die?"

"No. My bride lives. And you didn't let me finish." He snaps his fingers. "That's for interrupting."

My fingers frantically claw the smooth flesh sealing my lips.

"As I was saying, the contest also ends if five competitors die during door selection. In that case, the sixth can no longer search for the door and wins my hand by default."

So, out of six, only two can possibly live—one who goes home and one who marries Kedar—if being his wife counts as living. Worst birthday ever.

He snaps his fingers, restoring my mouth. "We're done here. Take Anaya to the other contestants."

I'm unsure who he's speaking to until a growl sounds from behind me. Spinning around, I'm face to snout with a crouching, house-sized, slobbering, sharp-toothed black dog with burning red eyes. I scream and stagger back into another of the beasts.

"Daisy and Rose are good hellhounds and won't hurt you unless I command it," Kedar says. "Follow Daisy. And don't forget your bag."

One of the beasts, Daisy I presume, huffs and moves past me, heading into a hallway on the right. Rose gives me a nudge and almost knocks me down. I snatch up the torture bag and follow Daisy down the hall. Rose's slimy drool stretches toward my head. I dodge to avoid it. A decaying hand reaches through the glowing, pulsating, blood-red wall. I yelp and stumble into Rose who nips at me. Scrambling between her legs, I avoid becoming puppy chow, but more hands grab from the opposite wall. One latches onto my arm, its papery flesh scraping like sandpaper on my skin.

I scream, prying at the fingers.

Rose barks. The hand releases and vanishes into the wall. Daisy growls and continues down the hall. It seems like an eternity of eluding the hands and drool before we reach a door.

After gingerly moving around the hounds, I turn the handle, pull, and step inside. Oppressive heat pushes me back a few steps and one of the beasts shoves its slobbery snout against my back. I tumble into the room and sprawl onto the floor, my bag sliding away from me. A sudden breeze leaves a whiff of rotten fish and mold behind. I gag several times.

"Stop, or I'll puke again," someone says.

I lift my gaze to my fellow contestants.

"Anaya? Is that you?" one of them says.

How do I know her? Then I remember. Our twelfth birthday party. I force a smile. "Hi, Layla."

She grins, helps me to my feet, and hugs me tight. I don't hug back.

"You two know each other? That's not fair," one of the others says.

"Oh, give it a rest, Gloria," Layla says, releasing me. "You've whined about how unfair this is since we got here five minutes ago."

"It *is* unfair," Gloria mumbles.

Layla rolls her eyes. "This is Beth, Pam, Gloria, and Terri." Layla points to each in turn. "Ladies, this is Anaya. We became friends in kindergarten when we found out we have the same birthday."

"And our friendship ended when you lied and embarrassed me the night of our twelfth," I say.

Layla blushes. "Anaya, I—"

"Can the drama," Terri says. "We aren't here to make friends. I'm finding that door and getting home, and the rest of you better stay out of my way."

"We all want to go home," Pam says. "The door doesn't belong to you."

"Enough squabbling," Kedar's disembodied voice bellows.

We jump and some of us scream. Kedar laughs. "Let the contest begin."

We don't move.

"Go on," he demands.

"Where to?" Pam asks.

"Wherever in Hell you want to," Kedar yells. "Go. Find souls. Torture them. Pick a door and hope for the best."

We stare at each other.

"Shall I call the hounds for motivation?" he growls.

Beth, Terri, Pam, and Gloria exit out the door. I retrieve my bag and follow, but Layla grabs my arm.

I jerk away. "What's your problem?"

"That's the door we entered," Layla says. "I think it's the wrong way."

"Look around. There's no other door."

"I know, but when the hounds led me through the hallway, hands reached through the walls to grab at me."

"Yeah, me too. So what?"

"So, if the hands can reach out, maybe we can get in."

"Into the walls? What for?"

"Well, where there are hands, there are souls, right? And I didn't see souls anywhere else, did you?"

"No," I admit. "I'll try the hallway . . . thanks."

"Wait," Layla says. "Maybe there are less grabby souls in the walls here."

"That's an interesting theory," I say. "Best of luck to you."

Layla's shoulders slump. "I hoped we could team up and find the door together. Two heads are better than one and all that."

I narrow my eyes. What's her angle?

Then I get it. My fists tighten around the torture bag's handle. "This is because you know I can detect lies, isn't it?"

Layla blushes. "Partly, but it's also the whole torture thing. If we take turns, we'd each have to do it less."

She has a point.

"But then what?" I ask. "Only one of us can go home."

Layla shrugs. "Rock, paper, scissors?"

My ears aren't tingling, but I don't trust her. Still, less torturing sounds good.

"Okay," I say.

Layla grins and reaches toward the nearest wall. Her hand slides in, and the rest of her follows. If only I were dreaming and could wake up and enjoy my birthday instead of participating in a stupid, backward contest where losing is actually winning. I sigh and push myself into the wall after her.

The intolerable heat increases in the tunnel-like, dim space. I blink several times, waiting for my eyes to adjust. Sweat rivulets trickle down my back and between my breasts. Hell totally sucks.

"Layla?" I call.

"I'm here. Just follow the corridor."

I hurry around the bend.

"I worried you changed your mind," Layla says. "Look. I found one."

She gestures to a pale, withered, human-shaped thing huddling against the wall.

"Do you know where we can find the door home?" I ask.

"Mebby," the soul croaks. It spits, but no saliva comes out.

"If you tell us, we won't torture you," Layla offers.

Its black eyes dart between us. "Won't be sayin' then."

"You want us to torture you?" I ask.

It shakes its head. "Can't say if ya don't though. Rulezies."

Layla sighs, opens her torture kit, and pulls out long nosed pliers. She frowns. "What do I do with these?"

I shrug.

"Fingerynails," the soul wails. "Why'd it gotta be fingerynails?"

Layla grimaces. "Fingernails?"

"I think you're supposed to pull the fingernails out," I whisper.

Blood drains from Layla's face. She sways but doesn't pass out. After a few deep breaths, she grabs the soul's hand, clamps the index fingernail between the pliers, and pulls. The soul screams, and the fingernail slowly inches along the nail bed, tearing from the flesh, bleeding silver. I slap my hand over my mouth and swallow the puke rising up my throat.

The soul screeches. "Stop. Stop. I'll tell ya."

Layla drops the fingernail onto the floor, breathing hard.

The soul jerks its hand away, cradling it against its body. "Blue door. Blue door."

My ears tingle. "It's lying," I say behind my hand.

Layla turns to me, almost pleading. "You sure?"

I nod and the tingling subsides. Layla sighs and grabs for the soul.

"No," it screams, backing away. "No. I wuz lyin'. I wuz. It's red."

"Lie," I say.

Layla snatches its hand.

"Wait. I duzn't know the door. I duzn't know."

"Truth," I say.

Layla releases the soul, slams the pliers into her bag, and hurries to me. "That was terrible. And for nothing. I hope the next one gives us something."

Finding another soul doesn't take long. "Your turn," Layla says.

Everything in me protests, but I open my bag and pull out a small, five thong, barbed whip. What twisted mind invented this horror? The soul wails and turns its already scarred back to me.

"Where's the door home?" I ask.

The soul shakes its head and wails again.

I raise the whip over my shoulder. Deep breaths. Deep breaths. I can do this. I bring the whip down on the soul's back, but the force behind it results in barely a tap. The soul stops wailing and gazes over its shoulder, its black eyes questioning.

"Um. Where's the door?" I ask.

The soul stares.

Layla marches over. "Give me that." Snatching the whip, she brings it down hard on the soul's back. I scramble away from the silver blood splatter.

"Tell us where to find the door home," Layla demands, raising the whip.

"East," the soul screams.

Layla glances my way.

"True," I say.

"Do you know more?" She strikes again.

"Layla, stop," I say.

"We need answers," she says, whipping it again.

The soul screams louder. "White. It is white and gold. The handle is bronze."

I shake my head.

Layla hits it several more times. "Tell the truth."

"It is white. And gold," it says.

I nod.

"So, the handle was the lie?" Layla asks, raising the whip.

"Yes," the soul wails. "The handle is missing. Missing." It slumps over and sobs into its hands. "I know nothing more."

I nod.

Layla returns the whip to my bag.

"That was harsh," I say.

"Someone had to do it. There's no time for squeamishness, Anaya. We need to find the door before anyone else. New deal. I torture, you lie detect. Let's go."

Not having to torture? Yes, please. But it's unsettling how quickly Layla adapted to it.

The next soul knows nothing, but Layla sticks another bamboo shoot under its nail "just to be sure."

Layla chops off fingers, sticks bizarre devices where things shouldn't be stuck, and questions until she's satisfied each soul knows no more.

"Okay," Layla says, dropping her latest victim's dismembered ear onto the floor, her fingers and knife dripping silver. "The field of doors is to the east. Once there, we find the only chocolate bar door, face the door, and turn west. We look for a red door with a green handle, open that door, and we should see the white door covered in gold scrollwork that has no handle. That's the door home. Let's find another soul."

"No, I think we're good," I say, my voice shaky. "If we don't find the door, we can always return and torture more."

Layla sighs. "You're probably right. Let's go."

After walking for what seems like hours, we reach the field. Doors everywhere. In the air. On the ground. In the ground. Half doors. Full doors. Huge doors. Tiny doors.

Door after door after door.

Distant howls drift across the field.

Layla's eyes go wide. "Did Kedar sick the hounds on us?"

"Sounds like it," I say.

We sprint for cover, skidding to a halt near a blue door.

Gloria's soul stands over her crumpled body. "It's not fair. Terri pushed me in. She got Beth, too. Watch your back."

"We will." Layla pulls me away.

Our search leads to Pam's chewed and torn body near the chocolate door. "Damn hounds." Pam's soul points east. "The orange door is over there."

"That's the wrong door," Layla says.

Pam frowns. "It is?"

I nod.

"Stupid lying souls," Pam says. "Good luck."

"Thanks," I say.

Layla and I face west.

"Red door, green handle," Layla says, pointing.

We leave Pam and hurry to the door. Layla flings it open, revealing the white and gold door with no handle.

"I did it," Layla says.

I frown. "*We* did it."

"Whatever." She pushes the door, but nothing happens.

We kick it, pound on it, say "magic" words, but it doesn't open. Howling nearby makes us jump.

"Damn it," Layla says. "Let's go. We'll lead the hounds away and come back."

"Wait. Maybe we should knock."

"We tried that," Layla growls.

"But not like this." I step forward and raise my fist.

KNOCK.

KNOCK.

KNOCK.

The door swings open.

Layla grabs me and squeezes. Home is inches away. Layla lets me go and takes a shaky breath.

I fist my right hand and rest it upright on the palm of my left, ready to play. "Let's do this."

Layla doesn't reciprocate. I knew it. She's reneging on the plan. I shouldn't have trusted her.

"Layla?"

Layla steps away. "Go home, Anaya."

I stagger back. "What?"

"It's my way of apologizing for the twelfth birthday party fiasco."

Joy and relief rush through me. I'm going home.

"Thank you, Layla." I grab the door frame and pause. Just step through. Go home.

My shoulders slump, and I turn away. "You did the torture, Layla. You earned it."

Layla beams. "Does this mean you forgive me for saying I didn't hear the knocking that night?"

"You let them call me crazy and laughed along with them. That hurt. Still, on the stupid move scale, me ending our friendship that night is right up there with putting on this ring."

Layla grins and hugs me. I hug back.

"Stop," Terri screams, running at us. "That's my door!"

Daisy and Rose smash through a door several feet away, black tongues lolling, red tinged slime dripping from their mouths.

"Go. I'll hold them off," I say.

"You're a good person, Anaya." Layla grabs my hand and pulls me behind her. "Have a nice life."

She shoves me through the door.

"Layla, no," I scream.

Cool air caresses me. I'm sprawled on my dorm room floor, door wide open.

"What the hell, Anaya?" my roommate growls from her bed. "Why are you on the floor?"

"I . . . I had a bad dream."

"On the floor?"

"I sleepwalk?"

"Whatever. It's barely after midnight, and I have an English exam at seven. Shut the door and go back to bed."

One year later.

11:59 PM.

I don't know why I'm awake. It's ridiculous. It's over. But what if?

No. It's not going to happen. Not again. Not ever.

12:00 AM.

KNOCK.

KNOCK.

KNOCK.

I gasp and rush to the door.

"For you," Gloria's soul says, handing me an envelope.

"Uh. Thanks."

She smiles and vanishes.

I close the door, open the envelope, and pull out a black card embossed with red roses and red text:

Your presence is required at the wedding of Kedar, the Demon King and Layla, Queen of the Damned. Please put on the enclosed ring.

Scrawled at the bottom:

As much as I want to see you, Anaya, you can't come. Kedar
wants you as his pet. I have removed the ring, so you won't
be tempted.

Love, Layla.

About the Author

JM Stradling is the author of the magical, fantastical, dark, mysterious fiction.
She's also an artist, photographer, baker, gamer, pet wrangler, mom. Get a
glimpse into her worlds by following her on Instagram @joanstradlingauthor
or @joan.of.arts and visit joanstradling.com.

PORTRAIT
OF A
VAMPIRE

HAYLEY HAWTHORNE

Tonight, I have to kill the man I love.

The carriage jolts to a stop, the wheels sliding on the snow covered street.

I glance up to Inspector Warren Henshaw who sits across from me and press my back hard into the velvet seat to avoid brushing his knees. Being this close to him makes me want to vomit.

The glow of his cigarette illuminates his cruel, gray eyes as they bore into mine. I've noticed the way he watches me the past few months with unmasked lust. I had to act fast, hoping my proposition of marriage would tempt him to agree. It did.

"If you're successful in extracting him on your own, the promotion's yours. I'm a man of my word."

I yank my gloves on. "As am I."

He breathes out a cloud of cigarette smoke in my face as he leans forward.

A cough racks through me, and I fan the air.

The bastard laughs. "You'll have to get used to it, pet. And I'm afraid I'm not going to want our engagement to be a long one."

He grips my knee and squeezes hard. I bite down on my tongue to keep from wincing. "And remember. Not a word of this to anyone. Ever. You won't like the consequences if you do. There are dozens of agents that would kill to take out a target like him."

I remember being so excited when I was accepted into Covert at Scotland Yard. But now I regret it more than anything. Because it led me to him. No, not the vile man in the carriage with me.

But the man living inside the mansion just outside.

I stare out the carriage window, fogged with the frigid December night. I have to do this. Any other agent would torture him and arrange a public burning in Trafalgar Square. Whoever kills him will be elevated to a near divine-like figure in society. But I'm not bringing him in alive.

He reaches and opens the carriage door. "Get it over with."

I step out onto the snow covered cobblestones and walk to the front door of 51 Earls Court, the home of a wealthy London gentleman who happens to spend an exorbitant amount of his wealth on art. Little does he know that an "original" oil painting of an unknown Count from Marseilles hanging in his gallery isn't that of a man.

No. It's a portrait of a vampire. And an alive one, at that.

Raoul Durand. Public enemy number one. Wanted for helping vampires escape England and seek asylum in France.

I glance side to side before I enter. The street is empty. The only sound is the soft hiss of the gas lamps and the whisper of snowfall. I pull my wand from inside my coat and trace the lock at the door. It clicks open, and I step inside.

The house is dark, silent. Like it always is this time of night. For the past year, these nights have existed outside of time. A fantasy I created, and one I allowed to turn into more. And now my heart is paying the price.

I make my way up the grand staircase to the art gallery on the second floor.

The sting of tears prick my eyes. "I'm such a fool." I whisper.

I tried so hard to keep leads from developing that would bring a Covert agent to him. I destroyed early intelligence reports when I could. But Warren discovered him yesterday. I don't know how, but he did. I overheard him talking with another agent about his location, so I had to act quickly.

Opening the door to the gallery, I walk in, careful to keep my footsteps silent in the cavernous space.

Taking a seat on the bench across from his portrait, I fix my eyes on the floor. I can't bring myself to look at him just yet. My hand finds its way to the inside pocket of my coat, and I pull out a small, leather bound book.

The initials on the front, R.D. Raoul Durand.

I run my fingers over the soft, worn leather of his personal diary. I came across it in the evidence department at Covert. An agent found it on the streets in London where Raoul dropped it while he was on the run. Curiosity got the best of me, and I read the first few pages. And then I couldn't stop. I learned he isn't a monster. Not at all. He wants peace between magical communities, not division and hate. He wrote about his rage when he learned of the rules that keep witches subjugated under warlocks in England. Witches like me. And back in Marseilles, where he was the leader of the vampire community, he worked tirelessly to influence that same worldview in his subjects.

I knew then that I had to protect him. So night after night for the past year, I risked coming here and sneaking in at the midnight hour, knowing the household would be asleep. Witches aren't allowed to conjure powerful warding spells, but I did the best I could. And as the nights went on, I began to talk to him as I put my wards up. I told him how much I hate the laws that keep our kind afraid of one another, and that knowing someone shared my beliefs made me feel less alone in the world. Some nights I would look into his eyes, and tell him that I long for a free world for magic folk where we can co-exist. That his dreams are my own, and if things were different, then we could be friends.

And then as time went on, more forbidden things. That he's the one I think about at night as I fall asleep. That I dream about what it would be like for him to touch me, hold me. *Devour* me.

Rising to my feet, I walk up to the gold, ornate frame. I still cannot bring myself to meet his eyes. I know he's in a deep sleep and has never once been aware of me. All of the other vampires that have been found by Covert and extracted from their portraits awoke confused and near catatonic, their last memory being when they were being trapped. Some were given a quick death, but most tortured and burned at the stake. I can spare him that. I can make it quick.

I bring my wand up. My hand shakes, and my eyes well with tears.

"I can't do this." I slump to the floor.

Think, Constance, think. How can you save him?

"I've never known you to give up easily." The voice echoes throughout the room. The tone is hypnotic and dark, near musical. My training kicks in. That's the voice of a vampire.

I whirl around, panic electric in my blood. The door is open. I couldn't have been followed. The street was empty.

"Who's there?" I feel cold air at my back and turn around, trembling.

Inches in front of me is a devastatingly handsome man at a towering height.

My wand clatters to the floor as I open my mouth to scream, but his hand covers my mouth before I can make a sound.

He says, "Mr. Fisher is quite the snorer, but if you scream, then we both are done for."

Two things happen at once. I notice the glint of fangs as he speaks. Next, my gaze darts over his shoulder to the very empty and Raoul-less canvas. My eyes fly back to the vampire holding me, and I go rigid as shock locks my limbs.

Vibrant garnet eyes, near glowing. A faint scar extending from his left brow to his hairline. Raven black hair tied at the nape of his neck. That shamelessly alluring mouth.

Raoul.

"It's a pleasure to meet you, Constance," he says with a grin. A small shiver goes up my spine. His voice is deeper than I imagined it would be.

"Please calm down. I won't harm you." He kicks my wand out of the way, and grins wider. "Just in case you try to hex me."

If only he knew what I thought of him. Thank the Mother, Father, and all of the higher powers above that he doesn't—wait. *He said my name.*

"Before I remove my hand, please promise me you won't scream."

I nod.

He releases me and takes a step back. His gaze trails up and down me, and a look of wonder passes over his face.

I try to catch my breath. "How do you know my name?"

"Ah," he says. "One moment."

He pulls a pocket watch from his waist jacket, and says, "*Heure de Minuit.*"

My French is rusty, but I believe he just said midnight hour.

The acrid smell of smoke fills the room. He just used time magic. One of the main reasons he was hunted.

I start to stutter. "You . . . how . . ."

"We only have an hour, I'm afraid."

I push at my temples. "I am losing it. I have completely and utterly, lost—
"

"Constance."

This can't be real. Raoul cannot be standing here saying my name like he knows me. This is a trick of some kind. I run and pick up my wand and point it at him.

An expression of hurt crosses his face.

He says, "Midnight has stopped all across London for an hour. Please. I want to speak with you."

"How did you get out of your painting?" I ask.

His mouth quirks up in a grin. "I always could. I just didn't choose to until tonight."

"That's impossible," I snap.

He laughs. It's a pleasant laugh. The tone is deeper than his voice.

"Covert doesn't know everything about me. One of their brightest agents does, though."

I feel my face go bloodless. *Could he know I read his diary?*

He cocks his head at me. "Seeing you through the canvas was always distorted. I thought I knew what you looked like, but I was wrong."

My breath freezes in my lungs. He could see me? For the past year?

I start to back up towards the door.

My voice shakes as I say, "Don't try to flatter me. I know what you're doing. And if you knew the things I said about you every night I had to come check to make sure you were still contained, you'd tear my throat out."

His face turns to stone, and his throat works as he swallows. "We both know that's a lie."

Dear God.

I start shaking my head, and the air squeezes out of my lungs. If he heard me, then he heard me say how I dreamed of a world where we could be together. How I desired him.

I spin around and run as fast as I can out the door of the gallery. My shoes clack against the marble floor as I fly down the grand staircase.

A shadow appears in my peripheral, and wind roars in my ears. I skid to a stop to keep from slamming into him as he blocks the front door. How is he so fast?

He holds his hands up. "I know I've given you quite the fright."

My voice comes out in a tremble. "Just get out of my way and leave me be. Leave London and save yourself."

He grins, fangs glinting in the moonlight. "You took up all the conversation this past year. It's only fair that I say a few words."

I shake my head and say, "I don't want to hear anything you have to say. If what you say is true, you have an hour before your spell is up, and they will hunt you down and burn you at the stake."

"Will your fiancé be the one to light the pyre?"

So he really did hear everything.

I try to reach around him to turn the handle. But he grabs my wrist and spins me until my back is up against it. His face is inches away from mine, and for a moment I can't think.

The scent of him, real. His breath against my face, real.

The desire in his eyes, for me. Real.

He tucks an auburn curl behind my ear. "Let me help you." He says, and a shiver laces up my spine as his thumb traces from below my ear and then slowly across my jaw.

How many times have I dreamed about this? What it would be like to touch him. For him to touch me.

He clears his throat and drops his hand. "I know of the deal you made to try and keep me from a terrible death. I have connections. You don't have to run."

"How can I trust you?" I clench my wand in my hand.

"We can make the midnight sailing for Marseilles at the docks. I'll be out of the magical wards. Once we reach Marseilles, I can offer you asylum. You have my word."

I bark out a laugh. "We? Are you mad?"

He smirks. "I'm not the one who talked to an oil painting every night for the past year." He smooths his hands down his vest. "I do have that effect on people, though."

My jaw drops, and I have the sudden urge to knee him in the groin.

His eyes darken, and the heat flares in his eyes.

"That's the first time I've seen murder in your eyes." He bends down, lips hovering just above mine. "I do believe I like it."

He reaches around me, opens the front door and walks outside.

I spin around and gasp at the scene in front of me. The snowfall hangs in the air, still as night. There's not a sound to be heard. I've never witnessed magic like this.

Raoul turns around and meets my stare. "Walk with me. I promise I'll answer any question you ask."

It would take me a lifetime to ask him the questions I want to ask. I follow him, but keep a few steps back.

"Why aren't you trying to kill me?" I ask.

"The same reason you couldn't kill me moments ago."

My heart flutters behind my ribs. "Wait. Please, just stop."

He turns and faces me.

"The Obsidian spell that backfired a year ago that trapped all illegal vampires in portraits. Every vampire that has been found was in a deep sleep before they were extracted and . . . killed. How have you been awake?"

"You," he says.

"I'm afraid you need to be more clear." I cross my arms.

He grins. "Obsidian is a sinister magic, as you know. But unpredictable. I was terrified when the spell contained me and began to force me asleep. I feared if I ever woke that the hatred and cruelty that comes second nature to my kind would be all I'd feel. But then I started to have dreams. Or at least, I thought that's what they were. A young woman's voice. Flashes of a beautiful face. Bright, crystal blue eyes. And then one night, I woke up."

He starts to walk towards me slowly.

"And I soon realized the girl from my dreams was real. And as she read my words back to me from my diary, it reminded me of who I am and that goodness is always worth fighting for. It kept me from going mad."

He places his hands on my shoulders. I want to lean into him and never leave.

"I cannot let you sacrifice yourself like this. If you don't leave London, Warren will find you. You know he will."

He takes my wrist, and his thumb skates over my pulse.

"Leave with me. Now. Please." His voice cracks as he says it.

"I can't . . . I . . ."

He cups my face in his hands. "What do you want, Constance?"

You. But I can't bring myself to say it. Because it would be too good to be real. He would be taken from me somehow.

He frowns. His gaze snaps to my wrist, and he pulls my glove off. "That gemstone on your ring . . ."

I look down, and black smoke is swirling inside the gem. I don't even remember putting the ring on.

Raoul growls out, "They used Obsidian on you."

"That's impossible. Obsidian was made illegal after the revealing spell backfired."

His voice quivers as he says, "Constance, run. Run now."

But it's too late. The black smoke shoots from my ring, and four Covert agents appear.

Raoul pulls me behind him. His fangs snap as he says, "I'll go willingly. But first give me your word that no harm will come to Ms. Rapier."

"Now why would I harm my darling fiancé?" A chill races up my spine at the familiar voice. Warren walks from behind us and steps in front of Raoul just as he throws silver chains around him and yanks him to the ground.

"No! Please!" I reach towards him, but Warren shoves him towards the other agents who bind his wrists with more silver chains.

Warren looks at me with fury. "Did you really think you could fool me with your nightly escapades? I've had you shadowed for weeks now."

Raoul groans in pain, and my heart shatters when I see the silver chains burning through his clothing, the scent of scorched flesh turning my stomach.

This is all my fault.

Warren steps behind me and bands an arm around my stomach. His other hand encircles my neck.

An animalistic growl vibrates through Raoul.

Warren laughs. "Vampires are such possessive creatures. That's when their bloodlust is fiercest. You played your part well, Constance. I was counting on you seducing him out."

Raoul's eyes have gone wholly black, fangs elongated.

"I'm not sure what would be a finer end for you, Raoul Durand. Torturing you myself before you're burned on the pyre?" Warren brings his mouth to my ear and bites down hard. Revulsion courses through me. "No. I think I'll have my way with Ms. Rapier in front of you. Over, and over again."

Raoul pulls against the chains, the silver burning through him down to the bone.

"Please, stop!" I scream. I pull against Warren's hold with all my strength.

"Enough of this." I feel the tip of Warren's wand at my back, followed by a shock that sears through every nerve ending.

The world goes dark.

***

I stir awake. In an instant it all rushes back. Raoul, alive. Raoul captured.

My head lolls to the left. I open my eyes, and my vision comes into focus. Looking through the window by me, I see Trafalgar Square. The snow is falling in sheets, and a pyre has been built and prepared.

He is going to die, and it's all my fault.

I groan as pain radiates through me. My wrists are bound behind a chair, throbbing and chafed.

I bring my head up and see Warren sitting at his desk. I'm back at Covert headquarters.

He is spinning a black, iridescent stone on his desk like a top.

Obsidian.

An animal noise of pain sounds from my left. Raoul is chained to the chair with the silver chains.

My voice comes out in a croak. "Warren, let him go, please. He's dying. I'll do whatever you want."

"You're in no position to bargain. I can take whatever I want from you."

Raoul's pocket watch is sitting on top of papers on his desk. If I could somehow get to it, maybe I could use it.

Warren sees me eyeing it and picks it up, dangling it by the chain. "He was the last vampire alive that could wield time magic."

He slams it on the desk and smashes it.

"As you saw earlier, Obsidian is *nothing* compared to vampire magic. I stopped it completely."

I grit my teeth. "That magic belongs to witches."

All of a sudden, the gas lamp on Warren's desk snuffs out. In the next second, the flames in the fireplace douse as if water was thrown on them.

The clock above Warren's desk begins to click out of rhythm, and then the hour hand starts to move backwards. The gray dawn of the morning outside darkens into night.

The scent of smoke fills the office. Magic. *Raoul's magic.*

Warren jumps to his feet and points his wand at Raoul.

"What is this?" Warren yells. A look of panic flits across his face.

The hour hand stops at midnight, and the ticking stops.

A flicker of shadow appears to my right, and my binds loosen. I look to Raouls's chair, and it's empty, the silver chains on the floor.

Warren makes a choking sound. I turn around, and Raoul has him in a chokehold, fangs at his throat.

Raoul says, "Advice from a monster to a monster. You only show your true power when your enemy thinks you're beat. That pocketwatch was a bluff. The power was with me alone all along."

My gaze drops to the Obsidian on his desk. A memory flashes from something I read in Raoul's diary. Obsidian was made from the blood of witches, and only witches can use it and control it fully. It was a truth I was never told by Covert. And to think it has been here under my nose this whole time.

I can feel the energy of it pushing against my mind.

What do you wish? A feminine, ethereal voice says, the Obsidian tugging at me.

I can feel the twisted, dark abnormality of it. A lump forms in my throat, and a heavy sadness pressed on my shoulders. This was once a pure power, but now it's been twisted into a magic that can't be trusted.

I can give you anything you desire, dearest. Tell me, the Obsidian says.

I can feel her pain. Her torment. There's only one thing I could ever command it to do.

"Be at peace," I say.

Warren struggles against Raoul's hold. "No, stop!"

A haunted sigh breathes throughout the room, and the stone begins to crack. Warren screams. My mouth goes dry as the same cracks in the stone appear on Warren's skin. With a burst of shadow, they both disappear.

Raoul rushes to me and brings his hands to my face. "Are you all right?"

I nod. "Yes. I wasn't sure if that would work."

"You're brilliant, you know that?"

He leans down, and the air rushes from lungs. His lips move against mine as he says, "Hold on tight."

Before I can reply, the room blurs out of focus, and we're falling. He pulls me close, and he laughs as I scream.

The roaring stops, and I feel the ground beneath my feet. He brings his hands to my shoulders to steady me. The brackish scent of the Thames wafts in the air, and several grand ships bob in the harbor in front of me, their rigging like pen and ink against the moonlit sky.

"Last call for Marseilles!" A ship attendant yells.

I meet Raoul's gaze, and his face goes grim. "That schooner on the left is headed to Dublin. Ireland is neutral, you'd be safe there. I have a friend who could help set up a life for you. A home by the sea. Wherever you'd like."

My heart soars in my chest. He remembers me mentioning how I'd love to live by the sea. "You'd do that for me?"

His eyes heat. "Don't give me that much credit. I am one breath away from doing the indecent thing, throwing you over my shoulder, and taking you to Marseilles with me."

A thrill goes through me at the thought.

He lets out a harsh breath. "But when you love someone, you honor their choice."

My eyes fill with tears. "You love me?"

"Ever since our first midnight."

I'm smiling. I'm crying. "I still barely know you."

He smirks and leans forward, mouth hovering above mine. "It's a four day journey to Marseilles. Plenty of time for us to get acquainted."

I stand up on my tiptoes, and my mouth meets his. His lips move against mine hesitantly, carefully at first. Then rougher, harder. A molten heat pounds through me, and I tighten my hands in his jacket and press myself closer. He pulls away, chest heaving.

His voice comes out gruff as he says, "I have one condition."

I raise an eyebrow "Oh?"

"We're going to need two cabins."

I run my fingers over his lips and he shivers, pupils dilating. "And if I don't agree to your terms?"

He smiles wickedly. "Ms. Rapier, you may just kill me yet."

About the Author

Hayley Hawthorne is a fantasy romance writer. She loves writing characters who prefer to stab each other before they want to kiss. Her stories feature strong, independent heroines who navigate dark, romantic settings. When not writing, she can be found reading enemies-to-lovers romances, watching anything Star Wars & Avatar: The Last Airbender, and dreaming of her next travel adventure. You can follow her writing journey on Instagram: @hayleyhawthornewrites.

SPECULATIVELY SARAH

CHRISTINE WILCOX

The cool evening breezes flowed across San Jose like fingers combing through long, silky hair. Pearl watched Sarah rock in her favorite chair on the second-floor balcony of her home while the world dimmed, the moon's light emerging degree by degree from the dusk blue of the sky. Sarah watched and waved as the carpenters and journeymen walked the path to the carriage house, lugging their toolboxes and tired bodies to the Model-T's she had given each of them in the spring. Sarah did things like that.

Pearl, Sarah's nurse first but also her friend, stood in the room behind the French doors that led to the balcony. She waited until Sarah rested her head on the rocking chair before deciding to interrupt the moment. Pearl knew how much Sarah loved when the calendar flipped from August to September. When she was a girl, she told Pearl her birthday celebration on the first of the month always brought a swirl of excitement. Now that she was well into her eighth decade, her love for the time of year had less to do with marking the passage of time and more with the thinning of the veil between worlds.

The thinning veil made everything so much easier.

A conversation about the veil forged their unique friendship, owing to being a beau's "plus one" at Sarah's 80th birthday celebration three years and three days ago. The forgettable man had wanted to impress Sarah by bringing a genuine, field-tested psychic into her sphere. Now, Sarah only remembered it was the day she and Pearl met. Pearl had been in her circle ever since. They were each a force of nature in a world dominated by men, and they knew it.

Pearl slipped silent steps onto the balcony behind Sarah's chair. "It's quite a sight when you see them all together, isn't it? Reminder of a hard day's work done."

Sarah's eyes flew open wide, and her spine snapped straight as she sucked air into her lungs. "Good heavens. You shouldn't scare an old woman like that. You could have killed me, and then where would I be?"

"You asked me to meet you here, remember?" Pearl replied, lowering her eyes, and biting the insides of her cheeks to keep from smiling. Sarah's face had a softness about it tonight that Pearl hadn't seen in their many conversations. Always so hard at work on her life's purpose, Sarah rarely enjoyed the complete stillness of a moment. She gifted everyone who worked for her a charmed existence. "Is that all of them? The workers?" Pearl asked.

"Yes. All thirteen." She paused and scanned the horizon, as if reading something secret in its shape. "Since John died, it's been harder to keep up with it all. He did so much . . ." Sarah's voice trailed off. She stared up at the waxing moon without tilting her head, to abate the tears that would have flowed otherwise.

It was one of the favorite tricks Sarah had taught Pearl. *"Looking up stops tears from flowing. Isn't that interesting?"* Pearl remembered her saying this once when they were in deep discussion and a particular memory rendered her teary-eyed. *"If we look to the heavens, our eyes physically cannot cry. Doesn't that tell you where love comes from and goes to, my dear girl? And our bodies know it! That's where our eyes can look to stop the tears. Toward love."* Pearl's heart warmed at the memory. The trick had come in handy for Sarah, especially when the nervous chatter about her house became grist for the gossipers' mill.

"I'd like to just sit here for a while. We don't need to chat," Sarah said, leaning back to give the rocker some sway.

"Of course. I'll keep an eye on the time," Pearl replied. She watched Sarah drink in the moonlight of her world. Pearl's gifts gave her a unique perspective on gratitude. Would everyone in the world be more grateful, more loving if they knew the expiration dates of those they loved? Or their own? They celebrated Sarah's 83rd birthday quietly just 3 days ago, and Sarah had said nothing of the impending date. She didn't change her schedule or try to do more things than she normally did. There were no grand gestures. She let her life stand as it was. But twilight had long ago faded, and midnight was approaching. Pearl wanted to give Sarah time to ready herself. She bent down to whisper in Sarah's ear. "Are you ready?"

"Is it time?" Sarah asked, shifting her feet to stop rocking.

"Yes," Pearl whispered. "We don't want to be late." She questioned in her own mind why she bothered mentioning not wanting to be late. She didn't know what Sarah's plans were, other than she was to remind her of the list.

Sarah grabbed the ends of the armrests and hoisted herself to the seat's edge, planting her feet on the balcony floor. Her gnarled left hand reached for her cane. She closed her eyes, inhaled, and pushed herself up at the top of her breath, exhaling in a burst when her legs had to support her.

Pearl helped Sarah steady herself by placing her hands on her shoulders. The old woman gained her balance and turned toward the doors to her home.

"How's your arthritis?" Pearl asked.

"It's been worse," Sarah replied. "I've kept trying to learn how I might force its exit from my joints, but the esteemed Dr. Augustin Jacob Landré-Beauvais hasn't been forthcoming."

"To be fair, he only gave it a name, not a cure. And he's been dead since the year after you were born."

"That's no excuse," Sarah said, stopping. Her eyes widened as they landed on a grandfather clock. "Does that say it's nearing eleven o'clock? Oh my. Time is of the essence."

Pearl followed Sarah at the only pace Sarah was capable of: slow. "Would you permit me to try something I've only just learned?" Pearl asked.

"Now?"

"It isn't something I could have planned for, but I think you are the perfect candidate."

"I cannot resist being in the vanguard of furthering research. Try away! What must I do?"

"Still yourself. I'm not sure this will work yet." Pearl positioned herself behind Sarah. She took slow, deep breaths and envisioned Sarah moving fluidly, without arthritis, surrounded by radiant light. She moved her hands from Sarah's shoulders down her back, past her hips and knees, stopping at her ankles, which she held for a moment. She repeated the process two more times, pausing at the major joints, envisioning a flow of energy going easily through Sarah's body. "How do you feel?" she asked when she finished.

Sarah had stilled her own breathing while Pearl worked. "My dear girl, what have you unleashed? I feel fifty again!" Sarah said, taking a few easier steps forward and completing a twirl that made her skirt flutter. "What have you done?"

"Something I learned from that Indonesian healer who visited yesterday. While you were resting, we had a lengthy discussion about the body's capabilities. He wanted to help."

"So much time wasted on drilling Landré-Beauvais and an Indonesian healer could have cured me in an afternoon's time?"

"To be fair, it isn't a cure. It's an adjustment, and a temporary one. Though I believe with time and attention I could bring about more prolonged results." Pearl stopped the sinking feeling in her gut from pushing tears to her eyes as she looked at Sarah, who would have no more time.

"I can't wait to hear more of it in the coming years. You know we must continue our discussions. We will find our way. I'm sure you will change medicine for the better! Yet now we must make haste to the Séance room. After all these years, could you imagine? Missing my own date with destiny and all because of a waxing moon."

"Do you have your list?" Pearl asked.

"Of course, I have the list. When have I ever been without the list? It's right here," Sarah said, slipping a hand into a discreet pocket on her full skirt. Pearl watched the hand frisk under the fabric as Sarah's eyebrows pinched together. "Or maybe here." Her other hand slipped into the opposite pocket and the same frisking motion occurred. Sarah began patting her body down, starting on her bodice and going down to her thighs. "Oh hell, what did I do with it?"

"Where were you when you last had it?"

Sarah's eyes fixed on a corner of the room. "Let's see. When I woke, it was already afternoon. Jane came to help me dress, and I put it in my pocket." Her eyes scanned back and forth, as if typing out directions dictated from her mind. "I went to the Hall of Fires."

Shuffling past her bedroom and into the Conservatory, Sarah paused. "I've always loved this room. The industrial pipes balanced out against the woodwork. The earthiness of the ruddy painted floors. The creams and greens. I think I'll come back here first afterward."

Pearl nodded. "I would certainly spend time here." She gazed through the greenhouse roof to the moon slipping across the sky. "But we're losing time to find your list."

"To the Hall of Fires!" Sarah charged forth again with vigor, so much that Pearl almost lost her in a corridor before seeing her outline against an orange glow in the hallway. "You've got the fireplaces going," Pearl said.

"I've kept them going these last few weeks. At odd hours when the pain becomes more than my mind can calm, I've made my way here." Sarah glanced around the small rooms and at the glowing fireplaces. A houseman slept in a chair in the corner.

"Why's Tom here? I thought he only worked in the orchards?" Pearl asked.

"He's deaf as a post, but always the first to smell bacon when it's two minutes away from being done, so he's responsible for keeping the fires going and the house from burning down."

Pearl giggled. "You've always been such an astute observer of a person's strengths."

"You give me more credit than I deserve with people. I was so shy. It was hard for me to get to know people. I always needed help in that regard," Sarah replied, looking at Tom while her head angled towards her shoulder. "He's a good man. He's been a good friend to me." She slid her hand to the wall and turned on the light switch, launching the sleeping Tom to his feet.

"Good evening!" he hollered before he'd had a chance to wake up or clear his throat; it came out a bit garbled. "I'll have the fires roaring in no time." He stumbled forward a bit until Sarah stopped him.

"That won't be necessary, Tom. I'm only here to see if I might have left a small book."

Tom paused and rubbed his eyes. "There's only the book there." He gestured toward the seat of a chair.

Sarah nodded, but said, "That's not it. Mine is quite small, like a deck of cards."

Looking around at the corners of the room, he said, "It doesn't seem to be here. May I assist in the search?"

Sarah paused, gazing at the fire. Her eyes followed the flicks of flame licking the firebox bricks' sharp edges. "No, I think I've sorted out where I might have left it. Thank you, Tom. Have a wonderful life." Flustered, she shook her head and said, "I mean night. Have a wonderful night." She swept out of the room, Pearl trailing behind her.

"I think I remember where it might be. Life begins and ends at the Doorway to Nowhere."

Pearl caught her own brow furrowing. "What were you doing there today?"

"Admiring the view. And I might have been hoping to scare a few people who were lurking and staring from across the road." Sarah replied. "The speculation that whirrs about me because of my art project of a house is delightful. I can't wait to see what they say once I'm gone."

"You won't care what they say when you're gone. You'll be on to another adventure."

"I'm sure I'll find time," she replied. The pair rounded the corner into an odd section of the house. The room wasn't finished, and at one end was a doorway to the outside with nothing on the other side but open air.

"Why did you keep that door there when it sparked so much negative attention?" Pearl asked, staring at the darkened portal. The room still had gaps between the framing and the wallboard. The only paint was on the window trim.

"You never know when it might be easier to go through than trudge upward," Sarah replied. "It allowed us to deliver lumber and other supplies to the second floor without issue. It made sense at the time. And there it is. My little book." She shuffled over to the windowsill where it sat.

"It's a miracle you remembered where to find it," said Pearl.

Sarah smiled. "Not really. Only my imagination is big. My life is quite small here." She pointed her index finger to her temple and began waving it as she spoke. "My mind ambles where my body cannot. To east Asia to explore the inner chambers of the Egyptian pyramids and down to Antarctica. I stretch my wings like the Great Sphinx and fly over the world. My earthbound body has a routine that permits such fascinations, all of which are confined to this level of my house. I sleep as late as I please. I wake in a fine room of my own design in a building that reveals new secrets to my waiting ear every time I listen. I steep in the Hall of Fires if my joints demand it. I make my way to the rooms I love when I'm able, but most importantly, I open the doors of the Séance room for great works to continue, and I close them so as to leave the balance undisturbed, save a few payments owed."

Pearl smiled. She had known no one like Sarah and felt the odds were lacking she would ever meet her equal.

Sarah gazed at the moonlight streaming into the room. "My body will end, but my imagination will have no end. I will spark the curiosity and conversation of generations going forward with this masterpiece." She flourished her arms easily to the space around her and toward the Door to Nowhere. "One could not ask for a better legacy."

Pearl nodded. "And we have the list, correct?"

"Yes, we have the list, and it's five minutes shy of the door opening."

The pair wove their way through hallways and doorways into the nondescript room that had a bell mounted to accommodate Sarah's 4'10" height and limited, arthritic reach. She looked to a clock mounted on the wall near the door, and at precisely midnight, she rang the bell three distinct times.

Sweeping open the door and settling at the humdrum table in the middle

231

of the room, she closed her eyes and announced, "Into this space I invite those with good intent. Those with messages yet to be heard. Those with aspirations unmet. And here, easy will be their words. I ask the archangels to be with me to the east, to the south, the west, and the north. Stand guard and let our energy bring forth more love, peace, and knowledge into our minds."

Pearl looked to the corners of the room. She expected something to happen. When nothing did, she asked, "What now?"

Sarah chuckled. "I secretly hoped opening the portal would cause the whole house to lift into the sky, as the great pyramids once did when their energy sources were correctly applied, but clearly there is another path for me to take later. Although, we have an appointment I need you here to witness."

"An appointment? With whom?" Pearl asked.

"An old friend who has helped me keep unscrupulous people at bay. He's a seeker of sorts, too."

"Is he expecting me to be here?"

"I don't see why it would matter. You're another seeker."

"Yes, but I'm the seeker who told you the missing numbers etched on your vision of your headstone. He might take exception to that."

"You gave an old seeker a gift. Nothing more. You and he are among the few I've let see the true purpose of this room. I call it the séance room to appease those who aren't intelligent. It was never about spirits. No one became possessed by dark forces, nor were tables raised in midair or other such nonsense. I had many things to learn, and it provided the conduit, but nothing as important as the penultimate lesson my work taught me: love is the energy that goes on. It is persistent and eternal. It's found everywhere and in all things, especially where and when you least expect it. Like at your 80th birthday party where you encounter a new, dear friend." Sarah reached for Pearl's hand and pulled it to her cheek.

A small thump emanated from the door behind them. As Sarah turned, it opened on its own. A black cat sauntered into the room.

"That door doesn't have a floor on the other side." Pearl said, gazing wide-eyed at the cat.

"I know. I must jump from the sink in the kitchen below and balance on the tiniest of thresholds," the cat said, tracking Pearl's widening eyes.

"Ovinnik, lovely to see you again," Sarah said as plainly as if Tom had walked in. Ovinnik strolled across the floor and jumped onto the table.

"Yes, the animal speaks," he said to Pearl before turning toward Sarah. "Why have you brought a stranger into our space, old friend?"

"Ovinnik, meet Pearl. Pearl, Ovinnik. Now you are no longer strangers."

"Fine, it's Pearl," he said.

"SHE's Pearl," Sarah corrected.

Pearl stared at the cat saying her name. She forced her eyes closed and opened them again. Ovinnik was still there. And still speaking.

"Fine. She's Pearl."

Sarah tipped her head at an angle. "And you need not feign caring about her. I know the only thing you care about is the list."

Pearl watched the cat crouch and settle in, a delicious grin on his face and big yellow eyes sparkling. She cleared her throat. "If I may ask, what is your work?"

Sarah folded her hands on the table. "Do you want to answer this question, or shall I?"

"Be my guest. I love hearing my story," Ovinnik replied.

Sarah cleared her throat. "Ovinnik is a creature who can bring both luck and misfortune. His humble beginnings were with farmers. Those who treated Ovinnik to the right foods would find their crops untainted and barns safe. Those who did not honor Ovinnik would find their crops and barns at risk of burning to the ground.

"The twist in this modern world of ours is the dwindling lack of barns, with which I can uniquely help, being an orchardist. Ovinnik and I became friends when I bought this acreage of apricot, plum, and walnut trees. And Ovinnik has been a happy soul, living in the far-flung sections of this house whilst keeping an eye on intent that may have otherwise gone unknown."

Pearl's brow furrowed. Who was this cat and why did Sarah need his help? And what was with that list? "What do you mean?"

Ovinnik's whiskers twitched, and Pearl saw a single eyebrow rise.

"Like workers and suppliers who fail to cut the mustard, darling," Ovinnik replied.

Pearl looked at Sarah and then back at Ovinnik. "So, you're her?" She waited for the cat to fill in the remainder.

"I think of myself as a karma delivery cat."

Karma. Pearl had heard the word before, of course, in her many years nursing soldiers from all over the world, but it was uncommon in the States. She paused for a moment and focused her breath of intention toward him to see what she could extract.

"Oh, aren't you delightful!" he cooed. "You're trying to frisk through my balls of yarn, aren't you?"

Pearl raised an eyebrow of her own. "How did you know that?"

The cat's mouth drew itself into a smile. "My dear, I may have paws in this world, but it doesn't mean my whiskers aren't drawing information from other dimensions." He rose to all fours, arched his back in a stretch, flicked his tail, and returned to sitting. "I am just what Sarah says I am."

Pearl asked, "So Sarah, I presume you're not here to conjure some portal to assist in your crossing over?"

Sarah's lips rose into a mischievous grin, and her eyes sparkled. "No, but I'm delighted that you thought I would try. It feeds perfectly into the eccentric narrative about me. I'm here because I promised to deliver the list to Ovinnik tonight."

"What is this list?" Pearl asked.

Ovinnik's face showed unanticipated glee. "Not what. Whom." He began purring.

Sarah placed her hands over the book on her table. "I have always prided myself on treating people fairly. Paying excellent wages—more than any wealthy man on this planet. Providing for the people and their families at every turn. At times, this attracted sophisticated thieves, which Ovinnik has an eye for ferreting out. When Ovinnik offered to expose those who made their way into my employ under less than honorable intentions, I promised him a sizeable reward: three names. The most unscrupulous, wealthy people who cheated me, stole from me, or lied."

"If he's got an eye for these types of people, why would he need a list?" Pearl asked.

Ovinnik's purring ceased. "I take from those who deserve to lose, and anyone who dared cheat Sarah deserves to lose as much as possible."

Sarah smiled. "Thank you, old friend. I've given this world every kindness, and in return, I've been labeled an eccentric crackpot, mostly due to the three names in this book who sought only to discredit me after I trusted them with my work."

"Who are they?" Pearl asked.

"My sweet friend, I know you too well to tell you. You would try to avert disaster if you knew who they were."

At that moment, Sarah pushed the book toward Ovinnik. She kept her fingers on one edge as he laid two paws down on the opposite side. Pearl watched as the book disappeared.

Ovinnik's eyes gleamed as he stepped towards Sarah and placed his forehead on hers. "I wish you peace. I look forward to our paths crossing again," Ovinnik said. And Pearl watched as he evaporated, too.

Sarah pushed back from the table and stood. "It's not yet two, but I think we can retire now."

"You're not going to tell me who is on the list, are you?" Pearl asked, slightly hurt at the lack of trust.

Sarah smiled. "Watch for news. Maybe about fires."

***

The next afternoon, Sarah slept through her typical wake up time. Pearl touched Sarah's face and watched a slow, contented smile emerge on her cheeks. As the moon slipped over the Conservatory's greenhouse roof that night, Sarah died.

When the news came out in the Modesto Morning Herald on September 7, "Sarah Winchester Dead at San Jose," Pearl loved that it mentioned Sarah's quiet, secluded life and philanthropy and discussed nothing of her eccentricity or eclectic home.

The following year, in September 1923, the city of Berkeley, California, saw a fire spark in the undeveloped grasslands of a canyon east of the city. Pearl read with fascination of the 640 structures—mostly the work of three prominent locals—that burned to the ground. A photograph showed the intersection of Scenic Avenue and Virginia Street after the fire was out. In the rubble beyond the bushes, Pearl could just make out the silhouette of a sleek black cat.

About the Author

Christine Wilcox writes essays and poetry about life and fiction about brilliant women who are ahead of their time and the societal norms they are born into. Happy word herder, defender of the Oxford comma, enthusiastic researcher of all things paranormal, and perpetual student of writing and life on this rock, Christine lives in Eagle, Idaho with her husband and two spoiled golden retrievers. Find her on Instagram at @christinewilcoxauthor and online at www.christinewilcox.com.

MIDNIGHT AT THE MASQUERADE

BRIDGETTE O'HARE

I sra had never attended an event like the Grand Masquerade Ball—an occasion that drew angels from all realms once every century.

Through the ages, she heard wondrous tales of the ball secondhand. Each time others spoke of the entrancing music, the joyous laughter echoing under the moonlight, she felt a pang of regret at what she was missing.

As an angel tasked with delivering dreams to slumbering mortals, she had been taught her duties were of too great a consequence to attend frivolous events. Yet, many nights, as she descended to Earth and whispered dreams into the minds of sleeping humans, she wondered if she was missing out on the enchantment of the legendary event.

This century, however, as the date of the ball approached, Isra made the decision to take a single night off from her duties and finally discover the splendor of the Grand Masquerade Ball for herself. She had hoped the tales hadn't embellished the experience and that this night would be worth the centuries of anticipation.

She was not disappointed.

The grand hall gleamed with an ethereal radiance, its marble columns winding upward until vanishing into the velvety night sky. Floating orbs drifted overhead like luminous moons, bathing the room in a soft celestial glow. Opalescent wings shimmered and fluttered as angels moved about the space, their laughter echoing off the intricate stonework.

She took in the splendor with wide-eyed wonder, feeling utterly out of her element, surrounded by eternal beings who had guided constellations and empires throughout the ages. An air of confidence she hadn't acquired surrounded them.

Self-consciously smoothing the silvery fabric of her ballgown, Isra tried not to gawk as a regal angel passed, her gown's train trailing iridescent peacock feathers. Another had adorned his robes with blossoms that bloomed into vivid color before withering away, only to be reborn again in an endless cycle that mimicked mortality.

A quartet played lilting melodies on harps and lyres from an overhead balcony. As the music swelled, angels danced, their graceful steps gliding over the polished marble floor. Laughter rang through the hall as the masked angelic beings shed their usual gravity and gave themselves over to exuberant revelry beneath the full moon's glow.

As midnight approached—the enchanting hour when magic was said to hold sway beneath the pale moonlight—anticipation built in the glittering hall. Tales stretching back centuries told of magical happenings and strange occurrences that revealed themselves at the Grand Masquerade Ball as the clock struck twelve. Angels manifesting new and unusual abilities. Walls vanishing as celestial landscapes and crystal caverns revealed themselves, then disappeared. Constellations reshaping themselves to unveil sacred messages.

No one knew what experiences the impending chimes might bring. And thus, a thrill of eager suspense ran visibly through the gathered angels.

Isra clutched at her filigreed silver mask, heart fluttering as the appointed moment drew closer. The very air seemed alive, thrumming with promise. She leaned against a marble pillar, not wanting to miss any fantastical occurrence by joining the dancers. Their steps weaved intricate patterns on the polished floor as the music lilted on.

At last, the first chime rang out, echoing off the vaulted ceilings.

The magic had begun.

Dancers all slowed to a pause, and a hush fell over the assembly. Three more melodic chimes followed, each intensifying the breathless sense of waiting in the room. Five. Six. On the seventh chime, the pillars began to glow a pearlescent light from within. Isra's own excited intake of breath mingled with the ninth toll of the bell.

When the final stroke of midnight resonated through the hall, a shimmering mist swirled through the air, pillars gleamed brighter, casting an ethereal glow.

Across the gleaming ballroom, illusions took shape slowly, then with greater speed. Spectral figures danced and twirled where none stood moments before. Scenes of fantastical creatures roaming misty forests and rocky cliffs lingered briefly before dissolving back into a silvery mist.

Gasps and murmurs of delight arose from the crowd as the angels marveled at the strange sights. Some reached out to touch the illusions, only to find empty air. Mystical music escalated as the mirages increased in frequency and vividness.

Then, as the last echoes of midnight faded, the phantoms began to slow their dance and thin into vapor. The music softened and the sights and sounds of the hall returned to their former glory, leaving the angels enchanted but wondering if it had all been an extraordinary dream.

Isra closed her eyes, attempting to memorize the moment just as a mesmerizing voice glided effortlessly like a blend of silk and honey from next to her. "May I have this dance?"

She turned to find an imposing angel clad in an elegant black suit with an iridescent sheen mimicking the dark luster of his arched obsidian wings that curved gracefully behind him. Their majestic edges seemed to absorb the ambient glow around them. Between those pinions hung a cape of the same light-drinking black material that matched his attire.

A silver mask encrusted with tiny glittering jewels rested above his finely chiseled features, obscuring his identity. Though initially startled by his bold invitation, Isra felt instinctively drawn to this mysterious stranger. He had an undeniable magnetism about his presence, a kind of quiet but powerful charisma. She studied the strong lines of his jaw, the sensual shape of his lips, hints of the beauty that lay beneath the mask. Everything about him spoke of confidence and purpose.

She hesitated, feeling uncertain and out of her depth. She was unaccustomed to such direct attention, particularly from one who exuded an aura of command and mystery. Yet, despite her trepidation, she could not resist the pull she felt. Steadying herself with a slight breath, she accepted the stranger's hand. His fingers were warm around hers, sending a tingling current up her arm that hinted at things yet to be revealed.

As they moved together, Isra was struck by how naturally they fell into the steps and rhythm of the dance, as if they had done this a thousand times before. He matched her movements with ease, guiding her along the floor with confident gentleness.

Despite having just met, dancing with this stranger felt intimate yet comfortable. A thrill of exhilaration ran through her as they twirled and stepped in flawless sync, their bodies responding intuitively to each subtle signal from the other.

Yet even as Isra relaxed into the pleasure of the dance, she found her focus entirely captured by the gaze of her mysterious partner. Though partly obscured by the mask, his eyes seemed to delve down to her very spirit. They were keen and intelligent, searching her face as if discerning truths she had yet to learn about herself.

When he spoke, his voice was low and melodic, crafted to command attention. "You are Isra, bringer of dreams," he murmured.

At that moment, Isra realized there was much more to this being than his alluring exterior revealed. Here was someone accustomed to peering beneath the surface and capturing insights in an instant that others took eons to uncover.

"Each night, you venture into the mortal realm and bestow visions upon them," he continued.

She held his gaze directly, no longer hesitant. "How do you know this about me?"

Questions hung unspoken between them as they moved as one.

"I have watched you," he confessed, his voice quiet, almost as if he hadn't wanted to admit it. "Watched as you crafted boats that sail unknown waters and gardens where lost loved ones laugh again."

How did this stranger seem to know her . . . and what did he truly want with her? "Who are you?" Isra demanded, even as she was helplessly drawn further into the rhythm of their bodies moving seamlessly with the melody.

"I am a friend," he said gently. "Or . . . I hope to be."

Isra tilted her head, studying the stranger intently as they swayed together. "You speak in riddles, sir. Please explain. How is it you have watched me without my knowing? Why have you observed my duties in the mortal realm?"

The stranger was silent momentarily as he expertly led them through a turn. "Curiosity drew me to you," he finally admitted. "I was intrigued by how you craft dreams, the care you take in gifting mortals what their hearts most desire. Curious to understand them . . . and you."

Isra pulled her lip between her teeth, then regained composure. "Those dreams . . . they were private moments. Sacred trust between myself and those mortals. I do not know you, sir. I cannot betray their confidence for the sake of your curiosity, or any reason, if that is what you seek."

He smiled beneath his mask. "Virtuous one, I applaud your discretion. Forgive me. But you have nothing to fear from me." He leaned close to her ear. "I do not seek to tarnish your virtue."

A shiver ran down her spine. "And yet you watch without permission," Isra countered with a trace of indignance.

"I never intended harm; I only wished to understand you better. Your dedication to your duties is admirable, and the beauty you—" the stranger hesitated.

"Simply saying hello would have been a more respectable approach to the matter," she replied.

"You are right to reproach me, of course. Perhaps in observing you, I hoped to recall how it felt to have a noble purpose." His voice grew wistful. "I have been where you have been and also where you dare not dream. I have seen the unseeable and know the unknowable."

Something in his tone gave Isra pause. "You speak as though you have lost your way somehow."

"In a manner of speaking." He stared off over her shoulder before returning his gaze to meet hers. "Let us just say the realm I inhabit now is . . . limited in its privileges. I envy those like you who can still brighten mortal lives."

Compassion stirred in Isra's heart. What injustice had this stranger suffered to make him sound so heavy with sorrow? Music swelled around them, but she barely noticed, focused only on the vulnerability in his voice.

A shudder ran through Isra, but she could not pull away, caught in his hypnotic presence. When the dance ended, they stood gazing at each other until those around them dispersed, and a fresh population of dancers surrounded them. Then he took her hand, bestowing a formal kiss upon it. Restlessness crept through Isra. This was no ordinary angel.

She opened her mouth to question him further, but he pressed a solitary finger to her lips.

"Until we meet again," he whispered. With a swirl of his cape, he disappeared into the crowd, leaving Isra with her curiosity and intrigue. Who was this stranger who knew her dreams as if they were old friends?

***

Isra drifted through the ball in a daze, stopping only to exchange pleasantries with friends, focused on her eagerness to see the mysterious stranger again. After some time, she spied him on a balcony overlooking the ethereal gardens below, his wings silhouetted against the fullness of the moon in the night sky. He appeared deep in thought as he gazed at the stars.

Isra slowly approached him. "The heavens are breathtaking from here," she said softly. "But I prefer to view them from Earth, amongst the mortal's dreams."

He turned to her, his expression unreadable behind his mask. "You find beauty in such a chaotic realm?"

"I do," Isra replied. "There is beauty in their hopes, their love, their fervent dreams. But I admit the mortal realm confuses me as much as it delights me at times," she said. "Their lives are so complex. Should it not be enough to simply exist peacefully?"

The stranger shook his head knowingly. "It is their struggles that give their lives meaning. They know their time is fleeting, so they fill it with fierce love, desperate joy, even reckless sorrow."

"But why?" asked Isra, turning to him. "Why seek out such turmoil?"

"Because it makes them feel alive. Their lives blaze bright because they know their flames will extinguish too soon," he said intently. "Consider how dull it would be to float through a bland, peaceful existence for eternity. There would be no poetry, no art, no passion!"

"Because it makes them feel alive?" Isra said skeptically. "They *are* alive. That hardly seems sensible."

He nodded solemnly. "Alas, matters of the heart rarely are sensible. Much messier than our orderly angelic lives, but also more vibrant!"

Isra furrowed her brow. "I confess, I do not fully understand such notions."

For a moment, he was silent, considering her words, staring into her eyes as if studying her thoughts. Then he spoke, his voice a seamless symphony of dulcet sounds, his words melodic.

"On tethered wings I venture down to mortal realms of joy and pain,

Where laughter weeps and sunlight drowns, and dreams bloom bright beneath their rain."

Isra felt herself drawn irresistibly closer, as if pulled by some invisible thread. The verse resonated within her soul. To avoid showing how affected she was by his words, she raised an eyebrow and offered a hint of jest. "My, aren't we the poetic one."

He chuckled. "I may have rehearsed that verse once or twice in anticipation of meeting you."

"Oh, so I'm not the first fortunate angel graced with such lovely words?" Isra teased.

"You wound me," he gasped in mock affront, then his tone lowered, his gaze intensified. "I give you my vow; those words were meant for your ears alone."

The distance between them closed, though she was unsure which of them had moved.

Isra pulled in a controlled breath. "I confess, your words stir something I have never felt. Like a door opening to a new, daring understanding that I'm not sure I will ever fully comprehend."

The stranger cupped her cheek with a hand, warmth surging beneath his touch. "You understand," he breathed, his face inches away, his gaze burning into hers. "You simply cannot fully comprehend something you have never experienced. Let me show you," he whispered and tenderly pressed his lips to hers.

Time suspended as a rush of fire burned through every fiber of Isra's being. She felt their energies mingle and intertwine as something fused them together on a soul level. At that moment, Isra glimpsed the world of mortal passions he had described—frightening and exhilarating all at once. Dangerous in ways she wouldn't have considered before. When their lips parted, she burned to know more.

Overwhelmed by raw emotion, Isra kissed him again, an aching meeting of lips under watching stars. Within that perfect moment, she felt closer to this mysterious stranger than any angel she had known.

***

After hours of walking the gardens and talking of philosophy, dreams, and all things between, the night sky began to show hints of the coming dawn.

Knowing the magical night was nearing its end, before he vanished with the sunrise, Isra wanted to see the face of the being that had bonded to her soul with a kiss. She removed her mask and began to reach for his when his hands slipped over hers, bringing them to rest on each side of his strong jaw.

"Please, the night is almost expired," she whispered.

He hesitated, tension in his frame. He lowered his head, then slowly removed the silver mask and lifted his face to look at her.

Isra gasped quietly. His beauty was beyond anything she'd seen, but a jagged scar ran down his chiseled cheek. "You—you are one of the Fallen?" she stammered. "But why? And how? How have you managed to be in attendance? I do not understand."

His eyes blazed with playful mischief. "I may have procured a favor from an old friend in order to attend. As for my circumstance, I was banished from the celestial realms for sharing forbidden knowledge with humans." He paused. "I thought I was helping humanity build great cities and new technologies that would bring them joy. I was unaware that I was choosing a side."

Isra's mind reeled. The Fallen were shunned as dangerous rebels who defied the Almighty. Yet her affection reached out to the hurting heart before her. The sincerity in his words and compassion in his eyes said he had not rebelled.

"We cannot change the past," she offered. "But that does not make you evil or unworthy."

He turned away. "I should not have ventured here tonight."

"But you did. All things happen for a reason. We must search for the lessons we are meant to learn to become who we were created to be."

"Maybe I was simply created to be charming and entertaining," he said with a playful wink in an attempt to lighten the moment.

Isra smiled. "And while you are certainly both of those, possibly in excess, maybe you were created to be so much more."

"I am what I am, Isra. I was foolish and blind," he sighed. "In my arrogance, I thought the knowledge I shared was a gift, that I was helping them. But I failed to see the deeper consequences." He looked away, unable to meet her gaze. "This scar marks me regardless of my intentions. It would be wise to forget this night we shared."

Gently, Isra reached out and brought his face back toward hers. "I will never forget. You know that isn't possible. You felt the bond just as I did," she said firmly. "One rash action does not define you. We have all made mistakes, trusted too much in our own wisdom."

She traced a feather-light touch over his heart. "Our Creator sees the true heart within. You may yet find redemption."

He shook his head bitterly. "The gates are barred to one such as me."

"Hope endures if you choose to seek it," Isra insisted. As if to confirm her words, moonlight filtered down around them, bathing them in a soothing glow.

Awareness of the fleeting time resurfaced.

"Please, tell me your name. I deserve to know the name of my soul bond," Isra pressed.

He turned to her, agony in his eyes. "Apolion," he offered softly. "But I should never have placed you in such a position as I have. You must let me go. Return to your realm before it is too late."

Isra shook her head defiantly. "It is already too late. "This—" She touched his scar tenderly. "—this may limit where your feet are allowed and where your wings may fly, but it changes nothing that has occurred between us this night, Apolion."

Apolion smiled at the sound of his name on her lips and covered her hand with his as it rested against his cheek. "You are innocent, untainted by the burdens immortality blended with rash choices can offer. Do not chain yourself to me and my cursed fate. It will only lead to sorrow."

"Then let us have this moment of joy before the sorrow comes," Isra insisted.

Apolion hesitated, then slid his hand to cradle her head and pulled her into a fiery kiss. As their lips met with new urgency, destiny shifted around them. This was no longer about right or wrong. Their souls had fused together for eternity. Only one force within the heavens could allow such a bond. It was that force alone that had the power to tear them asunder now.

Isra knew that force was the author of grace, forgiveness, and redemption. She vowed to somehow help Apolion remember.

They broke apart, hearts pounding, as the first hint of dawn glowed in the distance.

"I must go," Apolion whispered regretfully. Taking her hand, he kissed it in gratitude. "Whatever may come, you have awakened hope of a future unbound by the darkness I have existed in."

Isra silenced him with one last searing kiss. "I will find you again," she vowed.

"For your sake, I shall try not to be found." With that, he fervently pressed his lips to her forehead, then dissolved into shadows, leaving only a single ebony feather drifting to the ground.

Isra picked up the feather, its energy pulsing through her fingertips upon contact and burning trails through her lifeforce, halting only when it surrounded her heart with its warmth. At once, the energy thrummed a retreat as if searching for the missing element—searching for him.

"Challenge accepted," she whispered into the shadows.

A determined smirk grew across her lips; she donned her mask and began walking resolutely toward whatever unknown future awaited.

About the Author

Bridgette O'Hare is a native of North Carolina who survives on high doses of chocolate, excessive episodes of Supernatural, and copious amounts of snark. She spends her time in search of sleep, witty co-conspirators, and ways to unleash chaos upon her characters. For more Supernatural and Super-snarky stories with both romance and shenanigans, follow Bridgette on Instagram **@BridgetteOHare** and visit **www.BridgetteOHare.com.**

MIDNIGHT TREASURE

KT SWEET

O il lantern in one hand, small pickaxe in the other, Genna stared at the cave's jagged, tight mouth. Despite the vicious half-wolf, half-bear mutant beasts the mage had created, the ones pursuing their twilight meal, Genna had hiked the twisting mountain trail alone. Then she'd huddled in dense foliage by the cave, grateful to be the first to arrive. Half-starved and tiny for her age, no one paid attention to where she went. Stealth was her strength.

One night a year, the cave opened for the Treasure Hunt. One night the desperate came seeking the mystery prize, disregarding the dangers. Faraway, the church bells rang eleven times. The Hunt began. An hour was all she had. It must be all she needed.

The ground shuddered and bats exploded from the cave's mouth, fluttering wings stirring her hair and brushing her face. Harmless, peaceful creatures she'd long admired for their noiseless prowling that kept deadly insects from eating her little brother alive, yet she couldn't help ducking and screeching. They must be warning her, like her little brother. Diff's plaintive howl still echoed in her mind. *"Don't go. I can't lose you, too. I don't need the medicine."*

Only, his fingers curled so tightly she could no longer massage them open. Worse, his feet spasmed ceaselessly. The agony stole his mind and took him further from her each day. The mage's medicine was the one thing stopping the disease and Genna was the only one left to buy it for him. Fourteen years to Diff's nine, she was his sole guardian and parent. She must find the treasure and be out of the cavern before the church bells tolled twelve. In return for her giving him half the riches, the mage, Rorrel, had offered her potions for the rest of Diff's life. How could she refuse? Her hammering heart reaffirmed the stakes were beyond high.

The reminder that their ravenous street dog, Fierce, guarded Diff, soothed her. The mongrel snarled at passersby in between gulping down the last of her food. Her brother lay with the dog beneath their tattered shanty in the sweltering night's heat, by the rank-smelling town dump. It was the safest place for Diff after the townsfolk had called him demon-possessed and refused to help. Tonight, she'd change both their lives for the better.

Yet, she hesitated. Last year's sole Hunt survivor returned covered in grit, drooling, and vacant-eyed. Rumor held that the mage gave the man a potion to make him reveal the treasure cave's secrets. No one had ever seen the man again. A nauseating odor from the mage's burn pit hinted at his end.

Genna's empty stomach cramped, and she pressed her fist into it. *Never mind. The mage told her what she needed. Diff would never hurt again. They'd eat the best food.*

Once the stabbing ache passed, Genna stooped and swung her lamp into the cave's narrow opening. It lit just an arm's length ahead. Still, the view sent her thin frame quivering. Piles of white stick-like mounds clustered on either side of the cave's walls. Bones. The ones who hadn't made it back outside. Her hand shook, and the light clattered against the cave's mouth. She set it and the ax on the ground before dropping to her knees.

Holy One, give me courage. Diff needs this.

Stretched flat before the low entrance, Genna flinched at the sound of footsteps pounding the steep trail below. If other treasure seekers found her, they'd hurl her off the mountain like a sack of dry leaves.

Hurry! They mustn't know you're ahead of them.

On her belly, Genna dug in the axe and pulled forward. Her thin blouse shredded, and sharp objects scraped her torso. Grimacing, she stretched back for the lantern, swinging it ahead to light the way.

For Diff. For Diff. She repeated the words over and over, forcing herself over razor-like pebbles for what felt like a mile until her head bumped into a wall. *A dead end? The mage hadn't mentioned one.*

Genna pushed herself to her hands and knees. The lantern revealed the cavern ceiling high overhead and separate tunnels opening to her right and left. *Which way do I go?* As she climbed to her feet, angry words reverberated from the cave's mouth.

"Get away from that entrance. I got here first!" The gasping, gravelly voice belonged to Billit, the town banker. He'd cheated her and Diff out of the profit from selling her parents' home after they'd died. Said they didn't deserve it, despite having more than enough left after the loan was paid to buy Diff's medicine and rent a room. Hateful man.

"Scrawny sot, just try and make me!" Dreven, the burly, angry man who ran the tavern cursed Billit. He'd given food scraps to her and Diff until his wife left him. "This is my chance, and you won't stop me!"

"Please, men, don't fight. Let's work together."

Genna startled at the third voice. Why had the mage Rorrel come?

"See these footprints? That skinny little orphan girl went in ahead of us. She'll spring the traps, then we'll share the riches. Are you with me?" The mage's rumbling laugh boomed like thunder.

He'd sent her in to set off the traps and die. What a fool she'd been to think he wanted to help them. If the traps got her, Diff would suffer an agonizing death, all alone.

Billit barked out a laugh. "Mage, you're heartless. Good plan."

"A powerful magician like you should fetch it," Dreven jeered.

The mage coughed. "Strange magic like this takes a team. We'll all be rich."

Genna shook her head. Rorrel's voice sounded like an angry, chittering rat. What had happened to his usual melodic tones? Her gut tightened. *He'd used persuasion magic to make her do his bidding.* The cave unmasked his fakery.

What should she do now? Sagging against the hot dirt wall, sweat trickled down her forehead and back. If she survived, would the mage still make potions for Diff? Gripping her tattered shirt, Genna shut her eyes. *Holy One, guide   me.*

 She pondered Rorrel's instructions. He'd emphasized, "Take the tunnel towards the glowing light." She looked both ways. Only one path gleamed a soft gold. *Was it safe to run down that tunnel?*

Genna chewed her chipped nail, her rapid breathing making her dizzy. The arguing men's noisy forward progress kicked her into action.

Go! Stay low! She dove forward, wiggling like a snake, pushing the ax and then the lantern. The rocky path softened into fine sand.

Church bells clanged the half-hour mark. Genna winced. Even if she found the treasure, how would she get back out, past the men behind her? Had she come this far only to fail?

Stop worrying. Diff needs you. The Holy One will make a way. Taking deep, slow breaths, she rested her cheek on the gritty floor. Sudden, sharp blasts of air chilled her neck and back.

Thwack! Thwack! Thwack!

Genna's eyes bulged at the massive crossbow arrows embedded in the entryway behind her. Something or Someone non-physical had nudged her to hug the ground. Her tears wet the sand. *Thank you!* In the distance, a glimmering archway beckoned.

Dreven's harsh voice echoed in the cave. "If she gets the treasure, we can't let her keep it."

Rorrel sniggered. "No one misses street orphans."

Her heartbeat jabbed her ribs. Shivering, Genna dug fingers into the sand. What chance did she have against three grown men?

Slow them down. Break the lantern. Embed glass in the sand.

How could she find her way back? Yet, the nudge made sense. She blew out the flame, smashed the glass cover and stuck pieces into the path. The tunnel glowed more brightly now. Genna continued to slither towards the archway, clutching her pickaxe.

You're almost there. The memory of her brother's relentless convulsions kept her going.

At the archway, Genna studied the room. The large chamber held a wide stone table near the far end. Atop the table sat a jewel-clad box, its gems radiating rainbow-colored beams of light. The treasure! Just as Rorrel described. She clapped her hand over her mouth to cut off her excitement.

Rising to her knees, Genna had only a moment before the mountain shook and debris from the ceiling rained down. Rocks pelted her, and she gagged as dirt clouds darkened the room. Her tormentors' hacking coughs barreled down the tunnel. Good, they weren't doing any better.

As the billows cleared, Genna scooted into the chamber. The box remained atop the stone table. She pressed her back to a side wall, searching for the next trap.

Sudden shrill screams pocked her arms with goosebumps. She crawled back to the archway and gasped. Thick crossbow arrows pinned the banker and barkeep by their chests to the tunnel walls. Rorrel ignored them as he slunk past. His triumphant braying nauseated her.

"You used us!" Dreven's bellows matched his frantic attempts to remove the shaft. Moaning, he slumped, matching Billit's already still body.

"I don't believe in sharing." Rorrel wiggled toward her. "You should be dead, street rat." A cry of curse words followed the insult, and the mage lifted both hands in the air, bloody palms sliced by the lantern glass. "I'll get you for this!"

It was all Genna needed to hear. She dropped her ax and raced for the tall stone table, jumping as high as she could. The jeweled box remained just beyond her reach. She pulled back and again ran to the table and pulled herself up. Snatching the chest, she turned to jump down but crashed into the mage. Rorrel ripped the box from her hands, pulling her off the table. Genna lost her balance and fell to the floor. The mage kicked her head while hugging the treasure box.

Shooting stars seared her eyes until Genna rolled beneath the table to escape his attack. The chamber juddered, the floor heaving like a storm-tossed wave. Rorrel shouted and fell backward. The glowing treasure box flew from his hands and crashed against the archway, splintering. Gold coins flew everywhere. Genna scrambled out from under the table to gather them, but another jolt hit, and the stone table collapsed, just missing her legs.

Growling, Rorrel sat up, snagged her collar, and twisted. He dragged her backward, pulling so hard she couldn't breathe. "Too bad you won't see your brother again."

Oh, yes, she would. Kicking at the mage with all her might, Genna's ragged shirt ripped. As she got free, her hand slapped something solid. Her pickaxe. She clutched it, knelt, and swung it at him. *That's for Diff.*

The flat side of the pickaxe thumped his forehead. Rorrel howled. His eyes rolled back, and he hit the ground with a thud. How long would he be out? She needed to collect the coins and run back to the cave's entrance.

As she lurched to her feet, her eye caught a shiny object on the floor. The hand-sized chunk of stone sparkled, calling to her. She grabbed it. What was she doing? They needed gold, not a broken piece of the stone table. She tried to let it go, but the lump stuck to her palm. No matter what she did, the stone shard remained glued to her hand.

The chamber archway boomed, the exit collapsing on itself. Worse, Rorrel moaned, turned on his side, and pushed himself to his hands and knees. Genna shuddered. Trapped.

Another upward heave of the cave floor threw the treasure chest splinters in the air, their rainbow lights revealing broad fissures in the cave's far wall. A way out? She longed to run to one, but even just a handful of coins from the rubble would feed Diff. The mage was now her enemy. No more potion buying from him.

She knelt before the dirt pile, digging for coins one-handed. Pocketing what she found, Genna cringed as the church bells began tolling midnight. *One, two, three* . . .

Rorrel scrambled next to her, shoving her aside, paddling the dirt like a dog. The wild glint in his eyes forced her back. Tears burned her cheeks. Midnight. Leave or be added to the bone piles. She'd failed her brother.

Crying cleared her eyesight, showing her a wide fissure at the cave's back wall. *Did it lead outside?* She approached it, but Rorrel yanked her away and disappeared inside it.

Six, seven, eight . . . The church bells tolled on. Her head hurt and she swayed on her feet. *Holy One, I need to get back to Diff.*

She stood before the broad fissure, and a breeze cooled her face, reviving her hope. This led outside. Slick with sweat, she inched forward. The church bells gonged, n*ine, ten, eleven* . . . With a final push, she popped out into the night, tripped, and fell to her knees.

Darkness engulfed her. The ground beneath her hands felt smooth, like a well-worn path down the mountain. No sign of the mage.

The midnight bell tolled twelve. The ground trembled, signaling The Treasure Hunt had ended.

Her pocket felt almost empty. If only she'd collected more coins. She'd made it worse for her brother by coming. Rorrel wouldn't make potions for Diff, not after tonight.

Genna crumpled into a ball against the mountainside. *Holy One, Diff deserves a better life.* Still, she refused to give up. *Thank you, Holy One, for letting me return to my brother. I'll find a way.*

Eyes drooping and bones aching, one hand heavy from the peculiar stone shard, she passed out into a dreamless sleep.

***

Genna raced down the mountain at dawn, more confused than ever about the stone fragment stuck to her hand. The moment she heard Diff's agony she forgot her worries.

Pacing outside their shanty, her heart sickened at his attempts to stifle his cries. His worst spasm attack, ever. She must do something. *Maybe she could steal leftover potion.*

"Diff, I'm going to the mage. I'll be back soon."

Diff fought for breath. "No, Sis, don't. Not safe. I'll be all right." Their dog, Fierce, leaned into Diff's shaking frame, offering his strength.

Exhausted, Genna bit her lip to keep from weeping. *She couldn't just watch him suffer. She'd give Rorrel her coins. Maybe he'd trade for them.*

Genna forced herself to jog across town to the mage's home. It was quiet, the front door ajar, unusual since his potions business consistently bustled with servants and buyers. What if Rorrel hadn't made it back?

Genna slipped inside. In the front hall, the sound of deep, guttural sobs made her halt.

Who was that?

Moved by the haunted cries, Genna walked down the hall. She stopped before the mage's potion room. Someone was in there. She opened the door. Rorrel lay on the floor, grime-covered and whimpering, his bruised face etched with pain.

Genna blinked. "What happened?"

The mage's angry snarl made her turn to run.

"Wait! Where are your gold coins from the cave?" Rorrel's frantic tone surprised her. "Show them to me!" But he didn't move. What was wrong with him?

"You'll trade potion for my coins?"

"Where are the coins? Show me!"

Something in his voice made her hide her stone-glued hand behind her. Using her free hand, she reached into her pocket. Out came a clump of ashes that fluttered to the floor.

Rorrel keened like a wounded animal. "Nothing. I got nothing for all this!" His arms shook.

Genna looked closer, horrified to realize he hadn't moved because his twisted limbs prevented him from even sitting up. The dirt staining his clothes disguised clots of dried blood, broken bones, and other injuries.

Something inside Genna shifted. Rorrel looked worse off than Diff. How was that even possible?

"Mage, what happened to you?"

Rorrel's face knotted in distress. "On my way down the mountain, I stumbled off the path. My servants found me and brought me here." His lips curled. "The coins turned to dust in the light. I owed my servants back wages and couldn't pay them." He sucked in stuttering breaths. "They say I'm cursed. Now they won't come near me." He closed his eyes, tears wetting his face.

"Would Diff's potion help you?" Why had she even asked? Rorrel had tried to kill her for the treasure. What made her even consider helping him? *Because you're not like him, that's why.* "I'll help you make a potion to cure you if you teach me how to make Diff's potion."

Rorrel snorted. "You'll just trick me, make his potion, and run away. I know you street orphans, always out to cheat and steal."

Diff writhed in pain while Rorrel acted like he was the victim. A familiar ugliness lit his eyes. The same way he'd looked when explaining how to recover the treasure. He'd lied. It had nearly cost her life.

Genna's indignation burst into flames like a roaring furnace. "That's not true. I won't argue with you anymore because Diff needs help now. Give me his medicine. I'll return and help you mix potions to get you well, too."

"What's that in your hand?" Rorrel's squint held too keen an interest in her rock. For reasons she didn't understand, she knew not to tell him. "Protection from a mean street dog. He runs when I throw rocks at him." She swallowed her frustration. "Give me potion for Diff and I'll come back and make you some, too. Deal?"

Crashing noises came from inside the house. Rorrel squealed and Genna rushed out of the room to see what was happening. Servants were grabbing valuable items from the mage's living quarters.

"What are you doing?" Genna asked.

The former overseer answered. "He refused to pay us for months. We'll sell these things to feed our families. He's a terrible master, and he's done much evil. It's now come back to him. You should leave. He'll die soon."

The men gathered jewelry, expensive decorations, silver, and gold threaded cloth. Arms full, they left.

Genna watched, open-mouthed. They'd leave Rorrel to die without concern. The house fell silent, except for the mage's piteous sobbing. He'd mistreated so many, no one cared for him.

Holy One, he is a hate-filled man, but I can't abandon him. She returned to the mage's potion-making chamber. He remained on the floor, limbs askew.

Genna's mind raced ahead. She couldn't let him die, but how could she take care of him and Diff? Before she figured that out, she needed answers.

"What goes into Diff's potion? Tell me, now."

Rorrel pouted. "If I teach you to make it, will you get me something to eat? I'm so hungry." He whined like a child.

Genna knew well the unrelenting pain of hunger. Helping him was the right thing to do. And if it would help Diff, it was the best outcome.

"Yes, I'll feed you. But first, teach me. Diff's potion now, and more potion recipes over the next weeks. Everything you know."

Something shifted in the mage's face. "All right. See the big jars by the sink? Take the first two on the left and . . ."

Genna kept her rock-joined palm from his view. Working with care, her heavy hand steadied the vials and beakers while her unencumbered one measured and poured ingredients. After a while, the rock didn't bother her. Making Diff's potion filled her with joy.

***

The sign gleamed with fresh paint. "Genna & Diff's Potion House." The steady stream of customers reflected Genna's ability to diagnose and heal people. She'd reversed Diff's symptoms. They'd been working together for six months. All was well.

Except for the mage. His body remained misaligned, yet his symptoms hadn't worsened. His full-time caregiver reported him somewhat less surly, but the mage wasn't grateful like her and Diff. He sulked.

She and her brother treated the sick regardless of their ability to pay. Fierce guarded the cash box. Their loyal companion also gathered other street dogs to protect the house, day, and night.

Genna often visited Rorrel. A cranky man, he begrudgingly offered suggestions on new potions. Today he sat in his wheeled chair in the back garden, his wrinkled face upturned to the warm sun, eyes shut.

Don't expect anything from him. "Mage, how are you today?"

He grimaced. "Worse than yesterday. Haven't you found a healing potion for me?"

Genna frowned. "I've applied your suggestions, and Diff's, and read all your books." *What if he doesn't want to get well?* Was that a question to ask him? *Yes, ask.* There it was, again, that voice she'd first heard in the cave, then when she'd found Rorrel broken and alone in his home. The voice that had led her to this new life. *Holy One, what would help him?* Silence. All right, she'd ask.

"Rorrel, do you want to be well?"

He turned away, panic flashing in his eyes.

"I doubt I'll ever heal. Besides, you've stolen my business. What would I do?"

Genna shrugged. Fierce entered the garden and approached the mage. The large dog leaned his body into the old man's legs. Rorrel stretched his shaking hand to caress the dog's neck.

"Mage, you could teach others to make potions. Earn a living being an excellent teacher rather than what you used to be." She hesitated. "But you'd need to want to be that kind of person."

He grunted. "Ever since the day that rock fell off your hand, you've been picking on me to change." With a gnarled finger, he pointed at the garden and the new house extension she'd built for him and his caregiver. "You paid for everything, caring for me when I would have killed you without a worry, just like Billit and Dreven. Why help me? I've done nothing to deserve it." Petting the dog, his voice dropped. "I deserved to die. You wouldn't let me. Why?"

"Diff and I have been blessed. We share that with you. Besides, I can't imagine killing anyone."

The day she'd decided to care for him, she'd sold some of his possessions to pay for a helper and a doctor to look after him. Then she'd moved herself, Diff, and Fierce into the house. That night, the rock had dropped off her hand, fracturing into a thousand shards of pure gold. The cave's true treasure had been hidden in plain sight. They'd become wealthy, and she used the tiny shards sparingly to avoid gossip while running their business to help others.

Fierce growled and then licked the man's face before trotting back inside. Genna marveled at the dog's acceptance. Her street dog was particular about his friends.

The mage held out a finger to a butterfly fluttering next to him. "I've never been taken care of by anyone." The black and purple creature landed on his extended finger for a moment before flying away. "I could teach others for free. We don't need money, do we?"

Diff came to the door, Fierce prancing at his side. "Sis, the king's messenger just arrived. His heir is ill. They request your help to make the princess well."

Genna looked at Rorrel. "Will you assist Diff in making the more difficult potions while I'm gone?"

The mage's smile, crooked yet wide, lit his face. "If Diff will have me, sure. As long as Fierce visits me each day. He's my real medicine, you know."

Genna smiled back. "Good. I'll get my satchel. Wish me luck."

Rorrel shook his head. "No luck needed. You're smart and honorable. I see it in your eyes every day." He turned to Diff. "Let's cook up powder of salamander for parents to turn their little boys into lizards so they'll behave."

Diff guffawed. "Great, Rorrel, you'll put us out of business with those ideas."

Laughing, they left, Diff pushing the mage's chair.

Humming, Genna packed for the castle. Rorrel *was* healing. The best way—from the inside out.

The treasure had led them all to this unplanned season of restoration. A gift far better than gold.

About the Author

KT Sweet is an author of otherworldly quests who co-exists with two twelve pound rescues - a biscuit-making, gray tortie cat, and a clingy Bichon Frise. To meet beings and creatures tumbling into life-altering adventures, visit her website: www.ktsweet.com. Remember: Fantasy reveals hidden truths.

A
PRISONER'S
VOW

ROBYN BAKER

Thesking is dying.

The news repeats throughout the week in hushed whispers from the servants. He is not a kind man but he is the only father I've ever known. When my true parents signed my marriage contract to their son and heir, Prince Greyvor, soon after my third year, I became a royal ward.

More like a royal bauble. Kept pristine and guarded.

"Pay attention, girl!" My pianoforte tutor claps her hands together, pulling me from wandering thoughts and missed notes.

A knock at the door interrupts my playing. Several servants come through with bolts of cloth.

My tutor demands answers. "What is this? Lady Coralena and I . . ." Her purpling face turns white as the prince enters my rooms.

"You are dismissed." Price Greyvor doesn't look at the old woman. Instead, he looks around my rooms as though he forgot they were here and doesn't care for what he sees.

I stand and dip my head at my betrothed. He's handsome and his blue eyes, so different to the amber of my own, reflect no kindness as he wipes a hand through his short red waves. It takes all of my training to give him the amenable smile that is expected of me, even as my stomach twists with anxiety.

"Good morning, Your Highness." I breathe. "I was not expecting to see you today." *Is the king dead?*

He gestures to the bolts and servants still standing in my rooms. He says blandly, "The king is going to die within a fortnight. It has been decided that you and I shall wed in four days so that I may have a queen beside me during my coronation. The seamstress will be along shortly to begin fitting you for more appropriate gowns." His cold eyes rove over my soft frame. I fight the urge to tuck away any loose umber curls while under his scrutiny.

Four days. The twisting in my belly turns violent.

"We will make the announcement tomorrow evening to the court. Do try to close your mouth by then." Disdain twists his voice.

I snap my teeth together, embarrassment warming my pale skin, and stammer, "Of course, your highness," while lowering my head at his abrupt exit.

Four days.

I rush through my quarters to the bathing room and slam the door closed. Very nearly missing the porcelain basin, I retch my breakfast until I am empty. A knock from Gabriela sets off another round of illness and I tell my lady-in-waiting to go back to the sitting rooms.

You knew this was coming! This was always going to be my fate and yet I can't help but feel as though I've been run through with a sword. I have spent my entire nineteen years learning how to be the perfect wife for one man. I eat what he eats, wear the colors he likes, and master the songs he expects me play. I don't even know who I am beyond him. This family and their titles were always meant to be my fate but now, more than ever, I don't want it.

I've never really wanted it and always held on to the hope that I would be forgotten if he perhaps died on a distant battlefield.

This time, Gabriela doesn't knock before entering the bathing room and closing the door behind her.

She takes in my current state. Gabriela has been my lady-in-waiting since we both came of age at thirteen. We spend many hours a day together. She is the only person I truly like here.

She nods once and whispers, "You will not be his queen, Coralena. You must escape here."

"Escape? Gabriela, you know better than I that there is no way out."

"I will get you keys but you must promise me that you'll disappear."

Suspicion and confusion battle each other in my mind. "Why?"

Gabriela sighs. "Because I am in the prince's confidence, and *I* will be Queen."

Gabriela and Greyvor? My mind overloads with questions and a flicker of betrayal—not at the loss of him, but from the years of friendship with her now in a new light. "You?" She nods, offense taken. "I mean, you love the prince?" I quickly add.

She scoffs. "Of course not. He is foul, but we are . . . close." She grasps for the right word. "With your marriage contract void and the imminent coronation, he will look to me to fill your position. I have made sure of it."

I'm stunned. I stare at the woman like I am seeing her for the first time.

"I will bring you the keys at midnight. Be ready to flee." With that, she opens the door and walks out, leaving me with so many questions.

How long has she wished to take my place? Has she always planned for it? Can I trust her? Do I even want to escape and where would I go? The rare occasions I've allowed myself to imagine a different future, I always fantasized about the adventures of seafarers, like in my books.

It is that sudden hope for a new destiny, a dream come to life, that pushes me forward. Gathering my composure, I rinse my mouth, and straighten my spine before opening the door and walking back to my sitting room.

The seamstress and her team of servants set to work around me. I take this time to wonder at escaping. I cannot simply walk out of my door as there are always two guards standing just outside. All my life, I've been told that they are here to keep the future queen safe. If I were to open the door right now, they would be pleasant enough but they would stop me from leaving, and instead bring me anything I should desire, which is usually just books.

Then there is my balcony. The open square of the Grand Gardens stretch out below my fourth level accommodations. There are always people and guards strolling the gardens and even my twice daily walks through the maze-like rose bushes and orchards are supervised by my guards and Gabriela.

The castle itself sits in the middle of its own island with high walls and a vast moat surrounding it and only one bridge in or out. But getting off this island won't matter if I can't even get out of the palace. It is designed to be a labyrinth of corridors and rooms interspaced with the enclosed outdoor areas.

I'm left to my thoughts until the final pin is placed and the seamstress quietly exits with maids and cloth in tow.

At last, alone with Gabriela, I walk to the balcony, looking to the gardens below. Soundlessly, my lady joins me and we watch as a group of noblemen walk below us.

"I know so little of this place. How am I supposed to find my way out of here when I've never even seen most of it?" Defeat weighs me down.

Gabriela flicks a piece of crumbling stone from the wide banister to the grass beneath. "Yes, we've done a lovely job of disguising your prison as a home."

My prison. How easily she voices that which I never dwell on. "Why is that?" I ask, no longer allowing myself to justify them.

"They like to keep their treasures close." She answers. "And they have many unique possessions hidden away here. This place is a prison for many."

I take in my friend, wondering who she really is. "How do I get to the bridge?"

She exhales. "You don't. You would never make it there and even if you did, there are more guards on the walls and at the gates than in the halls."

"How then?" Why has she put this plan in motion if there is no hope?

She lightly elbows my arm and gestures with a nod when I turn to her. "The only way out is to go down." Her gaze finds my own and she whispers. "Get to the rooms below us. They are empty. Leave them and you will find the servants' halls between the knights. Take them down until you reach the darkest, straightest path. At every divide, take two lefts, one right, and repeat." Her blue eyes bore into me.

I repeat her instructions in my head, memorizing them. "And then?" I ask.

"You will come out to a large cavern. There is a door with a mercreature carved around the handle." She pauses. "I've never been through, but I'm told that it leads beneath the river."

"You could come with me," I suggest.

She shakes her head. "I have plans here."

When she doesn't elaborate, I nod. I have no idea what awaits beyond these walls, but I prefer that unknown fate to the one awaiting me here.

Without another word, Gabriela reaches out to give my hand a squeeze and walks back into my rooms. I turn, leaning against the stone railing, and watch her go.

"I will be back in a few hours to help you get ready for bed, Lady Coralena." She shouts when she opens the guarded door.

Turning back toward the gardens, I lean over the edge further than I usually allow myself until the balcony directly below is visible.

***

I pull the end of the rope through the final loop and tug it tight. It took knotting together over half a dozen of the curtain holdbacks, but I have my rope. I coil it beneath my cloak on the balcony, hidden in a pool of darkness from the starless night. It's nearly midnight.

I should be sad or perhaps relieved to bid these rooms farewell, but I cannot muster any emotion beyond excitement for a new life. *Where will I go? What will I do? Who will I become?* These questions circle my thoughts. I'm drawn to the sea, where the horizon stretches with no end.

"Lady Coralena?" I startle at Gabriela's call, my purse nearly slips through my fingers but I clumsily catch it, coins and jewels clanking. I step out of the shadows and into the dim candlelight. She stops at the edge of my room to the balcony. "Are you ready?" Her voice is soft.

"I'm ready," I say with more confidence than I have and recite her earlier directions aloud. She confirms with a nod.

She holds out a short chain with two keys attached. "This one opens every door." She holds the nondescript iron key up then releases it.

"What does the other one open?" I ask, eyeing the black key.

"The dungeons, I think. I didn't have time to ask before I slipped him a sleeping tonic."

I want to ask who she speaks of, wondering if it's the prince, but time is of the essence as the bells of the clock tower sound with the first ring of midnight.

The sense of urgency rushes through us as Gabriela pushes the keys into my hand. "There's not a place in this world that you haven't read about in your books. You're smart and beautiful and you are meant for so much more." She smiles and releases my hands. "Go now!" She orders and steps back.

I grab my cloak and throw it around me. Snatching one end of the rope, I knot it around the bottom of a pillar and tug it tight. With another ring of the bells, I scramble atop the banister, perching like a chicken. Easing down to stand on the outside of the railing, I drop the coil of rope, the end swaying further above the balcony below than I had hoped.

I lower myself inch by inch down the rope until my foot brushes the top of the new banister. With the final midnight toll, I jump down to the balcony, the sound muffled by the bells. Hoping that Gabriella was right and the rooms are empty, I rush through.

Soundlessly, I open the door leading into the hall. Pushing away the shock of an unguarded door, I take in the empty hallway and spot two shimmering knights on display. I dash for them, my heart beating with fear. Between the hollow sentinels is a narrow door. I push it but nothing happens. Then I see the small keyhole and pull the keys from beneath my cloak. There is no going back after this. Sweat beads beneath my hood. I glance around the still empty hall before risking a deep breath to steady my nerves, unlock it and dart in.

The tight hallway is dark with the occasional soft glow of candlelight coming through vents at the top of the wall. I follow Gabriela's directions as I reach fork after fork—left, left, right, left, left, right, the winding descent noticeable in my too-quick steps.

Coming up to another divide, a soft glow moves from the left—my next turn. Faint voices carry through the hallway, growing louder. My stomach drops and my knees nearly buckle as I stop. Even at this hour, servants and guards are expected to attend to the palace's needs. It has been sheer luck and timing that I've made it this far. But now, I have no choice but to go the wrong direction. Hurrying away from my path, I try to outrun the voices, praying to all the gods that I'm not running toward something worse.

Moving as fast as I can in this darkness, I don't see the black door as I collide into it with a painful thump. Bouncing back, I freeze, waiting and listening as long as I dare, praying that no one is on the other side of the door to have heard me. Instead, it's the voices I left behind that continue to follow me. My heart threatens to beat out of my chest, but I can't wait anymore. I test the handle and finding the door locked, I slide the iron key in. It doesn't fit.

Panic makes my hands shake as I feel the cold metal of the black key. The one that might go to the dungeons. *What am I supposed to do?* Go back and be caught, stand here and be caught, or go forward and probably be caught. Only one option still has an unknown outcome.

Slipping the black key into keyhole and twisting, I push the heavy door open. Relief floods my body at the empty, larger, sconce lit corridor. Quickly closing the door behind me, I silently continue forward, looking for a place to hide until the danger passes. Dampness and chill seep into my bones and I gag on the pungent stench of filth and feces as I slip around a corner. The faint torch light from the hallway illuminates iron bars along either side of the path.

Heavy silence fills the small dungeon. There are no guards here but neither do I hear prisoners as no one makes themselves known. I allow myself one breath of relief before realizing that the men behind me have only one direction to go. Here. Fingering the black key, I swallow the deranged cry that strangles me with the irony of the situation, peek into the darkness, and unlock the first cell.

With a muted *snick*, I am locked behind the iron bars and thick stone.

Moving backward into the darkness, I pull my black cloak tight around me.

"Are you my assassin, then?" A deep, rough voice asks from the shadows.

Whirling, a scream escapes my lips before I cover my mouth with both hands, biting into my palm. Stumbling back in terror, I trip and land on my bottom, my hood falling around my shoulders.

A slumped figure stands up from his place against the far wall. He moves slowly into the faint light and I gracelessly scoot away. He's tall, bearded, and too lean. His dark hair falls to his wide shoulders in a tangled mess.

"Please," I beg with a choked cry.

Low voices echo from the entrance to the dungeons.

I'm suddenly torn, wanting to call out to the guards for help but also terrified at being found trying to run away. The man notices my hesitation, looking from me to the approaching men.

"Get behind me." He whispers, holding a dirty hand out to me. When I don't reach for it, he promises, "I won't hurt you. But something tells me that they will." This jars me from the war within myself and I make the impossible decision to trust the devil I don't know.

Not taking his hand, I stand up and rush to the back corner of the horrible cell and crouch down. I pull my hood back up and sink into its shadows as the prisoner moves closer to the iron door.

Two guards step into view, one carrying a torch and the other holding a bucket. I hide my face in my knees and try to control my trembling.

"What's this then? What was that shout?" He barks.

The prisoner answers, "There was a rat."

The guard laughs. "Oi, you hear that? Shifter's afraid of a rat!" The men continue laughing.

Shifter? My body tenses, lungs ceasing to work.

"No." The prisoner says in a steady, deep voice. "The rat was afraid of me."

The men stop laughing and a chill ripples through me.

Stories about the deadly Shifters from the far away mountain kingdom fill my mind and blood fills my mouth as I bite my cheeks to keep from calling out to the guards, suddenly very sure that I've made a terrible mistake.

The second guard speaks. "Well, then you won't be needing your meal today." He throws the sloshing contents of the bucket on to the filthy cell floor before leaving as abruptly as they came. We wait until we hear the door close and lock before moving.

I stand on shaky legs, putting my back to the stone wall. "You're a Shifter?" My voice quivers.

"Yes." He pauses. "You are safe. Safer than you would be with them, I presume." The man says softly. "We're not the beasts of your stories." He steps closer. "I was sent here as an emissary."

"An emissary?" Shocked at the civility of him and the gentleness of his voice, I peel away from the wall.

He nods. "And what about you?" He looks me over and I'm very aware of how I must appear—too clean, too well dressed.

"I am running away from a fate I did not ask for."

He nods. "We can help each other. You get us out of here," he gestures to my pocket holding the keys, "and I'll get us beyond their reach."

Having a Shifter for an ally would not be the worst plan. I take only a moment to debate and conclude that I am already in too far to back out. "There is a tunnel that leads under the river. I was trying to find it." The tremble in my voice eases. "You will take me far away?" I confirm.

He takes my hands in his and I flinch at the sudden movement. "Yes. My word is my vow. I will take you anywhere you wish to go."

"I want to go to the sea." I declare with a surprising amount of confidence. The man smiles and gestures for me to unlock the cell.

"Call me Emrys." He bows.

"I am Coralena." I reach my hands through the bars and feel for the lock, inserting the key. The metallic click echoes through the dark. "Is it true what they say, that you can change into any creature you desire?"

I push the cell open and exit, standing aside as he follows. "Not quite." He smiles. "I can only summon two creatures. It is the ancients that can summon any they wish."

"Interesting." I accidently whisper aloud as we reach the black door. "Why didn't you shift when they captured you?" I wonder.

A human-like growl escapes him. "They caught me off-guard and have kept me weak."

I gasp and unconsciously recoil. "The blood. That's true then? I've read that Shifters feed on humans."

Emrys levels his brown eyes on mine and speaks softly, as though to calm a frightened child. "We don't *feed* on them, their blood makes us stronger, heals us when we're hurt. It's given willingly and only what's needed." He assures me.

Not entirely assured, I nod and accept the risk. Still holding the key, I slowly unlock the door and carefully pull it open, listening for the voices of the guards.

"It's clear." Emrys gestures, "After you."

I lead us back down the hallway that I practically ran through until we come to the fork where I was supposed to go left.

"This way." I whisper, relieved to be back on the correct course. We wind down the corridors taking two more turns before we come to another door. This one a wide, wooden door.

Emrys steps in front of me and puts his ear to the wood. "I hear water." He pauses, "But no people." He tries the handle and then steps aside for me when it doesn't open. I unlock with the iron key and we step through, into complete darkness.

"Follow me. I can see in the dark." Emrys grabs hold of my hand, pulling me forward.

The sound of rushing water fills the space, drowning out all other noise.

"Where are we?" I ask too loudly.

Emrys grips my hand tighter. "It's a cavern with a river. There's nothing here."

Yes! Excitement has me bouncing. I was so close to the end before the guards pushed me off course. "You don't see a door?" I ask. "There's meant to be a door with a mercreature carved into it."

"Wait here." He releases my hand and panic twists my stomach at the thought of being left alone down here.

"Emrys?" I call out after a several pounding heartbeats.

"Here." His hand curls around my own and he pulls me to follow. "I found your door."

I nearly cry in relief and hold out the keys for him. He opens the door and leads us through.

My feet slip on small rocks and damp earth and my shoulders rub against a rounded dirt wall. I'm sure Emrys is hunched uncomfortably ahead of me. We walk in silence, gradually climbing upward.

"There's another door ahead." Emrys halts.

"What's wrong?" I ask, noting that he hasn't opened it yet.

"Voices." He whispers. "A lot of them."

No. I have come too far. I can't go back and I will *not* give up. "You can shift." I declare.

"I'm too weak." He breathes.

Right. I reach into my hidden purse and feel for the emerald bird pendant. Not giving either of us a chance to consider, I press the silver wing tip into the delicate skin over my wrist and tear through it. The pain is immense but my resolve is stronger, even as I gasp.

Emrys hisses. "Coralena!" He pulls my hand with the pendant away and holds my bleeding arm firmly.

"Drink it." I demand.

He growls at my method, hesitating for only a moment, but lowers his mouth to the ruined skin. The pulling sensation is strange but not painful. He stops as the first wave of dizziness swims through my head.

"Wait near the door until it's safe, then you will have to climb on my back." His coppery breath warms my cheek. "Don't be frightened of me when I shift."

I'm about to ask what kind of creature he will become when he silently opens the door to the early morning light. Towering trees fill my view, but within them are the king's soldiers.

Emrys looks to me, his brown eyes glowing gold, then runs out of the tunnel.

I stifle a gasp as the man shifts into a massive, shimmering brown dragon. He roars, expelling flames from his gaping maw toward the now shouting soldiers. With a lumbering run, he twists and whips his spiked tail into the group. Half the men flee and the other half are scattered in broken heaps. Emrys turns his enormous head to me and lowers himself so that I can run up his back. I don't hesitate.

Finding my seat between his leathery wings at the base of his long neck, I squeeze my thighs and squeal as he explodes off the ground.

I never look back as we fly into the sunrise, toward the infinite sea.

About the Author

Robyn Baker writes fantasy and romantasy books and takes a lot of pictures of her animals doing nothing. Join her on Instagram @author_robynbaker and visit www.robynbakerbooks.com.

BEAUTIFULLY CURSED

ANDREA D. LONG

What would it be like to dive into the sea and allow your body to slip away into the abyss? My arm casually hangs over the lifeboat, cupping seawater and observing as it trickles away through my fingers.

A robust guard keeps a vigilant eye on me, ensuring I don't leap overboard and flee. *Take a moment to glance around, my friend. We are adrift in the ocean's vastness at this very moment. Could you spot any sign of land? Because I certainly cannot.*

Gazing up at the radiant silver moonlight bathing in its brilliance, it's almost surreal to envision how something so celestial could conjure an entire island out of thin air. The locals refer to it as Cursed Island, and that's precisely where these imposing individuals are escorting me. Thanks to the Amnesty Village Council, I am about to embark on a three-month-long journey to and fro as punishment for my petty theft of bread.

Indeed, I am aware that my actions were morally wrong, and I knowingly violated the law. The irony lies in the fact that I didn't commit the theft for my own benefit. If it weren't for the abundance of children under Amnesty's care, children whose parents have mysteriously vanished, I wouldn't have taken that loaf to feed a famished girl. Having experienced the hardships of growing up without parents myself, I yearn to help them all. So, when viewed from that perspective, enduring three months of confinement seems like a trifling cost to bear.

Out of nowhere, a mist materializes, hovering above the water's surface. Abruptly, a powerful gust of wind tosses our boat around. Before my very eyes, the fog dissipates, unveiling an enormous island, dwarfing our village in comparison, crowned by an ominous castle perched atop a towering hill. Taking in the awe-inspiring sight, we row the lifeboat towards the shore.

"We've reached our limit. Time to disembark." The guard's laughter resonates with a touch of madness as he playfully rocks the boat.

Headfirst, I plunge into the shallows. Several burly guards on the shore join in, finding it all amusing, and in that moment, I miss home. Struggling to my feet, I wring the water from my long dress while avoiding eye contact. I hope to avoid giving anyone a reason to prolong my stay in this place.

The cool touch of dry sand sends shivers through my feet, while the midnight ocean breeze adds a chill to the air. As I make my way towards the pier, a striking young man with long dark hair stands casually by a lamppost, his eyes fixed on me.

"Brutus has a habit of making things difficult for new prisoners," he remarks, strolling over with a blanket in hand. "Here, take this. It should keep you warm."

This mysteriously handsome guy drapes the soft wool around me, and I find myself entranced by his voice, his allure, and the way his sea glass eyes gaze into mine.

"Thank you," I utter, while strangely, my knees weaken at the mere thought of another touch from his hand.

"Allow me to escort you to your camp," he says, a captivating smile gracing his lips.

Wait. Camp? I quickly avert my gaze, taken aback by the unexpected revelation.

Noticing my apparent distraction, he glances down, nibbling on his lower lip. "All the prisoners stay at Camp Moonfall," he explains, extending his hand towards me. "It's really not as dreadful as it may seem."

"I guess there's no harm in giving it a look," I reply, allowing him to take my hand.

The instant we touch, an incredible sensation courses through my body. Though I've never been one to believe in love at first sight, this undeniably resembles the emotions one might experience in such a situation.

Hand in hand we walk up the hill, and my heart flutters.

"Are you—" I hesitate to finish my question.

"A prisoner?" He raises an amused brow. "No. I'm here to look after the island and monitor the prisoners."

As we reach the top of the hill, a forest lies ahead, with a wooden plank hanging from one of its trees. It reads, "This Way to Camp Moonfall."

He points towards the sign. "Camp's this way."

"Yeah, I can see that," I respond.

As we step onto the mulched trail, the sound of crunching twigs fills the air. Moonlight filters through the broad leaves, and fireflies dance around us. Soon, lanterns come into view, illuminating a settlement of tents, wooden chairs, tables, and a campfire.

"I assigned you to tent number 5," he points towards a canvas shelter across the camp. "Your roommates are Ren and Dove. They're siblings."

"Thank you," I say, pausing, waiting for him to introduce himself.

He blushes slightly. "Cole. My name is Cole."

"I'm Quinn," I respond, extending my hand, but he doesn't take it.

"I know," he says, his smile growing wider as he turns away. "I'll be back to check on you tomorrow."

As I watch Cole disappear into the darkness of the forest, I realize I miss home a little less than before. Unable to suppress my smile, I dance with the fireflies under the glow of the full moon. This island may be a prison, but it also holds a startling sense of intrigue for me. Somehow, I yearn to know more about Cole, to feel his touch, hear his voice, and discover everything there is to know about him. I am a moth being drawn into his flame, unable to resist the perilous fate that might be waiting for me.

***

The break of dawn brings about the cheerful crow of a rooster and the contented grunts of pigs slurping up their food from the troughs. On cots nearby, a boy around my age and his younger sister peacefully slumber. Their unmistakable sibling bond would be evident to any observer, with matching curly brown hair and identical freckles adorning their cheeks.

Beyond the camp's boundaries, a bustling scene unfolds with girls and boys of similar age engrossed in their respective tasks. Some tend to the animals with care, while others diligently mend fences or prepare eggs and meat over a crackling open fire. In this lively atmosphere, if I were to shut my eyes, it would almost evoke the comforting sensation of being back at home.

"On their first day, nobody knows what to do." His velvety voice sends a shiver down my back.

On my right, he stands, clad in light tan knickers and a white tunic, with a spacious bag slung over his shoulder. Rays of sunlight cascade through the foliage, causing the red and blue highlights in his almost black hair to shimmer gracefully.

Spontaneously, I utter the first words that come to mind. "Good morning, Cole."

His eyes sparkle with delight upon hearing his name from my lips. "I brought you some things."

Cole gracefully hands me the bag from his shoulder. Inside, I find a pillow, another blanket, and a few apples.

"Thank you." As our eyes meet, his very essence intertwines with my fascination. Suddenly, I'm incognizant of the world surrounding us, pulled in by his mystery and charm.

"I'm keeping you from helping the others with camp." He withdraws his gaze, severing the connection.

The sounds of clanging pots, crackling fire, and busy bodies return. For a few seconds, I turn my attention to the girl fixing a kettle over an open flame.

At the mere thought of food, my stomach lets out an audible grumble. Returning my attention to Cole, I begin, "It's a good thing you packed apples in . . ." However, to my surprise, he has vanished from the daylight.

"Do you always have conversations with yourself?" The boy from my tent grins, revealing endearing dimples at the corners of his freckled cheeks, while his wavy brown hair partially obscures his eyes.

"Are you talking to me?" I ask.

"The name's Ren," he announces, casually putting a piece of straw into his mouth and extending his hand outward.

"It's nice to meet you," I respond with a curtsy. "Cole has assigned me to tent five with you and your sister."

"Dove will be so happy." Ren leans in, cupping a hand around his mouth.

"She bet me two of her apples that our new tent mate would be a girl."

"So now you owe her two apples?" I ask.

"Afraid I don't have any." He shrugs. "I've already given them all to her."

As if on cue, Dove runs up to her brother. "See, I told you we'd get another girl. So, pay up." She holds her hands out.

Ren crouches down. "And where have you been, little lady?"

"Xploring the wood. Why do you ask?" Dove wrinkles her little button nose in Ren's face.

"I told you to stay near camp. We don't know what's out there." Ren touches the tip of Dove's chin.

Dove widens her eyes and leans into her brother. "How we gonna find out if nobody takes a look around?"

"Dove--" Redness spreads across Ren's face.

"Alright, big brother, I won't go off alone." Dove holds out her hand. "Now, where are my apples?"

"I've already given you all my apples. And bananas and oranges."

Her head down and arms crossed, she furrows her little brows.

"I've got a couple of apples for you," I offer, reaching into my bag. Retrieving two vibrant red apples, I pass them over to Dove.

Her eyes light up as she snatches them from me. Without as much as a thank you, she takes off running towards the stables.

"Dove likes to feed the horses." He says. "The darn things eat better than I do, thanks to her."

I laugh at the revelation that a little girl just swindled me out of two delicious apples, then fed them to a horse.

"I'm Quinn." I place the bag inside of our tent, then take another look at everyone working so hard around camp. "Do you have a job?"

"Tent five is on firewood and foraging duty." He replies.

"Berries and herbs, right?" I follow Ren through the camp's border gate.

He hands me a basket. "Right. You forage and I'll gather firewood."

We spend the rest of the day doing chores, making repairs, and getting acquainted.

Once the sun disappears and night returns, I lay down on my cot. Ren has just finished singing Dove to sleep.

"Whatever did the two of you do to get thrown in here?" I ask.

Ren strokes his sister's hair. "We got a job working at the market restocking baskets of bread. The owner had to take care of something and asked if we would watch his tent. Dove was especially curious that day. She ran off, and I had to find her. By the time we returned to the bread tent, the owner had returned and all of his bread was gone."

"That's terribly unlucky," I respond with empathy.

"How about you?" he asks.

"I stole bread to feed an orphan girl."

"Wait, it was you?" He jests. "You're the one who stole all of our bread and got us thrown onto this wretched island."

We erupt into laughter. Once I regain my composure, I add, "It was one piece. And it wasn't your bread because you were already here."

Somewhere outside of our tent, a lovely voice hums a melody. "Do you hear that?" I ask.

"We call them lullabies." Ren lays his head down.

"Where do they come from?" I wonder.

"No one knows. Anyone who's chased after it has never returned to camp." He pulls a blanket over his shoulders. "You'd be best to just ignore it."

Those who know me will say that it's not in my nature to ignore anything. But after a busy day of work and becoming acclimated to my new surroundings, I'm tired. So, I let the lullabies do their part and sing me to sleep.

I wake up to a sense of unease, and as I glance around the dark tent, I realize Dove is nowhere to be found. Panic sets in, and I nudge Ren awake urgently. "Ren, wake up! Dove is gone," I exclaim, my heart pounding in my chest.

He sits up abruptly, his expression mirroring my concern. We search the camp frantically, but there's no sign of her. Then, as we approach the old oak tree at the edge of the camp, we spot a chilling message carved into its trunk: "She's mine now. Don't try to find her."

Fear and anger take root as we stand there, trying to process the implications of the message. Someone has taken Dove, and they don't want us to follow.

"Quinn, we need to come up with a plan," Ren says, his voice determined. "We can't let them take Dove without a fight."

I take a deep breath, trying to steady my nerves as I look at Ren. "Maybe we should ask Cole for help," I suggest tentatively.

Ren's eyes narrow with suspicion. "Are you serious? The guy is creepy. I don't trust him."

Ren's hesitation is surprising to me. Cole has been nothing but kind and charming.

"Well, I do. And he is very knowledgeable about the island. We'll need that to find your sister."

Ren hesitates for a moment, clearly torn. "Fine," he finally says with a heavy sigh. "But I'll be watching him closely."

I nod in agreement. "That's fair. He's probably at the castle, so let's start there."

We set off to find Cole, walking through the filtered moonlight of the forest. Understandably, Ren isn't much for words. Once we step into the open, the castle comes into view.

"Come on, Ren!" I take off running, until I see Cole, sitting on a giant rock, whittling a piece of wood with a small knife. His pretty clothes are tattered and smudged with dirt, and he greets us without looking up.

"Quinn, Ren. To what do I owe the pleasure?" Cole's chiseled jawline turns up, his eyes locking with mine.

"We need your help," I say, choosing my words carefully as I push my feelings aside. "Dove has gone missing, and we think someone took her. We're trying to find her, and we could use your expertise in these woods."

For a moment, he says nothing, just studies our faces. Then, he puts down the piece of wood and stands up. "Lead the way," he says simply.

Ren narrows his eyes, still suspicious, but he doesn't object. We explain what we know so far as we walk deeper into the forest, and Cole listens intently. He doesn't offer much in return, but I can tell he's taking it all in.

We arrive back at camp and show Cole the old oak tree with the message etched into the side of it. Cole's eyes go dark, and he turns away. "I'm sorry about Dove, but I can't help you."

"Why not?" I try to look into his eyes.

Cole clenches his fists. "There are things about this island that none of you know, and you really should keep it that way."

"You know something." Ren points his finger in Cole's face. "You're going to tell us where she is."

Trying to calm Ren down, I step in between them. "Yelling isn't going to bring Dove back." I look both boys in the eye. "Working together will."

As Ren takes a step back, I inadvertently stumble, getting my foot wedged between the rocks. In my clumsiness, I end up falling right into Cole's arms. His stare captures my gaze and my entire body is drawn into his warmth. It's as if our souls became entwined and we are one.

A hand touches my shoulder, severing the connection once again. And my heart aches with loneliness and abandonment.

Ren places his hands on his hips. "I don't know what's going on with you two lovebirds, but we need to know, Cole. Are you in or out?"

I look into his speckled eyes and plead extra for his help. Cole gives a deep sigh. "Alright. I'll do what I can. But first, you need to know what we're up against."

A surge of excitement rushes through me, and we eagerly trail behind Cole as he leads us back to the castle. The dark stone on the frame of the entryway shimmers with the same red and blue flecks in Cole's hair. As I step inside the castle, another sense of belonging encapsulates me. Except, this feeling isn't a good one, but more like a caged animal who has given up on being free.

Cole gathers a few swords and shields, handing us one of each. "There is a curse on this island."

Ren and I look at each other blankly. Then I turn to Cole. "Yes, we know that. It's an island that disappears an hour after midnight, trapping all those who remain on it."

"The curse is so much more than that." Cole sharpens his blade with a stone. "Do you know who put the curse on this island?"

"No one does," I reply.

"Wrong." Cole looks at me. "Long ago, a sea witch named Isadora used the full moon to cast a spell binding those who remained on this island with her. They became her sirens."

"Sirens?" Ren mocks the idea of it.

"Actually, Ren, it makes sense." I tell him. "Think about the lullabies. A beautiful voice singing enchanted melodies in the forest. All those who try to find it come up missing."

A realization takes hold of Ren's mind and where his skepticism began, fear takes over.

"How do you kill a sea witch?" Ren asks.

Cole furrows his brow. "I don't know."

"Well, do you at least know where to find her?" The agitation grows in Ren's voice.

"Isadora lives inside of a sea cave on the east side of the island." Cole fixes a sheath around his waist. "Finding her is not the problem."

"Then what is?" Ren asks.

"The caves are only dry for three hours each night, starting at nine o'clock. Then they fill up with water." He helps me fasten a sheath around my waste. "That's not a problem if you are a sea witch, because she can live in water or land. But if you are a human, caves full of sea water aren't your friend."

"Got it." I check my watch. "That means we need to defeat Isadora and rescue Dove by midnight."

"What time is it now?" Ren asks.

"Three in the afternoon." Cole and I sheath our blades. "We have six hours until you can enter the caves."

Cole assists us in every way he can, ensuring we are well-prepared for the challenges that lie ahead. I can sense that he is well aware of the perils we are about to encounter. I wouldn't be surprised if he has personally confronted the sea witch at some point in his past.

At eight-thirty, we depart from the castle and make our way towards the eastern shore. There, a rocky ledge provides a vantage point overlooking the tranquil sea, far from the island's center. Cole effortlessly leaps from one rock to another, displaying remarkable balance. Ren and I follow suit, cautiously gripping each rock as we carefully descend the steep cliff's side.

Near the base, a slender opening awaits, and we maneuver ourselves into its shadowy embrace, where every sound reverberates. Cole ignites a torch, illuminating the smooth walls of the cavern as I observe the hanging stalactites and rising stalagmites. The air inside is damp and carries a distinct chill.

We tread carefully around each corner, trying not to make any loud noises. My mind is consumed with curiosity and speculation. What could a sea witch possibly look like? Is she an enormous creature with tentacles and menacing, razor-sharp teeth? The uncertainty of the danger that awaits us only adds to the unease I feel as we press forward.

Towards the rear of the cave, a mesmerizing swirl of blue and red light dances above a shallow pool. That eerie feeling of connection floods over me once more. Echoing footsteps fill the air as a woman of chilling, unmatched beauty emerges gracefully from the cave wall.

"Quinn, my dear. I had hoped for your arrival," her speckled eyes exude adoration as she glides across the water, drawing nearer to me. "I've been waiting for you for a long time."

Ice-cold hands touch my cheek, leaving behind stinging crystals. Suddenly, with no need for an explanation, I recognize this wicked sea witch as Isadora. And I realize Dove was merely bait, a carrot used to lure me into Isadora's lair.

Ren directs his anger at the witch, shouting, "Where is my sister?"

Isadora's face twists into an evil grin, and with swirling hand motions, she extends her icy grasp towards Ren, turning him into a frozen statue.

"Mind your words around me," she warns, raising her hand in the air, admiring its graceful motion. "I have turned men into ice, salt, and even reduced them to a mere pile of ash."

"Why do you want me?" I try to suppress my anger.

"Once every century, this island discovers an exceptional human who possesses the most potent essence," she explains, pacing around me, carefully examining every aspect of my being. "And in this century, it is you who holds the island's cherished soul."

She then turns her attention to Cole. "In the previous century, my dearest Cole was the cherished soul."

Heartbroken, tears well up in my eyes. "What does she mean?"

"Quinn, I—"

With a raise of her arms, Isadora lifts Cole's feet off the ground. He spins slowly, and from his body, blue and red lights radiate, transforming his skin into a deep blue hue and his feet into vibrant red fins. As he spins, a harmonious melody emanates from his open mouth, enveloping everything around me.

Isadora lowers her hands, and Cole reverts to his human form, curled up and visibly shaken on the cave floor. He meets my gaze with shame in his eyes, and I sense his thoughts. He never wanted me to witness him in this state.

"He will recover." Isadora dismisses any concerns about Cole, putting her arm around my shoulder. "All my sirens favor mastery over their transformations," she explains, attempting to reassure me.

"All of your sirens? Are there others?" I inquire.

"A hundred thousand years' worth." The sea witch looks me in the eye.

"I have a deal for you. I will release Dove and let your friends leave this island alive. All I want in return is you."

"You mean you want me to become your next siren?" I clarify in a matter-of-fact voice. "And what if I say no?"

Isadora narrows her eyes, and with a wave of her hand, Dove materializes on the other side of the shallow pool. The sea witch then extends her sharp fingernail, scratching the little girl's body from afar. Blood streams down Dove's face, arms, and legs, causing her to emit a horrific scream.

"Okay, stop. Please. I'll do what you want. Just let them go," I beg.

Isadora clasps her hands together in delight. Dove's scratches stop bleeding and heal. The ice covering Ren melts and the siblings run toward each other.

A warmness covers me as Cole wraps his arms around my shivering body. "Are you sure you want to do this?"

Our gazes lock, forging an unbreakable connection between us. I offer a smile and share my feelings with him, saying, "I've never been so sure about anything in my life until I met you. From the very first moment I heard your voice and felt your touch, I knew exactly where I belonged. Even if it means transforming into a fire-breathing dragon, I don't care, as long as it allows me to be with you."

My body becomes weightless as I hover in the air. Looking down, I witness my long locks transforming, shimmering with rubies and sapphires. Gradually, my skin takes on an oceanic blue hue, and my legs glisten with iridescent scales, in beautiful shades of blue and green.

With his speckled sea glass eyes fixed on me, Cole willingly undergoes a transformation. The waves crash into the sea cave, carrying us out into the open waters. We plunge deep down into the abyss, entwined in each other's embrace. And just before we reach the ocean floor, our lips meet in a siren's first kiss.

About the Author

Andrea D. Long is an author of fantastical worlds and adventure. She writes themes of self growth, found family, and true love. When Andrea is not taming wild dragons and using her wits to outsmart some great evil, she is a mother of teenagers and teacher of the much shorter humans. All the while, she's blessed enough to brave the forces of life with a powerful wizard by her side. Follow the link, www.andreadlong.com, to discover all the magical things.

The Girl in the Garden

in the

Garden

HEIDI WILSON

Found: Fabulous Footwear

"Two nights past, the palace hosted a grand ball in the hopes of finding our beloved Prince Rylan a bride. When the night was over, a glass slipper was found on the stairs outside, with no indication to whom it might belong. If you know the owner—or if you *are* the owner—of this lovely shoe, please leave your information with your local palace representative, and you shall be contacted shortly."

I fold the newspaper with a sigh.

"Alliteration, Peters? Really?"

"It's eye-catching, Your Highness. We should start receiving responses as soon as the paperboys have finished their routes for the day."

"That soon?"

"People tend to move quickly when a chance to meet the kingdom's most beloved figure is implied."

Right. Not that I particularly want to meet anyone. Not after meeting *her*. The girl whose name I didn't catch. The girl who made me wish all of this weren't a giant ruse, meant to cover the fact that my marriage was arranged long ago, to a girl who left me for my cousin two weeks ago. Now my father is desperate for me to find a girl, any girl, to secure the throne.

So I'll have heirs.

I don't even know if I want children, but the throne needs an heir. An heir to follow me as I'll follow my father. And he's unlikely to live much longer. So the rush is necessary, as much as I hate it. But I'd rather not marry a complete stranger. Though the girl from last night would qualify. And there was definitely chemistry. So why can't I remember her name?"

"Are you sure an advert is the best way to go about this?" I ask, gesturing at the paper in my hand. "I met a girl. I liked her, and she can't be that hard to find, right?"

"Do you have any idea how many eligible ladies live in this city, let alone this kingdom, Your Highness? This is likely to be the fastest way to find the lady."

He's right. But that doesn't mean I want to wait that long. Perhaps I can find her first.

"Peters, I'm going out."

"Out where, sir?"

"To find the girl."

"Are you certain that's wise? You have no idea who she is, let alone where she lives."

"We have to start somewhere. I'll check with the representatives first, then local businesses, see if anyone has seen her."

"Do you even know what she looks like, Your Highness? It was a masked ball."

I curse under my breath. He's right, I'm not actually certain what she looks like, other than an impression of golden hair, green eyes, and the brightest smile I've seen since my mother died. She was perfect. And I definitely want to see her again.

"I'll figure something out, Peters. Are you coming or not?"

"*Not*, sir. I need to stay and deal with anyone who decides they should report directly to us, and you can check with the others while you're out. Take Lewis with you, though."

I nod. "Fair enough." Lewis is my second favorite of our staff. I'd rather have Peters with me, but Lewis is a good fellow.

The streets are noisy as we emerge from the palace gates, my head ducked so no one can see my face, our clothes nondescript, so both of us look like guards. It would not be helpful for me to be recognized right now. We'd be swarmed by ladies ready to lie to me and say they were the one who lost their shoe last night.

Sure, one of them might be telling the truth, but statistically speaking, that's unlikely. So I keep my head down and allow Lewis's horse to move slightly in front of mine to block anyone's view if they're looking too closely.

"What's our first stop, sir?" Lewis asks, careful to avoid using my real title, in case anyone might be listening.

"The closest representative office, I suppose, Lewis. That seems like the proper place to start."

The streets are emptier than I expect the closer we get to the office, and I frown at Lewis. "Where is everyone?"

"Storming the palace gates, I'd imagine, sir."

"Peters will be having a time of it, then." I glance around. The only figure near us is a girl, her back turned and her head ducked much like mine was, skittering away from us as if we're about to chase her down. Odd.

"Likely. It should be safe enough for you to go inside, since the streets seem rather quiet today."

We dismount and leave our horses tied to the gate. The little bell on the door rings cheerfully as Lewis pushes it open, and we both duck inside quickly. The small lobby is deserted. Strange.

I knock lightly on the desk and hear a small shriek, then a thud.

"Can I help you?" A voice squeaks from under the desk, then a hand rubbing a head of ginger hair appears, followed by a pair of inquisitive blue eyes that widen as they see my face.

"Your High—"

I raise a hand. "Please don't. I'm trying to travel incognito."

The girl looks terrified, poor thing.

"Of course, sir, I apologize. Can I help you with something?"

Lewis clears his throat. "We're checking in to see if you've had any responses to the advert from this morning, Leise."

She shakes her head, still rubbing at the spot she must have hit on the desk. "Not yet, sir. Though a girl did come in a few minutes ago and left a note."

"A note?" I frown. "For whom?"

"You, sir. Or at least, I'd assume it's for you. The populace don't tend to just leave notes for random people at palace representative offices."

"May I see it?" Lewis asks, reaching across the desk. "With your permission, sir. I'd rather check and make sure it's not some kind of threat."

"Of course." I nod at him.

Leise hands him the note, and he reads it quickly, his brow furrowing. "It's not a threat, sir. There's that at least."

"Then what is it?"

He hands me the slip of paper, and I flip it open.

Meet me at midnight.

The penmanship isn't familiar, but somehow, I know it's from *her*. The girl from the ball.

"Do you know who left it?" I ask, sliding the note into my breast pocket.

Leise shakes her head. "The girl wasn't familiar, and she didn't leave a name. Do you know her or something?"

I shake my head. "Not exactly. But I think she might be who I'm looking for. Did she say anything else to you?"

"Not that I recall. She just handed me the note and asked that I ensure it made it to the right hands."

The right hands meaning mine, I suppose.

"Do you know where she means to meet you, sir?" Lewis asks, frowning.

I shake my head. I don't. Not for certain. But I think I might have an idea.

"Wait, what did the note say?" Leise asks, peering over the desk at us, confusion crinkling her pixie-like features.

Lewis repeats the sentence to her, and I wander away, studying the artwork on the walls. I hear them discussing the note as I mull it over myself. Midnight. Likely in the garden. And likely tonight.

I probably shouldn't go. It's a bad idea. She's a stranger. It might be a trap. But I want to see her again.

My kingdom needs a princess. Really, it needs a queen. It's needed a queen since my mother died. But my father refused to remarry, and now he's dying. So it's up to me to take a wife. I don't know this woman. But I want to.

I just don't know if it's enough.

"What now, sir?" Lewis asks, turning away from Leise, who ducks her head, blushing a little. I wonder if there might be something between them. Or the chance of something in the future. It would be a good thing for both of them if there is.

"The next office, I suppose. We have time. Peters will be handling all the comers at the palace, so we should take the chance to ask the others while we have it. We could go back home, but then everyone will be fussing over me again. I'd rather have what space I can get for a short while longer."

"Very good, sir. We'll be off, Leise." Lewis nods at her, and she flushes.

"Lovely to see you, sir. Your Highness." Her red hair swings around her face as she rises into a brief curtsey. I wave a hand at her.

"Sit down, Leise. It's not necessary. I'm no one today. But it was lovely to see you as well."

"Goodbye, Matthew." I hear her whisper as I tug the door open.

"See you soon, Leise." Lewis winks at her as he slides through the open door before I can.

***

We aren't as lucky at the next office. It's flooded with girls and their mothers, aunts, and grandmothers. Women everywhere. I stay outside, lurking behind a tree, holding the reins of our horses as the clamor of female chatter assaults my ears. So many girls who think they have a chance. Or whose mothers want them to, whether the girls themselves are interested or not. I hear one woman who says she'll gladly cut off the toes or heels of her daughters' feet if she must, to ensure the slipper fits at least one of them.

I shake my head. Not a chance. The slipper isn't the true test, anyway. Just the easiest way to narrow the field of possibilities.

Lewis emerges after what feels like ages, shaking his head and proffering another note.

"It's identical, sir. And Jessina said the same thing Leise did. She didn't see her face, and didn't recognize her voice. Nothing was left besides the note."

Meet me at midnight.

I can feel my brows crease as I stare down at the script, identical to the last. My father would lecture me about premature wrinkles if he could see how much I'm frowning today. But why won't this girl just tell me who she is? Why won't she come find me in daylight, in public?

"Sir?" Lewis places a hand on my arm. "We should go."

I nod, folding the slip of paper again. "Of course. On to the next office."

The villages keep getting smaller the farther we get from the palace, and the crowds seem to get bigger. I don't understand, but perhaps all the people who live closer to the palace went directly to the gates instead of to the representative offices.

Another office, another note. Lewis takes this one, and I let him. The crowd is louder here, and I wish I'd waited outside the village. It's too much. I didn't want this kind of chaos. I just wanted to find the girl.

"Sir!" A voice rises above the clamor, and I see a guard running toward me. A guard who isn't Lewis.

"Yes?" I ask, lifting my head, hoping no one has noticed the royal guard speaking to me. I don't want to be recognized here.

"You need to come back to the palace, sir. Now. It's the King."

***

He's gone. My father died soon after I arrived last night. And I am the king. I hate the sound of it. King Rylan. It sounds wrong. People should still be saying King Markham, not Rylan. It wasn't supposed to be me. Not yet.

"Sire, we need to talk about plans for your coronation." Peters says gently, standing next to the throne. The room is empty, save myself and a few guards. I promoted Peters to my personal guard, doubling as my secretary and occasional advisor. He's been working in the palace longer than I've been alive, and is the only person I truly trust, though Lewis has been promoted as well, to the head of the Royal Guard.

I drop my head into my hands, leaning forward. The throne feels too large. The crown that I've worn since I arrived back home yesterday feels too heavy. And it's not even the official crown. Just a placeholder.

"I'm not ready for this, Peters."

"I understand, Sire. But it must happen. And then we must speak about your wedding."

My head jerks up. "What wedding? We didn't find the girl from the ball. And I'm not marrying a stranger." And I missed meeting whomever left the notes. I didn't leave my father's bedside all night, even knowing he was gone. I couldn't move. Couldn't think.

"You must marry. As soon as possible. Because the throne needs an heir. The line can't end with you. I wish we could have found the girl, but we can't afford to take any more time. You will be crowned within the week, once we hold King Markham's state funeral, and then you must choose a bride. It's not negotiable, Sire."

I know it isn't. But it feels wrong, planning my coronation, a wedding, when my father hasn't even been dead a full day yet. I knew it was coming. So did my father. But I didn't think it would feel like this. Everything feels wrong.

I stand, scrubbing my hands down my face. "We will discuss it later, Peters. I need an hour to myself, please."

"Of course." Peters claps his hands and the guards clear the room, leaving us alone.

"To myself," I reiterate. "That means you can leave me alone as well."

He frowns at me. "You are the king, and I cannot leave you unguarded."

I sigh. "The palace is surrounded by walls and giant gates, and there are literally four layers of guards between that wall and the royal chambers. I'm perfectly safe. Please, leave me."

He grumbles, but backs out of the room, leaving me alone for the first time since yesterday.

I am alone. And I am the king.

"What am I going to do now?" I whisper into the silence of the empty throne room. I know a reply isn't coming. But I wish for one anyway.

Eventually, the silence starts to bother me and I move through the side door out into the gardens. The garden where I last saw *her*.

The night-blooming flowers are just beginning to perk with the last light of dusk on the horizon, and I wander past my mother's roses, towards the small enclosed lawn surrounded by box hedges. The lawn where we danced. I can feel the guards posted around the perimeter watch me as I disappear between the bushes, and I know Peters will find me soon enough, but I need a few more moments to myself.

The light between the hedgerows is so dim that I nearly don't see the slip of paper on the ground, left in the center of the lawn. Somehow, I know what it is before I open it.

I'm sorry I couldn't stay. Or tell you who I am. Forgive me. I promise I'll tell you everything. Please.
Meet me here, at midnight.

She was here. How did she get into the palace? Confusion tangles my thoughts, but I know one thing for certain. I need to return here tonight. At midnight. Alone.

The rest of the evening is full of plans for my father's state funeral, my coronation, and evading questions regarding my wedding. I refuse to plan until I know for certain that *she* is the one I'll be marrying. And I should have my answer soon enough.

Peters isn't happy when I dismiss my guards as we reach my chambers. Discussions ran longer than I wanted, and it's closer to midnight than I wish. I'll have to be very quiet when I slip out. My guards don't need to know. This meeting is mine, not the crown's.

The clock shows less than five minutes until midnight by the time I'm dressed in the darkest clothes I own and sliding through the side door of my chambers into the garden. The guards are looking away, and I thank the heavens for that as I tiptoe past, heading for where I found the note earlier.

A shadow waits, sitting in the center of the lawn. A shadow with golden hair.

"You came."

The whisper is gentle, soft, and slightly shocked.

"I came." I reply, sitting down beside her as green eyes meet mine. Eyes that have haunted me for three days now.

"I'm sorry I had to run from the ball. I had to return the gown." I notice her hands twisting in her lap, toying with something. The mask, from the ball.

"Are you going to tell me who you are now?" I ask, reaching out to still her fingers.

"You haven't figured it out yet, Rylan?"

I jolt at the sound of my name on her lips. "Wait, you're not—"

She nods. "You remember me now?"

Her name is a breath. Barely a memory. A young girl with a bright smile, infectious laugh, and eyes the color of moss. My first love. "Isabelle."

The daughter of the cook. We were children together. I loved teasing her, and she had been so sweet and kind. I loved her. And then she disappeared.

"I thought you'd left the palace years ago. You came back?" I tuck a strand of her hair behind her ear. It used to be lighter, but I love the new, darker golden shade. Her eyes though, those are the same.

"I never left, Rylan. I just wasn't allowed to be with you anymore. You were being groomed to be king, and I was nothing but the child of the cook. I'm still nothing. But I thought, at the ball, I might have a chance to see you again. One last time. I didn't expect for every single thing I loved about you when we were children to be the same. I'm sorry I had to lead you on such a chase to find me, but there was no other way. Your staff would never have let you take a meeting with the daughter of one of them." She looks down at her lap. "And I'm sorry about your father. He was a good man, and a good king."

I sigh, staring down at the signet ring on my finger. "I have little hope of ruling as well as he did."

"You can rule just as well, if not better, Rylan." Isabelle's tone is earnest. I'd forgotten how passionate she gets when she believes something. "You're a good man, if the boy I loved is still in there."

Loved. She loved me. I had loved her, and then she was gone. Just like my mother.

"Isabelle, why am I here?" I ask, moving her chin with a finger to force her to meet my gaze.

"The shoe was mine."

"I gathered that." I frown. "But why am I here?"

She swallows, fidgeting with the mask again. "The ball was for all eligible ladies in the kingdom. I can't say I'm the most eligible or best option, but I thought you might give me a chance. I never stopped loving you. And I was hoping you might still care for me as well."

I chuckle. "Isabelle, why do you think I've spent the last three days looking for you, thinking about almost nothing but finding you? I might not have remembered you at the ball, but there was something between us. Something real. And I don't want to marry just anyone. My advisors are going to force me to marry, and soon. Within a month, likely. Because I am the king, and I need a queen. I'd rather marry you than a stranger."

Isabelle pokes me with a slender finger. "That's not a proposal, Rylan. That's not even a declaration of love."

She's right. I'm an idiot. I need to do this properly.

I turn to face her, sliding the mask out of her grasp, taking her hands in mine. "Isabelle, I loved you when we were ten. I loved you when we were fifteen and you disappeared. And I love you now, even with the awareness there's much I've missed in the last twelve years, and much that you don't know about me. I loved you when I saw you at the ball, and I nearly couldn't bear it when I couldn't find you. I think my heart remembered you, even when I was too blind to see the truth behind the mask. Marry me. Be my queen."

Isabelle laughs, leaning forward to press a kiss to my cheek. "You know I will, if I can. Your advisors have to approve. *My mother* has to approve."

"What mother doesn't want her daughter to marry a king?" I tease, tilting my head down, leaning to reach her lips with mine.

She smiles into the kiss, tugging on a curl around my ear. "I missed you."

I grin back at her as I pull away, poking at one of her dimples. "I missed these."

"Stop it!" Isabelle giggles, just like she used to when we were children, and my heart feels like it settles in my chest, like it's finally found where it was supposed to be, when I hadn't realized it was looking for anything at all.

She leans her head against my shoulder and I wish we could stay like this forever. Hopefully we can, soon.

"In the morning, I'll send someone for you. You have the other shoe, yes?" I ask, pressing a kiss to her forehead. She nods. "Then it should be a simple enough process. My advisors can't complain if you're the one with the shoe, and you love me. The rest can be worked out in time."

"I trust you." Isabelle flings her arms around my shoulders, pressing her face into my neck. "And I missed you. I love you. And I will see you in the morning."

"It is morning," I tease, claiming her lips with mine before releasing her. "Rylan—"

"Go. I promise I'll send for you as soon as the sun is up. I love you."

We both slip out of the garden, going our separate ways, but I feel lighter. She's real. And she's Isabelle. And I'm not going to lose her again.

***

The morning breaks with its usual list of meetings, but I tell my advisors to delay them all.

"I have news."

"News, Sire?" Peters frowns.

"I found the girl."

"The girl?"

"The one from the ball. Her name is Isabelle, and I intend to marry her."

"Who is this Isabelle? Where is her family?"

"Her family is here, in the palace. She's the daughter of the cook. I've loved her since we were children, and I intend to marry her. It will be good for the kingdom to see their queen as one of them."

My advisors start to argue, but I catch Lewis's eye over the crowd, and he winks at me. Did he know it was Isabelle the entire time?

Eventually, the chaos dies down, and my advisors calm, realizing I won't be dissuaded.

"Send for the girl. And start planning the wedding. There isn't much time. The crown needs an heir."

Isabelle appears like a vision, wringing her hands until she sees my face, then her smile could light the kingdom.

I mouth *will you marry me?* at her across the room, and she mouths back one word.

Yes.

We're married two weeks later, in the garden, at midnight. There will be a proper royal wedding later, but this one is just for us. The prince and the girl from the garden.

About the Author

Heidi Wilson is a born and raised California girl, full time legal clerk, and story obsessive. When she's not at her day job, she's usually writing, reading, or working on a craft project. For ridiculous amounts of fangirling over her favorite books and humans, and the occasional snippet of what she's working on, find her on Instagram at @heidiwilson.thehobbitkhaleesi.

THE FOX
THAT LOVED
A WARRIOR

AVALON WOLFSTONE

T he girl with the dark hair slowly unfolded herself from the toddler hidden beneath her. Their mother stormed out the door as their father settled in to enjoy the spoils of his raid.

The toddler sniffled, golden curls plastered to her wet cheeks. The older child pulled her young sister into her arms, despite the protest of her battered body, creeping to the back of the room to settle in the shadows. Thin arms clung to her neck, but the dark-haired girl didn't pry them away. She held her little sister close, rocking until the hitched breathing subsided.

"I'm s-s-sorry," a tiny voice whispered in the girl's ear.

Pulling away to look at her sister, the girl with the dark hair plastered a smile on her face. "You have nothing to be sorry about. I'm fine."

Golden curtains of hair framed amber eyes as the toddler shook her head, tears welling in her eyes, threatening to fall.

The older sister's eyes darted between their father draining his flask of amber poison and her sister. She couldn't cry while he drank.

"Would you like me to tell you a story?"

The toddler nodded.

"Okay, but only if you go to sleep and promise to be quiet."

Again, the toddler nodded, crawling into her older sister's lap.

Glancing at her father, the dark-haired girl lowered her voice before beginning.

"Once upon a time, there was a fox that loved a warrior . . ."

***

The crystalline fox glittered in the waning light as she stole into the dense forest, weaving around thick tree trunks, under exposed roots, and over the remains of an ancient tree the forest was slowly reclaiming. There was a lightness to her step as she neared the deep river shimmering almost as iridescent as she did in this form.

Almost.

She sniffed the air, glancing left, then right, before walking south along the bank until she found the promised alcove.

Settling in on a patch of sun within the alcove, the fox waited. Above, were dense trees and bush, making this a perfect hiding place, and a wonder that the sun penetrated the foliage. Surrounded by smooth stone walls on all but the side open to the river, it was a perfect place for two hearts to meet in secret. That opening darkened as a man's broad shoulders filled it. Water cascaded from his black hair into eyes a deeper blue than the darkest depths of the sea. He wore breeches of an unfamiliar material, and little other than what was required for the weapons strapped to his person. The beaded cuff on his right bicep, his only decorative article, marked him as the War Chief of the Sea Realm.

The crystalline fox launched herself into his arms the moment he settled, snuggling into his neck.

"Whoa." The warrior from the sea laughed. "Aren't you going to shift first?"

The fox squirmed in his arms, twirling back into his neck as answer.

"My love?" The warrior said.

At that, the glistening form of the fox melted away—snout shrinking into a cute nose, pointed ears receding into distinctly human ears, while the fur grew into earth brown locks of silken hair. The only hint of a fox left was her eyes. Brown with golden flecks they had a mischievous youthfulness to them like the cunning fox. The woman in his arms was beautiful, with a heart that beat for him alone.

Smiling, the woman wrapped her arms around the man's neck, drawing him down. "Is this better, love?"

The Warrior smiled, one hand on her rounded belly while the other drew her head to his. "Infinitely, wife." And he kissed her, long and deep, like a man drowning.

***

The woman sat, fingers attempting to braid her long hair. "Your son is eager to meet you."

The Warrior pulled her hands from her hair, kissing each before releasing them. He settled behind her, gently weaving locks into one massive intricate braid made up of smaller chains. "Oh? And when can I expect to meet him?"

His wife slid a sly smile over her shoulder. "Tonight."

Her husband's hands stilled. "Are you sure?"

She nodded. "Midnight. By the light of the full moon."

Joy filled the warrior to bursting, something he had never experienced before, not when he ranked first among the people of the sea. Not even when he was stationed as an advanced unit on land. None of those accomplishments came close to the elation he felt now, with the woman he loved in his arms, and the anticipation of the birth of his son.

Scooping his wife up, he spun her until she squealed in delight like a fox. "Gather your parents. We leave as soon as our son is born." Slowing the spin, the warrior stared intently into his wife's eyes. "Our family will avoid the coming war. I swear it."

A twig snapped.

The lovers still, hearts beating wildly as they strain to listen. After a few moments the warrior lowers his wife to the ground, taking a protective stance before her. He sniffs the air, damp earth and decomposing leaves filling his nose. He frowns, glancing at the bright green spring leaves surrounding them.

Winter smells.

The warrior closed his eyes, casting his mind wide, letting it ripple across their surroundings in wider and wider arks. Each ripple echoed in his mind when it collided with the landscape, forming a picture of their surroundings in his mind.

Sweat beaded on his brow, the ability taking far more effort on land than under the sea.

His wife's warm hands rested on his shoulders, easing the tension from them, and he gave another mental push cascading over the landscape.

Four men carrying bows, traps, and rope lit up in his mind up river.

Hunters.

The husband silently unsheathed a blade from his waist, but his wife's gentle hands slid down his arms, stilling his hands.

Her head tilted toward the sounds of the approaching hunters, a crease between her delicate brows. "They are far away, and there is no chance they heard us. Leave them be." She smiled at him.

The Warrior lowered his blade, but didn't sheath it.

They were getting closer.

Backing up until she was pressed against the stone wall, the wife shifted back into her crystal fox form. The couple couldn't be found together. Not by her people, and not by his. Too much animosity brewed between their realms.

Fox ears pressed flat against her skull as the hunters drew closer. They were tracking her. She had led them to their safe haven. And she would lead them away.

The Warrior glanced back at her, frowning, not reading her thoughts as easily in her crystalline fox form. She slowed her fox mind. *I will lead them away.*

No.

The fox puffed out her chest, sun refracting off the crystal in a dance of rainbows. *They're tracking me. They're from my village.* The fox stalked forward with a shake of her head, resulting in the softest of chimes. *Besides, what would happen if they found you?*

There would no longer be a threat, her husband thought matter-of-factly.

The fox pawed the ground. *No! They are good men! Men with families! You will not kill them. Understand?*

The Warrior stared at his fox wife. Finally, he sheathed his blade, crossed his muscular arms, and waited for her plan.

***

A mile deep into the forest, the Warrior peaked around a thick tree at the hunters who had naively followed the couple away from the river and their secret place.

This is stupid, the Warrior thought at his wife, eyeing the human hunters tracking her. He sent every ounce of frustration coiled in his muscles into the mental message and grinned when he could sense her yip at the intensity of it.

I'm trying *to focus here.*

She couldn't force her emotions through like he could, but he could still feel the eyeroll in his wife's response, and a little frustration lifted.

A glimmer of light flashed in his eyes as a sunbeam found his wife before she disappeared into another bush running wide crisscrossing tracks to confuse the hunters.

If you focused before, then it wouldn't be needed now.

I was excited to see you!

The warrior smiled. He couldn't be mad at her for that. Crouching behind the tree, he watched the four frustrated hunters. They were losing her trail thanks to all the backtracking. Sending a mental image of the hunters fumbling around in the thick underbrush, he made sure to lace this message with an undercurrent of pride. The dancing sunbeam that was his wife's mind shimmered in delight at the praise.

Okay, okay, okay! One more false trail! Then home! The fox's thoughts tumbled through the warrior's mind, faster than a swordfish.

Meet me at midnight? The fox called.

He grinned. There was no way he was missing his son's birth. *Name the place, my love.*

Joy danced through their minds, until neither was sure whose emotion it was.

Under the ancient weeping willow. You know it?

I do. The warrior smiled. *It's where you first kissed me.*

The fox wife leapt with the grace of a dolphin, blush warming her cheeks, and in turn, her husband's. *Then I will see you soon my love!* And the fox wife scampered off, out of her husband's mental range, taking her light, love, and joy with her.

***

The warrior, satisfied his wife was safe, turned, coming face to face with a taller, thinner version of himself. Only this version had sea green eyes.

"Brother. What brings you here?"

The brother's gaze trailed over the warrior's shoulder to the hunters beyond, before wandering back. "The Sea Council convenes tonight. They want a report." Jutting his chin at the hunters, he asked, "What are they?"

The warrior maintained eye contact with his brother. "My quarry."

Nothing moved between the brothers in the silence.

Finally, the green-eyed brother broke the stillness. "Will you be addressing the Sea Council then?"

The council only met at high tide . . . there was no way the warrior could address them and make it back to witness his son's birth. "No. You will address them. Tell them I am otherwise engaged in attending to their actual orders."

The brother's smirk didn't quite reach his green eyes. "Trying to get me replaced by having me insult the council on your behalf?"

The warrior was taken aback, but didn't let it show. His brother had always been by his side. There was no other he would consider to lead the tribe in his absence.

"Never, brother." He said, clapping a hand on his shoulder. "But the council needs to learn that nothing will get done if they insist on us dropping everything at their beck and call. And you, you were born to address them." Might as well have his brother start leading now; with the warrior tending to his family, he couldn't lead the warband.

The lines tightened around his brother's eyes, reminding the warrior of a tiger shark before it strikes. But he paid it no mind. That was simply how his brother was. A warrior though and through.

"Very well, enjoy your hunt." With that, his brother disappeared into the foliage as silently as he arrived.

Free of his brother, the warrior turned to the path that would take him to his wife and son and ran. But when he arrived at the weeping willow, his wife was nowhere to be found.

***

The fox awoke in a cage far too small, with a headache far too large. She coiled into herself, trying to remember what happened. She got caught in some vines . . . no. No . . . the vines entangled her, encircled her limbs and snout. Then the pain came.

So.

Much.

Pain.

Her mind had felt like it would rip in two. Then, blissful darkness.

And now she was here, in a cage. There were a lot of people around. Did the hunters catch her after all? Had she been that careless? No. Her husband would have ripped them apart first.

And where was he? *My love–*

Pain rolled through her mind, choking out her call and making her crystal fur stand on end.

Oh, no. There will be none of that. An ominous voice boomed painfully in her mind.

She couldn't place the mental voice, although it sounded oddly familiar. She had only ever heard her husband's voice in her head. Her people were incapable of the gift.

Someone knew who she was.

Someone from the Sea Realm.

Ears pressed flat, fangs bared, she readied to take off the hand of whoever opened the cage. Then she would flee. Her husband. She would find him. He would keep her and their child safe.

You would like to think so.

She pressed herself into the back of the cage, as if that could distance her from the intrusive mental voice in her head.

"Shut up!" She yipped.

Someone struck the cage until she was silent.

Laughter rolled in her mind. *He never loved you. Our kind isn't capable of it.*

The fox pressed her paws over her head, trying in vain to shut the voice out.

***

Blinding light from the setting sun filled the dark space of the cage for a moment as the fox was unceremoniously dumped on the dusty cobblestones. Stunned and disoriented, she didn't move as hands secured her.

Then the pain returned. Sharp and fiery in her mind. She yelped until a strong hand clamped her muzzle shut. She could feel her body expanding, the crystal turning to flesh as she regained her human form. More hands secured her arms and legs, dragging her down the street and pressing her against a wooden stake. Rough rope bound her legs, hands, arms, and chest. And then a knife appeared at her stomach.

"NO!" The fox woman thrashed against her bonds, but they held fast.

Another scream of terror and frustration ripped from her lungs before it was cut off by a hand. She struggled against it, but a rope snaked around her neck, cutting off her air. Eyes bulging, she struggled in vain to breathe.

"Now, now," a dark voice cooned. The same voice that invaded her mind earlier. "Let's make sure that's loose enough for her to gasp for air, but not scream. Yes?"

The strangling rope loosened enough to gasp for air. And she did. Again and again. But it wasn't enough.

Her pulse pounding in her head, she registered the knife at her belly again. The man holding it waited, letting the dying light glint off the blade a moment before he cut her baby out while she screamed. He handed the bloody, wailing child to a tall man concealed in a cloak. The only thing visible was the reflection of green eyes in the depths of the hood before the cloaked man turned away with her child and disappeared into the mist rising from the sea.

***

"My love will come for me." She whispered to herself with a grimace. She tried to comfort herself as sweat ran down her temples, body shaking. She knew he could find their son. He would save them all. He would come any moment now and save her, then they would live far away from this nightmare. She just had to hold on a little longer.

Cold steel pressed against her throat.

She lifted her eyes, locking on the man who ripped her baby from her. He was the butcher, the same man who proposed to her last spring; whom her parents turned down.

"This is the price of bedding a monster." The butcher said, sliding the blade across her throat.

Her eyes bulged as hot blood ran down the front of her dress.

A torch tossed in the kindling at her feet, ignited a fire that clawed at her limbs.

With her last breath, she gurgled past the blood, "M–my lo-ve will come for m–"

***

The warrior cursed himself for taking so long. His wife could be in real danger because it'd taken him too long to find where her trail disappeared and foreign tracks began. Those tracks led directly back to her town. He sprinted faster than he ever swam to get there before it was too late.

But when he arrived, there was a building on fire. And not just any building. Her family's house.

"No." The warrior breathed.

Not caring if anyone saw him, he dove into the house, reaching with his mind for his wife. But he couldn't feel her, and that terrified him. He searched every room, fire licking at him, smoke choking him. But all he found was her bound and dead parents.

He didn't have time to save the dead.

Leaping out of the house, choking on smoke, he spun, trying to get his bearings. And that's when he saw it. There, across the square, was a wooden stake on fire. And in that fire, his wife.

With a growl of rage, he bounded across the square and into the fire. Slicing her bonds in one swing, he gathered her in his arms and leapt from the fire. On the cold cobblestones, he smothered the flames with his hands before he noticed the blood.

So.

Much.

Blood.

Her stomach ripped open and empty. And her neck . . .

"No, no, no, no, no." The warrior pressed his hands to both wounds to stop the flow.

But it was too late.

He didn't hear a heartbeat.

Covered in her blood, he cradled her limp form, pressing her forehead to his own, and wailed for all three realms to hear.

A spark leapt from her mind to his. The last dying embers of her memories flashed before his eyes. A hooded figure who stole their son. The eyes of the man who murdered his wife. And her last. hope-filled words.

Her unwavering trust in him was a stone dragging him to the darkest depths of the sea.

Distantly, the warrior became aware he was surrounded. But still, he held his dead wife, lost in the repeating memories of her last moments.

When the first person lunged for him, he let them stab him, if only to feel it.

He didn't.

Turning, the warrior locked eyes with his assailant. The eyes of the man who murdered his wife. The man who'd killed the only light in his life. Face slack in fear the murder withdrew the blade, stumbling away from the Warrior, the sent of his wife's blood clinging to the weapon.

A film covered the warrior's eyes, tinting his world red. Detached, he wondered how that was even possible since he wasn't in the water. The film served as a transparent eyelid, but never worked on land.

But the warrior didn't care why it happened.

All he cared for had just been taken from him. And they would pay with blood.

***

Later, the warrior would say he didn't remember the details of that night. But that was a lie. He remembered everything. It was the same night he saw every time he closed his eyes. He spared no one in the town. Every man, woman, and child were guilty in his grief-stricken mind. And he killed without prejudice. Those who escaped were tracked down and dealt with in the same manner. They never escaped for long.

The stories that circulated regarding the massacre depended on who told it. Soldiers used it as proof that those from the Sea Realm couldn't be trusted. They were just savage animals, after all. Fathers used it to scare their daughters into finding a good, stable match rather than indulging the man who would whisper sweet nothings in their ears. But the women of the Realm? They romanticized it. Surely no one had ever experienced a love as deep as this man. And if anyone could heal his broken heart? Surely they would be rewarded with the same kind of devotion.

All the stories held an element of the truth, but all had been distorted by what each group wanted to believe.

In the end, it was a hopeless romantic whose mixed bloodline had caused her heartbreak of her own, who eventually came face to face with the heartbroken warrior of her fantasies. She pleaded with him to marry her, and if he did, she could make him forget all his pain. She would bear him a son to replace the one he lost, and he could finally forget his anguish.

***

"Meet me at midnight?" The young woman pleaded one night under the light of a full moon.

The heartbroken warrior was taken aback by his wife's words on a stranger's lips. "What?"

The woman smiled shyly, "Will you meet me at midnight? Beneath the weeping willow?" Her brown eyes flitted between his, waiting for his answer.

"For what?"

Lowering her eyes to the ground, the woman said, "To marry me. I know I'm not her . . . but perhaps . . ." She clasped his hands, meeting his eyes again. "Perhaps, we can help one another forget, just a little."

The warrior stared at those brown eyes, his wife's words echoing in his mind. And he thought, just for a moment, he saw a flicker of that fox spirit within the eyes before him. So, he agreed, wanting only to forget.

***

The girl with the dark hair stroked the golden locks of the sleeping toddler in her lap, her sky-blue eyes wandered the small hovel they inhabited until they landed on the drunken form of the heartbroken warrior. He was rigid in his chair, sea blue eyes distant, fixed on a time long past. His chiseled jaw clenched tighter than his fists around his drink.

The girl quickly looked away, lest those eyes fall on her again. Curling around her sister for warmth, the girl with the dark hair finished the story in a whisper as she herself drifted off to sleep. "But the boy, he was never found."

About the Author

Avalon Wolfstone is a dyslexic author, dragon-loving artist, and wilding cover designer. When she's not weaving enchanted realms together, you can find her rolling in the snow with her blue heeler mix who fancies himself a cat. Avalon spins dark vivid stories for the wilding in all of us, for light shines brightest in the darkness, and the stars outlast the night. Come chat books and art on Instagram @avalonwolfstone, an alcove for sassy bibliophile wallflowers, or enter the alluring realm beyond the pages at www.avalonwolfstone.com

WITH THE SUN

KATARA J.Z.

Rieke's muscles screamed in protest from rowing for hours through the rough waves. Freezing wind whipped soaked strands of hair across her face. She spat them out, the ocean brine coating her mouth. Distracting herself, she squeezed her eyes shut and recalled the brief conversation from three days before.

"How long—do I ha—have?" her father asked between hacking coughs.

The village healer studied her satchel, fingers thumbing medicinal herbs.

"How long?" Rieke demanded, arms tightening around her father's frail form.

"Two weeks at most."

Opening her eyes, Rieke glanced over her shoulder and huffed in relief. The cave's blue hue illuminated the cove a skipping stone's distance away. A few more weary strokes, and the boat's bow finally bumped into sand. Although the year's highest tide was still a handful of days out, the choppy waters of tonight's low tide had proved a harder challenge than the myths led her to believe.

Her freezing hands struggled to unclench, and, stepping out of the boat, her locked knees gave way. Collapsed on the silky sand she panted, trying to catch her breath in the chilly air. When the burning in her lungs subsided, Rieke propped herself up, exhausted arm trembling. Slowly, she stood on wobbling legs. Rieke didn't bother wringing water out of her hair or wiping sand from her clothing.

Peering beyond the boat, the only thing differentiating the obsidian bottomless ocean from the endless night sky was the peppering of winking stars and the two moons almost at their midnight conjunction. As her father taught her, she mentally calculated the time. She had forty minutes at most to find the life-saving item. The tides would turn soon, trapping her in the cove.

Grabbing the boat's small anchor, Rieke stumbled several paces toward the mouth of the cave, feet sinking into sand, and drove the hook into the beach. She carefully picked her way into the cave's stony darkness as the water lapped at the shore like sand through an hourglass on the shore behind her. Glow worms lay scattered on the ground, and when Rieke looked up, she found thousands more filling the ceiling and overflowing onto the walls, emitting a soft blue luminescence. She walked through a tunnel of stars.

At the first of what she knew would be many tunnel forks, Rieke trusted the path with the most luminescent creatures. After all, the myths foretold they would guide her. The worms created a low humming that damped her footsteps. She inhaled a deep, steadying breath, and a breeze of comforting sea salt embraced her rather than the mustiness she expected. Her hands trailed the cool, damp walls as plops of water droplets echoed from elsewhere in the underground space. They reminded her of the tears flowing down wrinkled paths on her stoic father's face when Rieke told him she was leaving.

Lost in her remembrance, Rieke slipped on the slick stone, reflexively darting out a hand to break her fall. She fell anyway, but did her best to avoid crushing any of the little glowing guides. As her wrist twisted beneath her, a flash of pain shot up her arm.

Her cry eclipsed the humming and dripping in the cave. Upon gingerly prodding her arm, a hiss escaped Rieke's clenched teeth. She didn't feel any broken bones, but her wrist hung limply. Suspecting a popped socket, Rieke steeled herself, and shoved the wrist back into place. A tear leaked down her face. While breathing heavily, several worms caught her eye. They inched further into the cave as if urging her to continue, so she rose, gently plucking a few of the more inquisitive creatures off her clothes and placed them back onto the ancient stone. Checking she hadn't forgotten anything, or squished anyone, she moved on, cradling her wrist. She had no choice. Her father would not die. She would not be alone.

She navigated a few more turns and branches, and then the tunnel opened into an expansive cavern. The inside of the subterrane could easily hold multiple of her father's single fishing boat—five lengthwise and three stacked. Moonlight filtered through a wagon-wheel-sized hole in the center of the ceiling, sending a surge of panic through Rieke. How much time had passed in the tunnels?

Rieke hurried into the room and skidded to a halt, a pungent floral perfume hitting her nose. She blinked in the sudden brightness. Moonlight touched upon the leaves and blooms of varied plants. She passed under clusters of pale white, flat flowers on vines that weaved in and out of cracks in the stone entrance. Silvery, spindly leaves brushed her bare legs. A conical light-yellow flower, whose petals resembled festival skirts, hung from a supporting tree, the delicate blooms stroking her cheek as she walked through. Jagged crystals suffused with inner lights of pink and red dotted the room around it.

She paused to finger the waxy leaf of an emerald-green plant with a fist-sized, closed bloom, and a lightning bug briefly alighted on her nose. It lifted off, darting from leaf to leaf, circumventing a form coalescing in the shaft of moonlight. As she watched it, the shape morphed into a gray figure that resembled a human from the shoulders up, with features as solid as a bank of fog. Rieke froze until an arm materialized and a skeletal finger beckoned her closer.

Squaring her shoulders—this was, after all, why she had come—she walked to the figure and knelt, folding both legs beneath her, head bowed.

"You seek that which heals," a gravelly voice intoned, reverberating through Rieke's bones as though it radiated from the very stone around her.

She spoke to the ground. "Yes, please. My father is sick he—"

"—he needs that which heals."

Rieke gulped and nodded silently. Sweat formed on her brow, and she couldn't tell if humidity, fear, or both contributed to her sticky tunic.

She held her breath, waiting for the figure to speak again.

"Hear my riddle. Provide the answer, and you will get what you seek."

> *I feel though you may think me unfeeling,*
> *I breathe though you may think me unbreathing,*
> *I present to only the mightiest tide.*
> *With the sun I flourish, with the sun I fade.*
> *I am in this room.*
> *What am I?*

The words the figure murmured rang old as time, and Rieke continued staring at the ground, her mind spinning.

The myths hinted at consequences, but Rieke needed confirmation.

"And if I guess wrong? If I don't guess?" she asked.

"Answer incorrectly, you remain in this cavern. Answer not at all, you are free to leave."

She nodded, the figure's answer reaffirming the myths. Rieke rose to one knee and risked a peek at the figure. It dipped its head towards her, and she recoiled. Sharp cheekbones contrasted unseeing, infinite eye sockets. It made no further motion at her, so she stood and paced around the room.

Overwhelmed by all the objects in the cavern, panic seized her. She couldn't do this. Her father was the thinker. He knew the stars. Knew the fish, the earth, the heavens. She could only sew nets, do things with her hands. But no. She had listened to her father's stories. She had learned to tell time from the moons. And when his body failed in old age, her nets and her shared knowledge of fishing brought in good money. She could do this for him.

Rieke mulled over the first two lines. She wandered over to a crystal and placed her hand on its rough, cold surface. Feeling and breathing implied living, which eliminated the illuminated rocks. The second to last line excluded anything outside of the cavern, thankfully.

"*I present to only the mightiest tide.*" Rieke understood tides but had no idea what presented to water, so she skipped to the next line.

"*With the sun I flourish, with the sun I fade.*" She crouched, absently watching a worm nibble a leaf. It wasn't a glow worm; they lived in a sunless cave. It also wasn't likely a moth or lightning bug. Based on dinners eaten with her father in the fields behind their cottage, moths and lightning bugs only came out once the sun disappeared. They also couldn't be the answer.

Looking around the room, Rieke concluded that the *something* must be a plant. The panic gripping her chest had subsided, but pounding in her head and throbbing in her wrist filled her head. The first part was easy enough, but she needed to focus.

"*I present to only the mightiest tide,*" she silently mouthed, pondering how it could apply to a plant. Plants grew, budded, blossomed, were pollinated, and fell, and the cycle had nothing to do with tides. The ocean scent faded the farther Rieke travelled through the tunnels, so these plants probably needed fresh water. The tides were salt water.

"Mightiest tide," Rieke muttered, unfocused eyes staring out the ceiling hole. She wracked her brain, and a memory bubbled up.

Under the rising sun Rieke sat curled into her father's side, both with steaming mugs in hand. From the safety of their porch, they watched waves as high as their cottage pound the village dock and moored boats. Fishing boats smashed into one another like seashells in a whirlpool.

"Why are they so big, Father?" Rieke asked, another whooshing wave hitting the dock.

"The Ocean King is angry," he said solemnly, sipping his drink.

Rieke raised an eyebrow.

He laughed, sputtering tea. "See there. Notice the moons?" He pointed at the horizon. "Once a year the two moons align with the sun, and the mightiest waves are formed. Us fisherfolk call it the king tide."

In the cavern, Rieke's eyes shot open, and she spun in a circle, searching.

King tides occurred once a year, and if the flower presented to it, that's when it must also bloom. She needed a plant not yet in bloom.

She pawed through shrubs and vines, ignoring the pain in her swelling wrist. Rieke's nose stung from the overpowering fragrances, and pollen from countless disturbed flowers filled the air. She sneezed and stepped back into a plant. Steadying herself, her fingertips grazed waxy, oblong leaves. Of course. She had touched it upon first entering the subterrane.

Rieke ran back to the figure in the moonbeam.

"It's that." She pointed at the plant with closed flowers. "The answer is the plant that isn't blooming tonight."

Time slowed as she waited.

The figure cocked its head without speaking. Two arms emerged from the shadowy depths, and between the hands floated a white flower with reaching petals the size of Rieke's face. Curious, she twisted her head. The plant she'd chosen remained, but the closed bloom no longer rested amidst the leaves.

A grin and breathy exhale escaped Rieke's mouth, her tightly wound body relaxing. She stepped forward, hand securely closing around the flower's fuzzy stem. Thin outer petals caressed her arm, and thick inner petals bobbed lightly.

Rieke turned to go, but the figure unexpectedly spoke.

"Do you accept the conditions?"

Rieke paused, glancing at the cave system entrance, and asked, "What conditions?"

"The flower is life. It will cure your father's illness, but if it leaves this cavern, everything you see in front of you, everyone you saw in the tunnels, will die. Do you accept the conditions?"

Confused, Rieke asked, "What do you mean everything here dies? It's a flower."

"It is life itself."

The figure slowly raised one arm. In sync, color drained from the cavern. A moth flying near Rieke's head dropped, hitting the ground, unmoving. With the arm fully extended toward the ceiling, the low buzzing of insects quieted, the slight breeze the plant leaves stilled. Complete silence filled the room except for the growing thudding of Rieke's heart.

Nausea churned in her stomach like being tossed at sea during a storm. "Isn't there another way? Another flower?"

"There is no other. Do you accept the conditions?"

Rieke quivered. None of the myths had mentioned this. They'd simply promised a cure for any ailment. Would killing some plants and bugs really be that bad? Taking life was nothing to seasoned fisherfolk like her.

Rieke buried her face in the fragrant flower, reliving a day with her father.

"Come see this, Rieke," her father instructed.

She scampered across the boat, rocking it wildly. Her mouth salivated, hoping for lunch.

"Careful." He put a steadying hand on her narrow shoulder, his other hand holding a substantial lobster. Her father flipped it over, revealing black dots covering the underside of the lobster tail.

"This lobster is pregnant," he said, answering her unspoken question and transferring the lobster to her.

"Can we still eat it?" Rieke asked, stomach grumbling.

"We could eat her, but it would be worse for us and for them in the future."

Rieke held the lobster, her claws snapping, legs waving.

Leaning over the edge of the boat, Rieke released the lobster into the ocean, and her father patted her head.

In the cavern, Rieke sobbed. Her legs buckled, knees hitting the ground. She only killed fish to eat, to sell and survive. She couldn't doom the lives of the beings in this cavern just for her father. He wouldn't want it either.

Rieke opened the hand that death-gripped the stem. The flower fell, disappearing in midair. Four pale, crescent-shaped divots left by her nails marred her palm. A puff of wind tossed the ends of her hair, and she raised her head. Vibrant tones recolored the room, and from the corner of her eye the moth twitched, taking off into the air. The closed bloom sat embedded in its plant. The moonbeam was just that, a column of light without any nebulous figure. Rieke had gambled and lost.

She lurched to her feet, careful of her wrist, and dashed back through the twisting tunnels. Even without the flower, she needed to get out of the cove before the tide returned so that she could spend as much remaining time with her father as possible.

Fatigued from sailing and rowing with the aching of her tender wrist, the days blurred together on her journey home. On the fifth day, the sun crested the hills just as Rieke's heavy feet stepped into the village. At the top of a grassy knoll, her childhood cottage sat undisturbed, and plodding up to it, her father's coming reaction played ahead in her mind. Disappointment hiding in his clear blue eyes, even though he'd smile approvingly of her decision.

She focused all her energy on dragging tired feet up the stone steps to her front door, missing the person waiting on the porch until they coughed.

"I'm glad you're safe," her friend and neighbor, Tevan, greeted in an off-tone voice but with open arms.

Rieke smiled cautiously and returned the friendly hug. She stepped past, and Tevan's hand shot out.

"Wait, Rieke," Tevan choked out, "Rieke, I'm so sorry, your father—"

"No," Rieke interrupted, shaking her head.

"It's only been eight days. He can't . . ." Her voice faded off.

Rieke pushed past her friend and rushed into the small cottage, into her father's bedroom.

He lay in his old wicker bed tucked neatly under a quilt she'd made a few winters past, hands interlocked peacefully on his chest. He could have been sleeping, except Rieke's agonizing sobs replaced his notorious snoring. She gripped his hands as hard as she had gripped the flower, barely noticing the consolatory pat from Tevan or their departure. Oblivious to the world, Rieke cried through the day and into the next. Rieke was alone.

The sun set, its rays pierced through a crack between wall and curtain, shining directly into her eyes and waking her up from fitful sleep. Rieke's parched tongue stuck to the roof of her mouth, so she reluctantly stumbled outside to fetch water from the village well. Her toes stubbed into a bucket left near the front door, and water sloshed onto her feet. Numbly, she dunked a cup into the water and gulped it down. The water hit her stomach, and it growled for the proper meal that Rieke had neglected to eat in recent days. A grief flag someone had hung flapped forlornly, grazing against the bucket and an upturned crate. Upon lifting the crate, she found a basket laden with dried meats, bread, and fruits. Thinking the meats and fruit too rich to handle, she snagged a loaf of bread and turned to go back indoors, but her body refused. Her floundering mind envisioned her father's cold body waiting inside, and her feet wouldn't let her cross the threshold. Instead, she spun and shuffled into the fields, the setting sun casting her world into shadow. Darkness surrounded her, and soon mist rolled in from the sea to extinguish the village torches.

Rieke ripped off a section of bread, laid in the field, and chewed slowly, staring up at the night sky. She closed her eyes as a gentle breeze rippled the tall grass and crickets chirped. Tonight, no lightning bugs or moons or stars shone, and the unbearable weight of loneliness crushed her like the blanket of enveloping darkness. More tears trickled down her cheek. She would never hear her father's hearty laugh, never feel his strong embrace, his bushy beard, his worn hands. They would never discuss the day's catch or knead dough for savory fish pies.

A feathery tickle on the back of her hand drew her attention, and, blinking blurry eyes open, Rieke gasped in astonishment; a little blue glow worm crawled along her hand. She sat up, bringing it closer to her face.

"I traded my father's life for yours," she whispered. She'd meant it full of anger, but it came out brimming with immeasurable sadness.

The small legs wiggled, and Rieke carefully cupped the creature close to her chest. She sat huddled around the worm, its gleam solely staving off complete darkness and loss. Her breathing slowed, and the tears ebbed to a stop. Exhausted again, and feeling calmer with the worm's light, she lay down, placing the creature safely on a nearby wildflower. In between fluttering eyelashes, she watched it inch down the stem.

Semidarkness greeted her eyes a few hours later, and the little guide was nowhere to be found. Waves crashed in the distance. Rieke stirred in the field, and a sparkle of lightning bugs diffused throughout the meadow. They danced in the long grass.

Gathering her strength, Rieke ambled back to the cottage. To her surprise, a steaming pot of stew awaited her. Rieke scooped a bowl, grabbed another piece of bread, and sat, leaning against the outer porch. A wave slammed into the shoreline.

Her village had cared for her father, for her, and she would carry on her father's wisdom forever. With the sun peaking above the horizon, Rieke's lips curled into a soft smile.

About the Author

Katara J.Z. is an author writing adult high fantasy. If you enjoy magic, immersive world-building, and a little bit of shenanigans, follow on Instagram @katarajz or visit https://www.katarajz.com.

The Tick-Tock Turner

Susan Burdorf

318

Chapter 1

"Time has no power over the one who turns the key."

That's what Gina's grandpa used to tell her whenever he went to repair the town's tower clock. Twice a year, or whenever there was a storm that damaged the clock, it was his job to make sure the town's main timekeeper remained in working order.

The town depended on the clock for more than just keeping time. No one questioned how the town and the clock were connected, but people moved slower, the sun remained stationary in the sky, and birds didn't sing or fly whenever the clock stopped. Gina often thought it strange that she didn't feel the effects when the clock didn't run properly, but her grandpa just smiled if she asked him.

"Time is our friend, not our enemy," was all he would say.

Gina loved her grandpa's big laugh, his bushy silver mustache that tickled whenever he kissed her on the cheek, and his twinkling brown eyes. They were all they had in the world, except for the succession of cats she seemed to attract. Since Gina's parents died when she was young, she and her grandfather had been closer than most all her life. But he only ever let her into the clock tower when with her, saying she was too young to understand its power.

Everyone in town spoke of the clock with reverence and awe, and she knew it was special. After all, her grandpa was adamant the clock always stay running. Their family had cared for the timepiece so long that no one could remember a time when a Gray had not been its keeper.

But sometimes, passing beneath the large black and white clock, Gina felt it watching her. She often wondered if she hadn't been born a Gray would she still be here in this town? Without grandfather, would she leave and never come back? Sometimes, tradition can become a millstone around the neck. The weight of everyone's expectations could take you over at the expense of freedom to make a choice in your best interest.

When she turned thirteen, her Grandpa began to teach her how to care for the clock.

"One day, Gina," he told her as he handed her the special tool he called the Tick-Tock Turner, "all this will be your responsibility." He said it with pride and, hands spread wide, bent in a deep bow as if introducing her to the clock. There was no question in his mind that she would do this when he was gone. Only, Gina wasn't sure that was what she wanted.

There were times when Gina wished she could leave the village behind and find the way to London or another big city. Her ties to the village were loosening the older she got, and she often dreamed of being in a city and wearing fancy clothes and going to parties where people danced and laughed, rather than in her tiny village. Here, the most exciting thing to ever happen was when the bull on the Butternut farm escaped and ran down the street with half the town chasing it.

As fascinated as Gina felt with the cogs, wheels, and turnings of the clock, she was also a little afraid of it. Small enough to fit her tiny fingers inside the gears to pull out leaves or sticks that blew into the works and prevented the ancient timepiece from working, cleaning it been her job. As she grew older, she took on more of the tasks Grandfather's fingers couldn't quite manage.

But there was one part of the clock he'd warned her to never touch.

"Behind here." Her grandfather had indicated one of the long slender rods that controlled the main mechanism that turned the clock hands. "There is a small box. Never open that. Never touch it. Never move it."

He would not explain why, just warned her over and over not to touch it.

"Time holds its secrets, and we hold ours." He never said more than that.

But now, Grandpa Tony's recent death meant the responsibility was hers alone.

Gina trudged up the seven flights of narrow stairs to the tiny room where the clock's inner workings were housed. Her cat Winston took off for a corner where the resident mouse ran for its life.

The lamp she carried was nearly out of oil, and she silently cursed under her breath for forgetting to refill it. But her heart was still raw and heavy with grief over her grandpa's death, and she wasn't thinking clearly.

"Winston," she said to the cat now in a corner grooming himself before his nap, "behave yourself."

Meow!

Gina set the tool kit and lamp on the floor. The clock was ticking faintly. Gears were shifting, moving very slowly in an odd hum. Obviously, there was a blockage. She mentally went over the diagram of the clock. There were only a few places that could be the cause of the problem.

She glanced out between the clock face and the frame the clock was housed in. She could see the town spread out below. At this time of night, most of the townsfolk were asleep. She could make out a few dark shapes hulking in the shadows and recognized them as the houses and barns of her friends and neighbors.

Up here, so high above the town she found the world to be a peaceful place. A place she could live forever. But then the memories of her grandfather's passing overwhelmed her, and she stifled a sob. Could she stay here alone? She had no one. None of the boys in the village had ever expressed any interest in her and the thought of being here with only the clock for company was not a prospect she felt particularly great about.

Perhaps it was time to pursue life outside of the tiny village.

The odd humming grew louder, and a small metal squeak reminded her that she was here for a reason.

She pulled out gloves and set to work. She hoped it would be a quick job, but that was unfortunately not the case.

An hour later her lamp grew dimmer and dimmer while she worked. The town sat asleep, and the moon, shining bright just a short while ago, now played peek-a-boo with thickening clouds. A storm was coming.

Minute by minute the hour drew closer to midnight.

Gina stretched. Yawning, she pulled the Tick-Tock Turner from her toolbox to see if the adjustments she'd already made had worked. A twist of the tool should fix the last of the problem. At least, she hoped so.

Having just turned eighteen, Gina had expected to be her grandpa's apprentice for many more years. The town's mayor had disagreed with her grandpa's decision to train her, but he'd argued successfully that there was no one else to take over when he left. No one expected him to be gone this soon. But a freak accident just a month ago had taken him from her, and now she was alone in the world.

Mayor French had sought her out after her grandfather's funeral.

"Gina, you'll be taking over? Your grandfather did explain to you the importance of the clock?"

Gina nodded. "Of course, he did. I can do it."

The mayor beamed at her. "Good, good. Because the Gray's have cared for this . . ." He looked over his shoulder at the clock that watched, silently, from its place of honor in the center of town.

"I understand."

The mayor rubbed his hands together as if grateful he was done with her. "Good. Good. Of course, we shall continue to pay you as we have your grandfather and those before you."

That, it turned out, had been for the town to supply her with baskets of food each day and the small cottage she currently lived in rent-free. Any other money or items she would need would be bargained for within the town. Her grandfather had done simple repairs to people's personal clocks and watches, and so Gina agreed to continue his work, seeing as that was the only skill she possessed other than her ability to charm cats, which she didn't suppose there would be much need for.

Stretching her back, she carefully stood and walked around the room. The clock was still not working. She'd tried everything. Not even the Tick-Tock Turner had been able to fix the problem.

She racked her brain, trying to remember the things her grandfather told her.

"Just slip your fingers back here . . . but never touch this." Her grandfather's caution came back to her.

The small metal box was at the very back of the clock, attached to the main arm of the system of cogs and wheels that operated the timepiece. What if her grandfather was wrong? What if that box was the problem? She hadn't gotten that deep into the clock yet. Maybe that was the very thing she needed to remove in order to fix it.

With renewed energy, Gina reached into the back of the clock. Everything else had failed to work. Maybe it was time to try something different. Her slender fingers soon found the small metal box her grandfather warned her about.

Aware that time was running out before the timepiece stopped altogether, Gina's desperation grew. She'd try anything to make sure the clock was repaired. If it wasn't working again by midnight, there could be consequences to the town. That was something her grandfather had drilled into her numerous times.

Midnight was the magic hour.

As Gina probed the small metal box, she felt a screw loosening. Before she could stop herself, she tugged, and the screw fell out into her hand along with the small box.

Gina sat back and studied the box. She traced the letters "AW" that were engraved on the top in ornate gold lettering. Dropping it into her lap, she carefully turned the piece over in her hand. She held the Tick-Tock Turner in her other hand. The small opening left by the screw matched the end of the tool. She slipped the device into the place the screw had recently occupied. It fit perfectly.

"Interesting," she said. She turned the slim metal rod and heard the satisfying *click* of it releasing the lock holding the box together.

For a minute nothing happened, and Gina's shoulders sagged. Then a bright flash of light caused her to shield her eyes and jump to her feet, spilling the box on the floor and sending the screw rolling away from her.

"Ah, thank you. I was beginning to fear I would never be free again."

Chapter 2

Gina opened her eyes. In front of her stood the most beautiful boy she had ever seen in her life. He had a wide smile and dark eyes that bored into her with curiosity. He was dressed in clothes of the finest silk and velvet but cut in a style that marked him as from a time long ago.

"What? Who?" Gina backed up; hands raised in defense.

The boy turned, stepping forward on legs that wobbled a bit.

"Oops. Guess I'm not used to being upright again." He stretched his shoulders and arms, laughing in delicious delight at the freedom of his movements.

"Who are you? Where did you come from?"

He smiled, and the space surrounding him shimmered as if he were composed of a layer of air that was not quite there.

"Ah, questions. Of course. Let me introduce myself. I am Anders Whitten, at your service."

AW. The letters on the box.

"And you?"

His voice was not unpleasant, but not quite normal, either. The words hung in the air around them like skittering leaves in a graveyard before settling into speech she could understand.

Gina shook her head to clear it. Looking toward him again she was surprised to see him still there.

"And you, pretty lady? What is your name?"

"Gina. Gina Gray," she said, her voice fading away as he hissed.

"Gray? Did you say Gray?" He took a step toward her, his expression shifting into darkness, his hand held upward in anger as if to strike at her.

Before Gina could react, her cat Winston leaped up, claws outstretched, and forced Anders backward.

Snarling and spitting, Winston glared at the boy.

"Now, now, little one," he said. "You don't want to hurt me."

Gina gasped as his words froze Winston in place. She could see the cat trying to move, muscles twitching, whiskers quaking, but nothing the feline did helped him get any closer to the boy.

"What did you do?" Gina said, racing to scoop the cat up into her arms.

"Oh, he'll be fine. I did him no harm." Anders's lips twisted into the semblance of a smile. To prove his point he waved his hand, and the cat shivered once then hissed again.

MEOW! MEOW!

Winston was not amused and struggled beneath Gina's grip to be let loose, but she held tight.

"Who are you really?" she asked Anders.

"More importantly," Anders said, walking around her while tapping his fingers against his chin. "How are you able to avoid my magic?"

Gina frowned. "What magic?"

"This," he said. In another demonstration of his power, he waved his hand and Winston froze in her arms.

Gina glanced down at Winston who couldn't move and shouted, "Let him be!"

"I think . . . not. I prefer the beast less mobile."

Gina held Winston tighter to her chest as she watched the boy walking around the room. Suddenly bored with her apparently, he was peering out the hole between the clock and the outside.

With an evil chuckle, he turned and walked toward her. Gina held her ground. He waved a hand around her, but other than a slight tingling in her legs, she wasn't affected by his magic and his raised eyebrows indicated he noticed. He was not amused.

"As much as I would like to stay here and discover all your secrets Gina Gray, I'm afraid I must go." He reached out with one long finger and traced a line down her cheek to her chin. Leaning close to her he whispered, "And I'm sure you have more than a few delicious secrets."

Gina instinctively backed up a step at his cold touch. A shiver ran through her bones. For a moment she felt as frozen as Winston, but it passed almost as quickly as warmth pushed out the chill.

"I have business to attend to in town. Good-bye." And with that Anders transformed into vapor and slipped through the hole and out into the air.

Chapter 3

He left so quickly, Gina had no time to react.

He was going into town.

The town that was sleeping.

The town that did not know of the demon she'd released into their midst.

What could she do to stop him?

She had less than an hour to fix the mess she'd created and no idea how to do it.

Setting Winston down, she apologized to him. "Sorry, Winston. I'll be back for you."

He squirmed and squeaked but couldn't do more.

She grabbed the box and the Tick-Tock Turner, shoving them in the pocket of her work apron.

Pounding her way down the stairs she raced outside in time to see the demon once more disguised as a human boy. He strode quickly down the empty street and around the corner.

She followed.

She caught sight of him as she reached the mayor's house. He disappeared through the mayor's door via his ability to transform into a shapeless vapor.

Having no idea what to do, Gina just knew she had to do something.

Glancing around but finding nothing that could help her, she tried the knob to the mayor's house. It was locked. Pounding on the door she managed to rouse a servant who opened it with bleary eyes.

"I must speak to the mayor immediately," she said and pushed past the servant.

Racing up the stairs she approached the mayor's bedroom as the clock in the hallway struck the half hour. It was eleven-thirty. She only had thirty minutes to trap the boy back in the box and repair the clock, or the town would suffer the consequences.

Pushing open the door, she found Anders in full human form leaning over the sleeping mayor and his snoring wife with a wicked smile on his face. He turned as she ran into the room.

Snapping his fingers, he watched in joy, and Gina stared in horror, as the mayor and his wife became smoke. Opening his mouth, Anders breathed in the vapor.

Without a word, he once again became shadow and sparkling light and slipped out the open window.

"Come back." She ran to the window to follow the shimmering shadow as it headed toward the clock.

If she couldn't convince Anders to get back in the box, or find a way to trap him there once more, her town would become his.

She had to stop this.

She ran back to the clock. Running up the stairs she heard Anders' angry voice.

"You have it, I know you do. Give it to me or I will kill you both."

"I don't know what you're talking about, demon," the mayor's voice said. "But even if I did have it, I wouldn't give it to you."

"Then you've condemned your wife to sleep forever."

Without thinking, Gina ran into the room. Barely looking at the mayor who, along with his wife, was apparently no longer smoke, Gina stepped in front of the sleeping woman, placing herself between them and the demon.

Anders frowned.

"Ah, the princess of time has returned. How nice. Move out of the way, please. The mayor and I have old business to attend to."

Gina didn't move.

Anders's frown deepened.

"I think not. I think your business is with me, actually." Gina smiled even though her insides were quivering like a thousand caterpillars were about to hatch.

Anders stilled and then turned the full force of his anger on her, but Gina didn't back down.

Instead, she advanced toward him. In her hand she held the Tick-Tock Turner which she made sure he could see.

The demon hissed, his eyes caught on the tool in her hand.

"Give that to me. It's mine."

She stepped just out of reach, slipping the tool into her pocket. "This is no place for you. Your home isn't here. Your time isn't now."

Anders laughed. "You humans are so feeble. Do you really think you can keep me in a box anymore? I have tasted freedom, and I like it."

The mayor pulled his wife closer to him, but Gina ignored them. She knew what she needed to do, and time was running out.

"The freedom you feel is fleeting. Freedom comes from doing a job well. From being part of what you do," Gina said. She walked away from the mayor and his wife and toward the clock, hoping to distract him.

She slipped a hand in her other pocket. The box was still there, solid in her hand. She needed to find the screw though. Even as she followed Anders with her eyes, she was seeking that screw.

Anders snorted. "Freedom's about taking charge."

Gina shook her head. There! The screw was in the corner. Now, how to get it? "Freedom's not about controlling those around you."

"Easy for you to say, little one. You *have* freedom."

Gina laughed. "Oh, do I? What do you know of my life?"

Winston the cat followed her with his eyes, still unable to move, poor feline—and an idea came to Gina.

"I'm as frozen in time as my cat is." Gina casually waved at her pet to draw Anders' eyes toward Winston.

Anders looked at the cat. "See how easy chains can be released if you wish it?"

Winston hissed and made as if to leap at him, but Anders waved his hand again, and Winston froze mid-leap.

The distraction allowed Gina just enough time to swoop down and scoop up the screw and slip it into her pocket with the box.

"So, what of your freedom?" the demon said to Gina. "Freedom can be taken as quickly as I snap my fingers."

He did so, and the room shifted. The mayor and his wife froze at Anders's command.

Gina smiled. "But you see, when you have a purpose, your duty is its own form of freedom."

Anders snorted. "You make no sense, little one." He walked toward her. "Do you feel freedom being trapped here in this small town as a keeper of the clock? You are no more free than me, are you?"

Gina hesitated. "I'm not a prisoner."

"Oh, but you are. Your family's been keeper of the clock for generations. You can no more leave here than I can. If you do, the town dies."

Gina licked dry lips and considered her answer. He was right, she wasn't free to leave, but did she even want to? The more she thought about it, the more uncertain she was of her dream to leave for the big city. Here she had the love of, and for, a town, a purpose to fulfill.

"I like my life here," she said, inwardly surprised that this was true. "I have a purpose, and that's my freedom."

"Purpose gives you freedom?"

Gina nodded, warming to the knowledge that she was happy here. "I know every day what I must do. I know every day that what I do helps others. That is my freedom. Acceptance of my purpose."

Anders snorted again.

"What is your purpose?" Gina waited for Anders to respond.

"I have no purpose. I'm a demon. I was trapped here many years ago, long before anyone here was alive. I was forced to become the town's clock."

Gina softened her voice. "You found a purpose. A reason for living. You found your freedom."

The demon looked at her in surprise, his human face shifting from vapor to solid as she pulled the box from her pocket.

Opening the box Gina held it out to him. "Your purpose, your freedom keeps this town alive. What greater freedom can you have, than to have control over time?"

Anders looked at her with understanding dawning. He glanced from the mayor to her and laughed.

"Oh, little one. I must be weary, for you are making sense."

Shocking them all he shifted into his vapor form and into the box which Gina then closed and locked with the Tick-Tock Turner. Attaching the box back onto the arm of the mechanism that controlled the clock, she screwed it back in place and then stepped back.

The clock began to move, creaking and whining as it picked up its normal rhythm.

BONG . . . BONG . . . BONG . . . BONG . . . BONG . . . BONG . . . BONG . . . BONG . . . BONG . . . BONG . . . BONG . . . BONG!

The mayor, his wife, Winston, and Gina walked from the tower to the street.

The mayor gripped Gina's shoulder and squeezed. "Your grandfather would be proud of you tonight."

"Thank you." Gina cuddled Winston close, burying her face in his fur to hide her embarrassment at the mayor's praise.

"And Gina," the mayor said before turning away, "you have the freedom to leave if you want to."

"The town . . ."

"The town will always be here," the mayor assured her.

Gina watched the mayor and his wife walk toward their home until they disappeared around a corner. The town was so peaceful now.

Looking back up at the clock, Gina realized she had all the freedom she needed right here, and there was no place else she wanted to be.

About the Author

Susan Burdorf is an avid reader, photographer, and lover of all things sparkly. Writing is a passion that is only quenched when THE END is written on the last page of a manuscript. Nothing says home to her, though, like the presence of her family. Susan encourages you to correspond with her and is available for public appearances at schools and conferences. Follow me on Instagram @susanburdorfauth or Amazon.

THE COURAGEOUS HEART OF THE DEEP

BRENNA M. KEENAN

Thessa woke with a start, freezing rain pounding hard against the windows of her family cottage. Her eyes widened at the moonlight peeking through the storm clouds, casting a long light across her quilt. She couldn't help her awe at the powerful entities that kept order for their kind as the torrential downpour continued on the thatched roof. Clearly, the Goddess Rayna was unleashing her displeasure with this storm— a heavy onslaught against the world.

Unable to return to sleep, Thessa lit a candle on her bedside table. Tiptoeing out of bed, she held the candle aloft as she made her way to the small kitchen. A warm glass of milk, that's what was in order.

Her petite frame, swallowed by a white linen nightgown, swayed slightly. Her legs wobbled as her footsteps fell on the worn floorboards, light brown hair frizzing in unbound waves over her slight shoulders. She hated how her hair reacted on land—at least in the water it was always undulating with the currents.

Two days on land had her legs aching for release in the water, where her muscles could finally form to their natural state. Thessa missed her seafoam green fin that was the perfect camouflage for shallower waters.

Tomorrow, she thought.

Tomorrow she would return to the ocean and, after what felt like an eternity, would be a self-sufficient Oceanid. Thessa used the matches by the stove to stoke a small flame on the burner—pouring milk into a kettle as she set it to warm. More skills that were begrudgingly required of an Oceanid.

The moonlight shone brightly in between the storm clouds. The full moon meant a night spent on land. Since turning thirteen, this was her second month alone in the family cottage. It was an Oceanid's duty to bide the tides of the full moon after coming of age, or so the legends said. Creatures lurked in the ocean's depths in search of adolescent Oceanids to steal them away. Bringing them to the Gods as retribution on the full moon.

Shivering, she pulled a crocheted blanket from the ottoman, draping the scratchy fabric around her narrow frame. Sighing at the unfortunate slow passage of time, she pulled the kettle from the stove and poured the milk into a mug.

While she longed for the water, she also enjoyed the peace and quiet the world above provided. *Land had its perks.* One, nourishing milk and an array of foods that she had never in her life expected to taste so good. The way humans were able to create so many things from the earth itself was quite impressive. No, she didn't mind being on land; the villagers she encountered were always friendly and helpful towards her, even when she asked questions—and she had many of them. She would never admit this to her friends, let alone her family. Her grandmother would get her fin in a knot.

This life on land was all new to her, but it didn't frighten her as it did for most of her kind, who hated land dwellers with a fury—a never-ending vendetta against mixing species and fear of the Gods' wrath. Most Oceanids preferred to stay in the water, including her family, sending her on her own to be on land where it was safer during a full moon.

The youngest of three older sisters, already matured and who all detested land, Thessa often felt like the angler fish of the family; her curiosity and lack of hate for humans kept her at fin's length with anyone around her, especially her family. Thessa and her sisters were raised by their grandmother, Queen of the Kingdom of Havfrid—who was bound to the kingdom, as were countless others in their royal bloodline—and given the territory to protect by the primal God Aegir himself.

Her parents had succumbed to what many royal bloodlines of Oceanids had before them—taken by the Gods to appease and prolong the prosperity of their kind. For millennia, her people existed unbeknownst to the land dwellers above until the Gods became angry that Oceanids were galivanting about with *humans*. Even so much as staying on land to be with them.

Of course, a couple hundred years had passed since the Gods fully awoke after Aegir's own son chose a human over his duties as heir. Aegir sent his floods and tremors to wipe the lands clean, not only of his son's lover, but all humans and half-breeds in existence. After all, the Oceanids were his true children of the sea, so the royals' sacrifices for their kingdoms' sake continued.

Legends say that Aegir's creatures roam the seas on the full moon in an endless search for young half-breeds that dare to exist outside his realms. Eyelids drooping, Thessa began to doze off on the ottoman—*who would be absurd enough to roam the ocean and anger them further?* Her own species didn't risk their young ones' safety on a full moon, and they were pure-blooded Oceanids. Havfrid provided cottages on land for families with young Oceanids, not fully of age and able to take on the transformation—places of refuge and safety from the seas and the creatures that lurked within.

Her thoughts faded as the rain pattered a lulling melody, and she began to dream.

She raced through the currents at a staggering speed, urgency in every flick of her tail. Even though she was not fully grown, her speed was outmatched by the other Oceanids her age. Her heart pounding in her chest, the water soothing in and out of her lungs. The ocean was pitch black, but she could see miles ahead of her with her Oceanid vision. A lens shielded her eyes as the black ocean grew deeper, more dense.

Unaccustomed to fearing her home, she couldn't help that fear right now. Something was after her, something big. The darkness surrounding her encroached further, feeling like a firm suffocation on her heavy breathing. She risked a glance behind, seeing tendrils extending toward her.

She knew she must keep going—they promised there would be a light in the darkness to guide her. Thessa pushed her muscled tail faster, shooting through the darkness, evading the long tentacles reaching for her.

Finally, she saw it. Pillars adorning a cave entrance, bathed in iridescent blue light, beckoning her forward. She prayed to the Gods to pass through unscathed as she entered the sizeable open-mouthed cavern.

A blue, glowing light expanded within the domed opening of the cave. Behind her, she heard the creature let loose a booming growl. Daring to look back, she cringed, seeing the fleshy grey body, with giant golden eyes and slit pupils staring at her, watching, waiting.

A screeching noise as if nails on glass emanated throughout the cave.

Thessa awoke with a start—rain still hammered upon the roof, and the wind howled at the windowpanes. She glanced at the clock on the fireplace mantle—past midnight. Her dream left her in a cold sweat, body aching as if she was swimming for her life in the deepest part of the ocean. Sitting up in the chair, she put a hand to her chest, trying to calm her breathing.

Screeeeecchhhh.

Startled, her hand flew to her mouth to cover her scream. The nails-on-glass sound that had awoken her filled the small cottage. She whipped around to the window directly across from her, praying it was a tree branch scraping against the glass.

She beheld what appeared to be a woman with wet, dark hair and unseeing grey-blue eyes holding Thessa's gaze from behind the glass and beckoning her forward with a pale, slender hand.

She held a primitive beauty but did not smile. Her hand continued to motion to Thessa. *To go outside? Or let her in?* Thessa spasmed in terror, but she did not scream. She had seen far worse creatures than a mere woman. *But what did she want?*

Head held high; she considered the situation and, to battle her nerves, decided it was simply a woman lost in the woods. *Was she blind?* Thessa had heard of that particular hindrance amongst humans but had never met an Oceanid who suffered from the ailment.

Thessa moved slowly to the door, watching the woman follow her outside of the windows. *Maybe not blind, then.*

The woman kept tapping. More urgently this time. With shaking hands, Thessa opened the door to the woman. Gasping aloud, it took every ounce of bravery not to slam the door in her face. The *creature's* face. This was no woman. She had a tall and slender female form, with an abnormally long cow's tail reaching behind her like an extension of a limb, and her back was covered in what looked like the bark of a tree.

"What are you?" Thessa internalized her groan at the question, but her curiosity got the better of her the more she stared at this being. A sense of calming trust washed over her as Thessa began speaking to it, almost a lull in the back of her mind to do anything the creature asked. The initial sense of danger was still there, nagging at her, prodding Thessa to wake up, but her compulsion to learn more was too strong, and she shrugged off the pestering fear.

"I am many things, child." The creature's ethereal voice lilted with the wind.

"Why have you come here?" Thessa knew that this was no ordinary encounter. She had never heard of such creatures existing on land. But, of course, she hadn't been here long enough to learn any human stories.

"The Goddess Máni has sent me to fetch you."

Thessa froze. *Máni, the Moon Goddess?* It pained her that the kingdom's oceanlings were unsafe, even on land. Her stomach began to roil as she tried to back into the cottage.

The creature noticed her hesitation and fear taking over and stepped closer to the threshold with a grace and surety that Thessa thought she would never personally master on two legs.

"You must hurry, young one. We haven't much time."

"Time for what? For Máni to take me as a *sacrifice*?!" Thessa's temper flared. If she was going to die tonight, she wouldn't go without a fight.

"*No, dear one,*" its voice carried a soothing calm. Thessa shuddered in surprise at the creature's voice reverberating in her skull. "You are of royal blood, a direct creation of Aegir himself. Only you can help Máni."

"What help could I be to a Goddess?"

The creature stepped forward, running a smooth hand along Thessa's cheek, gazing into her pale blue eyes. Where its touch lingered on her skin, Thessa felt warmth and assurance—that calm settling back into her bones. It wasn't going to harm her; the touch was laced with comfort and beckoned her to believe and follow.

"Come. She is waiting." The creature turned and began walking towards the deep woods behind the cottage, expecting Thessa to follow. Hesitating for a moment, Thessa took a deep breath before leaving the safety of the cottage, for it was never wise to insult the Gods, even if they were going to eat you.

Thessa's feet ached, her legs groaning as they moved deeper into the dense forest. Thessa didn't know where they were; she had never ventured elsewhere aside from the cottage and the village down the road. "I am a Huldra, as the people in these northern lands would call me," the Huldra's ethereal voice called back to Thessa as she blindly followed. They had to have been walking for what felt like miles, and with each step, Thessa could feel her legs growing more steady. She knew she could get better at this whole walking thing with patience. The Huldra chuckled in a cacophony of chimes.

"Interesting. Most of your kind do not wish to grow stronger on legs."

Confusion swept over Thessa's features, "Can you enter my mind?"

"I can enter the minds of many creatures and speak to few. It appears that you qualify. But *humans*. Well, I cannot cross into their minds." A slow, feline smile spread across her face.

The way she emphasized humans made Thessa's insides curl into heavy knots. The Huldra sounded like a predator reminiscing about their latest prey, and she was leading Thessa into a dark forest with tall trees whose branches were so thick that the pouring rain was reduced to a light drizzling underneath the canopy.

"Fear me not, child. I only prey on the worst kind of creatures."

"Oh? And who might they be?" Thessa asked as casually as possible.

"Why, men, of course."

Thessa raised her eyebrows at the honesty in the Huldra's response.

"We are here, Princess."

She scoffed outwardly at the title. Thessa knew she was a princess, but her three older sisters, her grandmother, and the entire kingdom had never treated her as such. And here she was, on some journey for the Moon Goddess. With one of her older sisters more likely to be Havfrid's heir, why did Máni choose her?

Thessa glanced around the small clearing where the Huldra had suddenly paused; the trees were tall, with wide trunks covered in green moss. She craned her neck but only saw a black canopy above. In the center, an opening to the sky showed the storm breaking, allowing bright moonlight to shine into a small pool in the middle of the clearing.

"What must I do?" Thessa asked.

"Enter the pool. She is waiting for you." The Huldra looked Thessa up and down expectantly before adding. "We are all counting on you." Again, that warmth and comfort emanating from the Huldra blanketed Thessa's emotions, convincing her to move.

Thessa watched as the Huldra entered the forest in the opposite direction; clearly, she wasn't planning to stick around. Gathering every ounce of courage she could muster, Thessa walked to the pool. The moonlight danced along the surface of the water.

She stood at the water's edge before entering the pool and fully submerging into the moonlight. Thessa inhaled deeply as the water triggered her senses. Her eyes adjusted, while her muscles transformed her legs into her seafoam tail. She smiled at the feel of the watery world around her— fresh water was always so pure compared to salt water.

Looking around beneath the surface, she discovered she was in a narrow corridor of rock; she dove down the passage with a rush of adrenaline before tunneling through an opening into a vast valley beneath her. Moss-covered rocks lay at the bottom of the cavernous lake. Most freshwater cities burrowed deep into the earth from ambiguous ponds above. She beheld ruins of an ancient city scattered across the floor in a circle. Thessa couldn't help wondering about the kingdom or clan that had once called this place home.

Casting her senses outward, she couldn't feel any other Oceanids in the vicinity or any other signs of life besides a few schools of fish. She swam to what appeared to be an underwater courtyard with a dais set in the center.

As she swam closer, a voice reverberated throughout the cavern, and she shot to the nearest pillar to hide.

The voice was misty as it echoed around her, repeating a rhyme in perfect timing.

"In the night's shimmer,
I take flight,
Guiding dreams with silver light.
Seek me here where the shadows hide,
Conducting the ever-moving tides."

It was a riddle. Obviously, the first part was the moon, but the second part . . . Thessa took in the vast cavern, looking for the deepest, darkest spot in the room. She spotted a dark tunnel entrance, pushed herself off the pillar, and swam swiftly into the tunnel. Partway through the rocky passage, a cascade of rocks blocked the remainder of her way forward. After quickly shifting some stones with the formidable strength of a royal Oceanid, she created an opening and squeezed herself through the cave-in.

A statue carved of deep granite with many fading cracks along the surface stood out in contrast to the black room. The figure depicted Máni in one of her various forms, this form that of a sea dragon wound tightly around an oval-shaped object. Feeling compelled to touch the blue-black granite oval that resembled an egg, Thessa reached toward it. The stone was smooth and cooler than the surrounding water. She rarely felt temperature changes while in the water. Upon her touch, the stone began to glow bright and blue, filling the cave with light.

She backed away, unsure of what she had just uncovered, when the voice continued.

"In the sacred glow, a stone awaits.
Moon's essence within it, an ancient trait.
To fulfill your purpose, sleeping souls,
In icy caves, dwell beasts untold.
Deliver the stone with care and grace,
Awaken the ones in frozen embrace."

Within the oval, a small stone was visible. The stone glowed bright blue as the riddle repeated throughout the underwater cavern. She could feel the stone's power; she dared not think about the repercussions as she reached her hand into the granite, convincing herself she wouldn't pass through the unforgiving stone. Yet her hand easily passed through, and she grasped the glowing stone within.

The moment her hand grasped the stone, a powerful energy coursed through her body as she perceived her fin glowing in time with the stone, just for a moment, before returning to normal. The stone changed to a dimly lit blue, and the reverberating words of the riddle faded into nothingness.

The riddle was straightforward . . . kind of.

The ice caves first came to mind, as they were sacred and hosted their dead. Awaken someone within the caves. *Yeah, seems easy enough.* She had never heard of waking anyone within the caves, and not only was it a full moon, the ice caves were holy and forbidden to anyone other than the acolytes.

Suddenly, her dream felt more like a premonition. With the moonstone clutched in hand, Thessa realized where she must go—*the ocean.* Shooting towards the surface, she began to make the trek a full day earlier than planned.

***

Every bone in her body fought against her entering the waves that vigorously crashed against the black-pebbled shore. The warnings she'd heard her entire life echoed through her mind. Aegir's creatures prowling for half-breeds, often mistaking the oceanlings as such. Not to mention, the ice caves were further north of the cottage, and she had never been there before. She had only heard tales of their location from the elders.

She held the stone to her chest, where it thrummed in time with the stammering of her own heart. Clutching the glowing blue stone like a lifeline, Thessa dashed to the water and dove in before she could think about what she was doing.

Her fin enveloped her legs, and she shot through the water sure and fast, allowing the thought of the stone to bring her strength and courage as she followed the decline of the ocean floor northbound.

Thessa sensed the creatures stalking the depths as she sped to the caves, noticing every flicker of shadows in the darkness. The stone still clutched in her palm was a beacon pushing her forward, but it also summoned the creatures to her.

As in her dream, she felt the creature's eyes following her before she saw it. Shadows clinging to it like a cloak, tentacles and suckers opening in a wide embrace. *The Krabat.* She swam faster, not knowing if she was even within range of the ice caves. A tentacle reached for her. She pivoted sharply, maintaining her speed as she evaded the grab. The booming howl of the Krabat echoed around her for miles, sure to ward off any other creatures from its chosen prey.

Panic gripped Thessa as she weaved through the blackness, evading the long span of fleshy arms as it continued to reach for her. The stone pulsed in her hand, distracting her long enough to receive a blow straight to her torso, knocking the breath right out of her.

Clutching her torso, Thessa attempted to dart away, only to sputter with each movement of her fin. Something was definitely broken—if not everything. Her breathing labored, and her fin limp beneath her, she was only a couple hundred paces from the oncoming slaughter of the Krabat. She knew full well that there had been little chance she would accomplish her quest when she entered the water. But still, she'd hoped she could be enough and that the goddess hadn't chosen wrong. It was the most faith she had been given in her short life.

Broken sobs began to erupt from her. She was never strong enough or fast enough. She had experienced more kindness on land than she ever had from her own family or people. The Krabat drew up to her, its vast head elongating eight spongey tentacles and wrapping a circle around her limp form.

Eyes glowing golden in the black depths, Thessa whimpered, hollowed out and empty at the realization that this was her fate. She hoped the moon goddess was happy with her belief in her, because Thessa was nothing and no one.

What a great choice, huh, Máni?

The Krabat grabbed her, squeezing tightly, producing another sob as the pain shot through her body from the firm hold. Thessa tried to hold onto consciousness, but the throbbing along her torso and fin threatened to pull her under.

Barely awake, her hand began to glow brighter, illuminating the Krabat fully, its grey-blue flesh scarred and spongy.

Thessa felt a warmth flowing through her, from her chest down through her fin. With a start, the Krabat wailed, releasing its hold on her as if burned. She looked at her hand that held the moonstone. A blue light emanated from within her skin and spread throughout her entire body. As if being knitted back together, she felt her spine shift, her ribs popping, and she cried out as the stone stitched her bones together.

When she realized her fin was fully functional, she swam with all her strength, and her hope returned. The stone in her hand guided her through the darkness of the ocean depths. The wounded Krabat gave chase, but Thessa was now faster and more agile. She weaved through the shadows, using her newfound strength and healed extremities to evade the creature's grasping tentacles. The Krabat's howls echoed far behind her at losing its prize.

As she approached the entrance to the ice caves, glowing columns carved from ice adorned the corridor. She could feel the energy of the moonstone resonating within her as she passed the crystalline doorway.

The cave's icy walls seemed to glow in response to the stone's presence. Thessa swam deeper into the caves, determination fueling her every stroke, letting the moonstone guide her. The deeper she ventured, the colder it became.

With the moon's power fueling her, the moonstone seemed to guide her every move, leading her through the labyrinthine network of tunnels until she reached a massive, frozen chamber adorned with symbols she couldn't understand. In the center of the chamber lay a figure encased in ice—a woman with flowing silver hair, her eyes closed in eternal slumber, and her hands resting on a protruding pregnant belly. Thinking back to the riddle, *souls* . . . it was plural. Thessa knew this woman and her child were the ones she was sent to awaken. With a trembling hand, she placed the moonstone on the icy surface. A brilliant light radiated from the stone, thawing the ice and melting away the frozen prison. The woman gasped for breath as she awakened, her eyes opening to reveal a dazzling shade of silver with deep streaks of green beneath.

Thessa only then realized the woman had legs instead of a tail. *She was human?* As the woman took in her surroundings, it appeared she could breathe with the aid of the moonstone. She couldn't be more than twenty years old, gazing at Thessa with a kind yet piercing stare.

"Who are you?" the woman asked, her voice echoing with power into Thessa's mind.

Not expecting her to be able to communicate the same way as her people, Thessa started. "My name is Thessa. I was sent here to free you."

A shifting shadow appeared then, slithering from behind the woman, who was still sitting on the dais. Thessa's eyes widened while the woman let loose a dazzling smile, staring into the eyes of the sea dragon that came to life before them from the depths of the cave. The sea dragon coiled around the woman protectively as she ran a hand along its scaly hide. Its slender body became brighter, white as the full moon above the surface. Sea-green eyes with slits for pupils stared deep into the woman's soul before looking at Thessa.

In her mind, Thessa heard a resounding "Thank you."

"From this moment on, Thessa, you shall be blessed by the Moon Goddess herself." With those words echoing through her, Thessa felt a transformation within her as she glowed brightly. The sea dragon and the woman watched as Thessa's fin shimmered with an iridescent glow. She could feel a new power coursing through her veins as her fin changed from seafoam green to a shimmering white that matched the sea dragon.

As the woman climbed astride the sea dragon, leaving into the darkness, Thessa looked around the icy cavern, realizing she was no longer just an Oceanid.

She had become something more.

About the Author

An aspiring author from a young age, Brenna Keenan aims to bring stunning fantasy worlds to life and create dynamic and relatable characters that readers can root for, all wrapped in concepts from mythology. She lives a nomadic lifestyle, wandering to her heart's content alongside her partner and their two rescue dogs. When she isn't lost in a fantasy world of her own creation, she enjoys the outdoors, hiking, camping, and finding inspiration in nature and folklore. She welcomes fellow adventurers to join her on an unforgettable odyssey through the magic of words. For upcoming projects, you can follow her on Instagram (@brennamkeenan) and visit wanderingwithpassion.com.

THE MIDNIGHT ORDER: AN ITZY ADVENTURE

CANDY GOOD

Princess Keera couldn't ignore the secrets of the midnight hour, not when they whispered her name. Her heart ached as her mind wandered to her dear friend and loyal lady's maid, Clara, who had vanished just the night before. Would the King, her father, be next? Or was she herself in danger? An early curfew had been imposed, considering recent events, causing turmoil as Cogswellians hurried home before nightfall. Yet the curfew couldn't keep Keera away from seeking answers, not when her loved ones were at stake.

With her long, black hair trailing behind, Keera navigated the bustling market. Her sapphire eyes were alert, though veiled by her commoner's disguise, the world around her was colored in hues of intrigue and caution. With each stride, the mechanical wings concealed beneath her cloak felt heavier. Whispers of fear rustled through the crowd like a chilling breeze. "The Midnight Order," murmured a vendor to his companion, glancing nervously over his shoulder. "They say they've taken the Itzys again, just like in the old legends." A chill ran down Keera's spine as she overheard the forbidden name, a name tied to terror and best left unspoken. She hurried on, but the whispers followed her, tales of shadowy figures and dark arts intertwining with the clatter of machinery. Her resolve strengthened; she knew she must uncover the truth, even if it meant braving the dangers of the night.

As the ominous chime of the curfew bell faded, Keera's spirited eyes caught sight of something extraordinary—an ethereal strand of indigo light, glowing as if stitched from the fabric of the night sky itself. It pulsed with specks of starlight, a celestial beacon that beckoned her like a Cog-Song Mer's call. Was this the elusive phenomenon tied to the ancient mysteries she'd heard whispered in hushed tones? With a deep breath, she unfurled her mechanical wings, weaving her way through dimly lit alleys and deserted streets. The strand led her to the forest's edge, a realm where the safety of Cogswell's cobbled streets and gas lamps gave way to untamed nature. With the gears of her mechanical wings humming, she summoned a final burst of energy, she reached out, her fingers mere inches away from the tantalizing strand, but it proved elusive, dissolving into wisps as she touched the boundary of the forest.

Frustration tinged Keera's determination as she decided to return to the castle. Though she had ventured out to unravel the mystery of the indigo threads, she knew that the scholarly wisdom of Professor Cain could not be overlooked. He had been her mentor and friend, a beacon in understanding all things Itzy. Her mechanical wings carried her swiftly back to the castle, not for retreat, but for counsel. The stakes were high; her people lived in a shroud of fear, and her friend, Clara, was still missing. It was time for action.

As Keera entered the castle library, she found Professor Cain already engrossed in his research, maps, and arcane texts. His face lit up at her arrival.

"Ah, Princess Keera," he said, standing up and nearly dropping his monocle in surprise. "Tag and I were just delving into some old Itzy myths and maps. See for yourself." He gestured towards Tag, whose gyroscopic eye was zooming in and out, meticulously analyzing a map spread out before him. "Curious timing for you to drop in, wouldn't you say? So, what mystery brings you here tonight?"

"Professor, your presence here brings me great relief," Keera said, a tangible sense of comfort washed over her. Their bond had grown from years of quests and adventures in Cogswell. This certainly wasn't their first shared challenge, and Keera felt her resolve strengthen, grateful for the steadfast guidance of her trusted mentor.

The library was a sanctuary of parchment and ink, its air tinged with the comforting smells of cigar smoke and aging leather. Spread out on the library table was an ancient scroll, its text as intricate and enigmatic as the mysterious threads Keera had been following.

She inched closer; her eyes fixed on the cryptic symbols that Professor Cain was diligently deciphering. "Professor, I'm convinced that the Midnight Order is behind these disappearances, including Clara. We must find the source of these indigo threads and put a stop to their actions."

Tag glanced up from the scroll he was reading, his eyes narrowing as he took in Keera's unwavering expression. "You're not thinking of going after this alone, are you, Keera?" Tag asked, concern etched in his features. "You know I won't let you do that."

With a knowing smile, Keera responded, "And you know I won't leave you behind."

Professor Cain stroked his white beard thoughtfully. "You're certain it's the work of the Midnight Order?"

"Absolutely," Keera replied.

Tag, whose gyroscopic eye momentarily paused its scanning of scrolls and maps, looked up in confusion "The Midnight Order? I've never heard of them."

Professor Cain gestured to a specific scroll and unrolled it with the care of an expert historian. "Ah, Tag, you're in for a lesson in Cogswell's darker history. Allow me." His voice held a note of caution as he began the tale, explaining to Tag the legend of the Midnight Order—a group of malevolent Itzys who nearly brought Cogswell to its knees with dark magic. They were stopped by a combined effort of Clockwork Oracles and Grand Tinkerers who created the Chronoglyphic Latchment, a complex device that sealed away their source of power.

Tag listened intently, his gyro lens stabilizing as he grasped Professor Cain's words.

"Their victory was not without cost," Professor Cain warned. "And facing them again could be even more dangerous."

Keera met his gaze, her brow arched in contemplation. "We have to try, Professor. We need to save Clara and the kidnapped Itzys. If we can find this Chronoglyphic Latchment, we might stand a fighting chance."

"It's a dangerous path we're taking," Tag whispered to Keera, setting a map back on the table. His lens zoomed in and out, a quirk revealing his hidden nerves. "But I'm with you, Princess. Together, we'll face whatever comes our way." His voice was steady, his commitment unshakable. Then, with a confident grin, he added, "I insist we take the fluralator. It can stun foes, generate shields, and even create temporary portals–it has saved my pistons plenty of times."

Professor Cain sighed, his features reflecting both admiration for Keera's bravery and concern for Tag's youthful grit. "Very well, my dear. But we must proceed with caution. In the coming battle, understanding and wisdom will be our weapons."

Together, Keera, Tag, and the professor poured over the ancient texts, unraveling clues about the Midnight Order's secrets behind their previous defeat. Candles lit the table that was covered in scrolls and maps, filling the air with an old paper scent. The distant tick-tock of a clock marked the passage of time, as the group's focus deepened on the Midnight Order's mysteries.

Finally, Professor Cain's finger landed on a passage, his voice breaking the silence. "Here, Keera! It's right here. The relic I mentioned earlier was indeed the key to defeating the Order centuries ago. It's known as the "Midnight Chrono-Crystal," a mystical gem infused with both technology and magic."

Keera leaned closer, a thrill of excitement running through her as she read the description. The Midnight Chrono-Crystal wasn't just beautiful; it powered the Midnight Order, allowing the wielder to send threads of darkness to do its bidding. Keera gasped. "It allows the wielder to ensnare an Itzy and make them disappear," her eyes widened with horror. The question weighed heavily on her mind: who would want to do this, and why?

The professor continued, "The text reveals the crystal was hidden by a select few. We must find who's reactivating the Midnight Order, if we are to stand a chance against them."

A newfound conviction surged within Keera. The Midnight Chrono-Crystal, that mysterious relic, held the key to understanding the indigo threads and saving her friend Clara. "For the sake of Cogswell and our friends," she declared, "we will find the mystery gem and stop the Midnight Order."

Professor Cain looked at her, his eyes reflecting a mix of pride and trepidation. He nodded, knowing that the path ahead was fraught with danger, but also knowing that they had no choice but to embark on this quest.

As the three finalized their plans, a sudden chill filled the room, the candles flickering wildly. Symbols that Keera had seen in the ancient scrolls seemed to dance in the shadows. Was it her imagination, or did the very air tremble at the presence of something unseen? The room grew colder, and a soft whisper reached her ear, a word that she dared not speak, a name that she had been warned never to utter. *Gulron.* The shadows seemed to recoil, leaving her breathless and filled with a sense of impending doom. The quest had begun, and the master of shadow was watching.

***

Some miles away, the master watched the three from the interior of his sanctuary. The dark room's stone walls dripped with damp as a chill wind snuffed out candles, leaving an unsettling silence. At the heart of this foreboding chaos stood a tall, grim figure, cloaked in darkness: Gulron, the master of shadows, absorbed in his latest creation—a cage filled with newly converted Itzys.

He turned to his lieutenant, a cruel smirk dancing on his thin lips. "The progress is satisfactory," he hissed, "The conversion is proceeding as planned. Soon, all of Cogswell will bow to my might."

"But Master, what about Princess Keera and her entourage? They're on the move," the lieutenant stammered, his voice laced with fear. "Whispers of their prying inquiries have reached us."

Gulron's eyes narrowed, his gaze lethal. "Let them come," he snarled. "They think they can unravel my plans, foolish interlopers. My ancestors were betrayed, and this kingdom should have been theirs. It will be reclaimed, and nothing will stand in my way . . . Nothing!" His voice echoed ominously through the chamber.

He approached a map of Cogswell, his fingers tracing the path of his dark ambition. "Prepare the guards and secure the fortress," he barked, his voice dripping with a sneer of sarcasm. "Let's make our guests feel welcome, shall we?"

***

Keera, Tag, and the professor navigated the haunting Dark Forest, a realm of secrets. With the stolen Itzys increasing and their mission's urgency heavy on their shoulders, they followed faint clues towards the Withered Wastes, barrens choked of life.

Two days in, they stumbled upon an old hermit, whose eyes were filled with age and wisdom. "You seek answers," he rasped. "But you tread a dangerous path. Gulron's shadow stretches far." Nevertheless, the hermit told them of the Veil of Nightshade, the passage that would give them access, and gave them cryptic guidance to find it, but he cautioned that it was merely the beginning of a nightmare they couldn't comprehend.

The trio thanked him, and he vanished into the forest's darkness.

Days turned into nights as they searched, guided by the haunting melody of sorrow's song. Finally, they found the Veil of Nightshade, a wall of darkness pulsing with malevolence.

"This is it. The passage to the Withered Wastes. Gulron's lair awaits us, and we must be ready," Keera stated, determination in her voice.

They crossed the Veil and found themselves in the Withered Wastes, a land poisoned by darkness. Standing on the brink of evil, they pressed on, knowing that the answers lay in Gulron's fortress.

The trio managed to make it through the dark forest, though not without its share of perils. If it hadn't been for the whispered warning of a hermit, they wouldn't be standing here on the precipice of the Withered Wastes.

"Keera, d-d-do you see anything?" Tag stammered, barely audible over the sound of gears humming from the fluralator. The device hung at his side pulsating with a soft, eerie glow.

Keera took in the ominous view through her Opti-multiplex goggles. She breathed in deeply, feeling the metallic chill of the optical interface as she adjusted the dials on the binocular lenses. "I see destruction . . . trees laid to waste, their limbs twisted and lifeless." Her voice was unnervingly calm. "At the edge, there's a crumbling fortress, guards standing at the entrance, but no other sign of life. This has to be it: Gulron's domain."

Tag's grip on the fluralator tightened, his knuckles white. The professor's eyes, half-hidden in the shadows of his helmet, focused intently on Keera.

"Any sign of Gulron?" The professor asked.

"No," Keera confessed. "North of us, there's a fortress, crumbling but still standing. It looks like an ideal hideaway for the Midnight Order. We need to get closer."

"But how?" Tag looked at the professor, a note of desperation in his voice.

"Leave that to me," the professor said, a wry smile breaking across his face as he unveiled a compact device from his pocket–the words Hide-O-Matic were inscribed on top. Two turns and a click, and they were all invisible, mimicking their surroundings. "Let's go," he whispered, we only have 10 minutes and then our cover will be blown."

They approached the looming fortress, the air around them shimmering and warped, mirroring the eerie forest. Heartbeats echoed in their ears as they crept closer to the entrance, cold and uninviting.

Keera took the lead as they entered the stillness of the den, navigating the dark-clad corridors. Rounding a corner, a dreadful sight met their gaze.

"Look," Keera said, her voice choked with disgust, "Those are newly converted Itzys." Cages lined the room, filled with once-vibrant citizens of Cogswell, now dulled and vacant. This madness was a stark reminder of

Gulron's reach.

"We have to find Gulron and stop this," Tag urged.

They soon found their enemy's lair, the heart of midnight itself. Shadows clung to corners as inky darkness draped over the cold, stone walls. A wooden table in the center held maps, notes, symbols, and plans of an un-waged war.

"Time's almost up," the professor whispered, eyeing a tiny dial on the Hide-O-Matic.

"Look. Over there." Keera's voice was hushed as she pointed towards the table. Her heart pounded at the sight of the kingdom's mapped landmarks, a directory of targets and victims.

"It's worse than we thought," the professor said, dread in his voice.

Just then, a chilling howl echoed through the room. "Innntruuuuderrrs!" Gulron shouted, his menacing form at the entrance.

Tag immediately moved into a defensive position, his hand going to the fluralator strapped at his side. Keera drew her own weapon, as her eyes locked with Gulron's. The professor, not really one for strenuous battles, gracefully slid under the table.

Keera and Tag squared off against Gulron. Her hand gripped the SteamLight Glaive, a sleek, collapsible polearm, steam-powered, with an edge sharper than a dragon's tooth. Beside her, Tag had the Fluralator poised and ready. They were a formidable pair against Gulron's shadowy menace.

Keera lunged forward, her Glaive slicing through the air, blocking Gulron's blows of shadow magic. She was a picture of resolute strength, her every move precise, fierce, and driven by a desire to protect Cogswell. The blade whistled and sung, as if it too was fueled by her conviction.

As the battle raged, time slowed. Keera landed a solid blow, knocking Gulron's breath away. For a moment, victory seemed within her grasp. "This ends now, Gulron!" she shouted, her voice echoing throughout the lair.

Gulron regained his bearings and sneered. "You have no idea what you're up against, girl." He waved his Staff of Eternal Shadows, and a hidden passage materialized, revealing the Chrono-Crystal's secret home. From this dark abyss, indigo tendrils lashed out toward them.

"Tag, shield up!" Keera shouted.

Frantically, Tag fumbled with his weapon. But instead of activating the shield, he accidentally hit the wrong switch, triggering a shimmering portal behind them.

"What have you done?" Keera cried out.

Seizing the opportunity, Gulron thrust his staff forward. "Your friend's mistake is my gain!" The tendrils intensified their pull on Tag, dragging him toward Gulron.

Keera fought with all her might, her SteamLight Glaive clashing against Gulron's shadowy attacks. But the draw from the portal behind her grew too strong. With her attention divided, Gulron used his staff to channel the portal's pull, aiming it directly at her.

"Keeeera!" Tag shouted, his voice tinged with regret and desperation, his eyes dimming to an indigo hue.

"I won't leave you!" she yelled back, digging her heels in, her glaive braced against the ground.

But despite her resistance, the vortex's pull was irresistible. With one last effort, she tried to reach for Tag but was abruptly sucked into the portal. Professor Cain, realizing the dire situation, took a running leap and followed her through the shimmering hole.

In an instant, the portal snapped shut, depositing Keera and the professor back in the castle library of Cogswell.

Keera staggered, her emotions a whirlwind of anger, loss, and regret. She turned to the professor, her sapphire eyes ablaze, and said, "We have to go back. We can't let Tag's mistake cost him his life."

The next morning, rays illuminated the library, contrasting Keera's defeated mood. Questions of her recent failure against Gulron tormented her. Fretting, she said to the professor, "Let's face it, professor. I'm not strong enough, or quick enough, to battle against the Staff of Eternal Shadows."

Doubt was her enemy now, whispering everything she couldn't do, tormenting her with the elusive answer on how to save her friends.

Finally, the professor spoke up, his voice gentle but firm. "Keera, my dear, there is no time for what ifs and if only. We need to work, so oil your gears, recalibrate your resolve, and let's get started."

Keera's expression was unsure. "I hate to bring up the obvious, but if last night showed us anything, it's that maybe Gulron can't be beaten."

The professor chuckled softly. "My dear, defeat comes in many forms, and a frontal attack on Gulron is not the strategy we need. It's time to regroup and strategize anew."

Keera's anger spiked, but she was intrigued by the professor's optimism and his new plan to defeat Gulron by deactivating the relic.

"I've been working on a schematic spell that could be our key to defeating him," said the professor. He unveiled the intricate blueprint of the schematic spell, designed specifically to neutralize Gulron's control over the Itzys. The symbols were a complex maze, requiring meticulous precision—a task nearly as formidable as Gulron.

Days blurred into nights as they tirelessly planned. Grief for Clara and Tag fueled Keera's efforts. Together they decoded the complex design, merging magic and machinery.

The professor paused, his eyes narrowing as he pointed to a specific glyph on the schematic. "Be very careful with this one. If mishandled, the dark magic will turn inward, and you will absorb it."

Keera's heart pounded at the warning, but she nodded with understanding.

The professor crafted a masterpiece of cast engineering imbued with the deactivation spell. Keera's heart swelled with hope and concern. "We're ready," she whispered.

They spent one last night perfecting every detail, aware of the risks and the complexity of the task. As dawn broke, they departed, fueled by their newfound insights and resolution. Their journey back to Gulron's fortress was as perilous as expected, but their determination never wavered. Finally, they reached the hidden door leading to the fabled relic. The professor paused, his hand hovering over the entrance, and locked eyes with Keera.

"This is it," he whispered gravely. "Everything leads to this."

She nodded; her throat tight, unable to speak for a moment, then she replied, "Open it. I'm ready."

The professor's hand trembled as he activated the entry mechanism, but nothing happened. They both stared at the door, confusion gathering on their faces.

"It should have worked." The professor's voice rose in disbelief. "Surely, this should have worked!"

Just then, they turned to find Gulron standing tall at the far end of the room. But he wasn't alone; Tag and Clara stood beside him, their eyes vacant and expressionless. Gulron's eyes gleamed with conquest.

"Did you really think it would be that easy?" he sneered; his voice full of contempt.

Keera's eyes widened. Tag! Clara! They were alive! She frowned. But why were they standing with him? One glance told her they were under some form of mind control. Her heart twisted at the sight, her mind racing, wondering how she would manage Gulron, deactivate the relic, and protect her friends.

"Gulron!" she shouted. "What have you done to them?"

Gulron smiled wickedly. "Done to them?" Sarcasm oozed from his words. "Why, they have joined ranks of the Midnight Order, my dear, ever dutiful and obedient, just as you will be." Gulron sneered, "Now, since you are so eager to defy me, perhaps I should teach you a lesson."

With a flourish of his staff, he aimed it at Keera, prepared to strike her down. But as he unleashed his spell, the secret door behind her creaked open, revealing a dark mysterious indigo gem hovering in the center of a stone relic. It glowed with the eerie light of midnight.

"Behold, the source of my power," he declared, momentarily distracted by the sight, his voice triumphant, gesturing towards the heart of the relic.

Quickly, Keera's mind snapped back to the plan, and she pulled out the device the professor had created, the one that would deactivate the relic. Her hands trembled as she connected it to the gem. Time seemed to slow as she dialed in the spell's combination, the entire room focused on her actions.

"You underestimate us, Gulron!" Her voice was filled with determination.

Taking a deep breath, Keera pressed the final button, a small glyph that came with a warning. Turning, she faced Gulron, grinning smugly, knowing that she had won. The contraption sprang to life, sucking the magic right out of the inner core and into . . . Keera.

"Nooooo!" she screamed. The realization of her mistake swooped down upon her like a cogswinged vulture; the indigo light was consuming her.

Except it was Gulron's face that twisted in panic as his power, not Keera, began to drain, the very essence of shadows abandoning his staff. Seeing a fleeting opportunity to escape, he turned to flee, only to be blocked by Tag brandishing his fluralator, his loyalty already shifting under Keera's control.

With a surge of newfound power, Keera quickly formed a portal to the netherworld. "You will never take Cogswell or harm an Itzy again." Midnight tendrils swirled and whipped, obeying Keera's command, and she cast Gulron into the void, his cries of rage and fear echoing as he was pulled into the abyss.

The room was swallowed by silence. The professor froze, struck dumb by the shocking transformation. In Keera's eyes, a dark fire danced. A gem formed on her forehead, pulsating with a dark glow as she basked in her sudden, inexplicable power. The Midnight Chrono-Crystal worked quickly, erasing all traces of the kind-hearted Keera they had known and loved, replacing her with something else entirely.

The professor's heart hammered in his chest, terror and uncertainty twisting his features as he stared at Keera. With trembling hands, he reached for the schematic spell contraption that lay scattered beside the stone relic. His thoughts whirred, desperation driving him to find some way, anyway, to reverse the nightmare that had just unfolded.

"Don't bother." Keera's voice was chillingly calm, her eyes filled with a cruel glow. "This power is mine, and I will not give it up."

The professor's eyes widened, realizing the full weight of Keera's transformation.

"To ensure my secret remains hidden," she said, her voice dripping with malice, "you will come with me." Tag and Clara stood motionless, their faces void of emotion.

The professor's thoughts raced. Cogswell had just rid itself of Gulron. They were ill-prepared for the impending rise of an Evil Itzy Queen. Acting quickly, he reached out and grabbed the fluralator from Tag's hand.

"Forgive me, Keera," he whispered, tears in his eyes, and with a determined pull, he activated the portal, its energy beckoning them closer. He grabbed Keera's arm, forcing her into the swirling vortex.

As they vanished, Keera's dark influence left Tag and Clara, restoring them to their former selves. They blinked in confusion, the room falling into an unnerving silence. The reality of Keera's transformation into the Evil Itzy Queen settled in like a cold shadow, leaving them with a chilling sense of loss and the stark knowledge that their world had changed forever.

About the Author

Candy Good, a creative virtuoso, intricately weaves tales of fantasy within the captivating realm of steampunk. Her vibrant narratives blend thrilling adventure with delicate threads of romance, transporting readers into worlds where gears mesh with magic. For more mesmerizing journeys and an inside peek into Candy's cog-driven universe, follow her on Instagram @CandyGoodWrites and visit her Facebook at https://www.facebook.com/candygoodwrites.

ENDLESSLY YOURS

JOELENE C. BROWN

F awna Florence sat with perfect posture in a gilded chair placed near the open window. The hostess of tonight's gala had even insisted a cushion be brought for Fawna to prop her feet on as she recovered from her lightheadedness. She watched the dancing continue in full force before her, a celebration of joy and life underneath golden chandeliers laden with crystals twinkling in the light.

The sweat that gathered on her brow mixed with the angry flush she felt blooming on her cheeks had been the perfect excuse for Fawna to use as to why she needed a moment of privacy. She delicately fanned herself and let out an overwhelmed little sigh in case any eyes were upon her. If anyone were to become aware that Fawna was in actuality planning a grand escape, it would be her demise.

An engagement between Lord Gregory Bodycombe and herself had just been announced to grand cheers from all those in attendance, which included the kingdom's wealthiest and most influential figures. Fawna's older brother had strategically planned every detail of the night's declaration, including leaving his sister completely ignorant that a man had asked for her hand in marriage.

Fawna seethed with rage at the audacity of her scheming sibling.

Her eighteenth birthday was only a mere three weeks away and then she would be of legal age to attain the inheritance left by her beloved deceased parents. Fawna could already feel the walls of a cage slowly trapping her inside the cruel world that Felix and a man older than their own father were constructing for her. Her own independence was being threatened by a wedding date that had been outrageously set in just two days' time.

Angry tears threatened the corners of her eyes, but Fawna rapidly blinked them away. Now was not the time to give into sobbing and self-pity. She had to think, and quickly. Felix had played his hand well, but Fawna was not out of the game just yet.

Since her return from finishing school, Fawna had become aware of her impending demise at the hands of her drastically changed brother. The unexpected death of their parents had unleashed a darkness Fawna had never expected in Felix. With all attempts at rekindling their bond failed, she had come to acknowledge the sad truth that he was now beyond her reach. And so, the outline of an escape plan had begun to form in Fawna's mind. She'd cracked the code to the family safe in the early hours one morning and over the course of a few weeks had been smuggling out parts of her great inheritance.

Tonight's engagement news, however, put Fawna in a troubling predicament. She could either rush her plans and take a chance at freedom before the night's end or risk going back to Florence House and withdrawing the rest of her money. But after meeting her new *fiancé*, Fawna believed the old nobleman to be a cruel being that her brother was soon to become.

"My darling, there you are." The voice belonged to Lord Bodycombe himself. Fawna clenched her teeth in disgust as she looked up at the man she was betrothed to. He hovered indecently close over her chair, his heeled shoes crushing the hem of her indigo gown as his large belly was thrust in her face.

"I say you've rested long enough," he cooed, placing a clammy hand on her wrist and jerking Fawna to her feet. "If you're to be the lady of my vast estate then you need to start doing your part. Not sitting about lazily whilst a party is underway."

Attempting to free herself from his grip, Fawna was pulled with more force than expected into the frenzy of party guests.

Take it one step at a time. One step at a time. She chanted to herself as they approached a small group of noblemen who stood hunched over from the weight of all their finery. Crisp black suits adorned with medals displaying their favors with the king and jewels covering each hairy knuckle flashed at Fawna almost mockingly. Towering over them all stood a smug-looking Felix Florence.

Fawna's brother was smiling so broadly that his unnaturally white teeth gleamed underneath the chandelier lights. "Ahhh and here she is now. My beautiful little sister." He gestured at her with a proud twirl of his hand.

A murmur of approval rose as half a dozen pairs of watery eyes looked over her silk-clad figure with varying expressions of desire. She barely bent her knees into a curtsy as she stood before this loathsome group. Felix quirked an eyebrow up in warning, but nothing was said of her lack in manners. Lord Bodycombe clung to her hand with his sweat-slicked paws, possessively stroking the sapphire newly placed on her finger.

A footman neared with a tray of crystal goblets and Fawna grasped the closest one, downing its contents without knowing what it was. She needed something to coat the taste of bile creeping up her throat.

"Let's have more dancing, now," Felix demanded enthusiastically. "Show these gents just how beautifully you can move."

Fawna threw a scathing look at her brother, not bothering to hide her repulsed expression. She knew he only wanted to feed the lust exhibited from the men and to keep himself in their favor. Felix simply grinned back at her in wicked delight and jovially clapped a hand to her *fiancé's* back.

Lord Bodycombe's beefy face paled with worry as he looked out at the musicians getting their instruments ready for what was sure to be another fast-paced melody. He did not disguise his relief when another gentleman stepped forward with his proffered hand. "May I?" he asked. The man appeared to be in better shape than her *fiancé*, but Fawna did not care for the dark gleam in his eyes.

"Indeed, you may," Lord Bodycombe replied and roughly thrust Fawna at him. Hiding her annoyed scowl to prevent Felix from lashing out at her, she allowed herself to be led to where the other paired dancers stood.

Ignoring the whispered gossip that swirled around her in a thick cloud, Fawna took in a steadying breath and looked straight ahead, just above her partner's balding head. Thankfully he was more adept at dancing than the old lord and Fawna was expertly spun into the frenzied dance by his gnarled, groping hands.

As the brisk melody poured from the skilled musicians, Fawna recognized the type of dance and knew that soon they would be switching partners. She bit back a smile of relief and hoped that the next man would be more respectful as to where his hands belonged.

Fawna twisted and twirled, her skirts flowing like dark water around her feet as she turned to face her new partner. A large, callused hand gripped hers familiarly, surprising Fawna and she looked up at the tall figure who appeared before her.

Henry Beachwood. Once a homeless orphaned boy taken in by her family and now a full-grown man. In the last few weeks, Fawna had not heard or seen a trace from him and feared he had left without saying goodbye.

"What are you doing here?" she asked as he pulled her into his arms and gracefully led her through the next steps without missing a beat.

His large frame was garbed in a new black suit, equal in its quality with those worn by any other man present. Fawna had never seen him dressed in anything other than tunics and dirt-stained breeches. Nor did she know he could dance, let alone so expertly. But here he was, doing so with a shaved beard and his dark curls tamed into an elegant hairstyle. Henry was the last person on earth Fawna would have imagined crashing a gala so boldly.

"I had to see you," he said, his breath warm on her face. It caused a shiver to run down her spine.

Fawna glanced over her shoulder for any sign that Felix might be watching, but the swarms of people in the too-small ballroom made it impossible for anyone to notice. As the notes of the song became staccato, Henry skillfully maneuvered them towards the outer edge of the room. And when the moment came for partners to switch once more, he clasped Fawna's hand tightly as they dashed from the dance floor amidst a flurry of gauzy skirts.

Tucked away in a dark alcove in the outer hallway, Fawna laughed in delight at their successful disappearance.

"Well, that was pleasantly unexpected." She grinned up at her childhood friend and felt herself momentarily transported to the days when they would hide away in the gardens, snacking on stolen treats and whispering secrets.

"I'll admit, it went far smoother than I thought it would," Henry said, letting out a sigh of relief.

Fawna gave him a puzzled look and replied, "To be honest, you are not someone I expected to encounter tonight. How, exactly, did you secure an invitation to such an event?"

He puffed his chest out proudly, stating, "A frivolous piece of parchment wasn't going to keep me from the free drinks and those delicious little pastries with the strawberry frosting."

Rolling her eyes, she playfully punched him in the arm. "You dressed in the finest money could buy simply to have some sweets?"

"Ouch," Henry groaned as he rubbed at his limb in exaggeration. "And yes, but I must say, you are the sweetest thing that I have laid eyes on yet."

Fawna's smile dropped and she bit the inside of her cheek to keep from lashing out at his words. Noticing her reaction, he met her gaze with a serious look of his own and softly said, "I did not mean to offend."

"I know you didn't," Fawna replied. She backed away a few steps and leaned against the stone wall. "I've been shown off like a piece of priceless chattel tonight. If my brother could marry me to more than one, I am sure I would be leaving with a flock of crusty old men."

"Forgive me, please." Henry moved forward, easily closing the distance between them. He enveloped her in a warm embrace and held her pressed to his chest for several moments. Fawna closed her eyes and pressed her head against his neck, breathing in the rich, comforting scent that reminded her of carefree years gone by.

"I've missed you so much, my little fawn," he whispered against the top of her head.

Remembering her earlier confusion when she had first seen him on the dance floor, she pulled away slightly to see his face, and asked, "Where have you been?"

He gently set her back on the carpet but kept her hands in his own before answering. "My position as the Florence House head gardener was terminated while you were away at school."

Fawna gasped in outrage. "Why would Felix do such a thing?" Temper flaring, she pulled her hands away, balling them into fists. "And why am I just now hearing from you?"

"Don't be mad, Fawna," Henry said as he stepped forward and covered her clenched-up hand with his own. Sighing, she let him take hold of her hand again, but refused to meet his gaze, her emotions churning with anger. "I would've found you sooner to say goodbye," he continued, "But my sudden dismissal included a guarded escort off the property. I had to have one of the servants gather my belongings for me."

"Well, you found me on the perfect night." Fawna shook her head and laughed humorlessly. "Did you hear the good news? I am to be wed in two days." The words tasted bitter on Fawna's tongue, and she wished for a glass of water to wash it away. "My inheritance that I was to receive in a few weeks will now go to my husband's coffers. And the title Lady Bodycombe is soon to be mine."

Henry snorted, his eyes crinkling briefly with mirth as he said, "There is no way in hell you can take on that name."

Fawna gave him a slow, mischievous grin. "Precisely," she said. "Which is why I have every intention of disappearing before tonight's festivities have ended."

Henry grabbed her hand and pressed it firmly to his chest, right over his heart. She could feel the strong beat of it beneath her fingertips. "You are not in jest? You would truly leave tonight?"

"No longer will I be someone's pawn to use for achieving fame and riches," she said fervently. "It must be now, or I fear it will be too late."

Feeling the encouraging squeeze of Henry's fingers, she swallowed the lump that formed in her throat and looked straight into his warm brown eyes. "Will you help me?"

"Fawna," Henry began, keeping one hand covering hers while he brought his other to tenderly caress the side of her face. "You know I have been endlessly yours since we met those thirteen years ago."

Fawna's breath caught at the declaration. Henry continued to brush his thumb against her skin as he said, "When we were children running in the sun through those fields and counting stars on your roof at night, I knew it then. I may have been just a boy, but I knew that in you I had found my true family." His eyes never wavered from hers, the unfiltered passion visible on his face. "I'd always planned to prove myself to your parents and convince them that I could be worthy of you."

"They knew," she whispered, voice hoarse with emotion. "From their actions all those years ago, I saw the love and pride that they felt for you. Mother and Father would be proud of who you've become."

Henry turned his face away for a moment and took a steadying breath. "After tonight, you'll never be stuck in this abhorrent situation again. In honor of your parents and my love for you, we will flee together and start anew across the ocean if we must."

Heart pounding in her chest, Fawna said, "With declarations like that you could just marry me. Then it would be impossible for Lord Bodycombe to lay claim to me." She had been joking with her words, but Henry was immediately shaking his head.

"Fawna," he said, "When I do ask for your hand, I don't want there to be any other reason for your 'yes' other than that you love me. When the day finally comes, I don't want anything to pressure you into saying that you'll be mine unless it's what you genuinely want."

Fawna opened her mouth to respond when the noise of the musicians came to a sudden halt, alerting them that the dancing had come to an end.

"I need to return," she said. "If Felix catches me now then all chances of leaving will be gone."

"Then there isn't much time," Henry said, leading her back to the arch that served as an entrance to the ballroom. "I will make my way to the stables at once to secure horses. You have a plan to get away from your brother?"

"Yes," Fawna firmly said as nervous butterflies erupted in her stomach. "It's imperative that we depart during the party's firework display. At midnight. It will provide us with the cover we'll need to leave unnoticed," she added as raised voices began moving in their direction.

"Then I will see you soon, love," Henry promised before he quickly disappeared in the opposite direction.

The room that had once been alive with music and the tapping of dancing feet was now in a chaotic uproar. Fawna attempted to slip into the ballroom unnoticed but the cheery voice of the hostess instantly cried "Miss Florence!" The room quieted as all eyes turned in her direction.

Heavy footsteps came towards her and then Felix was there, pushing his way through the crowd. "Where have you been?" he asked as he came to a lurching halt. His cold, gray eyes studied every inch of Fawna as she stood there before him.

"All the swaying from the dance had my stomach upset. I stepped away for some respite," Fawna said, her voice cracking in what she hoped was a convincing display of meekness to her brother.

Felix narrowed his eyes at Fawna. "You do not excuse yourself without notifying me first, understood?" he practically shouted, spit flying from his mouth.

Dipping her head in acknowledgement, she cast her eyes down to the ground, hoping the submissive act would ease her brother's foul mood. A set of shiny, black heels stepped on the hem of her ballgown yet again, as Lord Bodycombe pressed uncomfortably close against Fawna's back.

"I say, is she ill?" he asked, disgust evident in his voice. He pressed a handkerchief to his face as though he were terrified of catching whatever sickness he believed Fawna to have.

"Forgive my sister's condition, my lord," Felix said. His voice immediately took on a soothing tone as Fawna watched her brother's expression morph into a winning smile. "It appears that she could not handle herself properly while out on the dance floor. I must beg your forgiveness while she takes a few moments to compose herself."

Beneath his charming grin was an air of malice that Fawna had become very familiar with in the past months. Not wishing to provoke him further, she bent into a deep curtsy while continuously reminding herself not to look too gleeful as she walked away. With Felix's "permission" she would now have the time she needed to enact her escape plan.

Moving through the throngs of people, Fawna kept the timid mask securely on her face. Once she passed through the doorway that would take her to the lady's powder room, she let out a sigh of relief and wiped the perspiration from her temples.

No longer bothering with the façade, Fawna lifted her skirts and ran into the private chamber, latching it securely behind her. The maids had brought up the necessities she had packed in the event of a wardrobe malfunction, and Fawna easily found the mahogany case with her name engraved on top.

Packing a bag full of belongings would have made her plans obvious, so Fawna had resorted to the bare essentials. Instead of silk and cosmetics beneath the box's lid, lay two days' worth of food rations, threadbare clothing, and what money she had claimed as her own from the family vault.

Without hesitation, she tore at the laces going up the back of her heavy gown. It loosened on her chest, and Fawna gladly freed herself of the suffocating indigo fabric. She unfolded a wrinkled gingham dress from the box and slid the thin material over her head. It settled softly on Fawna's shoulders in a soothing kiss of cotton. She pulled the worn green hooded cape over her shoulders and then placed her feet back in her slippers. There would be time to find proper footwear later. With her light blonde hair pulled into a thick braid, Fawna felt confident that her new ensemble would have others believing she was a simple peasant.

She stuffed her ruined gown as best she could behind a long tapestry and then picked up her wooden box. Opening the door tentatively to be sure the hallway was clear; Fawna pulled the hood up over her head and hurried down a servant's staircase. The wooden stairs brought her to the main floor with a door leading outside to her left.

Fawna stepped out into the cold night. Chirping crickets and muffled laughter floated on an early winter breeze. Keeping low to the shadows, she crept towards the direction of the stables.

It took a few minutes before the black silhouette of the building came into view. Her chest expanding with relief, she looked around for any sign of Henry when a twig snapped behind her.

Twirling around, she saw a familiar face but not the one she hoped for.

"Felix," she said breathlessly, panic clamping down painfully on her lungs.

"Out for a midnight stroll, sister?" His tone was mocking and sinister, not an ounce of the Felix she had grown up with in that voice.

Lifting her head high with a confidence she was fighting to hold, Fawna said, "I will not be forced to marry that swine."

"As your guardian, I say otherwise," Felix replied as he prowled towards her.

"And as my brother, you should have known I wouldn't give in," she countered.

Felix was close enough now that she could see his expression from the glow of the full moon. His eyes were cold as he surveyed her clothing. "Rest assured; I have been waiting for something to go amiss. Your behavior tonight was almost too perfect."

"Why can you not leave me be?" Fawna had to attempt just once more to find the brother of her past. "You and I are all we have left of our family. Father would never approve of this arrangement."

"Father isn't here anymore," he said coldly. "I make the decisions now. And as your better –"

A loud smack cut off his next words. Felix's head jerked forward, a pained cry releasing from his lips. Henry stood behind him, his fisted hand still raised with knuckles red from the punch he had thrown.

"You filthy drudge," Felix cried. "I'll have you horsewhipped for that." He made to lunge at Henry, but Fawna was quicker. Swinging her wooden case with all her strength, she caught her brother in the temple with a sickening crack. He dropped to the ground in a heap.

Fawna knelt beside him, adrenaline coursing through her veins as she looked for signs of life. Felix's chest was still steadily rising with his breath. Relieved, she stood without sparing him a second glance. She felt certain Lord Bodycombe would be on the hunt for Felix the moment her absence was noticed.

A bright golden flash lit up the starry sky followed by a giant boom. It was midnight.

Henry immediately stood before her. "We must go. *Now.*" The urgency in his voice set Fawna into motion.

Together, they ran to where Henry had a horse tethered to a tree. He hoisted Fawna up onto the saddle and quickly swung up behind her. One large arm wrapped around her waist securely as he flicked the reins and set his horse trotting swiftly out the back gate. Fawna clutched her little box and watched with disbelieving eyes as the gaudy manor faded into the background.

The lights of the city were almost completely extinguished due to the midnight hour, allowing for their departure to be cloaked by the black sky. A small bubble of joy rose in her chest, but Fawna shoved it back down. The weeks to come would be a struggle with Felix tearing the kingdom apart in search of her. She would rejoice and celebrate her freedom when she was finally of age and no one would ever be in control of her choices again.

As though sensing her thoughts, Henry bent his head low and said, "We'll be riding throughout the night. I'm sorry, but we should cover as much distance as possible before stopping."

Fawna voiced her agreement. The love and protectiveness in his voice reminded her of what family and security felt like.

"Any regrets?" His whispered words tickled her ear.

Fawna twisted the sparkling sapphire off her finger and tossed it out towards the nearing tree line. "Never." She repeated his own words that had earlier taken her breath away. "I am endlessly yours."

Henry hugged her firmly to him, a quick kiss pressed to her cheek as they made their way further out of the city and towards a new start together.

About the Author

Joelene C. Brown is a registered nurse who currently works as a school nurse and instructor. However, her first love is in creating stories. She makes her home in Northwest Arkansas with her husband and cockapoo. To get to know her more and find updates on Joelene's writing, follow her on Instagram @joelenecbrown.

Mirror at Midnight

Suzanne E. Alexander

S ash made herself take a look. Today was the day she and Drew were
going to talk about moving in together, and she was nervous enough
already. Now was *not* the best time for her to get stuck behind a tractor,
but she couldn't pass it without checking her rearview mirror.

The knots in her stomach grew tighter as she quickly glanced behind her.
Good—no cars. Except now one was coming towards her in the other lane.
She would have to look again.

Usually checking her car mirrors didn't bother her so much—it's not like
she would see herself in them. But today it was a nerve-wracking reminder
of the upcoming conversation with Drew. If they were going to live in the
same space, she was bound to wonder why Sash didn't want any mirrors in
the house.

Clenching the steering wheel, Sash shifted in her seat. How was she even
going to explain it? She had resisted looking into any reflective surface if she
could help it since she was seven years old. Sure, she'd seen herself in
pictures. The girl in the mirror may have looked similar to her, but *it wasn't
her*.

Sash rubbed her forehead and inhaled deeply, pursing her lips before she
exhaled and recalled the day she had confirmed her suspicions about her
reflection. The Other Girl in the mirror had always done everything Sash did,
but she didn't really look like her anymore. The changes had been subtle at
first, but one day Sash *knew* something was off. She remembered taking out
her school picture and comparing it to the girl in the mirror. The Other Girl
had green eyes, and light freckles were starting to splash across her nose.
Sash's eyes were blue, and there were no freckles on the girl in her school
picture.

Of course she had gone straight to her mother, who had promptly
gripped Sash's shoulders and shaken them, insisting that the Other Girl
looked just like Sash and making it clear she "never wanted to hear about
this nonsense again." Sash let out the breath she'd been holding and
wondered just how similar Drew's reaction would be. Would this ruin their
relationship the way it had ruined the one with her mother? Sash had never
been able to confide in her mother about anything after that–to the point
that now they hardly ever spoke. Mom didn't even know Sash was gay, and
thanks to her parent's religious views, she probably never would. Sash
clenched the steering wheel and grimaced. She *really* liked Drew, and didn't
want to lose her. But they couldn't go forward until this mirror girl was out
in the open.

Avoiding the whole issue hadn't been too difficult until now, and she was
actually pretty good at it. She didn't wear makeup, and her hair was cut in a

simple style that Sash could do herself without the need for a mirror. Although, the few times looking couldn't be helped, she'd noticed more changes: the Other Girl's hair had gradually turned to a bland shade of red. And she was thinner. In fact, the older Sash became, the less the reflection looked like herself in pictures. And for the last few months, there was an angry look to the Other Girl's eyes that made Sash's heart pound.

But those moments were rare, and, at twenty years old, Sash's life was otherwise pretty normal. She had friends, a job she loved, and a girlfriend who actually could be The One. At least Sash hoped so. In fact, she was supposed to meet her in fifteen minutes.

Sash glared at the tractor still in her way and groaned. She had to get around this slowpoke. Bracing herself, she peered into the rearview mirror again—straight into the Other Girl's eyes.

Sash slammed on the brakes. Thankfully, no one was behind her.

She cursed and reached up to cover the mirror, only to realize it was pointed directly at her, not the back of the car. She frowned. How had it moved? Did the Other Girl have something to do with it? Nothing like that had happened before.

Carefully, Sash started driving again, refusing to look in the mirror even to fix it. Maybe she was just worked up. She probably accidentally hit it while not paying attention. Besides, there actually was a chance that Drew would believe her. They had met at a haunted house tour, after all. Drew loved all things spooky, and their relationship would never have gotten this far if Sash hadn't been able to trust Drew as much as she did, which was a lot.

In front of her, the tractor honked then turned off, and Sash pushed down on the accelerator. She could still make it and not have to speed. Sitting up straighter, she took another deep breath then slowly let it out as she tried to think of what to say.

Before anything helpful came to mind, Sash turned into the park and pulled in next to the picnic area. She stepped out and got the box of food from the back. The picnic was Drew's idea, and Sash loved her for it. For all Drew's interest in the supernatural and scary stuff, she was also all about rainbows and sunshine. She loved vivid colors and was one of the most beautiful souls Sash had ever met. It wasn't that Drew was always happy. It was that Drew's happiness was the kind that made those around her happy, too. Already Sash could feel herself smiling in spite of her nerves. Maybe everything would be okay.

She spotted Drew on her brightly-colored tie-dye blanket right away. Drew often said her favorite color was rainbow splashed in tie-dye, and her rainbow-tinted hair matched almost perfectly. Sauntering to her, Sash plopped onto her knees and set down the box. "I thought this was your favorite-I-can-never-get-this-even-a-little-bit-dirty blanket. Or is that a different one?"

Drew leaned forward and started to straighten out the blanket where Sash had messed it up. "This is the one, but it has a hole in it. So now it is a beautiful, but functional blanket, not an aesthetic one only."

"My favorite kind." Sash began taking out the sandwiches and chips that were her contribution to the picnic and smiled as Drew scrunched up her cute button-nose and struggled to open a second chip bag. "Did you find any diet Ginger Ale?"

Drew gave the still-unopened chips to Sash and opened the cooler. "I did. And, I found something else!" Drew reached into her purse and brought out a small item wrapped in a plastic bag. "Open it!"

Sash took the bag and drew out a rainbow-colored magnet with the words "Home Sweet Home" on it and giggled. "This is perfect. I love it!"

Drew grinned, her bright blue eyes sparkling. "So, I was wondering which refrigerator we should put this on—mine, yours, or one in a new place?" Sash forced her smile to stay in place as her thoughts raced. So far she had been able to keep Drew from coming over to her place, and Drew had never pushed back on it. But now that they were going to share, Sash couldn't keep her secret any longer.

Sash looked back down at the blanket and reached for her sandwich while her stomach did flip-flops. How could she bring up the mirror issue without sounding like she wanted to back out? She should at least confirm that she did want to move forward. "As long as it's *our* refrigerator. But before we discuss that, I need to talk to you about something else, and I'm more than a little nervous about it." Sash risked a quick look up to see Drew's reaction, and was comforted to see her scoot closer and take her hand.

"Is this something we can face together?"

If only! Sash gripped Drew's hand tighter, realizing just how much it would mean to not face this alone. "I hope so. I've only ever told my mother, and that didn't work out so well. Sash watched as Drew nodded. Drew knew about her uneasy relationship with her mother, but had never pressed Sash for details. She never pushed about anything. She had always just accepted Sash, and everyone else, for who they were. It gave Sash hope. She nodded slightly, took a deep breath, and dove in. "Have you ever noticed that I never look into mirrors?"

Drew smiled. "Well, I noticed that you don't seem vain like a lot of other pretty girls."

Sasha grinned and looked down. She forced herself to stay serious, and then calmly and slowly stated her 'problem'. "It isn't vanity. I can't even see myself in the mirror. I see someone else, and I don't know who she is."

Drew frowned. "What do you mean?"

"I mean when I see myself, it's not me. It's literally another girl–and she looks nothing like me."

Drew's jaw dropped. "Really?" Sash loosened her grip on Drew's hands and started to back away when Drew took them again and immediately apologized. "I'm so sorry. I'm not sure exactly what that all means, but I believe you.. How can I help?"

Sash let out the breath she was holding. "I'm not sure, but just you believing me is more than I ever hoped for from anyone." Sash paused. "You do believe me, right?"

Drew smiled and nodded. "I believe there are all sorts of things out there we can't explain or understand." She cocked her head. "But mostly I believe in you."

Sash sighed and smiled as a healing warmth started to replace the butterflies in her stomach. "That means so much to hear you say that. Mainly I just try to stay away from mirrors. I was thinking we could get a place with two bathrooms, and you could have the one with the mirror in it, if that's okay with you."

Drew nodded. "Of course, but . . ." Drew paused. "Haven't you ever thought of trying to find out more about who the other girl is?"

Sash considered. No, she hadn't. After the confrontation with her mother, she'd just tried to avoid the other girl and anything to do with her. She told Drew as much.

"So no one else can see her?"

"My mother couldn't. She just saw me."

Drew sat up straight. "Well I have a *ton* of questions! Like, what does she look like? Could she be related to you, like a ghost of an ancestor or something? Maybe a twin!"

"Well, we looked almost alike when we were little, but we don't anymore. Now she has red hair and green eyes, and freckles. She's been aging just like me, so I don't think she's a ghost. I have absolutely no idea who she is, and she's not a twin."

"Well, what does she do? Does she try to get you to come through the mirror?"

"She doesn't really do anything except mimic my moves like a reflection is supposed to. Except . . ."

"Go on."

"Well, for the last few months, her eyes have looked really angry. I mean, she looks mad whenever I see her."

"When do you see her if you don't look at mirrors? And why is she angry?"

"It's not just mirrors, it's any reflective surface, like a window. I can't always avoid it. And I have no clue why she's angry."

Drew scrunched her nose again and looked thoughtful as Sash exhaled. Already she felt lighter and was beginning to feel almost excited at the prospect of solving this with Drew. Then she remembered the incident with the rearview mirror, and her heart sank. What if something bad happened from poking around at this entity? Sash picked up the magnet and blinked back tears. She really wanted theirs to be a "Home Sweet Home," but she didn't want to risk anything happening to Drew. But then, what did she know, really? Nothing.

Suddenly Drew squealed. "I know! We can try taking a picture! You haven't tried that yet, have you?"

She hadn't. At least not since she was a kid. She hadn't tried anything since then, really, but avoidance. "I haven't tried that, but I don't have any mirrors in my apartment."

"We can try it in mine, if you like. I won't push you."

Sash picked up her sandwich and took a bite. The idea scared her. "But what if someone gets hurt? Poking at this could make it worse. She might try something, and I don't want anything to happen to you, especially because of this." Sash told her about the rearview mirror.

"Wow." Drew fell silent, and both of them quietly finished their sandwiches. After Drew took her last bite and finished her coke, she spoke up. "If you're concerned about something happening, then I say we get help. Actually, I know someone who knows things about stuff like this. She's very spiritual and very nice. And she's *not* judgmental."

"What do you mean, spiritual?"

"Well . . . she calls herself a Seer. Sort of like a psychic, but she also has a PhD and is a Licensed Mental Health Counselor. Her name is Deena, and she's more like a grandmother than a therapist. You'd like her."

Sash thought for a moment. "Let's try the picture first; maybe that will give us some evidence. Then perhaps we can talk to Deena. At least I'll meet her to see what she's like."

"Great! Do you want to go to my house now, or would you rather wait? I don't want to rush you or anything."

Sash considered as she and Drew cleaned up the remnants of their picnic. With the possibility of finding answers hanging over her, continuing to ignore this seemed less of an option. "We can try now if you like. But what if something happens?"

Drew grinned. "Then we call Ms. Deena. She'll be glad to help, and she won't treat you like you're crazy or anything."

Sash nodded and they walked to their cars. She put the picnic box back in hers and then turned around to face Drew. "Aren't you nervous, at all?"

Drew put her arm around Sash and gave her a squeeze. "To be honest, I'm more excited than nervous, but I also want to help you solve this. Do you really want to spend the rest of your life avoiding mirrors and not really knowing why? What if avoiding this is what's making her angry?"

Sash's eyes widened. Why hadn't she thought of that? Her entire focus had been on staying away from it. Maybe because, until now, she had faced it alone. Telling Drew had opened the door to doing something about it, and now Sash could not go back. "You're right, and I can't go back to the way it was before. But promise me we'll be careful?"

Drew smiled. "I promise. And we won't do anything that makes you uncomfortable. Okay?"

Sash opened her car door and turned around to face Drew. "Okay. I'll meet you there." As Drew walked to her car, Sash started her own, put it in reverse, then froze when she remembered that she hadn't fixed her rearview mirror. Quickly she reached up and pushed it the other way, then adjusted it, making sure it didn't face her. She shook her head.

Why couldn't she do this simple task like a normal person? Was she a normal person? What was she getting Drew into?

But what was the alternative?

A life without Drew. A life without answers. Sash stopped at a red light and tightened her grip on the steering wheel as she felt a slow burn ignite in her stomach. Why shouldn't she have a normal life? She started to look up at her mirror but stopped. She couldn't do it. Sash let out a loud, frustrating sigh as she gunned the accelerator.

As she pulled into Drew's place, she imagined she was coming home. Drew's car was already there. Was Sash doing the right thing? What if this made it worse? Sash looked over to grab her purse and caught a glimpse of the rearview mirror and shuddered. Doing nothing had made things worse, too. Sash got out and slammed the car door shut, suddenly determined to get some answers.

When Sash walked to the door, Drew opened it and let her in. "I had just enough time to cover the mirror by the door. I thought we could use the one in the bathroom for this."

Sash followed Drew. When they walked in to face the mirror, she took a deep breath, closed her eyes, and raised her head. "I'm ready." Drew took her hand and squeezed it, and Sash stood quietly until she heard Drew take the picture. "Do you see anything?"

"Well, you look like you in the mirror. Let's see what the picture shows."

Sash bent her head down and opened her eyes to peer at the phone. Drew held it down and opened the picture. It looked like Sash, but her eyes were open. And angry.

"I thought you closed your eyes?"

Sash felt sick. "I did. That's me but those are her eyes! See?" Without thinking, Sash looked up at the mirror. While they watched, the Other Girl raised her hand, and banged on the mirror. Thankfully, it didn't break.

Sash and Drew both jumped back. Drew recovered first. "That wasn't you. You didn't do that. It *looked* like you, but you didn't raise your hand. *She* did." Drew started to raise her hand to point but put it back down.

Sash looked at Drew. "You saw her?"

"Well, I saw you, but the mirror-you was doing things the real you didn't. I *really* think we should call Ms. Deena. Is that okay? Can we call her now?"

Sash closed her eyes and nodded. Drew took her arms and led her out of the bathroom. "I'm so sorry, Sash. Do you think taking the picture made her angrier?"

"I don't know. Why could you see what she was doing but not see her?"

"Maybe only you are allowed to see her. At least she didn't break the mirror, so that's good, right?"

"Yes, but I'm starting to feel a lot better about talking to Deena, so if you want to call her, go ahead."

They walked to the living room and sat down while Drew scrolled through her contacts. As soon as she started the call she put it on speakerphone. It rang once.

"Hello? Drew? Did something happen? I felt something just a few minutes ago."

Sash looked up at Drew and her eyes widened. Drew smiled and began talking.

"Ms. Deena! My friend has a problem I think you may be able to help with, and it might have just got a little worse. Can you help?"

"You both come right over, dear. And tell your friend not to worry. I'll try to help in any way that I can."

"That's great! Thank you. We'll be over right away!" Drew hung up the phone and looked at Sash. "Are you ready? Is this okay?"

Sash was more than ready. Watching the Other Girl hit the mirror had cinched it; she knew she would need help going forward. She also knew she could never go back. Ignoring it certainly had not made it go away.

They took Drew's car. Sash avoided the mirrors and was quiet while Drew drove and called Ms. Deena to explain what was going on. How did the Other Girl do that? What else could she do? What else *would* she do, and how could they prevent her from doing it?

Soon Drew turned onto a gravel driveway that led into the woods. Sash hadn't even noticed that they had driven out of town. Ms. Deena's house was surrounded by trees, and beautiful flowers lined the patio in front of the door. Just as they got out of the car, an older woman with long white hair, wearing a tank top and a long skirt, opened the door and walked towards them.

Ms. Deena hugged Drew and then opened her arms to Sash. Without hesitation, Sash accepted the hug. It felt wonderful, and she imagined this was definitely how being hugged by one's grandmother would feel. "Thank you for helping me. For helping us."

Ms. Deena pulled back. "I've been helping Drew's family for a while now. That's how we met. Drew's mother was a client of mine, and in time, her and Drew became like family."

"Is that usual, getting close to clients like that? I apologize if I sound rude, but I thought therapists weren't allowed to get, like, personal or anything."

"Well, I am a therapist, but I'm also a Mama Bear, and sometimes the best therapy is the love you get from family. The problem is, not all families are willing to love unconditionally. Now, family doesn't have to be related by blood, and my family grows as it needs to, and only with consent on all sides."

Sash stopped as they came to the door and looked up at Ms. Deena, who put her hand on Sash's shoulder. "Drew explained about the mirrors, and I've covered them up. I do have one mirror out, but it's a special hand mirror, and it can't be used against you. You are safe here."

They walked into the house. The living room looked like a cozy cottage in soft roses and creams. As they sat down, Ms. Deena smiled at Sash. "I'm not sure what Drew told you about me, and I'm not a full psychic. Now she told me what happened, but do you want to tell me more about it?"

Sash looked at Drew and took her hand. Quickly, she told Ms. Deena about the Other Girl, the confrontation with her mother, her life avoiding mirrors, and what had happened at Drew's house.

Ms. Deena smiled and picked up a hand mirror from the end table and set it in her lap. "It sounds like this Other Girl may be getting tired of being ignored, but I think I can help you find some answers. Are you ready to get started?"

Sash nodded her head. "Yes. I want to get this done. I've had to deal with this for so long." Tears began to run down her face. Now that there was hope, she didn't want to have to live like she had been. She knew she wanted a relationship, but she hadn't realized how badly she wanted family. She took the mirror Ms. Deena offered.

Sash closed her eyes. She didn't want to look, but in her mind she saw her anyway. Knowing she had to keep going, Sash braced herself, raised the mirror, and looked straight into the eyes that should have been her own.

They weren't angry. Her expression was bland, then surprised. Sash opened her mouth wide. So did the girl in the mirror. She moved her head back and forth, up and down, and blinked her eyes. Her reflection did the same. As her face relaxed, so did the face in the mirror. Sash looked into her eyes, wondering if they would turn angry as before. While she wondered what to do next, the girl in the mirror spoke.

"Midnight."

Sash dropped the mirror and kicked it away when it fell on the floor.

Ms. Deena stood up and retrieved the mirror. "What happened?"

"She spoke . . . I mean, I didn't *hear* her, but her mouth moved like she was speaking, and I *knew* what she said. It wasn't me . . . I didn't say anything, did I?"

Ms. Deena shook her head. "No, you didn't, and your mouth only moved when you opened it wide. What did she say?"

She said "midnight."

"That makes sense. Midnight is when the link between our world and the spirit world is strongest. Is this the first time she's tried to speak to you?"

Sash nodded her head. "Yes, but I can't think of a reason."

Ms. Deena looked at her watch. "If she wants to try something at midnight, I say we do this tonight. I can prepare a place here where we can talk to her, and she won't be able to hurt you."

Sash looked at Drew and then at Ms. Deena. "You can protect us if she tries anything?"

Ms. Deena smiled. "I get the sense that you are not in danger, but yes, I can prevent her from being able to act out anything."

Sash nodded agreement and she and Drew stood up. It was getting late, so Ms. Deena led them to the bedroom and told them to get some rest while she "made preparations."

Sash and Drew laid down on top of the bed, facing each other. Sash smiled at Drew and started to close her eyes when she felt Drew take her hand. When she opened them, Drew smiled at her. Neither one said anything, but closed their eyes to rest.

At 11:45, Ms. Deena came into the room and told them it was time. They walked down the hall to a room that was mostly empty. A large circle with some odd symbols around it had been drawn on the floor. Ms. Deena sat at the edge of the circle, put the mirror in her lap, then motioned for the girls to sit.

When the clock struck twelve, Ms. Deena passed the mirror to Sash. "When you look this time, ask her name."

Sash took the mirror and gulped as anxiety started to swim around in her stomach. What if it was a trap? She looked over at Ms. Deena, who was smiling warmly at her, and she realized that she trusted her. Suddenly, she felt calmer, and resolved to accept this and move forward. Sash looked in the mirror and was amazed that the Other Girl no longer looked angry. In fact, she was smiling.

"Tell her my name is Cara, and I am ready. I promise I will not hurt you," the mirror-girl said.

Sash repeated what Cara said, to which Ms. Deena nodded and spoke some words Sash didn't understand, then raised her voice. "Cara, we bid you to come to our circle, to tell us your purpose, and to do no harm." After uttering more weird-sounding words, she looked at Sash.

Immediately Sash felt something *pull* out of her body. Something shimmered in the circle, then slowly became Cara, the Other Girl. She turned and looked at Sash. "I'm sorry, I didn't mean to scare you. I'm supposed to look after you, to help you, but I've been locked in for so long, and you only ignored me."

Sash was shocked. "What do you mean, help me? How have you *ever* helped me?"

Cara turned to Ms. Deena. "I am supposed to be her guardian, bound to her family for over 300 years. I can't do great things, but I can protect in small ways. Sash's mother rejected me because of her husband's religion. I was locked in limbo. When Sash was born, I was passed to her as usual, but I was still trapped. I couldn't even talk to her until she accepted me." She turned again to Sash. "I'm sorry I was angry, but I have long been in the dark unless you looked in the mirror, and it has been years since you have done so willingly."

Sash was confused. "Three hundred years? But you were a child, like me."

"I presented as a child to be your friend so you would not be afraid. This is usually how it is done. But I could not explain anything to you, and your mother would not."

"But I don't need a guardian, do I?" Sash just wanted a normal life.

Ms. Deena looked at Cara. "How did you enter into bondage with this family?"

Cara looked down. "I was an adult servant of a very important family. When the . . . relationship I had with one of their grown daughters was discovered, I was sentenced to die. Only because my love threatened to end her life if we were separated did they spare me. I was bespelled to be guardian to my love and her daughters, and their daughters, for she was forced to marry another in order to save my life."

Drew spoke up. "Wow, that's harsh. Can't we do something?"

Ms. Deena nodded at Sash. "You can release her, I think. Without locking her in the dark."

Sash looked up at Cara, no longer afraid. "I can release you? Just like that?"

Cara smiled and nodded. "You must say my full name. It is Cara MacCallery."

Sash couldn't believe it was that easy. "Cara MacCallery, I release you from the bondage to our family."

Suddenly Cara began to glow. "Oh, Thank you!" She looked up as the light became brighter until they could no longer see Cara within it. Then, just as quickly, the light rose up through the ceiling until it was gone.

When Sash looked down, she saw the mirror next to her. Carefully she picked it up and held it up to her face. When she saw her face—*her own* face—she stood and burst into tears. As Drew and Ms. Deena wrapped their arms around her, their smiles filled the mirror.

And there were many more smiles to come.

About the Author

If you like YA Fantasy, please follow Suzanne Alexander on Instagram at @suzannealexandercopywriting for more stories and book-related content.

HERE
AND
NOW

KAYLA KING

Together they teetered on the precipice of an ending. It would take only one word to push them over the edge.

Like *goodnight*.

Or worse, *goodbye*.

Niles forced both to stay hidden beneath his tongue, unwilling to part ways in this rain.

Simple as that.

If they kept moving, the fallacy that this was an ordinary day might last. Neither mentioned the people they'd lost, though they were supposed to remember the dead on Holloweaves.

Thunder cracked in the distance. But Camryn didn't startle at the sound. She tipped her face to the night sky. "Seems like there's a storm every year on this day."

"It's like the sky knows." Niles bent to the sidewalk, scooping up a handful of rainbow confetti. He hated this time-lapse material. It meant the names of the dead wouldn't begin to degrade until after midnight. Just another Holloweaves tradition.

He let the colorful bits fall from his hand back to the damp concrete. As soon as this persistent drizzle turned into a downpour, it wouldn't matter what he did or didn't say.

That would be it.

This walk would be over.

Another October 31st spent on his own; that's what Niles had to look forward to as the veil thinned, allowing all the potential versions of who he might be someday to haunt him.

But if Camryn wanted to head home now, he'd tip an invisible hat. He'd say *tomorrow* instead of relinquishing the farewells now gritted between his teeth. That finality contrasted the last hour spent wandering desolate streets of their city together as everyone else celebrated Holloweaves.

Only now, his smallest toe was crammed in the corner of his sneaker. The canvas material soaked through from the storm, and the space inside tightened with every step.

"We should probably take this next train." Camryn pointed to the station up ahead. "Otherwise, we'll be late."

He couldn't join Camryn the way she wanted tonight. "The Holloweaves party isn't meant for me, Bishop." Niles noted the look of pity as it crossed Camryn's face, furrowing between her eyebrows.

"But this whole day celebrates those we've lost." Water dripped down Camryn's chin and neck.

Without pause, Niles followed the path of another raindrop until it disappeared against the thin t-shirt now clinging to Camryn. The fabric started the color of dust before darkening to lead. Almost like a bruise. This rain had a ripple effect, changing her hazel eyes from blue to green. This sudden shift in shade confounded Niles. But the abrupt torrent from above weighed him to the spot, promising this phantasmagoric illusion was anything but.

Niles bowed his head. "My parents didn't die like the others." He took a step closer, worried the storm would steal his words before Camryn had a chance to hear them. "I don't get to take solace in speaking their names with everyone else. I have to remember them alone. I mourn them alone." It was impossible to know where tears ended and rain began, both trailing down his face. He wiped at his eyes anyway.

"But your parents are gone." Camryn tucked hair behind her ears. The once chestnut tendrils dampened, more like shadows. "The how of it all doesn't matter."

Niles ran a hand through his own hair, working out the moisture from the thick ochre strands. "It does to me. And I have to do this my way."

"So, I guess this is goodnight then?" She hesitated several heartbeats before taking a step toward the train station.

Goodnight.

Not goodbye.

Clear difference there.

But this wasn't the jovial parting Niles assumed would punctuate their time together. A small wave was all he could muster. "I'll see you tomorrow?"

Camryn nodded and returned the gesture, striding down the confetti-filled street.

He was through the main door of his building in less than four minutes. Though he'd anticipated this solitary ascent to his loft, the quiet grew louder after every step, rattling around in his head. Niles had never been one to wish away time. But tomorrow couldn't come soon enough.

Once inside, his eyesight adjusted to the space without needing the overhead light. It was a remembered feeling, shifting right toward the bathroom. He started the shower now, giving the water time to heat while he grabbed a towel from upstairs.

Usually there was safety to be found in darkness. But every night for the last week, distorted memories disturbed the nothingness he used to see in sleep. It'd been the same for Camryn. *Untethered.* That's what she called it yesterday.

Because being plagued by dreams meant dying.

And they were alive.

They were not afflicted with somnium. They would not be taken into endless sleep by that dreaming disease.

They would survive.

Together.

Back in the bathroom, he switched on the light. Moisture clung to the mirror, revealing a warped version of himself bound in the glass.

His dad used to tell him stories about how dreamer demons looked like the grown versions Niles would be someday. They would wait for midnight on Holloweaves, fingers like stingers capable of infecting him with the dreaming disease as punishment for eating too many sweets before sleep.

Terrifying shit to tell an eight-year-old.

Someone, somewhere, really thought this a necessary tradition on October 31st when dreaming was horrific enough every other day. Dreams paralyzed victims in sleep, beckoning them to exist in a world that would never be real. And okay, PSA? Adulthood will haunt you until it's too late to go back.

Like, what?

It was enough that Holloweaves borrowed from the traditions of before times with the idea of ghosts and unfinished business. From his research, no science had proved whether the veil became more tenuous between dreams and reality during this time.

If his dad were still alive, maybe he'd offer the same bedtime warning. But both his parents had been gone for just over a year. Niles wiped his hand across the mirror to return his reflection back to the him of here and now.

He slipped the damp shirt over his head and tossed it to the polished concrete floor. A knock at the front door echoed once and twice and again.

This couldn't be real.

All the usual people who could be on the other side of the door were elsewhere tonight. He gripped the counter. Stories of ghosts crossing between worlds on Holloweaves were only desperate attempts at resurrection. Nothing more. Even if his parents somehow made it back, he wasn't sure he wanted to see them as they would be.

Silence returned. He released his hold on the counter and unbuttoned his jeans.

Knock.

Knock.

Knock.

"Niles, is this your place?" Camryn's voice was muffled by the running water.

He buttoned his jeans and turned off the shower. "Just a second." Before opening the door, he yanked his shirt back over his head. "This is a surprise."

"Might be one of the first times we've agreed on anything." She shivered, wrapping arms around herself.

He took a step back. "Can I grab you something dry to change into?"

"Do you always sit in the dark like this?" She stopped a few steps inside.

With a smile, Niles flicked on the switch, and overhead light pooled into the center of the loft but struggled to touch the corners.

"Hmm, I pictured your place gloomier." Camryn left her shoes by the door.

It was hard not to laugh at the irony, but Niles kept his composure. "Interesting since you've been the dour one this year. Not me."

Camryn didn't argue, just meandered into his living space without acknowledging how it bled into the kitchen.

She paused at the painting. Her hand hovered over the collaged scraps of handwritten letters and unmarked envelopes before tracing the outline of the golden infinity sign. "Looks like honeybee wings."

Niles studied Camryn the way she did the painting. "If you get close enough, you can see my parents in each opening of the symbol. But the translucency makes them look like ghosts."

"And all these words?" Camryn turned toward him.

He ran a finger over the bottom of the painting. "Since my parents died, I've been writing them a letter every day. Now I think it'll just be my Holloweaves tradition. One letter. That's it." He turned away from the painting, leaning against the kitchen island a few steps away.

"But if you stop writing the letters, won't it feel like they're really gone?" Her words were soft, as if the admission weighed too much.

Niles forced hands into his pockets. The denim was still damp. "Don't do that. Don't pity me." His voice edged with a mix of sadness and frustration, coming out more broken than he intended.

"You'd rather I make this about me? Because my mom is the one who facilitates every detail of this day for herself, wiping out any trace of Gram in the process." Camryn pinched the bridge of her nose.

Turning back to the painting, Niles cleared his throat. "Why did you come *here*?" What he really wanted to say was *stay*. But he needed to know why.

"I know what it's like to grieve alone. Even in a room filled with half the city, all of them waiting to speak the names of their loved ones. But only the arboretum's eaves ever listen. There's no understanding in that. It's hollow." Camryn tucked a wayward curl behind her ear. More waves had appeared as her hair air dried.

Whatever the reason, Camryn's presence meant sharing his grief. He'd done it alone until now. And yeah, the world wasn't kind. Everyone was marked by that truth at one point or another. But his time had come so soon. And now Camryn wanted to meet in this barren land of loss.

Niles looked down. "Never thought of it that way. I guess no matter how you spend it, this is a lonely day."

"Most of it anyway. Gram always made Papa Leland's favorite foods and drinks. My dad promised he would keep up the traditions, adding tea and fortune cookies for Gram after she died. I guess he forgot."

Without delay, Niles nodded toward the stove behind him. "I don't have any fortune cookies, but I can make tea." He searched her face for acceptance, noting the way she shivered.

"Let's get changed first though." He started toward the stairs.

384

Silence crept between them, but Camryn kept her distance until they reached the top step. She leaned against the iron railing separating the lofted bedroom from the living space below.

Niles handed her a rust-colored sweatshirt and black boxer shorts. "You can get changed in the bathroom."

Once he heard the door click shut downstairs, he stripped off his own clothes, quickly replacing them with a pair of dark grey sweatpants and a faded teal t-shirt covered in flecks of paint.

Back in the kitchen, he started water to boil, and grabbed two mugs.

"Better?" Niles looked up when Camryn emerged from the bathroom.

She crossed the space, stopping in front of the windows at the closer end of the loft. She blew on the glass, drawing a flower in the condensation. "Much better." She'd contained her hair into a braid down her back, but she pulled the end over her shoulder now.

"What would Gram like best? I have lemon, ginger, peppermint, chamomile, or cinnamon." He popped the lid on the tin of tea pods.

Stretching arms above her head first, Camryn then joined him at the counter. "Lemon. If that's okay?"

"Of course. This is about remembering. It's a nice way to honor your gram." He unwrapped two tea pods, dropping them into the bottom of each mug. Both began to fizz and steep after he poured hot water over the top.

Camryn took the mugs toward the couch, setting one on each end table. "Did you write your letter yet?"

"I usually do it closer to midnight and it's only 8:07 now." Though he'd changed clothes, the chill still lingered in his bones. He shivered before grabbing a blanket for each of them.

Camryn curled into the corner of the couch, legs tucked beneath her. "What do you say in your letters?"

He wrapped the blanket around his shoulders. "Whatever needs to be on the page. That's the nice thing about envelopes. They keep your secrets safe."

"Like you, then?"

Niles tried to keep the smile from his lips, but there was no stopping the effect those words had on him. The blanket slipped from his shoulders. "We'll need—" He tried to find his way back to the previous thought, but retrieved the pens and paper from their usual spot without explaining, chest tight. "To write the letters."

Camryn grabbed a pen and pressed a finger to the tip, dotting her skin with a dark speck, almost like the inverse of a star. "I think Gram would like it if I wrote my letter like a reimagined myth. Maybe Icarus?"

"I don't know much about myths." Niles tapped his own pen to his temple, trying to draw out the perfect way to start. *At least someone will remember you, too.*

After sipping from her tea, Camryn cleared her throat. "Icarus was trapped in a maze until his father made him wings out of wax and feathers."

She tipped the mug to her lips. "His father warned Icarus not to fly too close to the sun. But of course, he did. How could he not? When the wax melted, he fell, and perished at the bottom of the sea."

"That story is depressing as shit. Why would you reimagine your gram in that?" Niles waited for her to meet his eyes.

Instead, she picked at a loose red thread on the plaid blanket. "Gram thought she could outwit somnium with stories of before times and her book of myths. What was supposed to be her escape was probably the thing that killed her instead. Just like Icarus." She twisted the end of her braid around her right finger. "It's called hubris. And sometimes I hate her for it." Camryn's amber complexion paled. "No, wait. I didn't mean that."

"It's okay if you do." Niles touched a knuckle to the back of her hand once and twice and again. Three was Camryn's pattern for calming down. He noticed, even if she didn't think he did.

She grabbed his hand. "How can you miss someone so much and still feel so angry?"

"Since blaming the universe is ineffectual, we have to push everything back to those we lost. And it's messy and it hurts more times than not." He yawned, but returned to his letter.

Camryn did the same.

The scratch of both their pens brought tingles to the base of Niles' scalp, lulling him as the minutes passed, and words began to blur.

* * *

This one means forever. Niles traces his toe over the symbol for infinity. Water laps at the edge of the swimming pool, inviting him in. But now is not the time to dive below.

Everything must end.

Tonight darkness is porcelain, so easy to shatter if Niles blinks three times at the moon. He'd start all over again to bring his parents back.

"Would they have said goodbye if they'd known?" Camryn materializes at the edge of the pool.

It doesn't take long for Niles to reach her. "Before the fire?"

"Before everything." Camryn yanks him to the depths before he has time to hold his breath.

At the bottom of the swimming pool, colors scheme and weave into something new. The blue underbelly of the pool transforms into the cosmos.

"We shouldn't be standing in the night sky down here." Niles blinks, and the moon disappears.

Camryn extends an offering. "Would you like tea while I finish your wings?"

Niles spins the saucer in his hand, tracking the gilded symbols surrounding the cup. Champagne. Cardigan. Clock. "Make sure you never miss me for too long. That's how people become ghosts and memories become a haunting."

"It's almost time." Camryn rips at the pages of a book. The spine is left between them

like a carcass. But she makes no acknowledgement of the desecration, only folds the sheafs into feathers.

Before Niles can protest, the feathers find a home against his bare back.

"You were wrong before." Camryn pulls his arms out to reveal his wingspan. "If you were really gone, I think I'd always miss you." Her tears turn to threads of red when she cries.

In an effort to rework fate, Niles attempts to unspool their lifelines. He plucks once and again and more, creating duplicates for each of them. But here they all wait; different versions of Niles and Camryn from other times of when and who they might've been over the last seventeen years.

"She's right." A familiar hand brushes against the side of Niles' face.

The gesture feels only like moonlight. Niles doesn't want to call this what it is, won't let the word unreal *spill from his mouth like gin into a rocks glass."Mom?"*

"We came to say goodnight." His dad steps forward. "No matter what happens next, you'll remember. Because you must."

When his dad pulls him into an embrace, Niles recalls the weight of it beyond the subtle breeze prickling at the back of his neck. "My parents are dead. They belong then and there." He wraps Camryn in his wings. "We have to get back to the here and now. This is just a dream."

* * *

Gone.

His left arm.

Niles tried to lift it, but there was nothing.

"Just a dream." He screamed the words.

But, no.

A whisper.

Too quiet.

The edge of the couch dug into his neck. Overhead light absent. Had the storm knocked out the power? He tried to find familiar shapes in the dark.

Camryn.

His left arm was pinned beneath Camryn's back. Using his other hand, he pulled the limb to himself, shaking it in the hopes of getting through the next few minutes of pins and needles without too much discomfort.

Wishful thinking.

He bit his lip to keep from muttering expletives that would be sure to wake Camryn. No need to put her through this same confusion until he figured out what happened.

Just.

A dream.

The truth sank in his stomach. But how long? Niles checked the time. Not yet eleven. Less than two hours until Holloweaves would pass. Was that all this was? Ghosts and unfinished business? Or had the veil between this

387

world and dreams thinned enough to let him and Camryn share the space together?

"You're gone." Camryn murmured and turned over. Somewhere in the time of sleep, her hair had unloosed from her braid. It tumbled past her shoulders.

Niles brushed the back of his hand down her arm, trying not to startle her. "I'm right here."

"Not like Icarus." She shifted off the couch, disappearing into shadows. "Tell me again how to cry to the old gods. When someone dies, wane of moon delivers the news because they know how to bring back the dead. You told me so." Her voice echoed from a distance and sounded, what was that word again?

Untethered.

Footsteps echoed on the stairs until they didn't anymore.

Niles followed after her, grateful he knew every inch of his loft, even with the lights off. He only stopped when he caught sight of her silhouette.

One step back, and she'd careen down the steps.

"Camryn, you're sleeping." Niles grabbed her wrist, trying to pull her toward safety. "It's only a dream, and now it's time to wake up."

She gripped the edge of the railing instead, pulling herself up. "It's time to leave." The words ricocheted and fell to the floor of the loft.

But Niles wouldn't let her do the same.

In an instant, he wrapped his arms around her from behind, and yanked their full weight back to the bed. He shushed her through the scream now tearing through her throat. That sound cut deep into his bones, nestling in the same place where the memory of his mom's last moments lived.

"You're here?" Camryn curled around into his arms, pressing her forehead to his shoulder. "I thought you were gone forever."

Niles stroked a hand through the wild waves of her hair. "I think it'd be safer for us downstairs." He held her hand until they reached the bottom, flicking the light switch up and down to no avail.

For the next thirty minutes or so, they broke down everything they'd seen in sleep, cross checking on separate scraps of paper. It didn't feel safe to sort this out any other way.

Now the flickering glow of candles they used to illuminate their words on the page held Camryn in their half circle. She looked so soft in that light, as if unraveling from her corporeal form.

Like a ghost.

But she accepted fresh tea when he offered her the cup. This time, he chose peppermint. Less than ten minutes before today turned into tomorrow, and they needed to stay awake.

Instead of sipping on the steaming liquid, Camryn pressed the mug to her chest. "What if this was all a hallucination?"

"I have to say it. You know I do." He set their pages side-by-side, identifying the similar things they'd seen. "That was a dream, both of us tangled up there. Together."

Camryn pulled Niles up on the couch beside her. "Do you ever wonder what it must've been like in before times?"

"Like the stories your gram used to tell?" Niles stretched, trying to forget the feeling of stories feathered against his back.

Though Camryn smiled, the look didn't have staying power. "Most days, I hear Gram in my head, but I can't remember if that's what she really sounded like."

"Sometimes I try to remember how my dad said my name in the morning, but it's not there anymore. How does that happen?" Niles turned to face Camryn, willing her not to look away.

She gazed up to the left before her eyes returned to Niles. "The ancients wrote of a river in the Underworld. When you died, you were meant to drink at the water's edge to forget your life before. So even though we get left behind when someone dies, at least we get to keep living. Eventually, we get sunny days."

"But it's all shadows for them," she continued. "Much easier to forget. Move on. Pretend you were never living at all. Learn to love the darkness instead. And maybe the day you forgot the sound of your dad's voice was the same time he lost the memory of being your father."

Niles shifted closer. "I hope not." He stood and stacked their pages on the counter. "I don't think there's any universe where someone could forget you, Bishop. Least of all your gram."

"It's almost time." Camryn closed her eyes and exhaled.

Those words were familiar, but the quality was different outside the world of dreaming. Everything sounded muffled there, like being underwater. "Three minutes."

"So much has changed. And I've been so desperate to get back to who I was before the start of all this, but now I know, she's gone."

Niles strode to the window. "It's like those old versions of us are dead." He looked back, desperate for her to understand.

"Maybe we should say our own names, too." She pushed open the window and climbed out to the fire escape. "Seems silly not to speak them directly to the sky."

With a nod, Niles followed behind. It'd stopped raining while they slept. The world smelled new again. "So we leave who we used to be there and then."

"And we stay here and now." Camryn counted down the next sixty seconds.

Midnight.

At last.

Together, they spoke the names of their loved ones.

Niles searched the stars for their faces, but they didn't live there. He took

389

in a breath before releasing his name in a whisper. "Niles Mead."

"Camryn Bishop." Her voice wavered with the same softness, disappearing with the confetti.

They said their names like a goodbye.

Because it was.

Because it had to be.

About the Author

Kayla King (she/her) is the author of These Are the Women We Write About, a micro-collection published by The Poetry Annals. She is the founder, Editor-in-Chief, and contributing writer for three collectives: Pages Penned in Pandemic, The Elpis Pages, and The Elpis Letters. Kayla's work has been nominated for a Pushcart Prize and made the Backlash Best Book Award shortlist. Her fiction and poetry have been published by Firewords Magazine, Sobotka Literary Magazine, and Capsule Stories, among others. You can follow Kayla's writing journey over at her website: kaylakingbooks.com or on Instagram @kaylakingbooks.

Hemlock Queens

Julie Fugate

F *orce majeure* is French for Act of God.
Fancy words for mountain kids who go barefoot and have a southern twang.

Yet, this is how they explained what my twin sister and I are. Unexplained miracles. They pronounced us dead before we were even born. Our mother was told we would be stillborn. Instead of baby showers and room preparations, our parents bought us plots and headstones by the church.

We came into this world premature but alive.

We survived.

We'd steal through the trees and visit ourselves at Ivy Hill Memorial in Tennessee. No bodies beneath our feet, but our headstones always marking our future.

Mary Day.
Beth Day.
Beloved Daughters
Happy in Heaven
Laughing with the Angels

We read it aloud together.

My sister, Beth, smiled at our early immortality.

I considered why we were rejected by Heaven.

MARYBETH DAY

We may be identical, sharing thin noses and eyes too big for our fine features, but we are not the same.

The worst part about being a twin is that the world tries to rate one of us above the other. So, we fought back by keeping our appearance exact.

I'm a bit taller, so she wears heels to school.

She's a little skinnier, so I'm the one who sacrifices a second helping of mama's pie to maintain an exact weight.

This carries right down to the freckles and scars we bear.

Make-up when possible.

Cutting as a last resort.

Our personalities take more work.

She's bubbly to a fault, and I'm mirthless with a temper.

Our reward. The two became one. Mary and Beth were now Marybeth Day.

Until now, the summer before our senior year.

We made a bold decision.
Separate summer adventures.
Separate friends.
Separate lives.
Divorces and remarriages in our family gave us options away from our Tennessee home.

I chose a beachside bungalow near the ocean with an absentee aunt. The land is flat, and bright compared to the swell and fog of the Smoky Mountains. I've gotten used to the changes in scenery and my body. The sun has lightened my strawberry hair, which I wear in braids, while my fair skin has been browned. There are now additional freckles across my nose.

Beth chose our artist uncle in a suburb about an hour outside of New York City. She craved a different brightness in her life—fame and fortune.

I'm not there to curb her reckless side, and she's not here to push me into unwanted adventures.

We check in every week. Quick texts.

I sent her a variety of seashells which included a bleached sand dollar.

She responded with a potted plant full of blooms and an odor of carrots. It was over two feet high and the small white petals in tight convex circles reminded me of snowflakes, even if they had a tiny purple dot in the center. With it came a photo and a name—Queen Anne's Lace.

The picture is her, or me, in a two-piece bathing suit, her body dotted in the same white clusters as if she's tattooed from head to foot.

Then, a few weeks before we were to return home and reconcile our looks for school, came the late-night text from my twin sister:

Force Majeure.
Midnight.
Our Lady.

Our personal code word for a mandatory meeting.

In Tennessee, we'd find each other at our graves and talk about our miseries and troubles. That is where we made confessions with no fear of anyone eavesdropping. There's an added location, so she hasn't gone home.

The graveyard she references is near Uncle Ron's house.

After making my travel plans, I text back tomorrow's date.

In my worry, I try to call. It goes straight to voicemail.

Not being able to reach her has stolen my appetite and sleep. What is so important? Is she in danger? Why won't she answer?

It's why there's a taser next to my flashlight in the pocket of my light rain jacket when I take a taxi the next night.

My chatty driver, who's disappointed in my evasive answers, drops me off in front of Our Lady of Peace Cemetery with thirty minutes to spare.

There's no indication anyone is here.

The weather is now drizzling, dark clouds playing peek-a-boo with the moon. A glow emanates from a faint light at the highest point where a building stands. White stone and pillars. What's most striking is the large angel standing on top, wings stretched out and a sword in his hand, as if watching over all the dead.

That's where we will meet, I'm sure.

The path is paved, barely wide enough for a small car, as I trudge up past headstone after headstone.

By the time I get to my destination, the storm has picked up. The door to the mausoleum is locked, but there's an overhang that wraps around the entire building.

Once I'm sure I'll stay dry, I push my hood off my head.

Midnight comes and goes, but my sister doesn't come walking up the road.

I'm about to call for another ride and go to my uncle's house when, over the drone of the raindrops, a footstep splashes in a puddle behind me. "You're late," I say mid-turn.

There's a red umbrella pulled low, but the thin shape of my sister's body is all wrong. Thicker, hairy calves are between sandals and baggy shorts.

"Who are you?" I put as much menace into my voice as I can.

The red dome tilts back, and the guy's face is delicate like a doll's. Honey-brown skin. Puppy dog eyes framed by thick eyelashes and brows with high cheekbones and thin lips. His chestnut hair is pulled back into a ponytail at the nape of his neck. Long bangs hang over one eye. "Your sister sent me," he says, his voice a smooth tenor.

Liar. She'd never use a proxy. "Prove it."

His lips widen into a white, toothy smile. "She told me you're the careful one." He tilts the umbrella back and spins it in his hands, shedding pellets of water.

It makes me notice all the colorful friendship bracelets he's wearing.

"Your name is Mary," he says. "I'm Trevor. Beth's boyfriend."

Boyfriend. It shouldn't surprise me, but it does. She has had a ton of crushes over the years, which makes her the boy crazy one. Each boy is placed in the category of flirting, kissing, maybe the one. No one has ever landed in the forever column for long. I don't believe she's ever met a forever guy. Where does Trevor fall? "Why are you here and not her?"

He runs his fingers through his bangs. "I'm the one who sent you that text."

This gives me pause. "You? She told you about . . . how to send a message to me?"

He nods. "And about Barry."

I draw in a quick breath.

He holds up his hands as if in surrender. "She swore me to secrecy." He winks. "We were exchanging romantic histories."

Another lie.

"Why should I believe you?"

One step backwards.

Grip the taser in my pocket.

I'm ready to flee *or* fight.

He gives me a sorrowful grimace and shakes his head. "You're right. Details. Her first kiss was with Barry." His brown cheeks flush. "Then later . . . your first kiss too . . ." He ends that last statement with an apologizing popping sound with his mouth.

Chills slither through my body. Maybe she did tell him. How much has she changed over the summer?

"We were entertaining Mary Jane," he adds. "If that helps."

It does not. "Is that why you sent the text? Is it drugs?"

"I'm hoping you can find out." He frowns. "A word of warning. She's sick. Acts strange. You're my last hope."

"What do you expect me to do exactly?"

"Get her to agree to work with her uncle. Tests. Treatment."

"My uncle the artist? Shouldn't we take her to a hospital?"

"She won't go. Plus, he's a brilliant man. As smart as any doctor."

Despite Trevor's assurance, I don't like any of it, but I give him a simple nod, my finger caressing the case of my taser. I'll find out what's going on, but I don't know Trevor, and if it comes down to him or my sister . . . well he better not get in my way.

GRAVE SECRETS

Grave secrets are a pact Beth and I created when we were kids. It meant secrets we take to the grave, never to divulge to another living soul.

Barry was one of the few boys we both had a crush on. The popular, handsome athlete that all the girls drooled over at school. She was determined he would be her first kiss and seduced him one night at a party. Excused herself in the middle of their make-out session and then sent me in.

Maybe it's a twin thing, but we wanted our first kiss to be with the same boy.

No one ever knew, not even him.

Until now.

Trevor has his mom's car and drives us to Uncle Ron's house.

It's an old Victorian home with a large front porch. It reminds me of a dollhouse we had as kids. Three stories. Lots of A-frame little roofs.

I stomp up the wooden steps and rap on the door. I'm about to do it again when Trevor proffers up a key.

"No need to wake up your uncle," he says. "This was under the planter."

I nod and step out of the way.

Inside, it's textured wallpaper and antique furniture. The only updates are the modern art that graces the walls. There's a collection of framed prints of a bright pink flower with red veins down the nearest hallway. The name Edunia appears above each one.

Trevor motions me up.

The stairs creak beneath my feet.

He beats me to the third floor and waits for me by a skinny door, the frame beat up as if it had once been boarded up and then ripped open.

My sister's room is covered in pale green wallpaper. She lies on top of a pink comforter in a princess bed with mosquito netting.

I'm already noting the differences between us.

She has on wild abstract pants and a tight black shirt. A ring gleams from her belly button, and a tattoo of those same small white flowers she sent me graces her left forearm. Diamond earrings glint from her earlobes. She wears the sand dollar I sent her around her neck.

What other piercings might be hidden from sight?

I'll be the one changing to maintain Marybeth's image, but right now I'm worried about the other modifications in her.

My salt-infused braided hair is frizzy but healthy.

Hers is dull. Paler skin. Big eyes. Jutting cheek bones.

"Beth," I whisper.

A hint of garlic permeates the room.

"Mary?" She moans while pushing herself up on her elbows. "Are you really here?"

Behind the netting, she is ghostly.

"Uncle Ron?" she asks next, her voice high and tight.

"He's not here," I respond.

Trevor, who is standing by the doorway, stares at me—at us, making note of the differences and similarities.

"You shouldn't have gotten her involved," her tone is sharp.

He winces.

"It's okay," I say. "We only had a few weeks to go, anyway. I'm glad he texted me if you're sick."

"Not sick," Beth emphasizes, picking a piece of lint off her shirt.

I nudge the netting aside to sit on the bed, but she covers herself with a blanket.

"Don't mother me," her muffled voice says.

"Then tell me what's wrong."

"Nothing."

I twist toward the doorway to ask for some privacy, but Trevor is gone. The door shut.

"Back away," Beth says.

"I don't care if you're contagious."

Silence.

Smoothing the tail of my braid, I move over beside a white dresser.

"Happy?" I huff.

Beth slings the blanket off and emerges from the netted bed. "I'm not really sick."

My pointed look is enough to elicit an eye roll.

"You caught me on a bad day. I've been having some severe digestive issues this past week. It's this room he's locked me in."

"Uncle Ron locked you in this room? It was open when we arrived."

"Was it?"

I did lose sight of him on the stairs. It was long enough to use a key. "Why?"

"The wallpaper weakens me. The plants don't like it. It's laced with arsenic." She pulls on gloves that go up over her elbows like Rogue wears in X-Men. Then she moves over to a narrow window, pushing the framed glass up.

"He put arsenic in the walls?"

"Not him. He bought it that way. Years ago, the well-to-do were all into this new green dye. This particular color was created by using what they didn't know was poison. This room has been closed up for years, but now he's using it against me." Her butt sits on the windowsill, her body folded at the waist.

"What are you doing?"

"We have to go."

"There's a door right here," I gesture.

She swings her legs through the opening. "It's locked," then pulls her head outside.

A moment later, I'm twisting the knob, but it doesn't budge. "Trevor," I call, but there's no answer.

I spin around, but Beth is gone.

I'm poking my head out the window now, where she stands on a small ledge on the edge of a steep roof. "What's going on?"

"This place has changed me. I'm no longer Beth or Marybeth. I'm Bethedunia."

She's not making any sense.

"Uncle Ron isn't who we thought he was."

What I know about our uncle clicks through my brain. Artist. Bachelor. Always sends separate birthday cards with money. Brother to our father, but they aren't close. We've been told we met him when we were too young to remember.

I'm about to ask another question, but I glance down.

We are three stories up with nothing but grass and bushes below.

It's no longer raining, but everything is wet.

Beth is already on the move.

The lightning gives me better glimpses of her. She shimmies over the roof, a lattice of plants like the one she sent me, their apple-sized heads cupped like inside out umbrellas toward the sky. She uses their exposed roots and stems like a rope ladder.

Along the back of the house, metal and glass rise even higher—a greenhouse.

With every electric flash, she's further and further away.

Then, there's a crack, and when the sky lights up this time, Beth slips.

Her feet slide over the edge, then her legs, but a tangle of plants has somehow looped around her wrist, keeping her from going completely over.

The light is gone, but the dark blob of her body makes it back up to safety. When she reaches the next window there's a bunch of those plants stuffed underneath the wooden pane. She jimmies it up then she's gone.

Moments later, the bedroom door is open, and she's grinning wide. "Did you see that? I've been planning my escape for a few weeks now. I wasn't sure it would work, but it was so easy."

"Easy? You almost fell to your death. Why did you take a risk like that?"

Her grins fades, "For you. He had no right bringing you here."

Whatever is going on, Trevor must be in on it. "Bringing me here for what?"

"To kill you."

EDUNIA

"Our uncle wants to kill me?" I breathe out.

"Essentially."

"That's crazy."

She winces for a fleeting moment. "He knows I'd do anything for you. I'll be forced to once again cooperate. If only to protect you."

"Cooperate how?"

"I'll show you. Come on."

"We need to call the police."

"They won't believe us."

My head is pounding. "Let's get out of here first. Then we'll figure it out."

"I can't. Not yet," Beth insists. She begins to glide down the stairs. Nothing could be that important.

I try to stop her, to talk some sense into her, my fingers touching the curve of her neck and shoulder.

She gasps and wrenches away, staring at me in horror. "Don't touch me!"

I'm so taken aback I'm frozen, my arm still extended, as if time itself has stopped.

Her lacy gloved hand grasps mine. "No, no, no. We'll get down to Uncle Ron's lab—"

"What are you talking about?"

All of Beth's attention is on me. "How do you feel?"

"Confused," I admit.

"No weakness? Dizziness? Nausea?"

Maybe she's delirious.

"How?" Beth muses with relief.

My fingertips brush the pale five-petal design of the sand dollar, leaving a purple cast on its porcelain surface. Then, it jumps.

Beth gasps, grasping her necklace and the purple fades. "That tickled. What happened?"

My nose is now a few inches away from it. "It moved, but that's not possible. They can't live without water, and I'd found that on the beach. But it's like it came back to life for a moment."

She takes a quick intake of air. "Did you get something from Uncle Ron?"

I furrow my brows. "No. But you sent me a plant." I'm not ready to tell her it got knocked off my nightstand, and I ended up covered in dirt and petals while some bug living in it bit me.

Her eyes widen. "Not me. Him. He sent you one of the phases of his research."

"The plant?"

She rips off one of her gloves, steadying herself before reaching out one finger. "Touch my skin again."

This is ridiculous, but I hold my breath before pushing my own up against hers.

Her skin is cold and clammy but then warms.

She breathes out a sigh of relief. "I feel better now." Her fingers entwine with mine as she practically drags me down the stairs despite my quiet protests.

We pass the prints of Edunia that I noticed earlier.

"Uncle Ron's work was inspired by that plant," Beth whispers. "A genetically engineered petunia endowed with human DNA."

"You're kidding."

"It's called bioart, and that particular experiment represents acceptance of others."

"Is that what Uncle Ron does?" I always assumed he was a painter or a photographer.

"Kinda," she said. "He works with biomaterial, clothing that's made of plants. But it doesn't last. He's been trying to fix the regeneration issue."

We enter a large kitchen with yellow walls and old, pale green appliances. When she opens the back door, instead of a yard, it's a huge greenhouse. The structure is over three stories tall with opaque glass and rows and rows of waist high planters full of the same plants.

Beth takes a deep breath. "Welcome to my palace."

Sweat has popped up on my upper lip. "Is it always this warm?"

"Is it?" Beth asks breathing deep, then doing a spin on her toes. "Stay here." She skips over a few rows before disappearing behind some large plants.

I'm distracted by a large poster of the same picture Beth sent. Me, but not me. In this one, she's in a dancer's pose, covered once again in those tiny white clusters, like body paint, except in 3D.

There's a rustling in the row Beth disappeared in.

I'm smoothing the end of my braid again as I step over water hoses and dry roots.

No Beth, but the umbel flower heads sway.

The Queens Anne's Lace are up on tables, regal atop their tall, green stalks. Their white circular heads are at eye-level, twisting like the spinning teacups at Disney, cupped like an umbrella with a single purple dot in the middle. When I brush along the hairy stem, my finger comes back sticky.

Further in, the stalks change. They are smooth with purple spots, and it makes me wonder if they are diseased. The blossoms aren't as tight, as if they are stretching out for freedom from the pack, and they seem to bend my way. I reach out and something inside the petals prick me, leaving a speck of blood on my finger.

"Be careful." Beth's voice echoes. "They have teeth in that generation." She comes around the corner, and she's covered in them, just like the poster. Except this time, they spin and crawl over her skin like strange bugs. Some of them drag spindly roots behind them until they weave with others. "You were supposed to wait."

"What are those?" I can't keep the horror out of my voice.

"These." Her lips stretch into a grin while the blooms on her body continue to regroup, soon creating ruffles layers and layers deep like a dress. Patterns form. Some red. Some purple. Soon all that's sticking out is her face. "They are like wild animals, but aren't they exquisite."

My arm itches, and some flowers are on me, doing the same thing. I scream as if they are spiders and start flicking them off.

"It's okay," Beth tries to tell me.

"Beth. Mary." Trevor yells.

My sister grabs me, pulling me into her living garment. For a moment, I'm going to suffocate, but it expands like a cage, leaving us space, and we are cocooned inside. Beth both hugs and tugs me down into a crouch, putting her hand over my mouth. We don't move as heavy footsteps stomp around the greenhouse, passing us, but not finding our hiding spot.

When he's gone, I whisper, "What is this?"

"Friends. They recognize you."

"They?"

"Uncle Ron did it," she says instead. "He's been working on a way to maintain the biomaterial of his clothing line. It began with the nutrient pack. Then he found a way to make the person wearing it the nutrient pack, but it works better when the plant is infused with their DNA. I agreed to be his model. His canvas. One of the first."

I'm shaking now. "You let him experiment on you?" When we talked about getting our own identities and experiences, I didn't mean this.

"He gave me a gift, but now he's trying to take it away."

"Is Uncle Ron trying to help you?"

"There are other ways to die than being put in the ground. When he found I'd been chatting with some influencers about his work, he took away my phone. Grounded me. Wouldn't let me leave. The last straw was when he read my diary."

"You have a diary?"

"On my phone. I started it at the beginning of the summer."

"Is Trevor in cahoots with Uncle Ron?" It's the only explanation of how he knew about our code. About our first kiss.

"Yes." Her tone was careful, with the slightest hint of hesitation. "It's been war ever since. I hid his research. Introduced a little Hemlock in with his Queen Anne's Lace. They look very similar." She sighs. "It backfired. Now I'm poison to everyone I touch."

As if to prove her point, she touches a beetle waddling by. It stops moving, falling sideways. Dead.

I poke at it and the legs twitch once again. It rights itself and continues on its way.

"You're the antidote personified."

A tremendous blast of light pierces our hiding place.

Trevor, with black gloves up to his shoulders, has ripped an enormous hole in Beth's mound of flowers. He pulls me out and holds a syringe up to my neck. "Where's the research?" He grinds out. "Tell me, or she's dead."

My neck bends away from the needle that's indenting my skin.

Beth steps out of her fortress of petals. "I'll give it back. Don't hurt her."

The entire greenhouse begins to sway, like all the plants are doing the wave.

The dress melts into a puddle of petals that seep our way.

"Call them off," Trevor yells, dragging me backwards.

A rope of plants lashes around Trevor's arm that holds the syringe and pulls. He howls, and blood runs down his forearm.

I fumble inside of my jacket, pull out my taser, and shoot.

Trevor's body stiffens before he falls, dropping the needle.

His body twitches until I let go of my weapon.

He groans already trying to rise.

I smash the syringe. "What is this guy's problem?"

"His problem is that he's Uncle Ron." Beth says.

"Trevor is Uncle Ron?" On top of almost getting killed, my mind is swimming through information overload.

Beth shrugs. "Remember the regeneration problem? In one of the phases, the side effect was a bio fountain of youth that made him younger."

Except younger Uncle Ron never makes it to his feet. He is changing. Several hemlock plants are attached to him like leeches, and they seem to be draining him of his youth, the gray reaching his temples, his skin spotting and sagging.

The end of my braid is now a smooth curl around my finger. "What's happening to him?"

"I was one phase. You were another. Then in his search to find his original research he found a way to make himself younger. The hemlock is recycling his energy, feeding on his blood to weaken him, trying to take back what he's stolen."

"Plants aren't carnivorous."

"Some are. They eat bugs, rodents . . . and now enjoy humans. Imagine if plants become the dominant predatory species. He mixed human and plant DNA. Gave them bite. Steals their regenerative process for his clothing line. Stumbling upon the fountain was an accident but messing with nature comes with a price." She wiggles her fingers as an example before pointing back to Uncle Ron.

The hemlock plants on him are losing the battle, shriveling into dry husks as he fights their attack, his body once again turning back the clock. "He can't do this."

"What do you think I've been trying to do?" She throws up her hands. "This is his life's work. He won't give it up."

All in the name of art, fashion, and now immortality. "So, this means . . ."

"Humans could live forever but would always be at war to be master. Not everyone would survive."

Young Uncle Ron sits up with a groan.

"Don't worry about him," Beth says. "He needs some time to get his strength back."

"Why do the plants respond to you more than him?"

She smirks. "I'm kind to them. They give us long life willingly. He takes. They've chosen us because I gave them a way to fight back."

Hemlock.

"He can't be what we are—Queens."

The high wave of plants now bend their stems as if bowing their flowering blooms.

Around me is a sea of white, bulging at the seams, the greenhouse a dam ready to break. My sister may be able to control them for now but for how long? It will change the world. "What are we going to do?"

"The plants understand the need for balance and sacrifice. We may need him, but the rest . . . burn it all down."

HEMLOCK QUEENS

Force majeure is French for Act of God.

Fancy words for a couple of mountain kids who died in a fire at their

Uncle Ron's house.

There were no bodies, and we were declared missing, presumed dead.

No one will ever know we survived.

Today, we sneak through the trees and visit ourselves at Ivy Hill Memorial in Tennessee. No bodies beneath our feet, but our headstones mark a future that will never come.

Mary Day.
Beth Day.
Beloved Daughters
Happy in Heaven
Laughing with the Angels

We read it aloud together.

My sister, Beth, beams at our early immortality.

I no longer ponder why Heaven rejects us.

Every part of Hemlock is poisonous from the seeds to the fruit.

We cancel each other out.

We make each other stronger.

We have a lifetime to understand it all.

Beth and Uncle Ron's war is over for now. We've come to an understanding. The original vampire plants with bite are also gone, with a few *pets* kept in the name of science. One day we may all need a cure.

He still pays the price for his youth. The same plants he needs still retaliates. It's a gruesome cycle.

We keep an eye on our maker of Frankenstein plants.

Another grave secret.

One more unexplained *force majeure*.

Our last transformation because we've found who we really are—the ones who protect the balance—Hemlock Queens.

About the Author

Julie Fugate is a young adult author who writes books about revenge, mysteries and nature gone wrong. Her short stories have won contests and her characters are fearless underdogs. For more adventures follow her on Instagram at @jfugatewrites and visit her website at juliefugatebooks.com.

THE
MODULE

SAVANNAH MANHATTAN

The bright day turned off at exactly midnight for New York. Silhouettes of parked cars cut through the fog, streetlamps flickered on for the nocturnal creatures, and the friends inside the Marney residence were digesting crab cakes and cold shrimp cocktails when Taryn Marney brought her black box downstairs.

She had to carry it with both hands. It wasn't large or imposing. The box was just heavy, as if it carried entire civilizations inside.

Sophia, her chosen sister, saw her and scoffed. "My God, you invited us over to play with a paperweight?"

Taryn moved her delicate china aside and eased the box onto the coffee table. Sophia, who Taryn always compared to a walking Virginia Slim, pointed at the box with her newly manicured forget-me-not blue nails.

Jennifer Talbot took her gaze off the original Charles Lyon painting of three buffalo Mr. Marney bought at Sotheby's and moved to the couch.

"Taryn, I'm intrigued. On the phone you said you had a party game for us. Is that it or is the rest inside?" Confusion swirled fluidly across her face and glassy eyes. As she spoke, she moved forward to investigate. The device stood on four elliptical feet, equidistant diagonally from the center. Taryn had told everyone it was a module. At least that was an educated guess. It was uniformly smooth, resembling an obelisk, and the living room around it seemed to disappear into the void cube, like it was a spatial negative. An anomaly of a bleak continuum. Along the bottom half stretched inconspicuous vents, yet no warmth or surge of color emanated from them.

When Taryn called Jennifer about it earlier, she mentioned Taryn sounded more excited than ever—almost in love—and to a certain extent, Taryn believed that.

"Just you wait, Sophia," Taryn said as she turned around and headed back upstairs. Sometimes her friends could be impatient. *They don't know the extent of its joy.* She played with it the first time when she found it in the attic during the mandatory residential cleaning.

National soldiers arrived with federal cleaners in every neighborhood once a month–or whenever reports came in on the tip line–to inspect and seize anything deemed "a danger to the American community." The inspections were never announced; their presence and battering rams of fists on the door were enough notice. That previous Saturday, Mr. Marney had been away at work when the inspection came, but Taryn had politely offered them tea as always. She had nothing to hide from her patriotic guardians. She couldn't fathom how anyone would want to go against their own land. The Father of The State broadcasted statuses of all international or domestic skirmishes they were engaged in. Burnt, salted, sepia skies and frail bombed buildings squatted in by ravaged and masked heathens was no way she wanted to live. How blissful it was to be in Father's arms. As far as she knew, if you plotted against Father, you should be cast out. They would end each stream with bombastic brass instrumentation and crashes of cymbals. The symphony of peace.

The towering soldiers in black, purple, and white sternly ushered the cleaners in, signaling to the idle vans running past the driveway. The soldiers changed each visit, in order to disrupt possible liaisons. They were covered with bulletproof mesh and heavy metal plates emblazoned with arrows and olive leaves. Helmets swallowed their heads, leaving a one-way screen for important communication. Thick, sturdy batons and long-barreled shotguns hung from side holsters, waiting to be used. Taryn's eyes widened in admiration as the soldier in front stepped forward.

"No worry, ma'm, we'll just see your ID and be on our way. We ain't comin' in." The voice crunched through static with stonewalled authority.

Taryn fished her ID from her purse. The soldier to her left—the captain, according to the badge on his chest—complimented Taryn on her youthfulness in the photo. She laughed dismissively and blushed. The cleaners were led upstairs where they probed in the dark corners with living light beams, fluttering from clear canisters, like a girl would use to capture a monarch butterfly.

Once they reached the attic, they opened the canisters and repeated the process. The cleaners monitored the light beam eyes on their handheld coms. Taryn knew they wouldn't find anything, and the inspectors came to the same conclusion. The cleaners returned the luminescent orbs to their glass home, and then placed them in a large zipper pack.

Downstairs, the soldiers signaled again to the vans to open the doors. The captain mumbled a meaningless apology to Taryn, then disappeared.

It was later Taryn found the module in the center of the attic floor.

How would the inspectors miss that? Did they leave this by mistake? Mr. Marney wasn't home yet, and neither the cleaners nor the soldiers brought a box.

She lifted it, groaning with the unexpected weight, and brought it into the bedroom. She set it onto the mattress. It sank into the comforter. Taryn inspected the smooth and metallic box, with a distinct impression that it looked wise beyond time. Around the module, humid and electric waves radiated outward as if it willed itself on.

The lamp on the nightstand crackled and shone remarkably bright. Taryn screamed and fell back as the video wall parallel to her rippled with cyan, yellow, and orange. A crimson glow hummed meditatively from the vents on the module: an *aum* of watts. Taryn felt a rush of heat travel up her legs and along her body as secrets and unrecognizable arcane sprinted through her mind, coaxing her to spill her psyche into the device. Taryn cried out as the pressure built and expanded. It was fearsome and incredible. She gasped and opened her eyes. Abruptly, the whirring and heat vanished. The lights leveled out. Stillness returned.

Taryn grabbed the foot of the bed and pulled herself up, stricken by the power she witnessed. Her knees felt suddenly weak and she ached with a compelling need to transfer the revelations she'd been exposed to. Leaning forward, she kissed the mouthpiece of the cube with zeal and breathed every regret or secret she thought to tell the maw's inner machinations. The release liberated her, as if the box pulled her soul from her body and swallowed it whole. She rested her head on the pillow, light-headed from pleasure. The last time she felt the same with Mr. Marney was a month or two ago, although she couldn't be positive. She couldn't remember much of anything at that moment.

I have to show this to the ladies.

Mr. Marney didn't mind that she seemed obsessive about her new discovery when she told him the next morning. He had his video screen and his art. That's all he ever loved these days beyond working at the State Department. He dismissed it as a silly relic due for an antique store somewhere in the lower edge of the city. Yet, his eyes told her he was uneasy.

"As long as I don't have to see it, you can do what you like."

***

Mr. Marney was in their bedroom, swinging a black rubber club in front of their video screen as Taryn entered. On the screen itself, a realistic avatar swung a two-thousand dollar Doroly golf club at the dimpled ball, flinging it toward the green. Taryn didn't watch to see where the ball landed.

Mr. Marney clicked a button on the club and turned to his wife. Onscreen, the golf ball was a white speck suspended in flight. Beads of sweat glistened on his brow. He sniffled and pouted his lips at her as she took a sleek, convex riser down from the top shelf of the closet.

"Taryn, love and dear of mine, should you really be playing with that?" He hardly finished when she interrupted. "Oh please, Mr. Marney, not again."

"I'm only saying, what if it, you know . . ." Mr. Marney wiped his brow with a kerchief in his lapel.

Taryn turned around to face her husband, indifferent to his words. "Yes? Turns me into a lizard?"

"Changes you. What if it changes you?"

Taryn scoffed. "Darling, that's your superstitious upbringing talking. You sound like a broken mirror."

Mr. Marney shrugged and clicked his club back on. The golf ball bounced twice and landed short of par. Canned spectators clapped. Mr. Marney chuckled softly. "They're so polite."

Downstairs, Patricia sucked a smear of cocktail sauce from the shrimp in her hand. A wet slurp escaped her mouth.

Taryn, Sophia, and Jennifer contorted their faces in disgust away from Patricia's view.

"Damn Patricia. Damn that woman for inviting herself," Taryn said with a stiff grin, before she asked, "Any champagne, dear?"

Patricia placed the empty tail on her plate as Taryn walked toward the kitchen. "Of course I wouldn't mind."

Taryn noticed Jennifer's lips quiver as she stared at the cube. Briefly, the house lights dimmed and returned to normal, but no one seemed to see them except Taryn. A poltergeist of excitement coursed through her, and she could barely wait for the crimson glow, the static mirage, and the warmth. *The warmth of its wisdom.*

"I think we could all use some," Deb piped up, lifting an empty flute. She slumped next to Jennifer and picked lint off her sun dress with the other hand. Together, the two women began to pet the face of the box. They laughed airily as Sophia scrunched her nose.

Taryn sighed and went to the liquor cabinet in the kitchen. This occasion called for her best bottle: one usually reserved for date nights with Mr. Marney. The bottle was still full.

Outside the shades of the kitchen window, the other houses in the cul-de-sac sat shrouded in the dense fog and dusk. Peering beyond them, Taryn narrowed her eyes to get a better view of the house in front of her. It was a two-story, cookie-cutter sore on the plot of grass it laid on. The Gladstones lived there. *Well, not anymore.* Mr. and Mrs. Gladstone were both executed by the state for espionage. Every time she thought of them, she found it strange they stooped low enough to betray their state. *Her state.* She shook her head, returning to the kitchen. She didn't want to linger on bad thoughts anymore, and the module summoned their strength as Taryn brought out the flutes of champagne. Deb downed hers quickly.

"So, your daughter is in Spain you said? Cat-a-lin-a?" Patricia asked Taryn. She hated Patricia's nasally whine.

"Remember, Patty, she's in Portugal." Jennifer was already done with her flute as well, and while staring at the box with an eager hunger, put the glass on the end stand. She appeared on the verge of an emotion that Taryn was already familiar with.

Sophia looked intrigued. "Isn't Portugal extinct?"

Taryn stretched the thinnest smile she could and didn't answer. She scanned the room until an odd silence hung like the fog outside. The module pulsed soundlessly and vibrations thrummed throughout the living room. Everyone was hushed, admiring the slowly cresting saturation of crimson heat from the opening.

"Are we ready? Remember what I taught you over the phone." Taryn's words fell hypnotically outward.

Sophia and the others nodded. The box patiently waited, its mouth facing the women. The ladies nested their flutes next to each other and gathered behind Taryn. Their auras needed to be fed.

Taryn felt long nails tap along her shoulder. She shrugged off Sophia and approached the relic slowly with the deliberation of a surgeon. Dark, potential energy pounded her chest. She knew between breaths it was only a plaything, but the arousal called for caution. Just as she did in the bedroom, she kneeled in front of the face and brushed her fingers gently along the box. Behind her, the rest of them watched and trembled.

She bent forward and pressed her lips into the open mouth of the box. It was just like she remembered a week ago, but the mouth was much warmer. She hated that she was kneeling there with nothing to do or say. The revelation from the bedroom visited her head as the heat traveled through her arteries. Disembodied guides whispered from outside the fold.

Share the lowest form of you.

She traveled the paths of her memory from childhood and on. Memories right after the initiation of Father and Empire. Memories of crowds gathered by infernal shepherds and kept in their houses, afraid. Memories of loss of love. Memories of atoms. The deepest corner of her wanted the panic and vacuity to be eradicated. She wished she never reported the Gladstones. She knew they never did anything. She just wanted to fit in with society. She wanted to please her husband and please everyone but now she wanted to please herself for once. Taryn shared her fear with the module's being, hoping for the grand release.

Opening her eyes, she gasped as a faint, igneous glow flashed and disappeared, catching her words and incinerating them, never to be again.

She methodically stood and moved aside in a haze. Sophia flipped her hair back and didn't wait for Taryn to finish stepping away before she eased into a comfortable position. Sophia whispered for what felt like countless minutes. Then the red glow snatched her thoughts. By the time it was Jennifer's turn, she was nearly weeping with anticipation. When Taryn put her arm around Jennifer, she whimpered and shook with electricity.

"What is this doing to us? We treat a box like a god. Now who are we?"

The Charles Lyon buffalo remained pensive, watching over them as they grazed on canvas. Taryn noticed through her bay windows that all the neighborhood streetlights throbbed and flickered. She hallucinated humid breath in her ear. No one was standing beside her. Deb and Jennifer were both worshiping the relic with gossamer hands and Jennifer was gently whispering into the maw. Her low, desperate breath was almost womb-like.

Taryn shuddered with wrenching disgust.

What are we doing? I want this thing banished the moment we are done. Perhaps she could ask Mr. Marney after his Masters Cup to chop the deviled artifact and build a nice fire. They could have peace and quiet from the crescendo of fanaticism.

All she needed was this last night with her mysteries. Then she wouldn't have any more curiosity. *Isn't that what we've always wanted? All the answers and none of the questions?* Until then, she had no choice but to give in.

***

Mr. Marney peered through the banister. He sneered as he watched the ritual, thinking how pitiful one artifact could turn a group of people. The ecstasy, the weeping and gnashing, the chaotic revelry; the performance was far more gomorrahan than he was comfortable with. He was going to ask his wife after the dishes were put away later to pack it up and ship the abysmal thing to the farthest location they could think of. That, or they could bury it.

On his way upstairs, he couldn't shake a chilling premonition. *Apocalypse, sacrosanct perversion, or is this a trend somewhere I can't fathom? Perhaps this is how Enoch saw the crystal palaces in the Gnostic Gospels. Awe and terror. He had to be taken away from corporeal existence to learn the truth of the universe. Is that the end here?*

He frowned, shifted the reverie aside, and took up his club again. The crowd on the emerald lawns waited for his swing. The avatars' blurred identities made great company. The audience clapped during his double bogie. He was eager for the admiration of the unseen spectators after a hole-in-one.

***

Downstairs, Jennifer lay hyperventilating on the carpet, having confessed to an infinite entity. Her satisfaction resounded around every wall. Sophia clacked her nails together. Her frown mourned Jennifer's overindulgence.

"It's over, Jen. The box is fed."

Taryn bit into another crab cake. She was ravenous with hunger. Deb and Patty's eyes were glazed over. Deb was falling asleep on Patty's shoulder. Patty called out to Jennifer. Jennifer was obscured by the table and the box.

"What's wrong with you, Jennifer? You never act like this."

Jennifer just giggled and bit her lower lip, a repressed force unlocked. All she managed was to slur her answer. "Mmm, I don't know why. I just think I'm the other half of a magnet bound to that . . . that . . ." Jennifer whipped an arm toward the coffee table where the module nested on the riser. She struggled to cope with what she experienced. She knew it was a divine intervention, but her face fluctuated between ecstasy and shame.

Patty, as if unaware of Deb's state, reached forward for the last shrimp. Deb snorted awake and rubbed her eyes, and Patty crunched into the shrimp with zeal. A strange cloak of euphoria hovered around the living room.

Taryn settled on the couch, exasperated but complete. Sophia murmured about how she needed to get her nails redone before she turned to Taryn, her expression embattled. "Where did you say you bought the game?"

Taryn yawned and picked at the empty shrimp tails on her delicate china. "If you must know, I found it in my attic. Sophia, don't you just feel euphoric?"

Sophia was taken off guard. "Oh. Oh, don't get me wrong, dear. Something feels different, that's for sure." The women all nodded in agreement.

Over the next few hours, they talked of the war and the newest broadcasts. Taryn led them out her front door past three, then hid the foul thing back in the closet while her husband took a shower.

I'll tell the others I sold it, or that I was too scared to keep it. No one should touch this again.

She was fast asleep when Mr. Marney came out of the bathroom in only a towel.

She didn't even process that the girls stopped calling about their special nights, or that she and the box mysteriously vanished days later in the night. Mr. Marney awoke to a whoosh of air coming from the closet and bed, and then nothing more.

About the Author

Savannah Manhattan is a poet and thriller/comedy writer in Los Angeles. She recently published her debut poetry collection called *There's Something About Theo*. You can find her on Instagram @savannahmanhattan for more.

Made in the USA
Monee, IL
23 December 2023

48376125R00234